B

A Wild People

Hugh Leonard is an award-winning playwright and screen-writer, and was Literary Editor at the Abbey Theatre, Dublin in 1976–77. His plays include the Tony Award-winning *Da* and Tony-nominated *A Life*, and his other works include the screenplay for the film *Widow's Peak* and TV adaptations of *Great Expectations, Nicholas Nickleby, The Moonstone, Wuthering Heights* and *Good Behaviour*. His novelisation of his 4-part drama *Parnell and the Englishwoman* (BBC) won the 1992 Sagittarius Award. He has published two volumes of autobiography, *Home Before Night* and *Out After Dark*. He lives in Dalkey in County Dublin.

A Wild People

HUGH LEONARD

Methuen

1 3 5 7 9 10 8 6 4

Published in 2001 by Methuen Publishing Ltd
215 Vauxhall Bridge Rd, London SW1V 1EJ

Copyright © 2001 by Hugh Leonard
The right of Hugh Leonard to be identified as author
of this work has been asserted by him in accordance with
the Copyright, Designs and Patents Act 1988

A CIP catalogue record for this book is available
from the British Library

Methuen Publishing Limited Reg. No. 3543167

ISBN 0 413 75960 1

Printed and bound in Great Britain by
Creative Print and Design (Wales) Ebbw Vale

For Paule, who died and took the fun out of it,
and with love, too, to Danielle, and my
gratitude to Gill Coleridge, who never gave up
when I came close.

There is a converted Martello tower by the strand at Killiney; but I have no idea as to who lives in it. In Tallaght, in west Dublin, a play was cancelled when a marquee was blown down in a storm, but I have forgotten what the play was and who produced it. These and other actual places and events are no more than a frame for the fictional portraits of Josie, Thorn, Shay, Greta and the other creatures of invention. In this book, the late film director Sean O'Fearna, mentioned but not met, is all too mischievously John Ford, who never did have a second wife. Without exception, every other character is fictitious.

HL

A Wild People

'The Irish are a good-natured people; they have many virtues, but their virtues are those of the heart, not of the head … Their strength of mind does not keep pace with the warmth of their feelings, or the quickness of their conceptions. Their animal spirits run away with them: their reason is a jade. There is something crude, indigested, rash, and discordant, in almost all that they do or say. They have no system, no abstract ideas. They are "everything by starts, and nothing long". They are a wild people.'

William Hazlitt, *On Good Nature*

Chapter One

At the Penders'

An October evening at the Penders' fifteen years ago is as good a time and place to start as any. To home in on it, it was the occasion when, just before going home, Andrew Hand said, mildly, 'I never read a book in all of my life.'

His wife Josie – for Giuseppina – said in her carefully stage-Italian accent, 'Do not mind heem.' We smiled, and one or two of us gave a small after-dinner laugh. It was as if Hand were reminding us of the heights he had attained without bothering his head with the codology of books and putting on airs. It may have been a friendly thumbing of his nose at those of us he regarded as self-styled highbrows. Or perhaps not; perhaps, when the audit was done, we were hardly worth a cocked snook to Hand, who could buy and sell all of us and not ask for change. For our part, we hardly saw him for the shadow his wife threw.

A year or so later, when I had become her lover, she told me, and the more intimately one knew her the less of a stage-Italian accent she had, 'If he hadn't inherited the business from his father, Andrew would hardly be fit to sweep the streets.'

It may have been her way of taking the sting out of any jealousy I might feel; but at least Hand did not dress like a fool. Once a year he went to London, not only to buy his shirts at Thomas Pink's and his shoes at Lobb's of St. James's, where his personal wooden last was Number H751, but expressly to meet a tailor from Hong Kong who showed him swatches of cloth. He made his choice, from the same narrow range, favouring greys or a dark blue with flecks of red. The tailor and his assistant measured him and affected to marvel that he never gained either an inch or a pound from year to year. He went to a gym twice a week and from January into February played golf for three weeks in Tobago. He had no excesses and was trim in all things. When the rest of us were sixty-five and fat or seventy and dead, Hand would still look a young sixty. He was a mild man, who (his wife told me) paid his dues by each year donating an equal sum to both the government party and the opposition. At the Penders', he drank little, listened indulgently to the gossip and began to peer at his watch at eleven. He was there, his manner told us, solely to please his wife, who was worth it.

There was a time when the Penders had given dinner parties for as many as sixteen. Their house was a semi-detached in Clonskeagh and had two downstairs rooms that were really one, running the depth of the house. Even bockety card tables were pressed into service, so that our hostess, Colleen, would sit at one end, with the cold glass of the french windows all but touching her back, while her husband Turlough was an ass's gallop away from her in the front room, with street lamps winking in over his shoulder. Their dinners were reckless, raucous, shouting, argufying, sprawling, poetry-spouting affairs that lasted until three in the morning or until the last heeltaps of Rioja were gone. The Penders' three children served and earwigged and helped Colleen in the kitchen until it was bedtime; then we formed a human chain to clear the last of the plates and, without prompting, poured our own wine. Turlough was part-owner for a time of Pender's Pictures, a gallery in Schoolhouse Lane; but when his partner asked to be bought out the cost of it meant short commons for the Penders. The dinner parties became fewer and the tables shrank in number until one sufficed, and the front room alone contained all the guests. It was no matter; Colleen still had her favourites, and among them were my wife Greta and I, and Josie and Andrew Hand, he who in all of his life had never read a book.

In spite of her name, Colleen was Maltese and a native of Valletta. She was christened Colette, and she and Josie had met long years before, when they were au pairs in houses on the same sylvan, money-dripping avenue in Carrickmines. They had hardly arrived than Giuseppina became Josie, and Colette, more mischievously, was renamed Colleen. As girls frequently do, they had become intimates at first sight. '*Amici per la pelle!*' Josie declared. And the story went that when Turlough first proposed marriage, Colleen turned him down. She could never, she said, marry any man with so unpoetical a first name. She changed her mind when he said that it was an Anglicised form of the Gaelic *Toirdhealbhach*. He wrote it down for her and said that if she still refused to have him, he would revert to the Irish and go to his grave blaming her.

In all, there were nine of us at table on that October evening: our hosts, the Hands, Greta and I and three others. There should have been an even ten, but JJ Thornton's wife had cried off; she was an actress and she had gone to Belfast to take over the lead in *Candida* at two days' notice, so Thornton had come alone. Everyone in Dublin has a nickname, and he basked in calling himself Thorn, perhaps because it carried with it an image of sharpness, unpredictability, danger. Until that evening, he and I had little more than a nodding acquaintance. We faced each other across the table, and I had the impression of being sized up before horns were locked.

The remaining two guests were Batt Kenirons from Ballyheige in County Kerry, and a litigious, sharp-faced red-head of 50 who had a perpetual bad hair day and, because of parents who had it in for her, was called April-May Macgreedy. Kenirons was a poet of some reputation; he was fat, with a mangold-shaped head, and his mouth was usually stretched into a smile that seemed to have been ironed there. Across the table, it emerged that he was working on a new version of Plautus' *Truculentis* – 'Without the laughs!' he warned us, bubbling at the nose with mirth – which

7

his friend Thornton was intending to stage in a Northside marquee at next year's Theatre Festival.

'Oh, are you a producer?' I asked Thornton with an Edna O'Brien air of innocent surprise.

Kenirons answered for him. 'Him? Erra, boy, he is another Walt Whitman. He is multitudes.'

Thornton smiled and gave me a look. I sensed that if my name was not already writ in black marker on his shit-list, it was at least pencilled in.

Colleen said out loud, 'You and Thorn, you are like two cats on a roof.'

'Boys will be boys,' my wife said.

'To coin a phrase,' Thornton said.

April-May Macgreedy, who was sitting on my right, sniggered.

Greta put down her glass so sharply that wine slopped on the cloth.

At this point whether to avert a row or take his opportunity, Andrew Hand said that he and Josie must be leaving. 'Oh, Andrew, eet is early,' Josie protested, a madonna to the tips of her steepled fingers. He relented, but it was his usual warning shot, and they would unfailingly be gone by twelve. His apology was always the same: 'I have an early start.' She gave a comic tigress growl of exasperation. We laughed and our good humour returned.

'Andrew, you always go home early,' Colleen said. 'Why don't you enjoy life?'

Josie said, 'Heem? Enjoy hees life?' She pointed a finger at her temple and pulled a trigger.

Andrew smiled and said, 'My wife is far too good for me. The world knows it.'

At this, Josie cried, 'No, no, no, no. Eet ees not true!' and went into an excerpt from *Lucia di Lammermoor*. She leaped to her feet, raced around the table and embraced her husband, to the accompaniment of words – endearments, presumably – uttered in Italian. She stroked him, kissed him on the cheeks and forehead and was back in her place within seconds. Andrew took out a handkerchief, smiled apologetically to the company and dabbed his face.

'Ah, lovely,' April-May Macgreedy said.

We all knew that indeed it was true: Josie was too good for him. She was so stunning that by general consent she was deemed unattainable. Even the banality of the name 'Josie' did not singe her wings and bring her tumbling down among the earthlings. She had poise, and she was immaculate. I saw her once, long before our affair began, sitting in an aisle seat on a flight to London, and she seemed grotesquely out of place, as if she did not belong with the coffined herd. Like her husband, she dressed quietly, but *her* clothes came from Via Tornabuoni and Via Calzaiuoli in her native Florence. At a dinner table she was too self-effacing ever to perform; instead and without an iota of coquetry she would hang on a man's every word. I know that when I had a story to tell, bumbling and all as I was, I might have been on a stage, with her as my besotted audience, a fan to the ovation born. Women liked her, forgiving her her perfections. They thought of her husband as a dry stick.

Josie Hand had more to her than the art of listening. She was a creature of fashion. She never let a talked-about book get past her. Watching a film, whether on video or at the pictures, she would weep, laugh and applaud. I once heard her snarl '*Farabutto!*' at a piece of cinematic villainy and, to my joy, she bit her thumb and thrust it towards the screen as if she were a Sicilian. She went in pursuit of whatever was the success of the moment, always eager to think well of it. And celebrity held her in thrall, not for its own sake, but because it argued talent. Once in London, as she and I were passing the upstairs sitting room of the Basil Street Hotel, she caught sight of Gregory Peck sitting in one of the chairs. For a moment, her nails dug into my arm. 'I must talk to him,' she said. I could get no further than 'Josie, for God's sake ...' when she was already into the room and telling

9

him, almost tearfully, what joy he had brought into her life. I saw the weary politeness of a beleaguered star give place to actual, if bemused, pleasure – she was overwhelmingly sincere. She came back to me within a minute. 'That is a memory to treasure,' she said. 'For him, too, I'm sure,' I said, meaning it only half in jest. She took what I said as a compliment.

That evening at the Penders', when someone mentioned a much-touted new *roman-à-clef*, *Love Among Our Own*, by the Ennistymon writer Emma Ring, Josie became animated and said: 'I bought that book today. Eet is on the table by the bed in my room, waiting.'

I felt a hard nudge from April-May Magreedy. She whispered out of a corner of her mouth the words, 'Did you cop that? "*My* room!"'

Josie heard her. Her forehead, smooth as alabaster, came around and she said, smiling and as if the remark had been addressed openly to her, '*Si, my* room. Andrew snores.' She blew her husband an affectionate kiss.

The Magreedy woman said, brazening it out: 'Andrew, you never do!'

He smiled. It was impossible to know whether he was embarrassed or not. 'Josie says I do.'

Josie said to the table in general, 'I cannot wait to read thees book. Eet is all about how Emma Ring had a great how-you-say *relazione* weeth that man in the North who made the bombs.'

'Now, now, no politics,' Turlough Pender said.

'Is not politics,' she said. 'Is *amore*. I have two books that I must read first, then will come Emma Ring.'

An image, which I at once put to flight, crossed my mind of her sleeping alone – and, yes, now I have it – it was at this point that Andrew Hand said he had never read a book in his life.

When it was past midnight and Josie had reluctantly let herself be led away, Kenirons said mournfully, 'A light has gone out of our lives,' and I, too earnestly, said, 'Yes, do you know, Batty, so it has.'

From across the table, Thornton gave me an amused look, and I stared coldly back at him.

'Greta, you'll have to watch that fellow,' he said to my wife, and she answered with a smile that came on and went out like a 20-watt bulb, 'Oh, I will.'

The departure of the Hands had left a vacuum which was slow to fill. Turlough asked Kenirons how the new play was progressing. The reply, in ripe Kerry, was: 'Erra, you must ask my im-pres-ar-i-o.' He rolled the r's, making finger food of it.

'It will be a milestone,' Thornton announced. 'I have the author's word for it. Yes?'

'Erra, you have, boy,' Kenirons said, beaming.

'Its brilliance will be exceeded only by my own modesty as I accept the Arthur Guinness Award as Theatrical Whirlwind of the Year.'

Colleen clapped her hands. April-May Magreedy said, quietly, 'Oh, delicious.'

'However, the notices will be merely respectful, except for the usual upwardly mobile pup, attempting to use a stiletto as a piton. The *Dubliner* will send its second-stringer, Seamus Lambe, who, if he happens to know even an iota about Plautus, will be ashamed to say so. "Baa-baa", as he is known, has a terror of affectation. In that fellow's lexicon, the unforgivable crime is to seem what he calls pass-remarkable. I'm told that he reads Tacitus and keeps it hidden behind copies of *Ireland's Own*.' He looked at me and winked. 'Right, Thady?'

He knew, and I knew that he knew, and he knew that I knew that he knew, that I preferred to be called TJ or even Theo. Because my surname was Quill, it was a tired joke to call me Thady, as in the old come-all-ye:

For rambling, for sporting, for football, for courting,
For drinking black porter as fast as you fill,

In all your day's roving you'll find none so jovial
As the Muskerry sportsman, the bould Thady Quill.

And, like everyone else, he was aware that Shay Lambe and I had been best friends for a score of years and probably knew, too, that we met on Mondays for a jar at Tish Merdiff's when he was not reviewing. Not to be drawn, I said, 'There's no fooling you, is there, JJ?' I knew that he liked, and he knew that I knew that he liked, to be addressed as Thorn.

He steamrollered on. 'So he will write a nice, friendly, careful notice which infers' – ('Implies,' I amended silently) – 'that Batt Kenirons has brought the classics to within reach of the ordinary, no-nonsense punter and out of the rarefied realms of ballsology. Am I right, Batty?'

'Bejasus, you are,' Kenirons said, warmly.

'You're a great charmer,' Thornton said to him. 'You ooze charm. Now there's an idea. I think I'll call you the Oozer.'

Kenirons went a dirty red with pleasure. Colleen wailed, 'Josie would love this. Oh, why is she gone home?'

Thornton, pleased with his little sally, and having given Kenirons a nickname that would probably be on his coffin-lid, wiped his dead-rat moustache and reached for the Rioja. Until recently he had been teetotal, and seeing him in drink was like watching a child with a new yo-yo.

Colleen told her husband to open another bottle. My wife adored Colleen. 'Mind, I like Josie too,' Greta said to me. 'She's terrific, but her mind is full of books and films and stuff I have no time for. Things that are more in your line,' she added, rubbishing half of my life.

It was impossible not to be enchanted by Colleen. She had a loathing of people who, she said in a rare lapse, were 'affectated', and she had a need to tell the truth without frill or furbelow. She did so not on principle, but as an addiction. 'She goes at it,' Kenirons declared in awed revulsion, 'like a bull at a gate.' Where another woman – Greta, for example – would put honesty in her purse when confronted by a hint of dissent, Colleen brandished the truth as if it were an extra fist. Once, when Turlough had given wall space at Pender's Pictures to an abstract, *Grey on Black*, by the Sligo artist Hilary Hosier, who was between galleries, Colleen said in the artist's presence: 'My God, it's horrible.'

To Turlough's disbelief, Hilary Hosier agreed with her. 'Horrible, yes, and what a very clever lady you are,' she said. 'It's actually a stark emotional image of the troubles in the North, but I thought it best not to be explicit. I wanted to avoid comparisons with *Guernica*.'

The occasion was a private view, and when the last of the plonk was gone, Greta and I took the Penders to White's of the Green for dinner, where they had one of their infrequent rows. 'A "clever lady" she called you,' Turlough all but sneered. 'Oh, yes, you're a very clever lady!'

'I said what I thought,' Colleen said.

'Fine. Keep doing it. Then I'll have no artists left, and we'll go broke.'

'Maybe that would be good.'

'You made a show of me.'

She said, flatly, 'I will not tell a lie.'

Turlough said: 'You hear her? This ... this Malteser' – I saw Colleen's knuckles go white at the jibe – 'is a guest in a country where, like it or not, the economy, the politics, the media and the arts are based on continuous and absolute falsehood. And she is too effing grand even to acknowledge the hospitality she enjoys here by telling one little white lie.'

'There is no such thing,' Colleen said.

'What is this unnatural vice of yours?' he said. His face was as tragic as if he were speaking of heroin, cocaine and drink, all in one. 'What is God's name is wrong with you?'

'She'll go to hell when she dies,' I said.

'You put a sock in it,' he said, and turned back to his wife. 'Did you ever hear tell of the proverb: "If you can't say something good, say sweet feck all?" Could you do that much for me? For *us?* Could you not sing dumb?'

'How dare you?' she said. 'That would be the worst lie.' She added, exempting present company, to Greta: 'For me, I mean.'

Greta said, 'Sure I know, love, I know.'

'Why don't you say it in Maltese?' I asked.

All three of them stared at me. 'Say what?' Colleen wanted to know.

'The truth. In Maltese. I mean, since nobody will –'

Greta was about to exercise her marital prerogative of calling me a bloody fool when Colleen put her hand up for silence. I could tell what was coming: she would say scornfully that a truth uttered in a language that no one understood was an hypocrisy and worse than any silence. Instead, she stood up from her chair, leaned across the dinner table, put her hands on my shoulders and, for the first and only time in her life, kissed me full on the lips.

On the way home, I concluded that, as a loyal native of Valletta, Colleen probably held to it that Maltese was a language as widely intelligible as English. Later still, as Greta and I were getting ready for bed, she said, 'That was very clever of you. I was impressed.' The compliment was so unexpected that I mimed the act of cutting a notch in the bedpost.

The Penders' dinner party broke up at two. A taxi came to take Thornton home to his restored Georgian house by the canal near Huband Bridge; April-May Magreedy, by now looking September-Octoberish, drove off in a farting MG two-seater; and Greta and I gave Kenirons, a non-driver, a lift home to Booterstown. Greta drove; I sat next to her, and the Oozer, in a spatial variation on Parkinson's Law, contrived to fill the back seat on his own.

'That fella Hand,' he said, 'is obviously not short of the few readies. Would it be what the Yanks call old money?'

'He's in tinned meat,' I said. 'Limerick ham. And I hear he has a controlling interest in a bottled water company.'

'Wicklow Wells,' Greta said.

'Jammy bugger,' Kenirons said. 'So tell us. What did his da do, and *his* da before him?'

Greta seemed to have it all off by heart. 'His father was a pork butcher in Dundalk, and the three sons, Andrew included, branched out into tinned meat . . . canned, the Americans call it. I know, because Josie told Colleen, and Colleen told me. Last month the Hand Brothers sent a whole shipload of low-grade ham to Nigeria.'

'They are so cute,' the Oozer said, 'that they could send it to Tel Aviv.' He leaned forward until the harvest moon of his face glowed between Greta and me. 'I'll tell ye something for free. If you went back another generation, I'd lay ye a pound to a penny that the grandda was farming pigs up the Carlingfords, with a bit of curly-tailed smuggling on the side.' He put a hand around the back of Greta's neck under her dark hair.

'Don't do that,' I said.

'Why, are oo jealous?' he cackled.

'Greta is driving.'

He laughed. 'Jesus, but aren't you the incurable romantic!' He took his hand away. He was drunker than I had thought. He said, 'From running porkers across the border to sporting a forty-quid haircut in only two generations. Greta, do you not think that's great?'

'Oh, marvellous.' She squinted at the road ahead.

'We're like the Jews in America. Universal Pictures brought me over, you know, to see if that update I wrote of *Antigone* could be made into a fillum. I was invited to a party at a house – erra, what house? . . . a mansion! – in Santa Monica. The host was one of them what-they-call boy wonders, and there *I* was: Batty Kenirons, brought up on forty acres on the shores of Akeragh

Lough, drinking out of a feckin' goblet by a swimmin' pool in a landscaped estate that stretched half-way to Mexico. Women drippin' joolery, and putting your eye out with their silicone tits, and may I die roarin' if there weren't two Japanese flunkeys serving shaggin' Mouton Rothschild. And yer man, the Hollywood big-wig, walkin' on the water of the pool. "Well, 'twas far from it you were reared," says I to him.'

I said: 'You said that out loud?'

'I had a mind to. And sure what could I lose? I mean, I knew the fuck-up that shower would have made of a Belfast *Antigone*. Ah, no, I said nothing. But that fella's grandda was gefilletin' fish in the Ukraine, and getting' a – a – a knout-hood from the cossacks.'

Achieving two puns in the same breath sent him into a spasm of wheezing. 'You know that, do you?' I said.

'You know it, too. Aren't you in the fillum business?'

Greta said, 'Now which way? I'm lost.'

'No, you're not,' I said. 'Go left at the lights. Then you're into Booterstown Avenue, and –'

'I know,' she said. 'Stop *telling* me!'

'Well, that's the Jews for you,' the Oozer said, 'and what I say is more power to their collective elbow. And aren't the Irish the same? From thatch to flamin' Foxrock, and from jackeen to gentry in two goes. Not like the Brits, the French and the Eyeties. That lot don't change; they don't need to; for them, the mould is set and long set. But us, now; once we shook off the …' – he wheezed again – '… the Yoke of the Saxon Tyrant, what did we do? We – wait now, 'tis on the tip of my tongue. Yis, I have it, and it is a word you could frame. We *reinvented* ourselves. Greta honeykins, isn't that a good word? And two generations of us was all it took.'

Greta took the turn into Booterstown Avenue with so vicious a swing of the wheel that he fell back in his seat. 'Don't,' he said, 'put me off me stroke. Look at us this evening. Andy Hand's oul' fella's oul' fella smuggled pigs ....'

I said, 'You have no proof of – '

'Don't argue with him,' Greta said.

'Proper order,' Kenirons said. 'Leave me be. Well, never mind the Hands ... sure we're *all* shaggin' upstarts. Turlough Pender will tell you, and no bones about it, that *his* da was a bus inspector, and the da's da before him was cleaning trams in the Dalkey tram-yard. Thorn Thornton's oul' fella was a solicitor's clerk that saved up to put him through Trinity, and the granny had a huckster's shop in Francis Street. Now the same Thorn has set his sights on runnin' the city. And he'll do it, too, Jesus pity us all. April-May Magreedy doesn't know where she was got or how she was got. Once upon a time, a thing the like of that was a skeleton in the cupboard. Not any more; the bitch boasts about it. You can't hear yourself talk to her for the rattle of –'

He began, raucously, to sing 'O dem bones, dem dry bones.' I pointed a finger, and Greta steered us into Kenirons' avenue, a cul-de-sac of trim houses with dormer windows. The Oozer broke off in mid-song and caught hold of my neck as he had done with Greta. 'And what about yourself?'

'Me?'

'You, you cagey bugger. Are you from lowly ancestors?'

'Lowly enough.'

'You see? And not a trace of it on you! I'm not talking,' the Oozer went on, unstoppable, 'about such shite as manners or accents or even the few bob. I mean we're light-years away from the farm and the red-brick terrace house and the –'

'This is your stop,' I said as Greta drew up.

'We're all totally *re-invented*,' he said again, enjoying the word, and added in the same breath: 'Ye'll come in for just the one.'

Greta said 'No' and I said 'We won't,' both together.

'I'm not saying it's a veneer,' Kenirons said. 'Anything but. I'm not saying, scratch the surface and a half an inch down you'll find the son of the cleaner of trams or the girl whose ma was a skivvy.

17

No, scratch all ye like and ye won't find them. They've been –' he belched softly – 'eradicated. "Dead and gone, and with O'Leary in the grave."'

'Sure,' I said. 'Goodnight, now.'

One hand clung to the back of Greta's seat. 'I mean, Jimmy Joyce and his blathering about the effect on the soul of "twenty centuries of authority and veneration." Nowadays, we would say that Joyce had his hash and parsley. What?'

'Absolutely.'

'We're a brand new race.'

'Good night, now, Batty,' Greta said.

He said, almost pleading, one foot out of the car and in a pile of wet leaves: 'Just a quick one.'

''Bye, now.'

We turned at the end of the cul-de-sac. The Oozer, when we again passed the house, was fumbling with his door-keys, and Greta slowed down until we saw the door open. For more than a year now, he had been a bird-alone. While teaching Irish litera-ture at a New England college, he had met and married a girl whom we knew by name: Belinda-Jo. After five years, she had left him, saying that she could no longer relate to him. 'She was on the plane and climbing out of Shannon,' he said, 'before I could find out what "relate" meant.'

'I would hate the idea,' I said to Greta, 'of going home to an empty house.'

She said, 'I know how he feels.'

Chapter Two

With Shay

Shay Lambe and I met every Monday evening in Tish Merdiff's. The well-to-do newcomers in our town – the runners-in and the culchies – probably paid little mind to the scrolled name above the door and on the windows. The true locals, including the upstarts of whom I was one, took a quiet proprietorial pride in knowing that a generation ago Tish had been the town whore.

Her surname was actually Meredith, but people of my parents' class were ill at ease with a 'th' at the end of words, whatever about the beginning, and could make no more of her name than Merdiff. She lived with her mother, who was her pimp, in a back lane off Rockfort Avenue and touted for business near the mailboat pier two miles away. I was old enough to remember her dimly and to have heard my father bid her a neighbourly 'Howayah, Tish ... ha'sh oul' day!' She wore a rakish beret and Bakelite earrings. Her lipstick formed an outsized cupid's bow, and she had a circle of vivid orange on each cheek. She was Church of Ireland, a distinction which, together with her unappetising appearance, helped to take the harm out of her. She was, on the contrary, looked upon as an asset, because in our town we liked to boast that we had at least one of everything. At any rate, not a word of protest was uttered when, long after she had died, white-haired and respectable at last, in England, Jack Fortune smartened up Grogan's pub and renamed it in her memory. On the day of my father's funeral, an old butty of his named Frank Flanagan insisted that I join him there for a pint, and the conversation got around to Tish. 'Your da,' old Flanagan said, 'was never one for drinking in pubs, but he used to say that to go up a laneway with poor old Tish you would need to be so ossified as to be impotent. I think he pronounced it, Lord have mercy on him, as "impudent". Whichever it was, I had never credited my father with that much wit.

When I saw Shay come into Tish's on the Monday after the Penders' dinner, I thought of the Oozer Kenirons' maunderings as Greta and I drove him home. Whatever about the rest of us, Seamus Lambe had not 're-invented' himself. He and his wife Brigid and their children lived a mile from Shankill, in sight of the sea, but he had never really moved away from the yellow glow of the Five Lamps, on the north side of town and caught in the girdle of the two canals. His long-widowed mother had recently died there in a small terrace house of red brick.

He and I could as easily have met for a drink close to his semi-detached with 'Massabielle' in faded paint on a name-plaque that hung crookedly from a surviving screw; or we could have found a pub at a half-way mark – the Ramblers' in Ballybrack, say – and done our colloguing there. Shay would not hear of putting me to the trouble of a ten-minute drive. For friends and neighbours alike, his kindness was an ever-flowing stream. He was golden-hearted and modest, and Thorn Thornton, for all his dinner-table malice, was right: Shay lived in mortal terror of seeming what he called pass-remarkable. He had never in his life carried a banner or poked his head over the edge of a parapet. In his entire make-up, he was guilty of only one affectation, and it was the belief that he was without affectation. He was nicer and less self-ish than I could ever be. Greta, who went shopping every week with Brigid, took pleasure in telling me so.

'When Shamy Lambe goes, God forbid,' she said once, '*he'll* have a big funeral.' For a moment I thought she was about to name a few of the likely mourners at my own paltry affair, but she let it pass.

Others, as she did, probably wondered what virtues I could

possibly have to make Shay look upon me as his closest friend. If I had to sum him up in a word, I would have called him a comforter. He was not a sycophant, never that; but you left his company assured that the pain in your chest was no more than muscular, that the tax inspector was an easygoing family man like yourself, that your rebellious eldest would, if left alone, give his bad company the go-by, and that the policeman who stopped you for speeding on Rock Road would by now have torn the page from his notebook. He achieved this, not in any facile way, but with quiet and reasonable argument, rubbing his right forefinger in a sawing motion up and down the side of his nose as he made a point. For years he had done nothing about his mouthful of bad teeth, and long after he had at last had them pulled, he continued to cover his mouth when he laughed. In middle-age, his hair was still tousled and fair.

He had contradictions. For a person in whom there was so much goodness, he owned up to an unholy liking for boxing matches at the National Stadium, the gorier the better. He adored western films, and the best of them all, he would tell you, was *The Wild Bunch* with its slow-motion goutings of blood. 'I love voilence,' he would admit cheerfully, and I took care not to correct him when he mispronounced the word or spoke of 'Eyetalians'; nor did I smile as he scornfully mimicked what he deemed to be a posh accent with an effete 'Doncher knaow!' Neither of us ever blundered into the *terra incognita* of the other's frailties. When our friendship was still young and raw, he liked to relive the final shoot-out in *Shane*, drawing an invisible six-gun and gunning down the villainous Jack Palance with a guttural 'Khrrrrgh … khrrrrgh!' I think it reassured him to see badness get its writhing deserts.

Another incongruity was that although he loved old songs and oft-told tales, he declared himself, when no one was listening, to be an atheist. He told me how, in his youth, his ma would give him sixpence for the collection plate every Sunday morning, and he would play truant, traipsing along the quays in all weathers, scavenging through second-hand barrows for books that by a fluke had escaped the censors' net. These days, on a tighter rein, he had no choice but to go to mass with Brigid and the kids, and once every month, she saw him off to the men's sodality. He went and took his place in St Anthony's Guild, because even if instead he mooched along the beach at Shanganagh he was certain to be saluted by a neighbour out walking a dog. His atheism jibbed, however, at sacrilege. When the men of the sodality shuffled towards the altar rails for communion, he became adept at taking the two quick steps that brought him ducking sideways through the door of what was, in more ways than one, the sanctuary. When he reached the church gate and the Bray road beyond, he may, for all I knew, have nursed an image of himself as Shane, dressed in buckskins and riding to the rescue of the homesteaders.

When I mentioned that I thought of myself as an agnostic, he was less than his tolerant self. 'You can't be,' he said with the air of a professional putting a flea in a dilettante's ear. 'That's like being an atheist, only watered down. In God's name, agnosticism is a load of rubbidge. No, no, grasp the nettle and own up to it. There's nothing and no one Up There.'

'Tell that to Brigid,' I said, and saw him shiver at the thought.

It would have broken her heart to contemplate a next world which did not have a sainted Shay in it, rubbing his nose at her. To have nagged him would be against the piety of her nature, but there would have been entire novenas offered up for his conversion; she would even have had the children gabbling through decades of the rosary for 'Mammy's very special intention'. She was neither a prude nor the conventional craw-thumper. Once, on the Lambes' yearly holiday in Connemara, she coolly sailed through my twelve-volume set – never read by me – of *Remembrance of Things Past* and, the following year, tackled the unabridged Pepys as if it, too, were a field for the scything. Books apart, her horizons ended with Shay and the four children. Getting six people into heaven was a massively full-time undertaking, and outsiders, God love them and with no offence, would have to fend for themselves, as would the housework and the mending.

To please Shay, she became part of our penny-poker school on Saturday evenings. Her unfeigned piety made us feel like cornerboys, and yet on one occasion I teased her. Over the cards, the subject had swung around to religion, and I asked, repenting of it even as the words came, 'Really and truly, Brigid, do you believe in God? No, come on.'

I saw Shay's eyes go narrow. It was what I privately called his John Wayne look: as if, while riding through Apache country, he had come across a ravished white woman. Not only was I poking fun at his gentle and adored wife, but at him also, daring him to hoist his colours.

Brigid replied very quietly. She said, 'Yes, I do. Because if there wasn't a God there would be no excuse for living in this rotten world.'

I had it in mind to say that it was none other than her God who had made this rotten world, but both Shay's face – he was all but grinding his new teeth at me – and the unaccustomed bitterness in Brigid's voice brought me up short. 'Well, trust you!' Greta said.

'Sorry,' I said, meaning it. 'I shouldn't have said that. People who live in glass houses ...' I have never had the gift of leaving well alone. As Greta swung her face towards me, the ceiling light blinked from her spectacles. 'Ah, there it is, the glass house!' I said.

She began to deal, causing the cards to snap as she announced openers: 'Queens or better!'

Shay and I first met when I was a clerk with Sunrise Insurance on Baggot Street. He came as part of a training course and was on his way to better things – two years later, he became an actuary –

whereas I ached to be quit of the treadmill. At lunchtime on his third or fourth day, I saw him sitting on Paddy Kavanagh's bench by the Grand Canal. He was juggling one of Brigid's sandwiches, a bottle of orangeade and a book. In my own experience, there is no surer way of attracting unwanted company in a pub or a park than to attempt to open a book; and of course the converse is true: if you sit without a crossword to solve or a book to read, you will die there of loneliness.

We were already on a nodding acquaintance. I sat next to him and, without preamble, fed him one of Joxer's lines from *Juno*: 'Whose is the bewk?'

To my delight and without looking up, he lobbed back Captain Boyle's reply: 'One o' Mary's. She's always readin' lately.'

We – he and I, that is – began there and then. I opened the snap-lid plastic box containing my own lunch of ham accompanied by coleslaw, which I hated, mixed with a thick paste of egg mayonnaise. Greta had set it out carefully on a paper plate under a wrapping of stretched cellophane. There was a bun, a dab of mustard, plastic cutlery and a white paper napkin. In contrast, Brigid had given Shay doorstep sandwiches of Irish Cheddar, which bulged from between the slices of bread like underwear from a burst suitcase. I scooped up a dollop of the yellow goo with my fork and flicked it over the edge of the lock, a few feet away.

To my delight, Shay said, 'They're playing the Mayonnaise.' It was the first half of a Groucho Marx line, and I completed it: 'The army must be dressing!'

I noticed that his shirt collar was frayed, and when he had finished his sandwiches he wiped his lips with a grubby handkerchief. He wore a blue serge suit over cracked black shoes, and in his breast pocket there was a row of two ballpoints, a pen and an eraser-tipped pencil.

'You'll want to watch out,' I said, pointing, 'or people will know what you do for a living.'

There and then was the first time I saw the narrow-eyed John Wayne look, and the friendship threatened to be stillborn. He said, stiffly, 'Thanks. I'm not ashamed of what I do.'

'That's not the point,' I said, making my escape, as he did on sodality Sundays, through the sanctuary door. 'The point is that what you do is none of their business.'

By next day the pens had moved out of sight. Months afterwards, in Searson's, I came back from ordering drinks at the bar in time to hear him say to the company, '... TJ told me it was nobody else's business but mine, and he was right.' I began to understand him. I had given him an excuse to get rid of the pens without betraying his self-image of an unspoilt chap whose da had died of TB in the consumptive forties and who had grown up a stone's throw from the Five Lamps. That self-image, his ideal of himself, was his only conceit. Although invisible to the naked eye, it was harder than a diamond. He was decent, ordinary, straight and honourable, and his most unforgiving judge was himself. A mutual friend told me that he had once given Shay a tip for the Derby at twelve to one. 'How certain is it?' Shay wanted to know. 'Absolutely cast iron,' the friend said. 'I got it from the trainer himself. It can't lose.' Nor indeed did it, but Shay refused to bet on it, holding that to gamble on a certainty was dishonest. In his view, the rest of us might fall many times, rise again and give ourselves absolution; Shay would not allow himself that weakness.

When we became friends, Greta and I had been married going on for three years, and he and Brigid for eighteen months. The women took to each other and went shopping together on Fridays, Greta trim and slim, and Brigid with her haystack hair that never saw a roller. Meanwhile, Shay and I gradually assumed separate roles in our friendship. He was a born bystander, and to him even my poorest cygnets were swans.

A stroke of good fortune enabled me to leave Sunrise. Out of my passion for old films, I put together a book called *Players of the Thirties.* It was not so much writing as a kind of annotated collage, and it celebrated the heyday of such supporting actors as Edward Everett Horton, Charlie Ruggles, Mary Boland, Alison Skipworth, Charles Butterworth and Herman Bing. When my Irish publishers went to the wall, an American bought the company and reissued the book in a coffee-table format, glossily illustrated and with the title changed to *These We Have Loved.* It became a success – nostalgia was in vogue just then – and when a follow-up, to be called *The Silver Screen,* was commissioned I handed in my notice to Sunrise. Greta was taken aback. That I had abandoned a pensionable job did not bother her in the least – we were still in love in those days – but she had married an insurance clerk and now had the faintly aggrieved air of a woman who had ordered rice pudding only to be served with a *crème caramel.* And she suspected that since I now enjoyed what I did for a living, it could not be work at all but a form of cunning retirement.

Shay's delight was unfeigned; it was as if I had turned out to be an O'Connor and an O'Faolain combined. There was no limit, he insisted, to how far I would go. 'Hey, *you* didn't write it,' I said, embarrassed, '*I* did.' He cackled with pleasure.

We are, as the apologists keep saying, a small country, and one man wears many hats. It was so in my case. I became a showbiz obituarist for the *Irish Record,* and as well there was a regular film spot on a radio arts show and a question-and-answer column of my own in one of the Sundays. *These We Have Loved* was reviewed in *Cahiers du Cinema* and I was invited to Bordeaux to sit on the jury of the *Festival de Nostalgie.* It was at an awards dinner that Turlough Pender introduced himself and Colleen. 'We're meeting quite a few new people,' I said to Greta afterwards. Aware that I was fishing for a compliment, she said, 'I've always preferred quality to quantity myself', although in the case of Colleen Pender she soon afterwards recanted.

Meanwhile, Shay and I slipped into our roles of Damon and

Pythias. Like schoolboys, we evolved a private language, using film quotes to repel intruders. He was supportive, subordinate, loyal unto death and the straight man of the act. The vanishing pens were not my only accomplishment; I taught him to drive, persuaded him to have his teeth pulled, and urged him towards the outer edges of the new world I enjoyed and from which he hid. At work, he moved upwards, but wore his eminence lightly. He acquired a new dark-blue suit, but his shoes were still cracked and his handkerchief a dingy off-white. He continued to say 'voilence'.

On a trip to London, I met the editor of the monthly *Playgoer*. He asked if I would be interested in writing an Irish newsletter: 'You know, thumbnail reviews of whatever plays are on.' I passed – theatre and the making of enemies in a town as small as Dublin was a hat I had no interest in wearing – but mentioned that a friend of mine, one Seamus Lambe, might care to have a try. When I attempted to endow Shay with a CV as glowing as it was bogus, the editor said, 'I don't give a damn if he can write or not, or what he knows or doesn't know. Just so long as he can deliver copy on time.' It would take a thirteenth labour of Hercules, I thought, to lure Shay another inch or so out of his shell, but to my surprise, he leaped at the idea. He made only one condition: that he could hug the shadows by signing his pieces 'JJL'. 'I always had a great *gradh* for the theatre,' he said, happily.

Without intending to, he and Brigid became a familiar sight at first nights. He took his trust seriously; and, even if she said that she wouldn't mind a cup of coffee at the interval, Shay thought it best that they should remain unobtrusively in their aisle seats. This had an effect opposite to the desired one, since it made them almost the only first-nighters visible in a sea of empty stalls. A Corconian designer of stage scenery nodded towards them on his return from the bitcheries of the Abbey bar. 'Crippled!' I heard him say in a great whisper to his inamorato. 'Can't walk.'

'Who? Which one?'

'Both, dear.'

I was annoyed for the Lambes' sake, and yet on the way home I mentioned what I had heard to Greta. She was just as indignant, but passed it on to Colleen. After all, we lived in Dublin.

Shay wrote his pieces in a careful Leaving Cert prose. 'All I know,' he said, 'is what Brother Athanasius dinned into me at the Presentation Brothers. "In writing a composition, let not the self intrude, boy! Stick to the third person singular!"'

Shay's opinions were benign for a time; then at Christmas I gave him the collected reviews of Max Beerbohm, which may or may not have been why his pieces acquired a fine edge of irony that could sting like a paper-cut. His editor paid him a derisively small fee without ever being aware that Shay would have done the job for nothing. He was as happy as Larry.

At an Abbey first night not long afterwards, I was introduced to Thorn Thornton. He said 'The very man!', took me by the arm and led me out of the bar and on to the small balcony so that we were looking down on the stalls. They were empty except for Shay and Brigid in seats K11 and 12. From that angle, it occurred to me that I might have a word with Shay about his short back-and-sides haircut.

Thorn said: '"JJL" of *Playgoer*. Right?'

'Pardon me?'

'I'm in the business, so I have a right to put a face on him. I don't much like fellows that snipe from under cover. Name of James Joseph Lambe? Seamus Lambe? He's a mate of yours, right?'

Without answering directly, I quoted Shay himself. 'He has a great *gradh* for the theatre.'

'It takes more than love, mate. A hell of a lot more.'

He released my arm like a policeman letting a drunk go with a warning.

Two years later, I was surprised to open the *Dubliner*, a daily paper, and see the name 'Seamus Lambe' appended to a review of a play by Alan Ayckbourn. 'When did that happen?' I asked when we next met at Tish's.

'Someone has flu,' Shay said, 'and they rang and asked if I'd fill in for him. And the buggers insisted that I use my name, did you notice that?'

'Yes, I did.'

'Apparently it's what they call house policy. No hiding behind initials or pen names. They insisted.' He turned to wave to the barman.

'They insisted,' I repeated.

'Um.'

'And you went along.' I was annoyed to find myself faintly jealous, as when a cat slides off one's lap and goes to another person. 'And what ever happened,' I asked, 'to Brother Thingy and the third person singular?'

'How do you mean?'

'Well, all of a sudden you're a star. I read your notice, and you used that hallowed phrase "Did these old eyes deceive me, or …?" Long time since I heard that one.'

He was too pleased with himself to notice my bad temper. 'Ah, Brother Athanasius is a long time dead. And sure it was time I started flexing the old muscles.'

The flu victim on *The Dubliner* either became worse and died or, which was the more likely, failed to sober up, for Shay became the second-string critic. He went to the fringe theatres or filled in when the chief reviewer – a dentist by profession and nicknamed McCavity – was indisposed or on holiday or had a *crise de nerfs* at the prospect of coping with a Pinter. Shay made it a rule not to discuss a play with Brigid until his notice was handed in. He had bought a second-hand Fiat by then and, after a first night, would park it under a street light outside the *Dubliner* office on Arran Quay, leaving it locked tight, with his wife safe inside reading a book while he hammered away on a typewriter in a corner of the news room. Finally, on the way home, they would swap judgements. 'Don't be cross with me, Shamy,' she would say in a little-girl voice if her opinion of the play, which was always both intelligent and forthright, differed from his. It was only her notion of love-talk. Shay was never cross with her.

Very well, then; it was the Monday after the Penders' dinner, and Shay came into Tish's. He saw me and raised a finger, first to me and then to Vincent the barman. After an incident at a wedding, his family doctor had warned him that he was allergic to alcohol, and now the pints he ordered were of ersatz beer.

This Monday, I had a small item of news for him. I said: 'I've put in for a job.'

'Tell me.'

'The interview is on Wednesday.'

'An interview? Serious stuff!'

I told him that the widow of the Irish-American film director Sean O'Fearna was endowing an archive in his memory.

'O'Fearna?' Shay said.

'He made westerns.'

'Oh, *that* O'Fearna! He did *The Seekers*. That was a great fil-lum.'

The position of archivist had been advertised in the national press. The salary was modest, not for lack of money but to make the job less of a magnet for chancers. The prestige was considerable, however. 'Archivist', like, say, 'historian', was a fat and fair word. I had applied and was on the shortlist.

'You'll get it, of course,' Shay said.

I smiled. 'You're incredible.'

'How?'

'I wish I was as confident as you are.'

'It stands to reason.'

He began to tick off on his fingers all the reasons why I was the only person for the job. I raised an opposing hand and did some ticking off of my own. My fingers and thumb all said the same thing: the plum, small as it was, would go to some politician's darling; a favour would be called in, and that would be that.

'Those days are gone,' Shay said, lying outrageously.

I was not to be cheated out of an injustice. 'Or else the Arts Council will have it sewn up.'

'Don't be such a misery. Who's on the panel?'

I had no idea. By now, Shay himself had earned a seat on many an interview board to do with insurance, and, between taking gulps of his non-alcoholic beer, he delivered a thirty-minute talk on the Art of the Interview. I could see why, in spite of being down at heel, he had risen so unfalteringly. In his soft-spoken way he could talk a hole in an iron bucket. By the time he had wound down, he was on his second pint and the job was in my pocket.

He said: 'What does Greta think?'

'I haven't told her.'

His smile was sentimental. 'You cute hawk, you. You want it to be a surprise.'

'Of course,' I said, 'and how well you know me!' Then, adding another lie to that one, 'No, the opposite. I don't like her to get her hopes up.'

Greta and I spoke of daily things; we shared jokes, we had screaming rows and louder silences, we even made plans, but in an emotional sense I could find no way into her. Within, if one could only detect a seam in the outer shell, there might have been depths to drown in or at the very least a shoal to run aground on. She might, like Shay, have been fiercely on my side; or she might have seen the job as one other net that would entangle her in a world she distrusted. I knew I could have asked her, straight out: 'Do you want me to get this job?' She would have shrugged and made a tiny 'Mmmp' that could equally have been a yes or a no, a question or an exclamation mark.

Shay and I parted at closing time. Our conversation had moved away from jobs and interviews. He enjoyed committing vicarious adultery, so I told him a tall tale about a London adventure of mine, adding a rich and false icing to a crumb of truth. Next, we talked about the current Oscar Wilde play at the Gate, in which Lady Bracknell was a Margaret Thatcher caricature. Shay was discoursing on the fashion for doing period plays in modern dress when a voice said, 'Well, the very man!'

I turned and it was April-May Macgreedy. It was the first time I had seen her since the Penders' dinner party, and her red hair seemed, now as then, to have been caught in brambles. I wondered again if it was a coiffure. She bore down on us and gave Shay an unhindered view of her back.

I said, 'Hello. This is Shay Lambe. April-May Mac-'

She said, 'Hello,' without looking at him. A notebook had appeared in one hand, a pencil in the other. She told me that she had been to see the novelist Deirdre Lynch, who lived in our town in one of the houses on the corner of the bay. She said, 'I'm doing a piece for *The Liar* about well-known people and the toys they loved as children.' The pencil was poised. 'So what about it?'

I said, 'Me? I'm not well-known.'

She said, 'Well, sure you'll do, you'll do.'

I said, 'Thanks all the same.'

Her face became small and sour. 'Oh, come on. Don't tell me you're too effing grand for fifty words?'

So I told her that my very favourite toy was a tiny sled my father had made for me. 'He painted the name *Rosebud* on it,' I said. 'And then he took it from me and burned it.' Over her shoulder, I could see Shay, who had a fist against his mouth and was rubbing the forefinger of the other hand up and down his nose. I felt the wetness of real tears come into my eyes as I told her how I saw Rosebud go up in flames.

April-May wrote it all down and said, 'Now that didn't hurt, did it?' She slapped her notebook shut and went back to her drink.

Outside the pub under a fat October moon, Shay and I fell about, shrieking. It was a good friendship.

On the Wednesday at a few minutes to midday, I reported to the Berkeley Court Hotel where my interview was to happen. I went to a suite on the fourth floor where a receptionist took my name and invited me to sit. She went into an inner room. To my relief, there were no others waiting, so I would at least be spared the humiliation of failing in public. After a moment, she returned and said, 'Will you go in?' I did so and discovered Thorn Thornton alone in the room and sitting behind a desk.

In my confusion I thought for a moment that he, too, was there to be interviewed. Then he said 'Good morning,' motioned me to a chair and placed in front of him what I recognised as my letter of application.

Chapter Three

At White's

Thornton sat, two fingers against his brow as he affected to read my letter. The weight of the world was upon him; he could have posed for a likeness of Beethoven revising his Ninth. He glanced fleetingly at me, and I knew it was play-acting. A half-minute is a long time when one is expected to writhe in suspense and as I was about to rise and walk – no, stalk – out in dignified silence, he said, 'Would you happen to know if Sean O'Fearna ever made a film with Jimmy Cagney?'

I told him, sullenly: yes; there had been a World War One comedy film called *Glory Road*, made in 1952. 'And two years later, pleading gallstones, O'Fearna was replaced on a film set on a navy supply ship in the south Pacific. He played the captain, but the star was actually –'

'Cagney's my favourite,' Thornton said, and added, 'You dirty rat.'

He looked again at my application, drummed his fingers on the desktop, and hummed a bar of 'Give my regards to Broadway'. Then he thrust the letter quickly into his briefcase and snapped it shut.

He said: 'Okay. Fuck it, you have the job. Let's have a bite of lunch.'

Greta would often remark on a certain mannerism of mine. In moments of unexpectedness, instead of showing dismay or pleasure, my face would lose all expression. 'Too cagey to show what you're thinking,' she said. Perhaps she was half right; anyway, at that moment, I imagine I could have out-frozen Buster Keaton.

Thornton, guessing that I was speechless, whinnied and quoted an exit line from his favourite film star: 'Made it, Ma ... top of the world!'

We took a taxi and were at Baggot Street Bridge before either of us talked. In a corner of my mind I had begun to wonder if this was perhaps an elaborate hoax. I caught him grinning at me. He said, 'Are you gobsmacked?'

'A bit.'

'By what? By getting the job? Or by me giving it to you?'

'Both.'

He said, 'I can imagine.'

We alighted outside White's of the Green. It was coming on to rain, and, as he paid the driver, Thornton caught my eye and nodded across the street towards the Green itself. 'There he goes, God bless him. Straight out of a bandbox and heading for his club.' I looked and saw Andrew Hand hoisting an umbrella as he loped along. He was as immaculate as ever.

'I wonder where herself is,' Thornton said. 'I know you see her as the Virgin Mary, so I hope you're not going to hit me a belt and lose this job before you're into it, but I had a most improper thought at the Penders' last Friday. That wife of Hand's ...'

'Josie?'

'You haven't forgotten her name? ... ah, good! She's so damned flawless that I wouldn't be surprised if her pubic hair resembled closely-trimmed Astroturf with a sprinkling of red dust from the Sahara. Now there's an image to hold onto.'

He took off across the pavement and was into White's ahead of me. As I followed him down the stairs, the head waiter was already leading the way to a banquette table marked 'Reserved'.

'Malachy, this is my guest, Mr Quill,' Thornton said. 'Mr Quill is the newly-appointed director of the O'Fearna Film Archive – OFFA, for short. It is a position, be well advised, which carries with it a handsome luncheon allowance.'

'Then Mr Quill will have to be well-looked after,' the waiter smarmed, returning Thornton's service. To me, he said, 'Congratulations, sir.'

I nodded thanks, reflecting that I was unlikely to become a friend with Malachy unto death. As Thornton and I settled in, I had a fleeting twinge, as from an old disquiet, but could not pin down the cause. I shrugged it away and took in my surroundings. Five men in dark blue suits, two of whom I recognised as Fianna Fail cabinet ministers, were in a corner, elbows on the tablecloth, foreheads almost touching in conspiracy.

'This, what I've landed you with, is a Mickey Mouse job, you do know that?' Thornton said. 'Or it will be, to begin with. It might be a stepping stone to better things, just the same as pigs might fly. And, like I say, your good lady – Greta, isn't it? – need never cook you another weekday lunch. An additional perk is, there'll be all the travel you like.'

'Travel? Where would I want to go?'

'Where? Well, Santa Fe for a start. Sure won't you have to pay homage to the Widow O'Fearna? Let's have a glass of wine.'

He signalled to an under-waiter. I felt my face go deadpan once again. I had been here and there in Europe for holidays and on business, but had never travelled further west than Clifden. An hour ago, my only commitment had been to spend the afternoon at home writing twelve hundred words on the films of Rouben Mamoulian; now, and without a US visa to my name, there was talk of Santa Fe, where Sean O'Fearna had died within sight of the Sangre de Cristo mountains.

The Buster Keaton face was at smiling point. Rather than give Thornton the satisfaction, I asked: 'Where do you fit in?'

'Me?'

He affected the surprised air of an admiral who had been asked if the stern of a ship was the pointed end. One of Malachy's acolytes came and was told, 'Colm, we'll have a drop of the Petit Chablis.' Thornton stroked the dead-rat moustache in anticipation. 'Excellent stuff. I'm thirty-three years old, the age at which

Christ died, and not until six months ago did I discover the pleasure of a quiet harmless jar. Did I put that in capitals? Allow me to do so. A Quiet Harmless Jar.'

He took a Mont Blanc ballpoint from his pocket and, turning it between his fingers, tapped it on the tablecloth, first the writing end, then the blunt. I was to find out that it was his prologue to a confidence. He said, 'I had business on the Coast recently and came back by way of Albuquerque. I rented a car and drove to Santa Fe.'

A saucer of olives arrived. I felt a twist of envy at the offhandedness with which Thornton had mentioned the place-names of legend.

'I'd read an item,' Thornton said, 'in the *Hollywood Reporter*. It said that the Widow O'Fearna was planning to set up a chair in the old fellow's honour at some New England university: Yale, maybe, or Brown in Rhode Island. I did a bit of mugging up on him, and it seems that the New York critics and the Hollywood begrudgers tore the tripes out of his last half-dozen fillums. He'd been making pictures, do you know, since the silent days. Well, of course you flaming well know; that's why you have the job. Any idea how many?'

'Silent films, you mean? Nobody knows. The first was in 1917.'

'Howsomever, the widow – Kitty O'Fearna, and a tough biddy she is, too – wanted him to have a monument. Not a statue of marble or bronze or such – hey, do you know he has an airport named after him in Wyoming? You do? Well, I didn't. No, she wanted something better, something longer-lasting. And while she was at it, she wanted to give the back of her hand to the phoneys and the highbrows that slammed his pictures.'

'His last films were all over the place,' I said. 'He was in his late seventies. He was tired, and for a lot of the time he was drunk.'

'Well, for Christ's sake don't say that out loud,' Thorn said, 'or you'll have us both in the brown stuff. I read up on those old films. I went through the reviews. I forgot the bad ones and learnt the other kind off by heart. And I paid a call on Kitty O'Fearna on her ranch out by the Pecos. What I mean is, I camped on her doorstep.'

As Thornton spoke, I saw in my mind's eye a handsome Spanish hacienda, set against a backdrop of desert and mountains with cactus and Jimpson weed and the Pecos river itself, wide and calm: the kind of setting O'Fearna used in his westerns. A lifelong habit of mine, perhaps childish, is that whenever I have a journey to take or a story to listen to, a film unrolls inside my head. I see the places and people, and they stay until the reality comes like a bailiff to evict them. In time, what Thornton said came true and I met Kitty O'Fearna, but not in New Mexico; it was when she came to Dublin; and she told me with amusement that the Pecos river was neither wide nor calm, but a rushing torrent no more than forty feet across.

No matter. As Thornton told his story, the pictures came, unbidden. Inside my head, I furnished the Widow's living room. I gave it a massive stone fireplace, with cattle horns over the mantelpiece on which were aligned O'Fearna's four Oscars. The sofa and armchairs were covered with buffalo hides. There was a Winchester in a glass case and a cavalry painting by Remington on the wall. In the movie house of my mind, the Widow herself, the keeper of the flame, was leathery and tough; she could have worn a poke bonnet and a gingham dress and stood at Fort Geronimo among the tumbling tumbleweed as the horse soldiers rode out.

Of course the reality proved to be that she was sixty-five and could pass for a citified fifty. She had been O'Fearna's second wife, a musical comedy actress twenty years younger than he, with all her toughness on the inside. I already knew that when she and O'Fearna were on location and arrived on the set by buckboard just after dawn, an old man – one of the survivors of the group that called itself the Sons of the Pioneers – played the mouth-organ and she sang either 'Red River Valley' or 'Yes, We'll

Gather at the River'. With Thornton, she was a cliff face without a hand-hold. She was used to hustlers; they came to feed like desert carrion off her husband's reputation, and she saw them off. When she consented to give him fifteen minutes and not a minute longer, she knew him for one more grafter, this time a Paddy on the make.

He talked to her about the later films and how underrated they were – 'autumnal' was the word he used. She was unmoved. He spoke about his idea for an archive. She had heard it all before. He reminded her that O'Fearna had, after all, been born in a thatched cabin near Letterfrack, and the archive would be her gift to his homeland.

She said, 'Mr Thornton –'

'My friends call me Thorn.'

She all but sneered. 'Mr Thornton … my husband no more came from Connemara than I did. He was born at Cape Elizabeth in the state of Maine. His father was a saloon-keeper in Portland.'

'Well, then,' Thornton heard himself saying, 'what if in return for your generosity –'

'Goodbye, Mr Thornton.'

' … What if, to convey their gratitude, the Irish government were to grant your husband citizenship?'

She said, 'Say again?'

Thornton said, 'I mean, of course, posthumously. Retrospective, that is. With full naturalisation papers. And a passport.' As she stared, he pushed further. 'I mean, he always claimed to be Irish. And you know as well as I do that the most quotable line from any Sean O'Fearna film is "When truth becomes legend –"'

Almost blurting it out, she said, ' … print the legend.'

She got to her feet and rang a bell. A servant came, a house-boy. Listening to Thornton tell it, I wondered if he was coloured. O'Fearna was always paternalistic towards the black people in his films. I remembered Stepin Fetchit in *Steamboat a-Comin'*.

Or – and I was becoming fanciful – the servant might have been one of his old character players: Hank Worden, perhaps, or Jack Pennick.

As if reading my thoughts and disposing of an interruption, Thornton said, 'He was a Jap.' He went on with his story.

The Widow told the servant that her guest would be staying for dinner. She asked, 'Is this your first trip to the South-West, young man?'

'Yes, ma'am,' Thornton said, slipping into the frontier vernacular.

She nodded towards the picture window. 'Well, there aren't any Apaches out there, not any more, but we still have rattlers, scorpions and Gila monsters. And I'll feed you to them if you bullshit me. Now this talk of making him a citizen ... is it a come-on or can it be fixed?'

Thornton said, 'I would say that our government would certainly wish to respond to so generous a –'

She said, 'Cut that out. I asked you, can it be fixed?'

'It can be fixed.'

White's had begun to fill up with the lunch crowd. Menus were brought with our Petit Chablis. Thornton sniffed and tasted the wine and nodded knowledgeably as if he had not been a teetotaller for all but the past six months of his thirty-three years. He told me he was a vegetarian: 'I don't mind eating fish as long as it doesn't look like the fish.' I pulled him back to New Mexico. 'Making him a citizen ... *can* it be done?'

Thornton said, 'No problem.' He nodded towards the group of politicians. For aperitifs, three of them were drinking pints. 'Any one of that lot could swing it quicker than he could pocket a back-hander. Making an honorary Irishman of a Yank who all his life had claimed to be a real one? Come on, now ... easy-peasy.'

'And that was it?' I said. 'Mission accomplished?'

He said, 'As good as. There was one hurdle left.'

Before the Widow and he sat down to dinner on the patio –

was the desert red at sunset, I wanted to know – they had what she called cocktails. 'I drink rye whisky,' she told him. 'You're Irish, so you get whiskey with an "e".'

Thornton wondered if he were being put through a kind of test. The stubby glass that was set before him had barely room in it for a topping-up of a half-inch of iced water. He took a sip. The spirits were raw and made his eyes water. He had never drunk either whisky or whiskey in his life and he wondered how much or how little of the stuff would make him stupid.

The Widow took an easy swallow of her rye; her insides, he thought, were lined with copper. She said two things, the first unexpected: 'For Chrissakes, choke on that and have done with it.' The second was what he had been waiting for. 'So come clean. What's in this for you?'

He told her, 'Absolutely nothing.'

From the look she gave him, it was his moment of danger. In his own words, he beat her to the draw. 'At least nothing tangible. I'm asking for reasonable and itemised expenses, but otherwise not a penny piece. And look, I'm sorry, Mrs O'Fearna, I can't drink this tack. I'd rather offend you with the truth sober than lie to you drunk.' He pushed the glass away. 'What I want,' he told her, '. . . no, scrub that . . . what I insist on, is full and absolute control, with authority to hire and fire, and no interference. It isn't a time-consuming job, so for now I'll do it free of charge. I'm not a fly-by-night; when I give my word I keep it, and I'll find you a good archivist, the best there is. Now, would you ever call Mr Moto and ask him to bring me a drop of dry white?'

Later, when I came to know Thorn Thornton, I realised that he had been in his element, his heart racing as he faced her down.

The Widow said, 'You still haven't answered my question. What is it you want?'

'With respect, nothing that has to do with you.'

She pouted, almost like a teenage girl. 'Secrets already?'

'Not at all.' Thornton crooked a finger and leaned towards her.

'Dublin, ma'am, is a small town, but in my Father's oven there are many pies, and I want a finger in every one of them.'

The widow stared at him, then laughed. It was a loud, full-throated bark. 'Is that it? Then all I can say is Christ help Dublin,' she said.

He grinned as he told me, proud of himself. I remembered Batty Kenirons in the back of our car rambling on about how Thornton's ambition was to run the city. 'And Jesus pity us all,' he had said.

Thornton raised his glass. 'So there you have it. How the West was won. And now here I am, and here you are. Good luck.'

'Personal question.'

'Shoot.'

'The Widow O'Fearna ... *can* she trust you?'

'Mm.'

'No, I mean honest injun?'

'As sure as my name's Cochise.' He laughed aloud. 'Hey, don't you know about me yet? Hasn't my honesty gone before me? I'm as straight as the proverbial – What's a die, anyway?'

Kenirons had mentioned that Thornton was a graduate of Trinity, so his ignorance was understandable.

'Singular of dice.'

'Get away.'

'And what about me?' I asked. 'Can I trust you?'

'Oh, yes. All the way and home again. Except maybe when I say to you: "Trust me".' He giggled, and again it was a whinny.

Over lunch, he told me he had ruffled a few feathers on my account. 'There was opposition. Other applicants. Committee freaks. The kind of gobshites who think the arts should be a democracy instead of a dictatorship.' He mentioned a few names. 'I told them you were the best man for the job, and that you're not to be interfered with. Finito.'

I said, 'I'll bet you told them something else, too. That you could handle me.'

He laughed. 'Who's the wise bunny rabbit, then? Oh, you'll get on. You'll be kept.' Then, in what I knew was a false show of candour: 'Well, of course I said I could handle you. That's how it's done.'

It was three-thirty before he called for the bill and said, 'Next time it'll be your turn.' He told me: 'I'm going to send you one of my girls. Don't worry, she won't seduce you. She's had a baby and can't go on working full-time, but a couple of hours a day will do you for the present. Name of Violet Mooney, and she's a topper. Why do you smile?'

'I know someone,' I told him, 'who would call her "Voilet".'

As we got to our feet, a man came over from one of the other tables. He was white-haired; his eyes were a watery blue, with extraordinarily long lashes. From my days with Sunrise I recognised him as an insurance broker. He put his hand out and said, 'The b'oul' JJ!'

Thornton looked at the hand as if it were broccoli on a tooth.

The man said, 'It's time we let bygones be bygones. 'S all water under the bridge, right? Good man yourself. Sure I was a prick in them days.'

Thornton, allowing me to precede him out, said, 'You're still a prick.'

Outside, the rain was down for the day. I said, 'Wait a minute. I have to know ...'

He said, 'More. Well, hurry it up. I'm getting soaked.'

I said, 'Was that a free lunch? You know what I mean.'

He said, 'You owe me shag-all. Now relax. Enjoy. This will be good for you. Stretch yourself.'

His hand darted out from the sleeve of his overcoat, shook mine and went back into hiding. Before turning away, he said, 'Oh, and I won't call you Thady again.'

It was not a bad exit line. As I watched him hurrying towards Grafton Street, head down against the rain, it occurred to me that except for the fingers his hands stayed out of sight like the head of a tortoise on the watch for a predator. All at once, I felt the same twinge as when he had introduced me to the head waiter, Malachy, but now I knew the cause.

He was nudging me forward into the light, just as I had nudged Shay.

Chapter Four

In 'Kate Fortune's Lane'

If you pressed your face hard against the glass of our living room window and squinted fiercely to the left, you could see down the length of Kate Fortune's Lane to Avourneen Road, where a wedge of Irish Sea and a fragment of island were visible in the space between two Victorian mansions, 'Aboukir' and 'Khyber'. Our house, half the size of either and unlikely to make old bones, was called – risibly in my case – 'Haven', and the estate agent's panegyric made mention of its far-reaching sea views, which was truthful inasmuch as on clear days and through the granite cleft one could see half-way to Anglesey. The ruins of five fishermen's cottages had been flattened to make room for two houses: ours, and the one next door, which was called 'St. Anthony's' because, as our neighbour, a borough councillor named Locke, said, 'He helped us to find it.' Mrs Locke, a nice little woman with a witch's chin, appeared from behind him and applied the icing to the saint's cupcake with 'St Anthony makes a great fist of putting his finger on things.'

We had been there a few years when, after a proposal by Sean Locke, duly seconded and carried, the council changed the name of our unpaved lane to Avourneen Mews, even though there had never been a stable within an ass's bray of the place. Greta said that the new name was 'nice'; then went burrowing into our thesaurus and enlarged this to 'sort of euphonious'.

'Do you not think so?' she asked.

'No, but I'll grant you that "euphonious" is euphonious.'

'You're so bloody smart.'

45

It seemed to me less than fair that Kate Fortune, whoever she might have been, should have her one small claim on posterity so rudely taken away. Out of badness, I enlisted the aid of a local sign-painter, who unscrewed the 'Haven' nameplate from our front gate and in its place put a new one. It said 'Kate Fortune's Lane', and at no extra cost was enhanced by dog roses entwined around and through the letters. The Lockes were not best pleased; nor was Greta. 'A house is not a laneway,' she stormed, almost quoting a madam named Polly Adler, adding, 'Anyway we don't even know what kind of woman she was.' At such propriety, I burst out laughing, and then so did she. She deplored her sense of humour and that she could never quite get shot of it.

When I arrived home after my lunch with Thornton, the hall telephone was ringing. Upstairs, where we as yet had no extension, I heard Greta say 'Bugger.' I called to her: 'I'm home. I'll get it.'

The voice at the other end was Shay's. He said, 'Well, tell us.'

I said, 'I landed it.'

'Of course you did. Stands to reason.'

For all his diffidence, he was the most sure-of-himself person I had ever known. I could not remember ever hearing the words 'I don't know' pass his lips, and now, in the most quietly maddening way, he delivered his rationale. The job was mine, he explained with exquisite simplicity, because it could not have been anyone else's. Again, he ticked off one reason after another, like a man removing pins from a new shirt. The other contenders, he said airily, were non-runners. When I told him, thinking to score a point, that I had been the only interviewee, he said, 'That's exactly what I say.'

A movement caught my eye, and in a corner of the hall mirror I saw Greta, who had come down to the half-landing and was, as she thought, standing out of sight. With one eye on the mirror, I interrupted Shay as he resumed his summing up. 'I can't talk now. I'll see you Monday.'

46

He said, as if the job were a new suit, 'Anyway, well wear.'

'Thanks.'

'God, it's great. Massive.'

As I hung up, Greta came down the rest of the way into the hall. 'Who was that?'

'Shay.'

'So why couldn't you talk to him now? What's so secret?'

'Were you listening?'

She said, 'You know I don't listen. I happened to overhear it.' Greta was adept at the practice of what, until sexism became a hanging offence, could be described as female handicrafts, except that she could not sew on a button and, unlike me, was a hopeless liar.

I said, 'I didn't want to have him on the phone all day. You see, there's something I couldn't wait to tell you. I have a new job.'

She said nothing for a moment, then: 'I suppose that was what kept you.'

'When?'

'It's going on for five o'-bloody clock.'

'Ah. Actually, I had lunch with Thorn Thornton.'

She said, 'Him? What has *he* got to do with anything?'

As usual, our morning post had not come until mid-afternoon, and she trod on my heels as I took the three envelopes from the hall table and walked into the breakfast room. There was a bill, an advertisement for double-glazing and a packet of readers' film queries for reply in my weekly column. Greta sat across the table from me. She said, 'I suppose you want me to get pliers and pull it out of you. What's this new job, then? Break it to me.'

I gave her a pocket-sized version of my day, leaving out the details of Thornton's adventure near Santa Fe. As the late Sean O'Fearna might have said, I cut to the chase and told her: 'There's to be a film archive, and I'm in charge of it.'

'I see.'

'An archive is a –'

'I know what an archive is.'

'Sure.'

'I'm not thick. It's ... things kept in a ... whatsit, in a cellar.'

'You could be right.'

She raised a hand and made curving motions above her head. 'In a vault, like. So what kind of fillums?'

'Do you know the name Sean O'Fearna?'

'You mean cowboy pictures?' she said.

'Westerns.'

'I see. Westerns.' She raised a hand to her face as if in a humane attempt to conceal a jeering smile. It was well done. It looked genuine.

Soldiering on, I told her that I would have an office of my own. 'So the good news is that I won't be under your feet all day.'

'The good news.' She tasted the phrase. 'Are you trying to make out that as far as I'm concerned this job, as you call it, would be *bad* news?'

'Well, you didn't seem thrilled to bits.'

'Do you mind,' she said. 'I've only this minute been graciously informed about it. How cute you were, keeping it to yourself.'

'I didn't tell you bec-'

'No, you didn't.'

'... Because there was the possibility ... no, the likelihood ... no, the certainty almost, that I would end up as an also-ran.' I was vexed by the realisation that I wanted her to be impressed. Adding a dash of hypocrisy that segued into sarcasm, I said: 'I didn't want to end up not getting the job, and with you bitterly disappointed. You would have been disappointed, wouldn't you?'

Silence.

'Well, wouldn't you?'

She donated an 'Mmmp.' Then: 'So what's Thorn Thornton's interest in it?'

'He's organising it.'

With joyous disbelief: 'He's never your boss, then!'

'Jesus, no. He's –'

'*Thorn Thornton*? Oh … my … Gawd.'

'He has no authority over me,' I told her, and the words, convincing on Thornton's lips, seemed feeble on mine. 'He's acting as an unpaid contact man, just so's he can show off. He's a figurehead.'

She said, 'Is that what he is? Well, you watch him.'

The note of concern was so unexpected that by way of encouraging a *détente* I told her about Thornton and the insurance broker, ending with 'You're still a prick.' She gave an unwilling smile. 'I liked that in him,' I said.

'Yes, go on,' she said, the smile evaporating. 'Make a hero out of him. That's all you need. He's a … a … a control freak.'

I said, 'Where did you get that?'

'What?'

'That expression.'

'It was in the paper. Someone in the Dail said it to someone.'

'Yes, well, you could be half right.'

She said: 'Half is too much. I'd mind him.'

Still at the table, I opened my film queries while Greta began getting the dinner. She took table mats from a cupboard and nodded at the correspondence. 'There's a place for those.' I gathered it up in silence and moved out and across the hall to my workroom which had once been our garage. A reader wanted to know the name of Hopalong Cassidy's horse. Another, trying to catch me out, asked what character actor's face was glimpsed on an election poster in a street scene in *West Side Story*. I typed out the answers: Topper and Joseph Crehan. A third reader wanted to know about an old Edmund Lowe film in which a mechanical doll nodded or shook its head when asked a question. I had identified it as a 1935 melodrama called *Best Man Wins* when Greta summoned me to table. By then my early excitement had turned to still water. What I had thought of as a challenge and possibly a new beginning no longer seemed to be so very much. It was like sex ten minutes after.

As I sat, Greta remembered to ask, 'This job, how much are they paying you?' When I told her, she said: 'They saw you coming.'

I said, 'There are good expenses.'

'Well, *I* won't see any of that, will I?'

Dinner was shepherd's pie. I thought how very pleasant it would be to throw it at the wall.

She said, 'What's up with you?'

'Nothing.'

'And is there an important name that goes with this?'

'Pardon me?'

'Something you can wear like a badge. I mean, we may as well squeeze the little we can out of it.' She had an uncanny instinct for homing in on whatever area would bleed the most. 'Will you be a director or a head buck cat or what?'

'They advertised for an archivist.'

The word was meat to the hungry. 'And that'll be you?' In mock awe: 'Gawny.'

'All right. Joke over.'

'An archivist.'

'Yes!'

'I'll have an archivist in the house.'

A scrape as I pushed my plate away.

'What's that in aid of?'

'I told you, I had lunch. I'm not hungry.'

'You what?'

'Sorry.'

'That's good food you're turning your nose up at. And I suppose you think it cooked itself.' Her voice rose to coloratura as I got up to leave. 'What do you take me for, to throw food back at me? Some kind of skivvy?'

There was no need to join battle; Greta could be relied on to move into overdrive without my help. It was what by my reckoning would be a two-day row; it would take that long before the anger subsided and the cistern had emptied, ready to fill again. She habitually slept on the left side of our bed and I on the right, with now and again an arm or a foot – a heat-seeking missile – straying across. Tonight and tomorrow, it would be as though every inch of her were nailed in place, as if, even while asleep, she would be black out with me. Through the closed door of my workroom I could hear her railing against the bad things of her life. I stuffed a paperback in my pocket, slipped out of the house and closed the door with a noise that was the soft side of a slam.

There was a sea-wind, and I had bungled my Captain Oates impersonation by not putting on a coat. On Avourneen Road, I passed a man exercising his dog. He said, 'That's a bitter one,' and I wondered if he was talking of the October cold or if he had a caterwauling wife at home. Perhaps he was some kind of archivist, a word that between Greta and me would henceforward be a tripwire. I had a premonition of the two of us at a party or a film premiere where I was introduced as the archivist for the O'Fearna Foundation, and I would not dare to meet her eye. What ailed the woman? It was a question that, asked down a thousand days, had become as smooth and worn as a stone in a stream. My only certainty was that, whatever the rows were about, it was not what the rows were about.

The nearest place out of the weather was the Amalfi Bar at the sea end of the town. Four or five men stood just inside the door, colloguing over a pint or a Jameson. They were on their way home for tea or dinner, whichever they called it, and they glanced at me as at an interloper. There is a story told of a Welshman cast away on a desert island. Over the years, he built two small chapels, one at either end of the island. When at last rescuers came and expressed puzzlement, he pointed at the chapel furthest away. 'That,' he said, 'is the one I don't go to.' In our town, it is the same with pubs, and the Amalfi was the one

I steered clear of. I nodded to the men and heard myself speak my father's east-wind greeting: 'Ha'sh old evening.'

No one answered. The loudest of mouth was Phil Higgins, who, unlike the others, would drink until his wife, nicknamed 'The Ambulance', came to take him either home or to the tool-shed where on summer nights he slept it off. I asked for a Famous Grouse and soda. The publican, Mick Sullivan, rotated a finger in his ear as if deaf, then, concluding the brief floor show, said 'We don't do Scotch.' He was, as I should have remembered, devoutly pro-Provo, and apart from his 4-litre Jaguar, his Church's shoes, his Burberry raincoat, his bay rum from Trumper's of Jermyn Street, his *Sporting Life* and *Daily Mirror*, his bets at Cheltenham and Aintree, his Scotch beef, his wife's cabinet of Wedgwood and his mistress in Islington, was resolute in banishing all things British. Rather than retreat and run a gauntlet of sniggers, I held my ground and told the landlord, 'If you do French, I'll have a Hennessey.'

'Oh, that's highly yoomorous,' Phil Higgins said in a stage whisper to his comrades.

Like him, the others were close to middle age and married. Did each husband and wife, I wondered, present a face of marital devotion to the world and go for each other's throat once the front door had closed behind them? Perhaps – and who could say? – every marriage was the same as mine and Greta's. Perhaps we were the norm instead of in the minority, and happiness was as rare as a tall midget. What if it were all a great, impudent world-wide conspiracy to pretend that the thing worked and cats and dogs were not enemies? I thought of my beloved Hollywood films of the thirties and forties, when we were all corrupted into innocence. The fantasies were dinned into us that the wicked paid for their crimes, that goodness was vindicated, that every falsehood was found out, that sex began, if it ever really existed, with a kiss followed by 'The End', and that love lasted to the end of time.

Phil Higgins informed his friends in a thick half-cut voice that he was going to the jacks and would they excuse him? I thought of George S Kaufman's retort to the same question: 'Certainly. The alternative would be too horrible to contemplate.' Like the coward I was, I cheated him of a jibe by leaving the pub while he was still ransacking his fly behind the door marked '*Fir*'. Outside, the wind had dropped, and yet rather than go home I made for Tish's at the far end of the street. I sat, ordered a Scotch and opened my paperback: an old favourite of mine, *The Lubitsch Touch*. The lighting was too dim for reading. Greta came off the page at me, and I wondered if she was working off her fury as she sometimes did by pounding the baby grand that had been our wedding present from her mother. Her favourite was Mussorgsky, and probably, peering through her glasses, nose against the sheet music, she was taking a battering ram to *The Great Gate of Kiev*.

Her family was musical. Her parents, George and Babs Comerford, had been part of the old Gate Theatre orchestra. His instrument was the violin, hers the cello. I once saw a programme from the 1950s; and, by way of overture, the quintet, crammed into the tiny minstrels' gallery, played a jig by Art O'Murnaghan and *Iphigenie in Aulis* by Gluck. The interval music was *My Love is an Arbutus* (arr. Redman), *The Snowy-Breasted Pearl* (arr. O'Connor-Morris) and the *Donegal Air* (arr. Coleman). In small print on the back page of the eight-page programme, the printers' name was given as *O'Leary Bros*, which was the firm where my own father worked until his death. It is, as I have said, a small country.

After the birth of Greta and her two sisters, Babs retired. She was not replaced; fashions were changing, and the Gate quintet shrank to a trio, then to an upright piano, and George moved to the Theatre Royal as part of the show band. It was the time of ciné-variety, with sketches, jugglers and a dancing troupe called the Royalettes. The music was brassy and raucous, and he was obliged to make fun of his favourite piece, Dvorak's *Humoresque*, turning it into a cod *danse macabre* when Eddie Byrne, as Nedser, staggered home legless to his nagging wife, Nuala, played in a frock by Noel Purcell. The conductor, Jimmy Campbell, whistled through his teeth, and George did two stage shows a day, the first one half sober and the second three-quarters ossified. Greek met Greek on the night he stepped out in front of a drunk driver on Burgh Quay when Greta was sixteen.

My own father was from Moone in County Kildare. My grandmother, widowed with six children to rear on a 30-acre smallholding, sent him to a cousin in Dublin where he was apprenticed to the O'Leary Brothers in Townsend Street and proved to be such a work-horse that in time he was made foreman. About my mother's beginnings, there was a mystery. She had been brought up, so she let on, in a children's home, but it was certain that she cleaned fish at the pierhead in Howth and in the evenings went to the tech and learned to cook. When she obtained her diploma, she found work at the Goodwill restaurant in College Street where the customers sat at communal tables and the cutlery was all but thrown at them, but a wholesome meal could be had – this was 1945 – for one and sixpence. My father went there every day; he asked her out, and they did what was called a steady line. Her want of a family did not bother him; he himself had never gone home to Moone – 'It might as well be the other moon,' he once told me. The only guests at their wedding were a few workmates from the printers' and the Goodwill.

They had two children, both boys. In an attempt to give my elder brother, who was delicate, the benefit of sea air, my parents moved to the village where Greta and I would one day find the house we – or, rather, I – called 'Kate Fortune's Lane'. Down at the harbour, there were fishermen and their boats. They taught Dinny and me, small as we were, to cast lines, to handle lobster pots and to steer boats into the four-knot current between the harbour and the island opposite. When Dinny, in spite of all, died, aged seven, my father's excuse was that the air had been too strong for him. 'Out that way, if it doesn't cure you, it kills you,' he said.

My mother was as dark as he was fair; however, it was Pa I took after in looks. She wept frequently, softly and inconsolably, without telling us why. She had done so even before their wedding day. If we asked, 'Mam, why are you crying?' the only answer we ever got was a broken-hearted: 'For what there's no forgiveness for.' We would say, 'Is it for Dinny?' knowing it wasn't, and the answer was a shake of the head and another sob. If ever we asked her where, once upon a time, she had come from, she would reply rhetorically: 'Where didn't I?' Which seemed true enough; a friend of mine who fancied himself as a kind of Professor Higgins, acknowledged defeat and said that her voice held a dozen accents, one piled upon the next.

When my father died, she sold up and moved into a condominium for elderly people, or senior citizens as they came to be known. At Hy-Brasil Lawns, named after the Land of the Blest in the Oisin legend, my mother played draw poker, stud and Cincinnati with the other residents. She was within easy call of Greta and me, and we took her for drives in Wicklow on Sundays. She liked the Rathdrum Valley and the Devil's Glen, but shook with fright when I once thought to drive up the Long Hill to Calary Bog on the west side of the Sugar Loaf.

'Where are ye taking me? Turn back.'

'Why, Mam? What's up?'

'I know this road.'

'What's wrong with it?'

'I'm telling the pair of ye. Turn round.'

'But, Mam –'

'Don't annoy the woman,' Greta said. 'Do as you're bid.'

It was either another mystery or part of the same one. I found a lay-by, turned and took the low road, and my mother wept softly all the way to Avoca.

The other day I came unexpectedly upon a photograph of

55

Greta taken perhaps thirty years ago. I almost wept, not because of what time had done, which is a common misfortune, but because it was like meeting a person who you at first think is a stranger. It was a posed portrait, taken perhaps for her birthday. Her face was quite clear, almost luminous, and she was smiling as if in expectation. If it was somehow my fault that her future never happened, then I know at last what mortal sin is.

We had a courtship that was like any other. We window-shopped or walked through the leafy web of roads that led to the sea, or we went to the pictures. On free evenings, I sneaked off to the Picture House, the Pavilion or the Astoria without telling her, guiltily spending money we should have saved towards getting married. Films were my life, not hers, but we had things in common: cycling to the Scalp and Glencree; whist and canasta, Patrick Kavanagh (Yeats was too effete for us), Fred Astaire, Dinah Washington, the Beatles, seeing Italian opera from the gods of the Gaiety, detective stories by Margery Allingham and Ngaio Marsh, stories by Maugham, Mary Lavin, JD Salinger and PG Wodehouse, bacon sandwiches at Tasty's, roller-skating at a rink off Grafton Street, and staying up until two or three reading *To Kill a Mockingbird* and weeping together when Boo Radley 'came out'. Often, if it rained, we watched television with her mother and sisters through an indoor snowstorm; it was preferable to taking Greta to my house, where my mother sat either red-eyed or in a sobbing fit like a regular Mrs Gummidge, with my father quietly saying, 'Now, now, Molly' without lifting his eyes from the *Herald*.

Soon after we were married, Greta cast aside the soft nets of courtship. Paddy Kavanagh, Wodehouse and roller-skating were a few of the casualties. We were childless and, as far as she was concerned, likely to remain so. After she had miscarried our first and only child, I said in an attempt to cheer her up that we might one day try again. Her reply was, 'I'm not going to be disappointed a second time, thank you.' Once, when I suggested that she might be happier if she had a part-time job to occupy her days, she replied that she had more than enough to cope with at home, thanks very much. Knowing her, I was not surprised when the idea took root; and before long she had engaged to work three afternoons a week at the Thorn Island Bookshop in the village. I asked 'Are you enjoying it?' and she replied with one of her shrugs and 'Mmmp.' Already, the doors into her were beginning to close. Later, I overheard her tell a friend that she would not give her job up for diamonds.

The loss of the child was not traumatic for either of us; we did not play-act and invent a surrogate offspring like George and Martha in *Who's Afraid of Virginia Woolf*. It was soon after I left Sunrise Insurance that the real change in Greta came about. She told me it was my imagination, and I thought so, too. When I came to know better, I waited for a sign to enter, like a lover who mooches up and down watching for the signal of a raised blind or an opened curtain. Perhaps she was sealing up the hope that was in that old photograph, or perhaps her house was empty. No one at home.

At any rate, it wasn't because of Greta that I went with Josie Hand. I would have done so anyway.

Chapter Five

At Poppintree

The day after my celebratory lunch with Thornton, I was interviewed by the journalist Roy del Rey, whose actual name was Willie Cooney. He and his wife, Madge, lived in our town and there had been three friendships: mine with him, Greta's with her, and ours with them. He was owlish, roly-poly and white-haired, and in middle age he left home and took up with a twenty-five-year-old black-haired Dominican postulant who played the *bodhran*, a one-sided drum made of goatskin which can be beaten inoffensively in a drawing room and yet is audible a half-mile away. It is usually not favoured by women musicians, or by either sex as a solo instrument; but Willie's new light o' love, Siobhan Ni Bradaigh, became much in demand at weddings as a change from the ubiquitous harpist, even if to an impressionable guest its rumbling might have seemed a portent of storms to come.

In appearance, Siobhan could have posed for the Abbey Theatre logo of a statuesque maiden with two Irish wolfhounds pulling her off her feet. She was with the Dominicans when she set her eyes and heart on Willie. None of us knew why, to use the language of apostasy, she leaped over the wall and landed on a fat little married man who was twice her age and had two scandalised grown-up daughters. Willie could not to save his life resist making a bad pun, and even in Siobhan's presence would chuckle that infidelity was the mother of invention. When he was taken to hospital with a lurgy of some kind, she was a barnacle, refusing to leave his bedside even when his estranged wife was visiting. 'He told me, wouldn't you know, that he had taken a turn for the nurse,' Madge said, 'and honest to God I wanted to hit him with the bedpan.' Once the affair had become serious, we saw him no longer. He turned up one Christmas Eve and presented us with a ceramic dish bearing the likeness of a fish. He said, spelling it out, that he hoped we would find a p-l-a-i-c-e for it, gave us a crooked smile and took himself off.

'What was that about?' Greta asked.

'I think it was goodbye,' I said.

Probably, Siobhan wanted Willie to have done utterly with his past life. In her mind, one of the great advantages of marriage – and she believed their relationship to be nothing less than that – was that it did away with the need for friends. We heard that they had obtained a mortgage on a semi-detached in Mulhuddart in far-flung Dublin 15 and had gone over to the Church of Ireland.

Thorn and I had no sooner parted after our lunch at White's of the Green than he put out a press release, which brought Willie, wearing his interviewer's hat, to 'Kate Fortune's Lane' at short notice and with a photographer in tow. Greta had continued to be what she called very great with the forsaken Madge – when it came to being a friend of the bosom, she had, as Boswell said of Mrs Johnson, an embonpoint of more than ordinary protuberance. She gave the cad Willie a smile that had splinters in it and made coffee. She and I were on day two of our row, but an outsider would never have guessed. 'This archive thing is great news,' Willie said, and Greta shamelessly all but sang, 'Yes, TJ and I are thrilled to bits.' He made no mention of what on his part had been a year's silence, but put his voice recorder between us and asked questions while the photographer moved around the room changing lenses and taking more pictures than would have been warranted by a fortnight in Crete.

After a while, Willie said, 'That's our lot,' and switched off the recorder. He stood up: 'I have to get back into town. The traffic is only brutal.' I knew that he had received his orders from the *bodhran* player; there was to be no lingering, no colloguing. Not allowing him an easy escape, I called out, 'Greta, Willie is off!'

She came from the kitchen and at once jumped in at the deep end. 'So how are you and, ah –' momentarily forgetting his inamorata's name, she hit a shoal – 'and ... ah, *herself* getting on?'

'You mean Siobhan? Fantastic. We're as happy as Larry.'

I thought that Greta would weep for joy. 'Ahhh,' she said.

'Bugs in a rug,' he said.

'Isn't that great?'

'Matter of fact,' he said modestly, 'we're expecting for April.'

As I reeled mentally, I took a look at my wife's face. A seismograph would not have picked up even a frisson of shock. As I have said, she was not a good liar, but her gift for insincerity was beyond reproach. She gave a great yowl of delight, and for an insane moment I thought she would hug him. She said, 'Well, God love the pair of you.'

As she was speeding him on his way, he added a postscript: 'Oh, and we've become the devils for style. Now that we've turned C of I, we're having the christening in Christ Church the first Sunday in May. So I only hope the new arrival won't be, if-you-know-what-I-mean, a late arrival.'

There were whole novenas in Greta's voice. 'Please God it won't be.'

She told him sternly to keep in touch and that he and she were not to be strangers. I watched and waved as he and the photographer reversed down the lane into Avourneen Road, and when I went back indoors Greta was almost dancing with rage, our quarrel quite eclipsed by the greater infamy. 'First the fuckin' *bodhran*,' she said, 'and now a shaggin' baby at his age. They'll never get a wink of hoorin' sleep, and the devil's cure to them.' It was not often she used bad language.

Next morning, Thorn Thornton's picture and mine were in the *Irish Times*, and the story was headed 'JJ Thornton Wins

O'Fearna Bequest for the State'. 'I told you,' Greta said. 'He's grabbing it all for himself. He'll be the hero.'

'Well, that's what he's after,' I said. 'He made no bones about it.'

In the American film world the news caused a stir, even meriting a paragraph in *Time* magazine, and I received a call from Mrs O'Fearna to wish me well. Her tone, while affable, put me in mind of the story about Joan Crawford, who on meeting the author of *The Great Gatsby* and learning that he was to work on the script of her next film, told him, 'Write hard, Mr Fitzgerald, write hard!'

There were legalities to be observed and my two-year contract to be drawn up. Thorn found a temporary office for both me and the secretary, whom Shay, whenever he had occasion to telephone, did indeed address as Voilet. Later I moved into a small suite in Temple Bar with a viewing room and a damp- and fireproof cellar for storing the O'Fearna films. I became friends with Liz Meara, who masterminded the Irish Film Centre, two streets away. She was tall and auburn and had troubles enough at home without my help. Within weeks we might have been joined at the hips. Thanks to her, I liaised with the British and Irish Film Institutes, and after months of gestation the archive came about. Greta, taken aback by the commotion, became Churchillian and declared that never had so much fuss been made by so many about so little.

The formal opening of the archive was planned to coincide with Sean O'Fearna's centenary. There was to be a week-long screening of silent films that had been feared lost, but the main event was to be the showing of a new colour print of *The Man from Innisfree*, shot by O'Fearna around Lough Gill and Benbulben. A great coup would be the inclusion of ten minutes of out-takes that had been found in the keeping of the producer's widow, a one-time ice-skater and rival of Sonja Henie. These consisted of a sequence where Maureen O'Hara was sexually interfered with under a Celtic cross in Drumcliff churchyard. As her assailant, played by Ward Bond, galloped away, she adjusted her torn blouse and panted, in homage to Yeats, whose grave was in shot: 'Horseman, pass by!'

'We'll call this the director's cut,' Thornton said.

'But O'Fearna never edited his sound films,' I told him.

'Bollocks,' he explained.

Mrs O'Fearna was to come from Santa Fe for the occasion, and the Minister for the Arts, who resembled an outsized leprechaun, was to present her with a certificate of her late husband's citizenship. The ever-busy Thornton had kept his word.

He and I had become friends, and with his actress wife, Prue, he came to our house and we went to his. I enjoyed the precocity of his twins, Adam and Niamh. Whenever he chose to flip the appropriate switch, Thorn could display charm and warmth. He was younger than I, but he became my helmsman. 'Never make an offer,' he said. 'Never, never, never. Always let the buggers come to you.' Greta's forecast was coming true: I was making a hero of him. On seeing the earnestness on my face, he laughed and punched my shoulder. 'I'll make a tycoon out of you yet.'

Among the other strings he had to his bow was Batt Kenirons' version of *Truculentus*, which was to be staged in a field between Poppintree and St Margaret's. That year, the Theatre Festival was postponed from October until the following March, and the delay suited Thornton; it gave him time to mount a production which would dazzle the town. 'Ziegfeldian' was his own word for it. Comedies from *circa* AD 194 were not in my line, with or without laughs, but I gathered that this one had to do with an avaricious whore for whose favours rich men ran themselves ragged. Kenirons called his version *Lust*.

'That'll bring them in,' Thornton told me over one of our lunches. 'The Oozer has moved the setting from Rome to present-day Guess-where. And we're doing it with masks. In Plautus there were four lechers; we're trebling up on that, and every one will be recognisable as a well-known cute hoor – a certain politician, a prelate, a pirate or some other consummate bastard.'

I said, 'I thought you wanted to be a pirate yourself.'

'That was only old guff. And as for the trollop ... '

'Go on,' I said. 'Break it to me.'

'I had in mind,' he said, 'to put a mask on her that would be the face of the rubber-heeled lady wife of a certain Garda superintendent!'

'You'd never get away with it,' I said. 'She'd sue.'

He sighed. 'I know ... pity. Well, not to worry. The Oozer has gone to town with the script. It is only coruscating. And we'll have a company of thirty, not counting musicians. And Mervyn Mendl to direct.'

'And you're doing it in a tent?'

'Do you mind? A marquee.'

'In March?'

'A month which by then will be going out like a lamb.' He gave me a sly grin. 'Would you like me to invite your dream girl?'

'Pardon me?'

'The Italian job. Josie Hand.'

'Get knotted.'

On the morning of the great day, the sky was clear, the air dead still. The word from Thornton was that the dress and technical rehearsals had been smooth. Rather than dilute the impact of the first night, he had forgone previews.

Greta said, 'We'll freeze in that tent.'

'They have heaters.'

She looked out of our kitchen window. The tree-tops and the wisps of spring foliage might have been painted on the sky. 'There's not even a leaf stirring,' she said. 'It's all gone quiet.'

'It's too darn quiet.'

'What?'

'Nothing.'

Later while going for the papers, I chanced to look across the Bay and saw what appeared to be faint shards of Wedgwood far beyond the isthmus of Sutton. I remembered my father saying, 'When you can see the Mountains of Mourne, it's a sure sign of rain.' Probably, from Killiney Hill to the south one could also see the hump-back of Snowdon. By mid-afternoon, the sky was darkening; by dinner-time, it was spitting rain and with a hooligan wind. Our tickets were marked 'Black tie,' and as we dressed Greta actually laughed. 'I think we're mad.'

We took the airport road out of town and cut west from Santry. It was, or should have been, early twilight, but we drove on headlights which picked up an arrowed sign that spelled out '*LUST*' in catseyes. 'Jesus, it's too much,' Greta said. By then the car was being buffeted by crosswinds with splats of rain, and there was a storm warning on the radio. Provident by nature, I took note that we had passed a possible bolt-hole, called the Poppintree Pub. Suburbs became country; there were more lubricious catseyes and almost at once a frenzy of fairy lights dancing above the road. We steered into a field and saw the floodlit marquee, with '*LUST*' again, now writ large in light-bulbs over the entrance. Under a jimmy-rigged awning, a band which looked as if it would have been more at home on the *Titanic* was playing Dixieland. 'Ah, God help them,' Greta said, peering out.

'Who?'

'All of them.'

'I thought you didn't like Thorn.'

She gave me one of her rare Mother Teresa looks. 'Well, I wouldn't wish this on anyone!'

As I got out of the car, the rain hit my face like a slap. Greta screamed as she stepped into mud. She was wearing an anorak and held the hood tight to protect her hair. We squelched along a churned-up track for fifty yards that seemed like five hundred. Outside the marquee, several men – I recognised one of them as Thorn – were trying to capture a loose canvas flap which snapped

like a whip. I slipped, bumped into a woman and shouted, 'Sorry.'
It was Josie Hand.

She was with her husband. She said: 'Hello. Isn't this marvellous?'

'You're mad.'

'But it's *theatre!*'

Her words were carried away by the gale. At the entrance to the big top – it had been hired, I found out, from a circus – a ticket-checker passed us through and told us: 'It's open seating.'

'No, it's not.' Thorn, or one of his several clones, had come up behind us. He wore a rainproof over his dinner jacket; his hair and the dead-rat moustache dripped water. He was delighted to see us with the Hands. 'Ah, all together like Brown's cows!' He seemed not in the least bothered by the storm. He told the girl to show us to Row A. 'It has cushions,' he said.

I said, 'You're not going ahead with this debacle?'

'Oh, shush.' Josie told me. 'You're as bad as Andrew. Both of you are wet sheets.'

'I wonder what she means,' Thorn said, leaving us.

The marquee was already half-full, and I recognised several regular first-nighters. The bullet-headed director, Marvin Mendl, was striding about as if he were wearing jackboots, shouting at the front-of-house staff and addressing them as 'You people'. The seating consisted of tiers of wooden benches, and the wind whistled through underneath. Battens of arcs and floods shivered overhead. Across the circus ring, there was the set: a cut-out panorama of Dublin. From left to right, one could recognise the silhouettes of the Wellington Monument, the Four Courts, the O'Connell Monument and the Customs House. In one of the aisle seats, which were reserved for critics, I could see Shay, on duty – the regular critic, McCavity, had craftily gone to the Abbey. Instead of Brigid, Shay had brought his daughter, Blanaid, who was taking a course in journalism at Rathmines Tech – the other girls were Maire, Dympna and Louise. On seeing me, he raised a finger.

In our town, all first nights, like Tolstoy's happy families, are the same. It is a continuous never-ending party, done in instalments, with the same faces and the same conversations. This evening, there was something new to be talked about, if one bellowed. The noise was terrific; the tortured canvas groaned and whumped louder with every gust. From outside, shreds of *Basin Street Blues* were borne on the gale.

'I wonder if we're going to achieve lift-off,' Andrew Hand said in what was for him a rare moment of humour, and probably I was not the only one to envisage the tent-pegs popping like corks and the entire marquee, wooden seats, audience and all, rising like a flatulent zeppelin above the fields of north Dublin. The wind was from the south-west, and I reckoned that within minutes we could be out over the Bailey lighthouse and heading for Liverpool.

I looked at Greta and saw that her face had become pale with fear. I was sandwiched between her and Josie, who turned her head and whispered into my ear, 'I am beginning not to like this.' Her breath was warm and, even in that place, arousing. I looked at her and she nodded, her face blank of any kind of coquetry.

There was a pummelling that was the strongest yet. The two tent-poles shuddered and leaped. Overhead a piece of canvas tore loose, flew up and made a crackling noise like gunfire. Rain came into the tent. The Dublin silhouette buckled. A woman screamed and several people leaped to their feet. A voice on the public address system said, 'Please keep your seats. There is absolutely no cause for –'

The voice broke off, and there was a loud crackling. Andrew Hand said, 'Nothing can go wrong, go wrong, go wrong ... ' I made to scowl at him, then saw that he was as frightened as I was. I declared a moratorium on my agnosticism and thought, 'God, not this, not here, not in a field in north Dublin.' I wondered if Shay, across the aisle, was still an atheist.

Another voice came through, and this time it was recognisably

Thorn's. He said, 'Ladies and gentlemen, may I please have your attention?' He paused, and I could have almost sworn that it was more for effect than silence. 'I much regret that acting on the advice of the Dublin Fire Department and the Gardai –'

'That's it, we're out of here,' Hand said without waiting for more. I knew how he had made his millions. He was first up and on his way, dragging Josie after him. She barked my knees and Greta's as they passed in front.

'Yes, come on,' Greta hissed. Others were on the move, thrusting arms into sleeves. It was a stampede in the making. Near the entrance, I saw Batt Kenirons for the first time. He was wearing a dinner jacket and had a handkerchief pressed to his eyes. Greta caught his arm. 'Batty, come on.'

He was snuffling. 'I can't.'

'Yes, you can. "He that that fights and runs away, may live to fight another day." TJ, make him come.'

It was the first poetry I had heard her speak since the days when she and I memorised Paddy Kavanagh. We dragged the Oozer, unresisting, out with us and caught up with the Hands in the car park. I said, 'There's a place called the Poppintree Pub a mile back towards Santry.'

Andrew said, 'Thanks, but we're for home.'

'No, we are not,' Josie said. Now that her composure had returned, her accent, which she had mislaid, re-thickened. 'Thees is an evening to talk about. We must deep our bread in eet.'

As the car squelched out of the field, Kenirons lowered the rear window, stuck his head out and looked back at the marquee. He burst into tears and said, 'Oh, me lovely play.'

Andrew and Josie followed us in their brute of a Merc to the Poppintree, which was an empty road-house biding its time for the completion of a new housing estate. First things first, we made a fuss of Kenirons, assuring him that this evening was only a postponement. The marquee would not blow away, and Thorn would try again, perhaps even tomorrow or the next day; and in any case there was always an indoor venue: the Point Theatre, perhaps, or Simmonscourt. I pressed a large Jameson into the Oozer's hand. He was brighter now. 'You're right,' he said, wiping his face. 'Sure Thorn would never be bested by such a thing as an act of God.'

We all laughed, except Andrew Hand, who, being a regular massgoer, only smiled. Other refugees came in and brought the storm with them. Everyone talked excitedly. Greta looked ruefully at her shoes, muddied and scuffed.

'Greta, *cara mia*, I walked on your feet,' Josie said. 'Eet was Andrew's fault. He dragged me after heem. He is such a coward.'

'Nothing of the sort,' Hand said. 'I prefer to call it presence of mind.'

We laughed, again. The mood was light-headed. The pub was a lifeboat, and we had survived a shipwreck. Admittedly the ocean liner was probably still afloat, but that was no thanks to the tempest.

Kenirons said: '"Stay me with flagons, comfort me with apples,"' and took a swig of his Jameson. He added, 'And while ye are at it, bugger the apples.'

I quoted Mildred Natwick in *The Court Jester*: '"The pellet with the poison's in the chalice from the palace. The flagon with the dragon has the brew that is true."' Nobody got it.

'Let me buy a round,' Hand said. 'Then Josie and I must be off.'

He was not a pub man. I pictured him in his club on St Stephen's Green drinking Laphroaig from Waterford glass, or perhaps at home sipping a medium-dry sherry before he and Josie had dinner. Perhaps, and not to speak ill of him, he was the sort of person who dined in the dining room. While he was at the bar, which was by now two-deep, Kenirons maundered on, telling us that his play would have set Dublin on its ears. 'But there are villains,' he said, 'who will always prevail because they have a great leg of the devil. And 'twas the devil that sent that shtorm.'

'Bosh,' I said.

'We will never get the better of them,' the Oozer said. 'They are invincible.'

Josie wanted to talk about the archive. She said, 'It weel be fabulous, *magnifico*.' As if she had heard a dissenting voice, she raised a hand. 'No, no, no, no, no, I can tell. Everyone speaks of eet. Everyone speaks of heem.' She pointed at me. 'But *scusi*! I am eegnorant. The man who makes the feelms .... ah ... ?'

'O'Fearna,' I said.

'I do not know why he ees importante.'

'Welcome to the club,' Greta said.

'These pictures, I see them on the television. They 'ave men who ride horses, and go chasing the Eendians, and they have guns and they go bang-bang-bang. Now I say to mself, "Giuseppina, thees man, thees ... O'Fearna – *bene!* – must be deeferent because my friend TJ Queel is not a person who weel waste his time." So you must explain it to me.' She slapped her hands. 'I know! I weel make a dinner. I weel have the Penders, and I weel invite a nice girl for Oozy.'

'Oh, grand,' the Oozer said, his mind back in the marquee.

'But not an American. No, they are too much like the engine of Andrew's car that makes of eetself a how-you-say? ... *una diagnosi* a thousand times a second, and so eet leestens to eetself only. Yes, I weel make a dinner ... I weel cook a *sarta di riso alla napoletana,* and TJ will seet here on my right and tell me all about thees O'Fearna.'

'Oh, he'll do that all right,' Greta said. 'Try and stop him.' She was usually careful not to let me down in company, but the wasted evening, the mud, the storm, and the marquee had made her waspish. Andrew, who was not one of nature's menials, had come back attended by a barman who began to set the drinks out on the table.

'You weel come to my dinner, Greta?' Josie asked.

'We'd love to,' Greta said. Then she did it. 'It will be a lovely change for us. Do you know, never mind my shoes and my hair, but he has that dress shirt on him for less than two hours, and now it's got to be washed and ironed. And guess who'll have to do it? Muggins.'

I said, 'Did you know that they named a whisky after my wife? They called it The Famous Grouse.'

It was the first time I had heard Andrew Hand laugh out loud. Kenirons guffawed, Josie made a reproachful face, and Greta reached out and tipped my whisky into my lap.

Perhaps it was accidental. If not, she repented it at once and said: 'Oh, I'm sorry.' Josie was at once in charge. In a moment, she produced a wad of tissues from her bag. 'Ees no problem!' She leaned over and dabbed at the front of my trousers. I was about to make an inane joke, when I felt her hand take deliberate hold of me.

She raised her face for a moment to within a few inches of mine, and I can see her eyes now as clearly as if it were not years ago, but last evening. The look lasted for two seconds or a lifetime; choose one. She said, and the accent was gone, 'It won't stain.' Only Thorn, who missed nothing, would have noticed, and he was a mile away.

Greta said, 'I didn't mean it, honest.'

'There!' Josie said, crumpling the tissue and dropping it into an ashtray. 'It is done.' And it was.

Chapter Six

In Thelma's Room

'Hello. It's TJ.'

'What is?'

'I am. TJ Quill.'

'So! What a time you pick. Andrew is coming home for lunch.'

'Listen ...'

'No, you listen. All morning you have been on my mind. I have said to myself, if he calls it is because he will have the wrong idea. And then I can tell him that I am not a tart. Is that the word for it? What we call *una sgualdrina*. Yes? So why are you calling me? Is it because you think I am easy?'

'Not at all.'

'Yes, you do. For else, you say, why would I do such a shameless thing?'

'I want to see you again.'

'Why?'

'Because.'

'Oh, now that is a good answer! "Because!" So tell me what "because" means. Do you want to take me to bed, is that it? ... Hello, are you there? You say nothing. ... Hello? *Pronto*?'

'Look, I grew up in a house off Pearse Street. Both my parents were –'

'My God, I tell him my husband is coming home, and he gives me the story of his life!'

'... the kind of people who went to mass and confession ...'

'Good! Oh, I'm so glad to hear it. And so are you saying to me that what I did in that place last evening was a *sin*?'

71

'Don't get in a wax. No, I am not. I'm trying to say that the kind of people I come from … I mean, the damn country I grew up in … I mean, I'm like all the rest of them. When it comes to sex, I make jokes. I find it harder to make truth … What's so funny?'

'I laugh for happiness. At last you are talking to me! So? You want that you and me will make truth together? No, no, my God, it is madness. I gave Andrew my most sacred and honourable word. Never, not ever at home. Not where he can be made the laughing stock. Because he is vindictive. If you … what is the word? … if you go across him … whoof!' A pause. 'So where are you now?'

'What?'

'Where are you calling from?'

'My office.'

'Tell it to me.'

'Do you mean describe it? Well, it has four walls …'

'Idiot.'

' … With photographs of Sean O'Fearna, and stills from his films.'

'Which you are to explain to me.'

'There's my desk and another one for my secretary. She can only work until noon, so she's gone home. That's why I took so long about calling!'

'So *that* is why? Ah, better and better! What else?'

'It's a corner office with two windows. It looks out on the backs of old houses. A bit slummy. On the far side of them there's the Ha'penny Bridge.'

'Okay, that will do. Now I can see you.'

'Point is, when can *I* see *you*?'

'You cannot. Go away. I told you, we will meet for dinner, and my husband will be there, and your wife will be there, and I will kill you with politeness. We will talk about books and your films – what in this place of savages they pronounce as "fill-ums" – and

72

who is sleeping with who, only whoever it is it will not be you and me –'

'Yes, it will.'

'*Scusi*? What did you say?'

'I said …'

'Don't whisper.'

'I said … it will.'

Silence. 'I see … *bene. Momento*!'

There was a small clatter as she put the receiver down on a bare surface. Weeks later, I found out it was so that she could make a gesture with both hands, striking them together with an up-and-down movement as if they were cymbals in a marching band. It was her way of disposing of a thing that was settled, done with: a meal cooked, a tear mended, an affair embarked on. After a second or two, I heard her voice again. 'And now I have business to finish. Have you ever heard of Key Biscayne?'

'Pardon me?'

'I have to go there. I tell Andrew that it is for a holiday. Do you know what he says? He wants to know if it has a good golf course! I will go there next week, and when the business I have to do is finished, I will come back and we shall meet.'

'But –'

'And meet and meet and meet! Now I hear my husband's car. In a moment, his key will be in the door. I must go.'

'Well, in that case –'

'Actually, I tell a lie. Andrew is not here. It is the last lie I will ever tell you. You must permit it, however, just this one time. You will find out that I am very romantic. I like danger, when it is safe. *Ciao*, darling.'

The line went dead.

The receiver, as I hung up, bore the damp imprint of my hand. My first emotion was confusion, next anger. I had been down this road before: as a twenty-year-old, cooling my heels outside a cinema and wondering if such and such a fair one would turn up or else send two friends to walk by, who as proof of conquest would report that the eejit was waiting. This was no different: a bored wife playing games and watching a randy fool jump through hoops. Josie Hand, the sublime Giuseppina, was a tease, a fantasist, perhaps, and that was the beginning and end of it. The next time I saw her, at the Penders' probably, she would smile and look through me as if the moment at Poppintree and this telephone conversation had never happened. And yet no more exquisite carrot had ever been dangled in front of a donkey. Her final '*Ciao*, darling,' lodged, refusing to budge, like a squatter in my head.

That afternoon, Thornton called from his office in Harcourt Street. In the previous evening's storm, trees had been blown down and roofs torn off. A motorist in Westmeath had been killed when a gate flew from its hinges, but the front page headline in the *Irish Times* was 'Hundreds Flee from Storm-Lashed Marquee'. (The *Sun* jibed: '"LUST" BITES THE DUST'.) There was a photograph of Thorn gritting his teeth and holding a guy-rope. Further down, there was a library picture of the Oozer in the classic pose of chin resting thoughtfully on hand in an attempt to conceal the existence of two other chins beneath that one.

At least there was a consolation: Thorn had taken another leap forward on his journey to celebrity. 'Look on the bright side,' he said. 'The hit show of the theatre festival is the one that never happened.'

'So what now?' I asked.

'How?'

'I mean what about "The Show Must Go On"?'

'Get stitched. Yesterday I had thirty actors, and by this morning they were all out looking for new jobs. And how many punters do you think would be mad enough to set foot inside a marquee after last night? Anyway, the state that field is in, a Land Rover would sink in it.'

74

'Poor old Kenirons.'

'What about poor old me? I'm out a bob or two, you know. And the insurance won't cough up. Act of God. Hey, they're telling a story about me. Do you want to hear it?'

'Go on, then.'

'Well, it seems that the devil – Beelzebub, old Nick himself – offers me a deal. He says, "I'll make you famous and rich. Whatever you touch will turn to gold. If you put on a play, it'll get rave notices and a six-month run. If you make a film it'll win ten Oscars and the *Palme d'Or* at Cannes." So I say to him, "I suppose you want my soul in return?" And the devil says, "I want more than that. This is a big deal I'm offering you, so I also want the souls of your old mother and your wife and your two children." And I say to him –' Here, relishing the punch-line to come, Thorn gave one of his hee-haws – 'And I say to him: "*What's the catch?*"'

He laughed again. An image came into my head of an O'Fearna film, with Russell Simpson as an old preacher quoting from Ecclesiastes as he told a group of dissolute cowboys that their laughter was as the crackling of thorns under a pot.

I said: 'You like that story, do you?'

'It's the image, you see. Mister Ruthless. I not only like it, I'm going to tell it tomorrow evening.'

'Tell it where tomorrow evening?'

'They've invited me on the *Late Late*. That's why I'm calling, to tell you to tune in. 'Bye, now.'

'Wait a minute. Tell me something else. Where or what is Key Biscayne?'

'Why? Are you going on your holliers?'

'Do you mean it's a resort?'

'Think of the letter Q, as in Quill. Miami is the round bit and Key Biscayne is the squiggle. Don't go there. Greta would only hate it. Try Ballybunion. 'Bye-ee.'

A week or so later, I saw Andrew Hand walking towards me in

Nassau Street and actually felt my heart stumble with guilt. Then I remembered that it was I he was looking at and not my depraved portrait locked away in the attic. He smiled; we shook hands; he asked me about the archive; I told him that the grand opening was three months off.

I said: 'How's your good lady?'

He said: 'Grand. She's in Florida with a girlfriend. Then she might go on to a Club Med in Martinique.'

'Oh, yes?'

'She never stops, you know. My mother, RIP, used to say there was a bee in her. In the meantime, I'm having to shift for myself.'

'You're looking well on it.'

'I get used to it.'

We parted, and I turned into Kildare Street. So the bit about Key Biscayne was probably not an invention. Even so, I could not see what kind of business would have to be disposed of before she and I could meet. I cursed Andrew; meeting him had drawn her out of a dark corner of my mind. The thought occurred that I was only around the corner from Turlough Pender's gallery, and an idea had half formed when I caught sight of a familiar figure walking in front of me. I hurried to catch her up.

I said: 'This is my day for meeting people.'

'TJ!' Colleen was pleased to see me.

'Not five minutes ago in Nassau Street I ran into Andrew Hand.'

'Do you mind if we walk quickly? I want to spend a penny, and the gallery is the nearest place that has a lavatory.' Colleen gave the word the full four syllables, loud and clear, instead of the usual three. A girl who was passing turned and smiled. 'I hope you will tell me that you are going to see Turlough?'

'I thought I might drop in,' I said. Then, returning to my favourite subject. 'Andrew says that Josie is in Florida.'

'She has the money,' Colleen said. 'Andrew is rich, and her

people are rich. I tell her that twice rich is too rich. She is restless. Do you know how many friends she has?'

'No, how many?'

She tapped her bosom. 'Me! That is how many.'

The gallery had only one customer, who was either deaf or admirably self-possessed, given that he did not start or look around when Colleen walked in, kissed Turlough and said loudly, 'I am going to use the lav-a-tor-y and then I will make us some coffee.' While she was gone, I exchanged small talk with Turlough as he walked me around. One painting appealed to me; it was of a girl peering out through a rain-mottled window. It was called *At Huband Bridge*.

'That's nice. A bit sentimental.'

'The price isn't,' Turlough said. 'Six hundred.'

'Wow.'

'For you I'd forego commission. Old Pals' Act ... four-fifty.'

'Greta would skin me.' I moved to the safety of turf-stooks in a Connemara landscape. 'By the way,' I said with the subtlety of a boot-print in a flowerbed, 'I bumped into Andrew Hand just now. He says the lovely Josie is away in Florida.'

'Oh, yes? Here, this one is interesting.'

'I wonder if she ... ah ...' – trying to make it off-hand – '... plays around.' It was a cornerboy remark, crass and repented as soon as spoken.

He said, 'Not half. Waiters, milkmen, gondoliers. She never stops.'

'Turlough, shame on you, that is not true.' Colleen, who made a habit of spoiling slanderous conversations, had appeared from the rear carrying cups on a tin tray.

'Yes, it is so.'

'No, it isn't.' She turned to the lone customer. 'Would you like a cup of coffee?' Without waiting for a reply, she said: 'TJ, do not mind Turlough. He leaves nobody with a rag of reputation. Josie is my good friend, and she does not go with men. I know and I

77

am telling you.' As I hovered between relief and disappointment, she added, 'Of course you have heard about the Romanian opera singer.'

I said, truthfully, 'I didn't know there was such a thing.'

The door slammed as the lone customer left. 'Well, Colleen, you got rid of *that* nuisance,' Turlough said.

She either missed or ignored the sarcasm. 'He was a baritone, a horrible man, who wanted Andrew to put money into his career, and for this he made to her an advance ... is that the word?'

'Advances?' I said.

'That was a bad time for her. And out of this, my husband makes up waiters and milkmen and I do not know what.'

She glared and hurled a word at him in what I assumed was Maltese. The subject was closed. We sipped our coffee, and as they talked of matters domestic I took my leave of the girl at the window that overlooked Huband Bridge.

Two weeks or so later, there was a telephone breakdown in the Temple Bar area, and I sent Violet-stroke-Voilet Mooney home even earlier than usual. I was thinking of treating myself to a bar lunch at Davy Byrne's when the office door virtually slammed open and the woman to whom I had not given a thought for at least ten minutes came in and sat, almost slumping, in the only chair other than mine.

Josie kicked her shoes off and massaged her feet. She said, as if she had just returned home from the shops, 'I am jet-lagged. I look like what the dog has dragged in, or is it the cat? Some animal. And I discover that your telephone is not working. So I drive into town and walk around Temple Bar looking at the names on doors. I am no good for walking; I think my legs are too short, but for your sake I do it. Then at last I have an idea. I go to where the cinema is, the ... what is it? ... the Irish Film Society.'

I managed to say: 'Film Institute.'

Details annoyed her. 'Whatever. They give me the address, and here I am.' I looked at her, wondering how long it would take for my Buster Keaton face to melt. She said, 'Well, I knew you would be surprised, but not like this.'

'Sorry.'

'You look good.'

'I feel fine.'

'I don't mean you look well. I mean what I say: you look good. There's a difference. Do *I* look good?'

'Very.'

'My God, such eloquence. So now are you going to speak to me or am I to go home?'

'How was Florida?'

Her face darkened. 'It serves me right for asking you to speak. Florida was bad, so very bad. I will tell you on Wednesday.' Probably, I looked at her stupidly. 'We will meet then, okay? So where?' In another moment, she would have snapped her fingers at me like a schoolmarm. Flustered, I mentioned a pub in Baggot Street, near the bridge.

'Are you mad? Andrew owns it.'

'Silly me,' I said. We settled on a quiet bar, recently opened, named the Nora Barnacle. She said, '*Bene*,' and leaped up, her energy restored. 'I must go. I have been away; so now I must start my life again!'

Andrew Hand's mother had been right about her Italian daughter-in-law; there was a bee in her. Down the years, whenever she and I had a lunch date, she would invariably look at her Rolex Oyster and drive off to attend to what she said were 'things to do'. I once asked her where she was off to on a particular expedition. If the question was put even half in jest, her answer was all in earnest, an angry 'My husband would not ask me that!' For a woman who supposedly had only one friend in the world, she kept remarkably busy. Perhaps to be without a flaw was a full-time vocation. I had a vision of cosmeticians, dieticians and an infinity of other icians, all doing their damnedest.

Waiting for Wednesday and with an emptiness in my gut, I

gave Greta notice that I had an engagement with an O'Fearna biographer who was passing through and that I would be dining out. She said it was well for some. I was in the Nora Barnacle at five to eight, and Josie arrived at a few minutes past. She touched my sleeve, opened her hand and showed me a door-key. 'It belongs to a woman I know called Thelma,' she said. 'Finish your drink and we will go.'

It transpired that this Thelma was an interpreter who worked in Brussels on weekdays. Her home was an apartment on Mespil Road, just yards from the pub. Josie, with her hatred of walking, drove us both there.

'This evening I am being false to Andrew,' she said, a tyre scuffing the pavement at the canal bridge. 'Years ago, I talked to him. I said, "You want a perfect wife. You want someone who will keep a nice house, who will be with you and make a smiling face when your horse is running at Longchamps, who will look beautiful and give dinner to your business friends. You want all that and more, but what you don't want is me. Very well. I will go my own way. I will do –" what is it they say? – "my own thing, but I promise that I will not put horns on you. Whatever happens, it will be in other places. Hokay?"'

'Did you say that to him?'

She smiled. 'In Italian, in my head, yes.' To my terror, she took her hands off the steering wheel and made her gesture of striking cymbals together. I need not have worried; I was to learn that whatever she did, driving excepted, she either performed it flawlessly or not at all. As we stopped outside a red-brick apartment block, she said: 'So this evening I am doing a bad thing. I break my word. But I am human. I cannot wait.'

Thelma's flat was one floor up. There was a Vuitton overnight bag on the living room sofa. Josie opened it and took out a black garment that resembled a full-length spider's-web. 'I don't like to wear other people's clothes,' she said, 'so I brought this here this afternoon.' She went into what I assumed was the bedroom. 'Be patient. I will call you.' As the door closed, I had a vision of Arletty, the eternal woman, in *Les Enfants du Paradis*. Or, not to delude myself, perhaps I should have imagined an Abbott and Costello farce, with the little fellow, Lou, being vamped by a foreign temptress – Lenore Aubert perhaps – and calling in panic for his partner, Bud: 'Chi-i-ick!' The thought occurred to me that I could still turn and flee to 'Kate Fortune's Lane' and Greta.

After a time, Josie called to me, and I went in. She looked, as she herself would say, good. She was standing by the bed wearing the web, and when the optimum effect had been achieved, she shrugged herself free of it. Unlike most other women, she looked as alluring naked as dressed. And yet I was irresistibly put in mind of Thornton's joke about Astroturf and red dust from the Sahara. She said, 'Why are you looking at me down there? I have very nice boobs, you know,' and indeed they were the breasts of cliché: proud, thrusting, superb, whatever.

Writing about it in the here and now, I ask myself if perhaps it is an Irish thing, this reduction of emotion to low comedy? In her case, no; never that. She made love – an absurd phrase, if you think of it – as if she were perfecting an endangered art. She did not abandon herself to passion or cry out; it was as tenderly done as if she were making me a gift, without stint or holding back. When it was over, she sighed and said, as if filling in a report card: 'That was very good, but it will be better.'

I said, with sarcasm, because offended: 'Oh, you mean it'll happen again?'

'Of course. I have been after you for a long time.'

'If so, I never knew.'

'If you had known, I would not have been after you.'

She remade the bed, swallowed a pill and rinsed and dried the tumbler; it was a perfect crime; we left not a trace. We went to a nearby bistro that served what passed for Greek food. She told me she was the most discreet person in the world and expected no less of me. I swore I would tell no one. She said, '*Impossible*! I know you already; with a secret you would explode. I will allow you to tell just one person, and that is all.'

'There's my oldest friend,' I said, thinking of Shay.

She said, 'Old friends get jealous. Why not Thorn Thornton?'

'Could I trust him?'

'No. But you could if you tell him he is the only person who knows. Then he would be afraid to be indiscreet.'

I said, 'And who will *you* tell?'

She said, 'Andrew', and my blood froze. She laughed and said, 'No, I will tell nobody. I am the Sphinx.'

I mentioned that I had met her husband in the street. 'He said you were in Florida with a girlfriend.'

She laughed. 'Yes, darling, I was there with my friend Mary, who lives in London. She does not exist. I make her up, for Andrew.'

'You mean you've been Bunburying!'

'*Scusi?*'

When I told her who Bunbury was, she was delighted. She clapped her hands: 'Mary Bunbury, who goes everywhere with me! Wonderful. You will teach me much. That will be one of the porks.'

I thought of her husband, the ham tycoon. 'Not porks … *perks*.'

'And now I will tell you about Florida.' She spoke quickly, anxious to have it over with. 'I had a friend in Key Biscayne. He was younger than I was … not too much, *comme ci, comme ça*. His name was Scott. Very handsome.' I felt the first stirrings of jealousy. As if with second sight, she said, 'No, no, it's over. Oh, my God, it is over!' I saw tears. *Was* it over?

This Scott, she said, was a lawyer in Miami. She had been in love with him for a year; then the affair went stale because of distance and other things. 'He had friends, who in the American way would spit on you if you smoked a cigarette, but they – what is the word? – they *used* cocaine. That was not for me –' a fastidious

82

shudder – 'I never like to go away from myself. And what was even worse, Scott asked me to leave Andrew and marry him!'

She said it with a stare that asked if I had ever heard of such a thing. I was not to realise until later that there were two Josies. Whenever I drove into town and went out with her, I was the same person who would return home at midnight and listen to music or read or talk to Greta, if she was still up and sociable. I was leading a double life, and so much the worst for me, but Josie was not. She lived two quite separate lives, without an overlap, keeping one or the other life in its box until needed. She told me once that she loved Andrew, and when I looked askance, she said, laughing, 'I am more than enough to look after two of you.' And it was true, because there were two of *her*. When Scott asked her to marry him, he was reaching out for Andrew's Josie, who was none of his business.

She said, 'He would not stop asking. I said no. He asked again, many times, and I knew I must tell him it was finished. And yet my heart was too soft. I put … the Irish have a word for what they do not want to do … I put it on the long finger. Then you happened, damn you, so I went to Key Biscayne to tell him.'

'You could have written him,' I said.

'No.'

'Or phoned.'

She shook her head and smiled slyly.

'What you mean is, you wanted to go to bed with him.'

'It was for the last time. What harm? I told him that it was goodbye. He begged me, he cried, he said that without me in his world he could not live. It was one in the morning. I left him and went back to my hotel.'

When she did not strike her hands together like cymbals, I knew there was more to come. I reached for the wine carafe, and she said, 'I think that already Andrew does not like you. He says you probably go to bed drunk.'

'I think Andrew is a gobshite. What about Florida?'

'At eight o'clock the next morning, two of his friends, young people like him – Clay and Sylvie – came to my door. They said that Scott wanted to see me. I told them no, that it was over and there was no more to be said. They insisted, I said no again, blah, blah. So I told them to wait downstairs. I got dressed, and I went with them to Scott's apartment. I was very angry.'

'I can imagine.'

'So I went into his room, and he was dead.'

'Sorry?'

'Scott had killed himself. He was lying there on the bed, no clothes on. So … ah so *patetico*. His eyes. Still half open, and white. And those two friends of his, they had wanted me to see what they wanted me to think I had done to him. Such cruelness.' Her eyes filled with tears again. Attempting to smile, she said, 'Forgive me, everyone will think this is your fault.'

She caught hold of my wrist, so tightly that it hurt. I thought not of her dead lover but of another Scott – Scott Fitzgerald, and how Gatsby was destroyed by 'careless people'.

Josie said, 'You don't think I was to blame, do you?'

Of course I told her no and meant it.

Chapter Seven

At Loggerheads

July came, and the arrival of the Widow O'Fearna was nearly upon us. I had written her often and at length to report progress, and she had replied, once or twice by telephone, or more often in blue-black ink on sky-blue paper. With a week to go, she called to say that she would not be travelling alone.

She said, 'My stepson, Tyree, has got a hankering to see the Emerald Isle. Can you reserve a room for him at my hotel or close by?' She began to spell his forename.

'Tyree' was a familiar name in the O'Fearna mythology. I said, 'I think I know how it's spelt. I'll bet that his godfather was Ben Johnson.'

She laughed; her voice was low-pitched. 'Say now, aren't you the clever one!'

On the Monday before they were due to arrive, Shay and I met in Tish Merdiff's as usual. He had a favour to ask on behalf of his second eldest girl. An agony of shyness overcame him; he hated to think that his request might be construed as pass-remarkable.

'You know,' he said, 'that Blanaid is doing this course in journalism. Well, she put the bite on me. The idea is, she has to get an interview with somebody who's well-known. She was wondering if there was e'er an old chance of getting a few minutes with this Mrs O'Fearna. So what do you think?'

I said, 'Well, you'll appreciate that I can't speak on behalf of –'

At once, he was in full retreat. 'Oh, look, no, forget it. You have enough on your plate.'

'No, listen, will you wait –'

'You see, I told Blanaid. I said to her, "Look, TJ is a busy man –"'

I let loose a snarl that made the glasses tremble on the bar. 'Will you for Christ's sake shut up?' And then, quietly, 'Shay, I've never met this woman. I don't know what she's like. However, I'll tell you what I'll do ...'

'Ah, sure we'll take the will for the deed.'

'Will you shut it? What I'm trying to say is –'

'No, it's too much trouble.'

I soldiered on. 'Blanaid can come to Thursday's press conference at the Anna Livia –'

'Ah, but sure that's great!' Give my friend a crumb, and he would call it a banquet.

'Shay, I'm not finished ...'

'She'll be over the moon. She won't know herself.'

I said, 'I'll split your head open in a minute, I swear I will. This evening, as soon as we've had our few jars, we'll go back to my place, and I'll scribble down a couple of questions Blanaid can ask. Something that'll maybe soften the Widow for an interview.'

By now, Shay was almost tearful. 'You're a good friend. I won't forget it to you.'

'Feck off.'

On Thursday morning, Thorn and I went by rented limousine to the airport. Thorn carried a bouquet of white roses. 'See what I've tied them with?' The question begat its answer; it had to be a yellow ribbon: more O'Fearna mythology. He said, proudly, 'You're not the only one who does his homework.' More likely, I thought, he had been picking the brains of the wall-eyed film critic of the *Dubliner*, a chap who firmly alleged that O'Fearna's cacti and box canyons were, respectively, phallic symbols and vaginas.

It was three months since Josie had given me permission to tell Thorn about her and me. Perversely, I had said nothing; I wanted to prove, to myself as well as her, that I was not what in Dublin

86

was called 'a mouth'. Now, passing through Drumcondra, and with a sliding glass partition between us and the driver, I blurted it out.

'I'm seeing Josie Hand.'

Thorn said, 'When?'

'Whenever I can.'

'You what? You jammy berk.' He giggled. He looked at the high wall on our right. 'And he waits to tell me until we're passing the very residence of his Grace the Archbishop.' He tasted the name, 'Josie Hand!' as if it were a sip of his beloved Petit Chablis.

I felt that a show of modesty was called for. 'I dunno what she sees in me.'

'I do,' he said. 'No offence, but Josie is a girl who likes a man who casts a long shadow.'

Laughing: 'A long shadow? Who, me?'

'Well, maybe not yet,' he said, 'but it's lengthening. And do you know, you'll want to have a care.'

'How?'

'If Andrew Hand finds out.'

'We're very discreet.'

'In this town? One morning you'll wake up and find a horse's head in your bed. No, scrub that. Bearing in mind her husband's vocation, it's more likely to be a pig's cheek.'

He did not speak again for some minutes. He said, 'We've come a long way, haven't we?' I looked out of the window; we were passing Collins's Avenue. 'Not that kind of long way, you thick! What I mean is, I'll bet your old fellow's notion of infidelity was half a dollar each way on a hundred-to-eight shot without telling the ma.'

'No. The very worst thing my da ever did was, he sneaked off on his own to see the Three Stooges, in person at the Theatre Royal.'

Thorn smiled. 'What was his trade?'

'Printer.'

'Is the ma still alive?'

'We saw her yesterday. She's great.'

'Same with mine. When she goes – and God send it won't be tomorrow or the next day – that'll be the gangplank taken up and the lines cast off. No more contact with the land. No ties with the little shop the grand-da had in the Liberties. Anchors aweigh, what?'

He had spent a weekend cruising on the Shannon with Prue and the children, which accounted for the nautical jargon. Sentiment sat strangely on the same Thorn Thornton who, so it was said, was cute enough to herd mice at a crossroads. I thought of his grandfather's huckster shop, and a memory came of Batty Kenirons raiméising in our car after the Penders' dinner party. It was not altogether true what the Oozer said on that occasion, that our entire generation had reinvented itself. Many had done so, but not all. There were those who, like Shay, preferred to cling to the homespun past, and there were others who fed off the best of two worlds. Politicians, for example, would hearken back to bog roads, whin grass, ceilidhes and the privations of the Seven Hundred Years, while, almost in the same breath, they rubbed shoulders with money-launderers in the Caymans. For the rest of us, James Joyce was our template. He had been the first to break free of the three great 'f's of Ireland: faith, fatherland and friends. Perhaps I had not his steeliness of purpose; at any rate, ridding myself of the first two 'f's was plenty.

There had been tailwinds over the Atlantic, and Kitty O'Fearna and Tyree came through the Arrivals gate even as we got there. Thornton presented the Widow with the roses and I looked on jealously as he actually kissed her hand, taking it by the fingertips and raising it to the dead rat. I made do with a handshake that earned me a goring from the rose-thorns.

'Aren't you the self-effacing one!' the Widow said.

It was a toss-up as to whether she was poking fun at my shyness or Thorn's showing-off. Perhaps both. She was a handsome woman in late middle-age, tall, slender, pinch-faced and blonde – which was a surprise, given that both her hand-writing and her voice were brunette. Her complexion was pale; whatever about New Mexico, she stayed out of the sun. She wore a figure-hugging jersey dress, with a leather jacket over it for travelling.

It was her companion whose appearance was the more striking. I calculated that a son of the first Mrs O'Fearna would have been at least in his forties, whereas Tyree could not have been above 30. He wore sun-bleached denims and a Stetson, rolled at the sides. I caught a glimpse of high-heeled boots of tooled leather. He was short and wide-hipped. He had an open razor of a nose, an olive complexion and eyes that were another kind of olive. I had seen hundreds like him bite the dust in O'Fearna westerns.

He shook hands and said, 'Call me Ty.' As he pushed a loaded luggage cart towards the exit, the Widow said, 'Tyree is a native American.' She followed him out, going ahead of us and giving Thornton a chance to whisper to me, 'Injun!'

In the limousine, Ty sat with the driver, and the Widow, Thorn and I wedged in behind. Tyree may have been one kind of vanishing American; Kitty O'Fearna was another: a cigarette smoker. She lit up a Chesterfield and looked out at the airport exit road, where there was a large *Cead Mile Failte* sign: the work, seemingly, of a drunken topiarist.

'I don't know what people here are going to make of Tyree,' the Widow told us. 'His mother was a Hopi woman. She still is. My husband met her when he was on location for *Fort Geronimo* and they had a thing going. He wasn't my husband then, of course: no way, José! At that time, he was still married to his Number One. And to begin with, Tyree wasn't called Tyree. He was given a Hopi name. Little Flying Fuck or something like that.'

She unleashed a small guffaw, which encouraged Thorn and me to go into fawning mode.

'Sean took him off the reservation, put him through high

school, made a Catholic of him and gave him a job as assistant director and stunt rider. Well, think of the alternatives. The boy would have ended up either as a drunken Indian or making silver bolo-ties for the women to sell to tourists on the plaza at Santa Fe. And it isn't easy for the Hopis. Where they live is surrounded by the Navajos, and those peoples don't see eye to eye. Right, Ty?'

Tyree, who to our surprise could hear through the glass panel, prodded the under-brim of his Stetson with a finger and said: 'Got it, mom.'

The Widow snuggled between Thorn and me. 'So break it to me, what have you boys got lined up?'

She already knew; I had sent her our souvenir programme. The week of silent films was already on its fourth day. There was to be a Friday morning press conference at her hotel, the Anna Livia off Grafton Street. All day Saturday, there would be a non-stop programme of O'Fearna sound films, demonstrating his diversity, and that evening there was to be a black-tie dinner at which the Widow would be presented with a passport in her late husband's name. Next day, there was to be a lecture, 'Print the Legend', delivered by an eminent journalist named Fintan O'Doul, who specialised in nearly everything. That evening, there was to be a gala presentation of *The Man from Innisfree* at Savoy One.

She said, 'When do I get to see the archive?'

'Now, if you like,' I said.

Tyree stayed in the car as Thorn and I ushered her past the brass plate that said *O'Fearna Film Archive*. She thought the office was under-furnished. 'Hate those chairs! And it needs a divan. Green leather. What's a film executive without a casting couch?'

I told her I had tried to stay within my budget. She said, tone-lessly, 'Shoo-shoo,' which I interpreted as 'Sure, sure.' I showed her the strongroom where the films were stored. A smaller room, grandiosely called the library, contained a shelf of videotapes and a bookcase that held everything I could find about O'Fearna: biographies, critical studies, published screenplays. Yesterday in its modest way it had seemed impressive; now, through her eyes, it was Mickey Mouse. She spent minutes looking at the book titles, tracing her forefinger along the spines. She straightened, sighed and said as if replying to a question, 'That's all there is. No, it won't do. Christ, no.'

As we got back into the limousine, she said to Thornton, 'Honey, would you be awfully offended if Mr Quill and I had lunch at my hotel? Alone, that is.' To me, unsmiling, 'You and I need to talk.' Thorn's look said what I was thinking: she was going to feed me and fire me.

As the car nosed up a cobbled laneway and into Dame Street, she said, 'Say, how would you gentlemen define an Irish-American film?'

Thorn, sliding out from under, passed it over to me. He said, using the name I hated, 'Thady?' I replied that one could make the definition as broad or as narrow as one liked. 'Think of Cagney. You could have *The Fighting 69th, Yankee Doodle Dandy, The Irish in Us, Shake Hands with the Devil, Angels with Dirty Faces*. Or you could have Pat O'Brien, with *The Last Hurrah*, or *Fighting Father Dunne*.' As for Barry Fitzgerald, say, and Sarah Allgood ...'

The Widow laughed and said that I ought to be on a quiz show. At the Anna Livia, Thorn took over the business of assisting her and Tyree to check in. He had a masterful style that I envied; he filled in the registration cards and presented her with the room keys. When she said that she would see him next day at the conference, he launched into a repeat of his d'Artagnan act, and I was maliciously pleased to hear her utter a negative 'Uh-uh' and draw her hand back out of range. To me, she said, 'They have a restaurant here?'

'One floor up,' I said. 'It's called Loggerheads.'

She laughed. 'You're a caution. One o'clock, then.'

On the hotel steps, Thorn said, lying through his teeth and from under the rat, that he had work to do. He paused to say, 'So what about that, then?'

'I think I'm for the high jump.'

He managed to look sympathetic. 'You're lucky you weren't scalped.'

With more than an hour to kill, I walked around the Green and found a bench with a single occupant, an elderly woman. I had hardly sat down than a drunken ruffian came up. He stood in front of me, hands in pockets. He swayed from the hips, knees buckling, scowled and muttered at me. Ignored, he held his ground and began to make small abortive lunges. I was not in the humour to be mugged, even incompetently. I said, as coldly as I could manage, 'Don't even think about it.' He bit his lower lip, muttered again and took off, weaving by the ornamental lake and made a staggering run at a duck. The elderly woman gave me a look and said, 'He was askin' you to move over. The poor shagger wanted to sit down.'

Too proud to reply, I got up and found another bench, out of sight. I pondered on how Greta and Josie would separately react to the news that I was now an ex-archivist. Josie was a snip. She would say that if the Widow O'Fearna had chosen to fire me, then more fool she. During the past three months, she had dinned it into me that I was a person of worth; otherwise – although it never strayed into so many words – why would a woman of her, Josie's, excellence waste her time? She was extraordinary. If I asked her opinion on any matter, I would hardly have launched into my opening address to the jury, than she, from the bench, would deliver a final judgement, accompanied by the crashing of invisible cymbals, to indicate that there would be no appeal. She had added an extra twelve inches to my height, and the bossiness was a small tax to pay.

With Greta, it was a case of *The Lady or the Tiger*? Open one door and she would spring out with claws unsheathed to say that she had told me so and that this was the price of me. (I dreaded the day when she would tuck the word *hubris* into her vocabulary). She would demand to know how we were now going to manage. Or, if I perhaps chose the other door, she would comfort me, call the Widow an old bitch and assure me that, in spite of all, she and I would hold the devil by the tail. Chance, as they say, would be a fine thing.

At 12.50, I walked back to Grafton Street and the Anna Livia. Over the way in England, there was once a maxim to the effect that the fool of the family went into the Church; the bistro, Loggerheads, was one more proof that in Ireland the same fool usually went to work in the kitchen of a hotel restaurant. I asked for a glass of dry white. The Widow, when she arrived, was alone; Tyree was off exploring the city. She was carrying a thin document case. She ordered a vodka martini and gave exact instructions to the waiter, who would, I knew, make a balls of it. From the menu, she chose something with parsley sauce; apathetically, I asked for rib-eye of beef.

I asked, 'How is the jet-lag?'

She said, 'I never get it. I take erbs.' This was my first indication that Americans pronounced 'herbs' without the aspirate. She looked at my still untouched wine. 'So what say we get down to business before we tie one on?'

My stomach turned over. Like cat-hairs, wisps of the past still clung to me, and I came from a time when losing a job was a stigma, like catching TB. She unzipped the document case and took out several pages clipped together. 'You know what this is? It's your contract.' Keeping her eyes on my face, she took a grip on the pages and tore them slowly across the middle. She crooked a finger at the waiter. 'Would you kindly put this in the trash?'

Although it was bad manners to do so before she had been served, I took a gulp of my wine. The thing was done, then; I was jobless, and whatever appetite I might have had had vanished. A silver lining was the certain dreadfulness of the food.

She said, 'What I want to do is renegotiate. A new contract, a new deal, new money. I propose to expand the scope of the O'Fearna Archive so that it embraces – is that a good word or isn't it? – Irish-American movies. Just like those you mentioned in the limo.' She smiled, letting it sink in. 'So you've got yourself a promotion, Buster, and how do you like them apples?' Buster was a good name for me; she waited, watching my Keaton face.

I heard words, mine. 'You have a hell of a nerve.'

'*What?*'

'No, let *me* say "What?" to *you*. What do you take me for? Somebody you can play with, some country mug, wanting to watch him squirm, letting him think he's going to get the boot?'

'Is that what you thought?'

Even as I spoke, I knew that the voice was not mine but Josie's. Some people – most people – believe their own CVs, and Josie, who herself had nothing to lose, had written mine. I heard myself say, 'Stuff your job. I mean, how bloody dare you play sadistic games with me? Coming into the archive, turning your nose up after I worked my sodding guts out for an effing year, telling me "It won't do."'

'Nor will it.'

The waiter came with her martini. She said, 'You'd better bring another one. This boy is a regular caution.' She looked at me, laughed and shook her head. 'You are very rude.'

'Sorry.'

'No, you aren't.'

'No, I am not.'

'And I'm not going to stuff the job but oh, boy, am I ever tempted! Sean O'Fearna would have kicked your ass from here to Christmas. But I happen to think that you and I can do business. Do you know the reason I –' She broke off to light a cigarette, using the pause as stage business – 'the reason I said "It won't do"? I'll tell you. In that bookcase of yours you have all the critical junk ever written about my husband – by Andrew Sarris, Joe McBride, Robin Wood, Mike Wilmington. And you have all the memoirs, books of recollection by people who worked with him: *Pops, Man of the West, The O'Fearna I Rode With* – Christ, my husband never got on a horse in his frigging life! Are you aware that there is not and has never been one serious, in-depth, full-length biography of that man? And that is why I said it won't do. Now I think it's a crying shame, don't you?'

I made no reply. Climbing down off a high horse required an expertise I had never learned. No doubt Thorn could manage it. The Widow took a taste of her martini, which was probably straight vermouth, and said, 'Jee-suss.' It took her a while to flag down the waiter, and ask him – it was an old joke – how he managed to get the donkey to sit on the cocktail shaker. She ordered a rye whisky, then looked at me blankly. 'Where was I?'

'You said it was a crying shame.'

'Yes, it is. So what about it?'

'What about what?'

She said, 'I want you to write the definitive O'Fearna biography. But hey, here comes the chuck wagon!'

We waited as two dishes under silver covers were wheeled in. The waiter whisked the domes away, one in each hand, like a conjuror milking applause and revealing a dead rabbit. There can be more than one reason for loss of appetite. You lose a job, or you get a job: either will do. Or, as in her case, it may simply be the food.

She watched her lunch congeal for a while, then said, 'I have my husband's letters, papers, shooting scripts. I own every movie he made as an independent. I'm laying this thing in your lap. I can open doors. I have contacts, people he knew and worked with, only you'll want to saddle up right now, 'cause the old-timers are going fast. Got it? You would be writing an approved biography, which does *not* mean that you would have to kiss ass. With my okay, you can go to a top publisher and write your own ticket. And don't take an advance of less than a hundred thou. So what do you say?'

I was tempted to ask, 'Why me?' but I remembered Thornton's golden rule: Never, not ever, go to them; always make them come to you. Then I asked, 'Why me?'

She said, 'I've read your stuff, all of it. You can write. You care about movies. No, more than that, you're crazy about them, and with you writing it the book wouldn't be just a chore. A labour of love. So I'll take a flyer. Now, will that do?'

Instead of answering, I looked the gift horse in the mouth. 'Would this be warts and all?'

'Come again?'

'What about the first Mrs O'Fearna?'

'What about her?'

'And the Hopi woman.'

'Hopi woman, Apache woman, Shoshone woman, Arapaho woman ... how many tribes are there? One of his squaws even had a name for him; she called him her "Little Big Horn". Jesus, how about that?' She laughed and thumped the table. Her parsley sauce did not even shiver. 'And it wasn't only Indians; there was the occasional hot *tamale*, like when he was shooting *The Vanishing Vaquero* and *Shoot-out in Sonora*. My husband was a once-removed Connemara Catholic; which meant that if a woman wasn't either Irish or white American, then screwing her was a venial sin, like gabbling a Hail Mary.'

A coin dropped. 'Warts and all ... hey, hey, I get it! Now come on, do you think this book would even get off the ground if I asked you to pull any punches? That man was a great movie-maker. He was also a bullshit artist. Talk to him about art, and he would say ...'

She and I quoted O'Fearna, together: 'I make westerns.' I had never heard O'Fearna speak, but her voice had gone into a mimicry that was not affectionate.

'He was a bastard on the set. He was an old bully, he kicked ass,

96

he liked pain just so long as it wasn't his. And in the evening he played poker and bubbled at the nose while the crew and the bit players sang *I'll Take You Home Again, Kathleen*. Then when he'd had his little cry, he went to bed. And if you think that bed was empty, then I've picked me the wrong boy!'

'What about you?'

'Me?'

'In the book.'

'Good question. By the time I came along, all his best movies were a long time in the can. But I was part of him, and I don't want to come over as an afterthought. Fair?'

'Fair.'

'Hey, this food is crud. Is there a real bar-room in this town?'

'There's Davy Byrne's.'

She was on her feet. 'So lead on.'

We walked into Grafton Street and crossed over to Davy's where the dish of the day was what the Widow read from the blackboard as beef stoo. We had a bar lunch and talked some more. I was light-headed. She said: 'Hell, I'm not going to call you Mr Quill. So what's your given name? Teddy? Was that what Thornton called you in the limo?'

'No, what he said was "Thady". It's a name in an old mock-heroic song; it comes from Tadgh, which means Timothy. I prefer TJ or Theo.'

'What did your folks call you?'

I bit the bullet. 'Thady.'

'Uh-huh. Well, you can call me Mrs O'Fearna.'

'I think I prefer the Widow O'Fearna.'

She slapped me on the back. I wanted to leave, find a telephone and pass my great news to Greta and Josie. It would be in that order; there was such a thing as protocol. And it seemed like a good time to mention Shay's girl, Blanaid, and the possibility of an interview.

I did so, and to my surprise the Widow's answer was a flat no.

'I thought that was why we were having a press conference, to cut out all that crap. No, I want to get out and see a bit of the city before Ty and I go west to the Yeats Country. Hey!' She snapped her fingers. Cigarette sparks showered. 'Now there's an idea. Why doesn't this kid ... uh ...?'

'Blanaid.'

'Funny names you got here. Why doesn't she interview Tyree?'

'Sorry?'

'I told you, he grew up with the Hopis. He worked with his father. He's had one hell of a life. He'll talk to her, sure!'

Well, it was a wonderful idea, and I told her so. I knew that Blanaid would be thrilled to interview Tyree. Apart from my gaffe with the drunk in Stephen's Green, that was the only mistake I made all day.

Chapter Eight

At Les Trois Cloches

'What did you do on Josie Hand?' Greta whispered.

'How?'

'Do you not see the looks she's giving you? Daggers!'

We were part of the crowd that had gathered in the Chapelle d'Iseult Room of the Anna Livia Hotel drinking coffee and paint-stripper before the press conference settled down. I glanced in Josie's direction, and yes, she was giving me a look that could have burned a hole in a surplice. Only Greta, I thought scurrilously, could have mistaken horniness for animosity. Once our eyes had locked, Josie came over, saying, 'Well, *hello!*', overacting as if we were the last people she had expected to see.

'We thought you were black out with us,' Greta said.

'Me? Are you mad?' Josie said. She affected to look around her, even putting a hand to shade her eyes, like an Indian seeking a stagecoach. 'I'm looking for Colleen,' she said. 'She promised to meet me here.' I received a mock-scornful glare as she added, untruthfully, 'Of course *he* deed not invite me. He ees becoming too famous.'

Greta gave a push-button response: 'Don't I know!'

A Telefis Eireann camera crew had turned up and was concentrating on the Widow, who, with Tyree in attendance, was the star turn. Thornton was talking to a woman journalist who was carrying a month-old infant suspended in a kind of sling around her neck. Somehow, she was managing the feat of eating an egg sandwich and taking notes at the same time. Thornton had appointed himself as greeter-in-chief. When I arrived with Greta, he had said, corner of mouth, 'So what happened at your lunch? Did the Widow give you the old heave-ho?'

I told him, sighing like a male Mrs Gummidge: 'She turfed me out on my ear.'

'Aw,' he said. 'Tough.'

Greta waited until we were out of his hearing. 'Did you not tell him your news?'

'Not yet,' I said, enjoying myself.

'I wouldn't trick-act with Thorn if I were you.'

'He'll find out in a few minutes.'

'Boys will be boys! Still, wonders of wonders, at least you told *me* about it.'

And one other person, I thought.

Now, as we waited with Josie for the room to come to order, Greta nudged me and said, 'Look.' I turned and saw a black-haired girl who had come in and, like the journalist, was carrying a baby in a sling. 'The place is a bloody creche,' my wife said.

Josie, sucking up to her, said: 'Oh that ees funny!'

She even linked her arm in Greta's. Mentally, I banged their heads together. In France, or at least in French films, having both a wife and a beautiful mistress was an accepted way of life, like owning both an oak-beamed home out in the country and a smart *pied-à-terre*. Only in a small back-yard of a country would one's wife and mistress not just meet but virtually live in each other's handbags.

As the dark girl went past, my one-time friend Willie Cooney came trailing after her, and I realised that she must be none other than the *bodhran*-playing light-o'-love. Their union had evidently been blessed, as expected. Greta gasped, happily scandalised, and poured the story into Josie's ear.

A hand plucked at my sleeve, and, as if my cup were not already overflowing, I saw Shay's daughter, Blanaid, who was almost trembling with excitement. She was clutching a notebook and pencil. She was nineteen, curly-haired, tall and still gangly for her age. She was accompanied by a youth who hardly came up to her chin. He was scowling. 'This is Duane,' she said. 'He was dying to come.' From the look of him, it did not seem so. As we shook hands, I noticed that his fingernails were bitten to the quick and there was what seemed to be oil ingrained under the skin of his hands and face. He said 'Howyah,' in a low, faintly disgusted voice.

I said, 'Greta, would you mind getting Duane a sandwich while I introduce Blanaid to Mrs O'Fearna and Tyree?'

The previous evening, I had called Shay and told him what the Widow had proposed: that Blanaid should interview Tyree. This had cost me at least another five minutes of gratitude. The coda was 'Brigid says she's saying a prayer for you', and Shay gave an affectionate chuckle at his wife's God-worshipping foolishness. Now the Widow kept her word. When I introduced Blanaid, she said, 'Bless you, my children!' and pushed her and Ty towards a corner of the room. I returned to where Duane, holding a bayoneted sausage, was darkly loitering. Turlough and Colleen had by now arrived, so that, less conspicuously, Greta and Josie were part of a foursome. I found myself thinking of a Father Brown story: 'Where does a wise man hide a pebble? On the beach. Where does a wise man hide a leaf? In a forest.'

Turlough said hello and asked if either Greta or I would be at home later on.

'Greta will,' I said. 'I have to look after Mrs O'Fearna. Why?'

He winked and put a finger to his lips. There was an actual hissing noise, and I saw that Josie was staring at him venomously. As Greta opened her mouth to ask what was afoot, a small bell was rung and Thorn said loudly, 'Could we all settle down?'

He beckoned to me, so that we sat, one on each side of the Widow, behind a table that was covered by a green cloth. Ballygowan bottles, intended for us, were rolling about, already empty. He introduced the guest of honour and spoke of her generosity. He would not, he said roguishly, be at all surprised if there was an Irish ancestor lurking in the green foliage of her family tree. When he mentioned what was already known, that Sean O'Fearna had been posthumously made a citizen of this sea-girt isle, there was the kind of applause which is peculiar to stand-up occasions where drink is served: the sound of one hand clapping. Thorn spoke of the archive, which, when complete, would bring together all of the director's films. After five minutes, he introduced Mrs O'Fearna.

She made a charming little speech. She said, 'I'm keeping the twenty-minute hearts-and-flowers bit for tomorrow's shindig.' There was warm laughter, not untinged with gratitude. She said: 'However, let me just say this. The archivist, TJ Quill ... ' She turned to me. 'Do you mind if I call you Thady?'

Everyone chuckled. Now publicly given a hated nickname, I managed the rictus of a smile.

' ... Thady has been doing such magnificent work that I want him to do a lot more. That's one of the reasons I have decided to extend the scope of the archive to include not just the work of Sean O'Fearna, but Irish-American movies as a separate genre of its very own. It will be the first collection of its kind, anywhere, and I think that my late husband, who so admired the work of his great colleagues – Howard Hawks, Raoul Walsh, King Vidor, Mike Curtiz and the rest of them – would have wanted this with all his heart.'

To my small credit, I managed not to nod in agreement. From what I knew about Sean O'Fearna, he was territorial and held that every director, himself and Ernst Lubitsch excepted, was a talentless bum. As the applause started up again, the Widow began to sit down, but changed her mind.

'Oops. One more thing. I am delighted to say that my friend, Thady here –' more chuckles, damn them – 'has agreed, with my warm approval, to write what will be the definitive – and, need I say, the best-selling – biography of Sean O'Fearna.'

There was an 'Ooh,' as if she had announced a raffle for a free holiday in the Seychelles. Now, after kissing me on the cheek, she did sit down. Flash bulbs went off and the Telefis camera came nosing at me. Thornton, so I was afterwards told by those who had a full-face view, did not even blink. His footwork was in the Astaire class and, as the applause grew, he topped it by declaring stoutly and loudly, 'Of course he'll write it! Who the hell else would do it?' I noticed that Josie had given Greta her coffee cup to hold, and her clapping hands were making noises like a child's cap gun.

There were questions from the floor, and Thornton fielded the inevitable one or two that were barbed. He was suddenly in a bad temper that was rapidly worsening. As was usual on such occasions, the questions and the wine dried up simultaneously. Thorn said, 'Anyone else? I'll take one more.' A tubby white-haired man came forward; it was Willie Cooney, who was spelling the *bodhran* player by proudly holding their new infant in the crook of his arm. He said, '*I* have a question.'

Knowing Willie, I could tell that a joke was on its way; his chins were wobbling. He said, 'Why is Mrs O'Fearna so anti-Irish that she pronounces "fillums" with just the one syllable?'

The joke was not meant to score off the Widow; it was a feeble attempt to poke fun at the native way of saying 'films'. There was forced laughter. Thornton motioned to the Widow not to reply. He said, keeping his tone light, 'Willie, I honestly haven't a clue. Why don't you ask your grandchild?'

There was a small groan from the audience, and Willie's face reddened.

Thornton said, 'Well, I think that's our lot. Thank you all, and safe home, or wherever.' There was a dribble of applause, and I saw Josie retrieve her coffee cup from Greta. Several journalists came to cluster around the Widow with private questions.

As I walked around the table, Willie was protesting to Thorn: 'I didn't come here to be insulted. What's up with you? What sort of a snide bloody remark was —'

Thornton said, 'Feck off, Willie, or I'll burst you.'

He walked away from both Willie and the *bodhran* player, who was beginning to cry. He came around me and blocked my way, facing me. He said, 'You're a cute hawk, aren't you?'

'How?'

'Keeping your good news to yourself.'

'Well, I didn't know if you'd be pleased or not.'

He took a step back as if to see me clearly. 'Say again?'

I said: 'When you thought the Widow was giving me the chop, you weren't all that much put out, were you? It was "I'm all right, Jack, I'm in the dinghy." You even made a joke of it.'

'Oh, grow up.'

'In fact, you did a runner.' Out of the corner of my eye, I saw Willie and the light-o'-love go from the room. She was still crying. 'And what's more,' I said, 'if you're mad at me, why take it out on Willie Cooney?'

'Fuck Willie Cooney. And you. And the horse you came in on. Certainly I did a runner, why wouldn't I? Same as when there's a road accident I keep walking. Who wants to hang around?'

'Jesus, you're good.'

'What's eating you? I was upset for your sake, and I made light of it. You're paranoid, you know that?'

'TJ! Thay-dee!' Greta, getting in on the joke of the day, was calling to me. Thorn, on the edge of a quarrel and a scene, suddenly pulled back. 'Listen, I'm your friend, and this is great news. Massive. Terrific. You deserve it. So c'm 'ere to me.'

He enfolded me in a bear-hug. I shivered, feeling the tip of the dead rat against my cheek. Out of embarrassment, I said, defusing the bomb, 'I swear, if you kiss me I'll kill you.'

He thumped me, grinned and went off. I had not been forgiven. People came up with congratulations. Among them was Josie, who solemnly pumped my hand up and down. '*Complimenti*! But what a beeg surprise!' She kept a straight face.

Colleen said, 'Are you hungry? Josie wants to take you and Greta and Turlough and me to lunch.'

'To celebrate,' Josie said.

There was a token protest from Greta. 'I've been telling her no, we can't, but she won't be talked to. She's awful.'

'Eet ees arranged.' Josie said. 'I have booked a table at Les Trois Cloches.'

As we left, Duane came up. He said 'I can't find Blaw.'

'Pardon?'

'Blanaid. She's gone off.'

I said, 'Well, she's doing an interview with young O'Fearna. Probably they're down in the lobby, where it's quiet. Tell you what, I'll have her paged.'

I did so, and joined our group. The five of us strolled along Wicklow Street to the restaurant. As I walked next to Greta, Josie positioned herself on my free side, squeezing my arm discreetly. Quite suddenly, Turlough called from behind, 'Hey, Josie, when did you have time to book the table?'

Josie said, 'I did eet this morning, from home.'

Colleen said, 'But that was before any of us knew that TJ would be –'

Josie's footwork was the equal of Thorn's. She segued smoothly into: 'Yes, yes, yes. I told them that today I would be meeting my four best friends een all the world, and I wanted to geev them a lunch. And of course now we have heard TJ's wonderful news on top of everything else –'

'*Thady's* wonderful news,' Greta said, old jokes being the best.

'... Well, we must have a bottle of Dom Perignon to celebrate.' With one bound, Josie was out of the woods and in the open.

Colleen said, one accent on the heels of another: 'Giuseppina, you are a howl.'

Turlough made a suitable baying noise. We were a happy fivesome.

Josie led us into Les Trois Cloches as if she were trailing a mink across the floor. Heads turned to stare, eyes loitered to admire, and I added the sin of pride to that of adultery. Greta whispered, grudgingly, 'She's gorgeous.'

I said, all but yawning: 'She'll do.'

Josie refused to allow us to be guided to a round table in the centre of the room; instead and cleverly, she chose one with a banquette where, avoiding contact with me, she could sit next to Turlough. She ordered the champagne, scowling when instead of Dom Perignon there was 'only' Veuve Cliquot.

'Poor Andrew is missing this,' Colleen said.

'Poor Andrew ees doing what poor Andrew does best,' Josie said.

'And what is that?'

'Looking after poor Andrew.'

We all laughed. During the past three months, Josie and I had been together on trips to London and Belfast. A nationalist would have argued that Belfast and Dublin were in the same country, but in matters of sex Josie was a unionist. We were on foreign soil, she told me; and so, when we shared a room on the fifth floor of the Europa Hotel, she was not breaking her undertaking to Andrew. At other times, we went to the pictures or a play or met for lunch in a Chinese restaurant in the inaptly named suburb of Stillorgan. We learned each other.

There was an evening over dinner when she asked, 'Why do you hold back from me?'

'Maybe it's to brace myself because one day it'll be over.'

She said, 'But nothing lasts.'

'I'm no good at letting go. I haven't the knack.'

She said, 'Then for my part, you'll never have to. I promise.' She rested her hand, which was small and rather fleshy, on mine. It was the only occasion we ever made physical contact while alone in a public place.

At Les Trois Cloches, after the champagne had been poured,

she thrust the wine list at me across the table and said, 'The guest of honour must choose.'

'Yes, Thady,' Greta said, taking her pitcher to the well yet again, 'you choose.'

Josie dropped her in-company accent. 'No, no, please, we will not have that. It is a horrible name. "Thady?" Ugh.' She mimed a double-spit over her shoulder. 'No, Greta, this is not good. Colleen respects Turlough, and I respect Andrew.' She was utterly sincere; there were, as I have said, two of her, wife and lover, and it was the wife who was giving us lunch. She reached over and squeezed Greta's hand. 'So you must respect TJ. You don't mind that I say this?'

'God, no!' Greta said, humouring the madwoman. 'Of course not.'

Josie was not finished. 'Then so why do you want to punish him?'

Turlough said, 'Josie, Greta was making a joke.'

Josie said, 'Oh, yes, I know that.' Tears came into her eyes. ' But you see I do not have a sense of humour. For me, it is matter of honour.' Her accent had returned; she pronounced 'humour' without an h and 'honour' with one.

I sat, both loving her and wishing that her tongue would fall out. She picked up a table napkin and dabbed at her eyes. Still talking to Turlough, she said, 'Well, let us say that I 'ave too leetle yoomour and the Irish 'ave too much. That is why you are all … what ees the word? Ah, *si*! That ees why you are all the time what you always will be. Bolleexed.'

The word was unexpected that we all roared and Veuve Cliquot ran out of Colleen's nose, which made it worse. She was mortified, and the laughter became the more out of control when Josie said, 'But I am serious.'

I looked at her and thought of the many answers to a question that I would never ask myself. I loved her because I was lonely; because I was lustful, because she thought well of me. She was imperious, vain, wanting in frailty and an incurable back-seat driver; and as reasons for loving, each one of these, the last excepted, was a because and not a but. She was beautiful; she was wise; her voice stroked me; she could tell you black was white and yet without ever ringing false. She put the silly romance of old movies into my life; I thought of a line addressed to Robert Donat on board a river steamer, 'The Danube is only blue to people in love,' whereupon the camera moves to an upper deck, and Greer Garson, looking down, says to her friend, 'But it *is* blue!' I possessed the world as it ought to be instead of as it was, and damned her soul should she ever go away and I should lose it. I loved her because she demanded respect for me over a stupid nickname that I hated for a private reason, because in the song Thady Quill was heroic and bold, and I was not. I loved her because she took what Greta had pulled down and built a new person from the pieces.

When the laughing stopped, the conversation was relaxed and warm. Colleen wanted to know how I would set about writing the O'Fearna biography. I said that there would have to be at least a year of preparation. The Widow would dig up a first-rate researcher, or perhaps two. Then I would need to travel, to New Mexico and O'Fearna's birthplace in Maine and visit his one-time homes in Santa Monica and Marin County. If Josie took this as a hint that we could meet in foreign parts, she was careful to give no sign. She loved to travel. She went Bunburying in places as far apart as Puerto Vallerta and Lombok. She called upon her sixteen-year-old daughter Silvana, who was at boarding school near Montreux, and she visited her elderly and ailing mother at home in Florence. For her, the world, like knowledge itself, existed to be mopped up. When she came across an absorbing book – by Salman Rushdie, for example, whom she adored and I loathed – she said, intending it as the very highest praise, 'I could dip my bread in it.' She dipped her bread in whatever she did and wherever she went.

On the days when we lunched together, my accustomed seat in the Mimosa Garden was facing the door. Whenever a new customer came in, there would first be a flash of light from the outside, then a human shadow on the far side of a stained-glass screen. I was never so besotted that I did not look up in case it might be a friend of Greta's and mine, or worse. Once, preceding Josie into Marraine's on Essex Quay, I saw two men sitting just inside the door. I whispered, 'Andrew is here.'

She laughed. 'Fool.'

'I'm not joking.'

On the instant, she turned and fled. Andrew Hand, attracted by the movement, looked up from his plate, saw only me, an acquaintance, and smiled. I grinned stupidly, waggled my fingers at him and went out into the street without a word to the *patron*. Josie was standing, shivering, by the quay wall at the Ha'penny Bridge. She was terrified of discovery, just as what I most dreaded was going down to certain defeat on the day that Greta found out and declared total war. But for Josie, there was also a fear of the unthinkable, that her two selves, both of them *sans pareil* and kept surgically apart, would someday meet.

At three o'clock at Les Trois Cloches I excused myself and left the lunch table. Josie squeezed out of the banquette and came after me, catching up at the cash desk. 'I am following you,' she said, 'on the pretence that you are very naughty and might try to pay the bill.'

'I couldn't afford it!' I said.

She smiled and wagged a finger under my nose so that Greta, Turlough and Colleen could see my chastisement. She said, for their benefit, 'Oh no, you do not do thees thing!' Then, softly, 'Today is a good day for you, and I am very proud. This is just between you and me. *Ciao, amore.*'

I caught the second half of the afternoon double bill at the film theatre and in a daze sat through *Riders of the Limberlost*. Afterwards, I found the Widow and Thornton having an early dinner at the Anna Livia. Strange, I pondered, that for a man who was carnivorous by nature, his staple diet was fish.

'Where have you been?' the Widow said. 'I'm a gal who likes attention.'

Thorn pushed the afternoon paper at me. Most of an inside page was taken up with *Liffey Log* – a gossip column written by 'Yer Man'. It was yet another nom-de-plume of the insulted Willie Cooney, and today's column, already in print, described the late Sean O'Fearna as a Hollywood 'Oirishman'.

'Read the whole thing,' he said. 'Willie Cooney says that you and I are a couple of half-baked dilettantes.'

'Terrible if it were true!' I said.

'This is all your fault.'

'How is it my fault? It was you who insulted him.'

'Because you got me mad.' He laughed. It was all a joke, his mouth said; although his eyes travelled a different road. 'Have a jar,' he said.

'Is this a rib?' The Widow was confused. 'I mean, fellows, gimme a break.'

That evening, I escorted her to a screening of *A Terrible Swift Sword*, which was acknowledged to be one of O'Fearna's master-pieces. It was midnight by the time I got home, where Greta, wearing her dressing gown, was waiting up. A large flat object wrapped in brown paper and tied with string, was leaning against the hall table.

'That came for you,' Greta said. She amended: 'I mean us.'

'Then you should have unwrapped it.' I tore the paper off. It was the painting I had seen months before in Turlough's gallery of a girl at a window, looking out through the rain at Huband Bridge. There was a card which said, 'Congratulations to you both – Josie.'

'Nice, isn't it?' I said lamely. Greta made no reply; she had a perplexed look and read the message twice over as if it were an anagram. 'I saw it one day months ago at Turlough's gallery. He must have mentioned to Josie that I fancied it.'

'You told her, didn't you.'

'About the painting?'

'No, about today. I know you did. This was bought before today ever happened. Turlough gave the game away when he asked if you'd be at home this evening, and you said no, but I would be. I saw the look on her face. She nearly ate him.'

'Meaning?'

'Meaning that I wasn't the only one who was told all about you and writing the book and, and, and, and, and whatever.'

'All right, then. So I bumped into Josie in town. Big deal.'

'I see.'

'You know I'm a bad hand at keeping a secret.'

'Liar.'

'Ah, now.'

'What's going on?'

'Nothing.'

'So why did she pretend' – mimicking – 'that eet was all a beeg surprise?'

'Oh, for God's sake.'

'Yes, you told her ... I suppose before you even told me.'

'No way.' That at least was a ha'pennyworth of truth.

'Huh.' For once, she was at a loss for words. I saw her rejiggling the anagram. Then, feebly, 'Well, I'm not having it in the house. Anyway, I don't like it.'

'Grand.'

When I came to bed, she was sitting up with dabs of cream on her face. By now, she had sorted herself out.

'What's going on between you and her?'

'Nothing.'

'That thing must have cost a hundred pounds.'

I thought of the asking price and all but laughed. 'Josie can afford it.'

'Well, I have her taped. She's after you.'

'What?'

'Jesus, are you blind? Now that you're a big fellow and all cock of the hoop and full of yourself, Josie Hand is setting her cap at you. The minute you gave up the good job, I knew this would happen. And I ought to have guessed when she came out with that shit about me not respecting you. The cheek of her. Oh, the rip.'

Relief flooded through me. With both ends of the stick to choose from, Greta had caught hold of it by the middle. All I could think of was that Josie, in the role of predator, could live with Greta's dislike more easily than I could survive a war of attrition, a ceaseless chipping away day by day until not even the lies were left.

'Yes,' Greta summed up, 'she's after you. And I suppose you're enjoying it.'

I said, 'Well, you wouldn't care anyway.'

Foolishly, I thought this would silence her, knowing that she would go through fire rather than admit – or pretend (choose one) – that she did care, but she had an answer. She said firmly, immovably: 'I'm not going to be made a jeer of.'

Next day, I found a space for the painting in my workroom, and Greta no longer said that Josie was gorgeous. She even found nice things to say about Andrew Hand.

'God help that poor man,' she said at breakfast-time, 'and us all the time having a down on him. It's so easy to misjudge a person.'

In spite of fretting about Andrew, her mood seemed almost lightsome. Perhaps, having slept on her conviction that Josie was 'after' me, Greta had come to the conclusion that she was being paid a kind of compliment. At any rate, as I sat down she said, carelessly: 'I did you a fry this morning.'

Chapter Nine

In the Tram-yard

The weekend came and the Saturday banquet was as grand and as dull as one might expect. The Minister for the Arts recited a piece of his own poetry and presented the Widow with proofs of citizenship in her late husband's name. 'He really *is* a leprechaun,' Thornton whispered to her. 'If you grab him and hold on tight he'll have to grant you three wishes.'

On the Monday, she and Tyree returned to Santa Fe, and that evening I was with Shay in Tish's, as usual. He was dismayed that he had not met the O'Fearna stepson. 'I remember Trooper Tyree in *Rio Pecos*,' he said, 'when he used his horse as a shield and brought down three Apaches with his Winchester.' He imitated the triple whine of a rifle, echo and all: 'Khrrrr-eee … khrrrr-eee … khrrrr-eee.' The more waggish of the three barmen clutched his chest and buckled at the knees.

I reminded my friend that Tyree O'Fearna was not a cavalry trooper but one of the Indians. He saw no contradiction in this; like Walt Whitman, Shay was large and contained multitudes. Blanaid had brought home to him a glowing account of Ty, who in her estimation was a thorough gentleman. He was the only boy she had ever met who wore a proper hat and when he showed her into the Frank and Jesse James Barbecue House in South King Street he held the door, doffed his Stetson and made a low sweeping bow.

'I'd have expected that,' Shay said. 'Politeness to women is the Code of the West, you know. And it's a damn sight more than she'd get from the Midget Mechanic.' That was his scornful nickname for Duane, who worked in a factory that made car tyres. 'Catch that bugger taking off his hat! I dunno what Blanaid sees in him. His ma is the sort of old one that's always looking for her rights and would make a holy show of you. I mean, I'm not a snob – God, no, never that – but they're not our sort.'

It was his twist, and he ordered a Famous Grouse for me and, for himself, his usual tipple of two bottles of alcohol-free lager served in a pint tumbler. He had been on the dry for two years following an incident at a wedding. The bride was the daughter of a widowed friend of ours named Jessie Vesey, and the reception was held at a hotel in Howth. It was long morning's journey into a longer afternoon, and Shay was deeply anaesthetised by the time the bride and groom left for a secret destination which turned out to be Kelly's Hotel at Rosslare. Of late, it took only a few drinks to render him legless; on top of which he became obstreperous, refusing to hand over the car keys to Brigid. At such times, she was never a whinger, but loyally said that Shay was tired and had not properly recovered from last winter's bout of so-called twenty-four-hour flu. And when he insisted on getting behind the wheel of their Fiat, she always deferred to him; wedding vows apart, it was, after all, a test of her trust in God, who had never let her down yet.

After the wedding breakfast, I found him swaying in front of an unattended bar. As far as I could make out, the barman had given my friend change for a five-pound note instead of a ten. Shay, who was usually soft-spoken to the point of inaudibility, was shouting 'Come out, you bastard!' at a closed door.

'He's probably skipped out the back way by now,' I said.

'No, he hasn't,' Shay said. 'He's in there, but I'll wait him out.' He was weaving about and bunching his fists.

'Shay, mate, listen. Don't let him spoil the day on you. It's only a few quid, forget it.'

I touched his shoulder from behind. His response was to swing around and throw a punch at me, which was so wildly misjudged that it went past, almost pulling him off his feet. He straightened up and came at me, half-crouched, ready to try again. His eyes had narrowed. He said: 'Back off.' I did as I was told, making a small gesture that said the hell with him. As he gave up on me for a poltroon – it was a word he liked – and turned back to resume his death-watch by the bar, I walked away in search of his wife. She was on the hotel terrace with Greta and Jessie Vesey, gossiping and enjoying the view of Ireland's Eye.

I said, 'Brigid, I think Shay could do with a smidgin of TLC.' For a moment, she seemed about to rummage in her handbag. 'No, I mean he needs looking after. He's in the bar.' As she went, white-faced, into the hotel, I called after her, 'And watch out for his left hook.'

Greta, who knew Shay's form, said, 'Is he bad?'

'Ah, no. Only ossified.'

A few minutes later, Brigid came back. Without waiting to be asked how Shay was, she announced, 'He's grand. All that ails him is he's jaded and he wants to go home. My God, he was up at five this morning with Dympna's toothache.'

Greta and Jessie made sympathetic noises; Jessie even asked if they had tried oil of cloves. Brigid sent a short-sighted glare in my direction; annoyance was as close to the sin of anger as she would dare to go. She said, 'TJ, what Shamy *doesn't* need is his friends stirring up trouble and making out that he wants minding when there's not a feather out of him.'

As she said her goodbyes and hurried away, I saw that Shay had come weaving around a corner of the hotel on his way to the car park. Greta and Jessie waved to him. He gave me a squinting look of undying enmity, drew a Colt .45, pointed it, fanned the hammer, shot me dead, blew down the barrel, twirled the gun and, all in one movement, holstered it. He went off with Brigid to find their car in the corral.

'That's put you in your box,' Jessie said to me.

God seemed once again to have done the right thing by Brigid, for Shay called me next day from work, safe and sound and as amicable as ever. 'That wasn't a bad class of an old do,' he said. He hummed and hawed, and it was clear that the last two hours of the previous afternoon were lost to him. He fished for details. 'Brigid isn't happy in herself. She says she was a bit short with you, and it's preying on her conscience. You know, she's very … um …'

'Scrupulous.'

'Exactly.'

He had to be told, and I got it over with, all at once: 'Shay, you were more than half cut, and when I put a hand on your shoulder you threw a punch at me. Brigid felt that I was –'

'I threw a punch at you?'

I should have known that in spite of his carry-on about loving 'voilence' he would be horrified beyond measure at having lashed out at anyone, never mind at me. As a character said in the most overrated play in Irish theatre, there was a great gap between a 'gallous story' and a dirty deed.

I said: 'Look, Shay, I'll be in town today. Let's meet at lunchtime at Paddy Kavanagh's bench, and I'll give you the full blow-by-blow version.'

'Blow by –? Jesus, don't say that.'

'No harm done, honest. Relax. Talk to you then.'

Which I did, as if I were an informer; for, even though I was telling him about himself, I could not shake off the bad feeling that I was carrying tales. After we had sat for a while by the canal lock, he went back to work, deeply shocked. We met on the following Monday, as usual, and I wondered if there would be more remorse. Instead, he all but sailed in and said, 'Brace yourself.' He ordered two bottles of what he called cat-pee. He had been to his family doctor, who told him that he had lost his tolerance for alcohol and must give it up. 'So that's the way it has to be,' he said with a shrug. He took a swallow of the yellow liquid in front of him, smacked his lips loudly and said, 'Aaah … disgusting!' So it had been ever since. On Mondays, we continued to meet and put the world to rights, and he downed several pints of the stuff as if it were the real thing. He bore his cross stoically. I had the uneasy feeling that in a small corner of his mind he looked upon it as a just penance for hitting out at a friend. It was, he might have said, the Code of the West.

That had been in what we thought of as old God's time. Now, from where we sat in the lounge of Tish's, we could see through a door opposite into the small public bar. This was the domain of regulars to whom comfort, polished wood and shaded lights were folderols. Among the more colourful regulars were a Provo, a malevolent retired police sergeant from Kerry, a bank manager whose wife, it was rumoured, had been mummified these ten years, a broadcaster who did educational programmes in pidgin-Irish, and a dealer in precious stones who, with his wife and other couples was reputed to enjoy throwing *après*-pub Spin-the-Bottle parties. There was also a wife-murderer – weapon, a coal hammer – who for want of evidence had never been charged. Probably, much as the others did, he frequented the public bar out of abhorrence of the even greater crime of affectation. Their talk was of either Gaelic football or, heretically, rugby. Shay and I would not have fitted in, which for his part was why he stoically endured the comfort of the lounge bar.

As he was enlarging on his theory that the Midget Mechanic was little better than a guttie, I became aware that a stillness had fallen on the regulars in the public. They were facing the outer door like dustcart men who had seen their first dead cat of the day. The intruder was, of all people, Thorn Thornton. He saw me, retreated into the street and came in by the lounge bar door. He was not, I knew, a frequenter of pubs or for that matter of our village.

He said, all in one breath, 'I had business out this way, two bits of business, in fact, and I called you at home, and Greta said it was Monday and that you'd be here. I knew what day of the week it was but I forgot where. Hello.' The salutation, uttered with the last of his breath, was addressed to Shay.

I said, 'Do you know Shay Lambe?'

'By sight, of course, and I read your reviews irreligiously. Hello, a second time.' Thorn smiled his Sunday smile and extended his hand, which was accepted as if it were a copy of *The Watchtower*. Shay, not himself knowing how charm was worked, always distrusted it.

When Thorn had ordered a Courvoisier and insisted on the same again for us, I asked: 'So what's this business of yours?'

'First of all,' Thorn said, 'you know of course that Edwin Eustace has snuffed it?' Old Eustace, the revered patriarch of an acting family, had been at the topmost rung of his profession, as proof of which he had not learned his lines for ten years. 'Well, I've been invited to deliver a couple of words – the proverbial *cupla focail* - at the funeral mass, so I paid Ginny Milligan to write something for me.'

Ginny Milligan was a best-selling novelist who lived grandly in our town, on Victoria Road. Thorn patted his breast pocket where the corner of a white envelope was visible. 'She came through,' he said.

I said: 'I would have thought that you'd have preferred to say a few words of your own. From the heart, like.'

'What heart?' Thorn laughed, his eyes inviting a response from Shay. If humour failed, he would try candour, flattery, wit and the fail-safe ploy of kindred spirits. He welcomed a challenge to his power to charm; the most rabid of Holy Ghost missioners could not match his expertise at making converts.

'And what's your second bit of business?' I asked.

'Ah!' – lifting his glass – 'I'll show you when we get these down us.'

Shay protested that it was time he headed home, but Thorn would not let him go unconverted. He led us out of Tish's and through the town to the old tram-yard. There, late as it was, two men with drills were prising up the last of the old cobblestones and with them the tramlines that curved into the high-gabled sheds. When I was eight, my father took me to see the last tram at the end of its slow journey from Nelson's Pillar. Thousands had turned out to bear witness to the end of an age, and the destination rolls, pirated from their spools, fluttered like streamers and bore what were for the moment names of legend: Stoneybatter, Inchichore, Chapelizod, Dartry, Donnybrook, Terenure, Ringsend, Sandymount, Dun Laoghaire, Dalkey. For more than half of his forty years; my father had never set eyes on a tram; even so, he was conscious that this, accompanied by the wailing shriek of engine whistles from the railway siding, was a kind of great death. The music of iron wheels on steel and the crackle and spit of the trolley against the overhead wires were stilled for ever.

The noise from the pneumatic drills was ear-splitting. I shouted: 'Nobody around here is going to get much sleep tonight.' Thorn uttered what I lip-read as the standard Dublin two-word reply to either complaints or criticism. Without saluting the workmen, he led Shay and me across the yard to the tramsheds. The place had for years been stacked with peat briquettes and builder's supplies; now it was empty.

'Welcome,' Thorn said, 'to The James Joyce.'

'To the what?'

He said, 'Do you know what Irish punters most enjoy?' If a broken chair or an orange box had been handy, he would have mounted it. 'A bloody good evening out. They want plain food and lashings of it – bacon and cabbage, Irish stew, Dublin coddle and colcannon. I'm going to give it to them.'

'You?'

'What's more, they want Dublin city in the rare old times. Bowler hats and stick-on whiskers, shirt-waists and feather boas, Irish dancers in black wool stockings, inflicted with St Vitus' Dance from the hips down and total paralysis from the waist up.

Tenors singing "Deh pale moon was rising above deh blue mountains." Sing-songs, with old come-all-ye's like "And the Band Played On", "Sweet Rosie O'Grady", and "When Irish Eyes are Smiling". They want June the 16th, nineteen hundred and four. Maybe they'll never read a word of Joyce, but they know enough to want Molly Bloom and Bloomsday.'

'A restaurant,' I said.

'With gaslight and melodeons. And don't give me any guff about how it's too far out of town. The Yanks will come out in their droves. I'll run a bus service from Jury's, the Berkeley Court, the Shelbourne and the rest of them. We'll be the Number One shore excursion for cruise ships. I'm telling you, this town we're standing in won't know itself.'

'Nobody else will know it either,' I said.

'Come again?'

'I mean it used to be a quiet place.'

'It still will be. No problem; all it needs is a car park.'

Shay spoke what were virtually his first words. 'Are you done with theatre, then?'

'Sorry?'

'With putting on plays.'

In the gloom of the tram-yard, I could make out a crafty smile. 'That's another little iron I have in the fire. Still, one thing at a time.' He turned to me. 'As far as I'm concerned, the archive has had its chips. It's getting too big, too messy. From now on, you're on your own.'

I was delighted to hear it. Meanwhile, Thorn had found a new approach road to Shay's good regard. 'I've been meaning to tell you, by the way – and I'm delighted to have the opportunity now that we've met – that you're a damn fine critic.'

'Thanks.'

'No, I mean it. You're … ah … Is there an adjective for "integrity"?'

'Don't think so.'

'Surely there must be. What about "integritous"? Yeah, that's not bad. Well, if you permit me, I'd say that applies to your good self. You, sir, are integritous.'

It was so brazen that I expected Shay to laugh out loud. Instead, he smiled, put his right forefinger alongside his nose and sawed it up and down with pleasure. Perhaps – it was too dark to see – he actually blushed.

Thorn invited us to join him for supper in a local *trattoria,* but Shay, using an all-purpose mantra of his own said, 'Thanks all the same, but I'll follow me star,' and went trotting off into the dark. His last gastronomic adventure, apart from special domestic occasions such as visiting and being visited, had been back in the days when, like the first vertebrate waddling out of the primeval swamps, the meal that was called tea evolved into dinner. He lived in, and enjoyed living in, a land beyond which there were dragons. Even in his drinking days, home had been a beacon. Josie had taken me to see Fellini's *Il Bidone,* and I was reminded of Shay when the youngest of the three swindlers, played by Richard Basehart, decided that he had had enough of living without self-respect and struck out for home and Giulietta Masina, muttering to himself '*A casa, a casa!*' So Shay, following his star, went off to 'Massabielle', and Thorn and I had *spaghetti bolognese* and shared a bottle of Corvo. As we sat down, I said, 'That wasn't nice.'

'What wasn't?'

'Twisting Shay around your finger.'

Thorn stroked the dead rat. I noticed that his hair, which has always been neatly cut, was now designer-tousled. He said: 'A fellow has to practise.'

The Widow introduced me by letter to her Los Angeles agent, who made an appointment for me with his London *vis-à-vis,* by name Leon Esterman. I went to see him; we got on well, and on the strength of the proposed biography my name was added to his books. 'This one,' he said, 'is going to be easy.' The next step would be to approach publishers and make a deal. I went home in high spirits.

Thorn called me at the office. When was I next seeing Josie?

'Tomorrow, for lunch.'

'Mind if I make up a threesome?'

'Why would you want to?'

'I keep running into you and her separately. I want to see what kind of a pair you make.'

'We usually meet out at the Mimosa Garden in Stillorgan.'

'In the sticks? Sod that for a game of soldiers. The Coffee House at one.'

In spite of its name, the Coffee House had a Michelin star and was operated on the *nouvelle* principle that if one did not go away with a growling stomach then one had not been properly fed. It was operated as a sideline by a bisexual dress designer named Patrick Flurry, and the bar area, known as the Pit, was an eavesdropper's Elysium. When I arrived, the first person I saw was April-May Magreedy, who was not merely a gossip in her own right, but hawked bits of scandal to a scandal sheet called *The Razor's Rim*. She was drinking champagne in the company of an ancient barrister whose eyes were so close together that they all but overlapped. He and she were plotting the strategy of their third libel action in eighteen months.

Thorn came in, dressed as usual in a dark blue suit and sober tie – I had a theory that he avoided sporting a pattern in case it might be used as a Rorschach test by DIY psychologists. He beckoned, and I followed him to our table. When Josie came in a few minutes later, I warned her that the Magreedy woman was on the prowl.

She was unperturbed. 'There is safety in numbers. She won't know which one of you I'm with!' She sat, smiled at Thorn and said, 'Well, now!' It was her acknowledgement that she and I were what a few years later would be termed an 'item'. Since he was in the know, she did not bother to employ what I called her what's-a-da-matter accent.

As our lunch progressed, Thorn played gooseberry in the manner of a kindly old Geppetto watching the antics of his favourite puppets. When he suggested that Josie was my muse, she all but blossomed. She turned to me, delighted: 'Am I?'

'I've got a funny idea you like this fellow,' Thorn said.

'I cannot keep my hands off him!' She said to me, 'Go away. Shoo. You are too near. Go to another table. *Mostro!*'

'*Mostro* ... what's that?' Thorn asked.

'It is my word for him. It means "Monster".'

She spoke of her daughter, Silvana, who had now reached the end of her final school year in Switzerland. She was for the moment visiting her grandmother in Florence, and in September and as a treat Josie would take her for two weeks to the Club Med at Cancun. 'Then I do not know what to do with her. She says she will not go to university, so she must find work, maybe with her father, but pig-meat is not very glamorous.'

'*What* did you say isn't glamorous?' April-May Magreedy had come upon us, unseen in spite of the red signal fire of her permanent bad hair day. 'And which one of these lovely men are you with and which one is playing the beard?'

'Josie is with TJ,' Thorn said, calmly.

For one hellish instant I thought: This is his revenge. I'm being repaid for letting on that the Widow O'Fearna had fired me and for making him so angry that he had humiliated Willie Cooney in public. Josie, her mouth half open, was for once speechless. It all happened within a couple of seconds, and Thorn's timing was immaculate. Just as an unbelieving delight was creeping into Magreedy's face, he said. 'TJ is giving Josie's daughter a job as his researcher. He's writing a book, you know.'

Magreedy said: 'Oh.' It was a very small 'oh'.

Thorn grinned at her. 'Had you going there, didn't I, petal?'

'Yes, it was very funny,' Magreedy said. She pulled her notebook half-way out of her handbag and pushed it back in again. The Cyclopean barrister was holding a chair for her two tables away.

When she had gone, Thorn thumped his fists on the table. He was ecstatic. 'I got her, I got her! If I say so myself, that was a lulu.'

Josie, breathing hard, was kneading her left breast. 'And now it is you who are the *mostro*,' she said. 'My God, when you said, "She is with TJ," I thought that I would die.'

'What are you doing?' I said. 'Making bread?'

She punched my arm. She said, 'I have never in all my life had my name in a newspaper. And suddenly to think that I might be in – what is it called? – *The Blade of the Razor?*'

'*The Razor's Rim*,' I said. 'Nice one, Thorn.' I made a chalk mark in the air.

He said: 'Did you think I was getting back at you?'

'Well, yes.'

He had, after all, remembered, so I knew the revenge was still to happen. And, of course, he knew that I knew. Josie was having a wonderful time; she had been taken to the cliff edge and had not fallen. Suddenly, she said '*Mamma mia!*' I thought that Italian women said this only in films when they were cooking dinner in the Bronx for Richard Conte. Nonetheless, Josie said it. She clasped her hands together. 'What a marvellous idea.' To Thorn: 'And I have you to thank. Don't you know what it was you said?'

Thorn said, 'Remind me.'

'It is so simple. I want to find a job for Silvana that is not pig-meat, and you, you wonderful man, you have said what it is to be.' We stared at her. 'My daughter will do for TJ what you said she will do. What is the word? She will do research for him.'

A small cold wind blew around one of the back lanes of my heart. Her smile dimmed when I did not at once share her excitement.

She said, 'Well?'

'Yes, well, we'll have to talk about it.'

'But –'

'Please, not here.'

She shrugged, letting it pass. As we were having coffee, Thorn said: 'You two are incredible.'

She said, 'Oh?'

'Tell me I'm out of line, but why aren't the pair of you together? I mean, I've never seen anything like it ... like you and him, that is. Why don't you shag your bonnets over the windmill and say "Bye-bye, Andrew ... bye-bye, Greta"? Christ almighty, you have something that'll never come again. Why don't you *grab*?'

I smiled at Josie; we were back on solid ground. 'He's a romantic old thing, isn't he?'

Thorn said, 'When I want something –'

'I know ... you grab, but –'

Josie interrupted. 'But TJ has a wife –' she never referred to Greta by her name – 'and I have a husband, and there were promises made. Perhaps they are not always kept, but a person does a person's best. There is a home and my daughter and my responsibilities. What has Andrew done to me that I would put him to shame? What has TJ's wife done to him?'

She had it off pat. I thought of her dead lawyer friend, Scott, in Miami and treacherously wondered if she had ever made that speech to him. She was looking at me for my contribution.

'Yes,' I said. 'And there's more than just a husband and a daughter. There's a car and clothes and that diamond ring, and sitting up front in aeroplanes. And holidays, and a big house and –'

'*Mostro!*' Probably to Thorn's astonishment, she shrieked with laughter and lashed out at me with her linen napkin, overturning a saucer and spilling the collar-stud of cauliflower that passed for vegetables. 'How dare you? *Mostro! Animale!*' People looked around, smiled and envied us.

As we parted, Thorn saw someone he knew in the Pit. 'Excuse

me,' he said. 'It's Gus de Paor.' There was awe in his voice. I caught a glimpse of a hairless head. De Paor managed a pop group or band – they were all the same to me – called The Prince of Darkness. I said, 'Tell me, Thorn, do you want to be Gus de Paor when you grow up?' and he suggested that I have sexual intercourse with myself. I found a taxi for Josie and went back to my office. In less than an hour, the telephone went.

'Hello.' It was Josie.

'This is pleasant.'

'Thank you. Listen.' I silently mouthed the words as she spoke them. 'About this job for Silvana. We have to talk.'

Chapter Ten

On the Esmeralda

'TJ, are you mad?'

'How?'

'Is that a tape recorder?'

'Yes.'

'Do you mean that you want to tape our conversation, yours and mine?'

'Oh, don't worry. You can take the tape home with you. Listen to it and then wipe it or throw it in the fire or whatever.'

'This is crazy. I think you have – what is the expression? – a slate that is loose. Why do you want to tape what we say?'

'Not what *we* say; what *you* say.'

'Ah. I see. And then you want me to go home or maybe sit in the car and listen to it? And what will I discover? I mean, am I supposed to say, "Oh, my God, are those my words? If so, I am a crazy woman!" Is that it? Is –'

A waiter came and took our order. We were in, or rather on, *Esmeralda*, a barge-restaurant moored at Little Venice. The trip to London was our first time away together in six weeks. It was early September and still warm, but Josie was a hot-house flower and insisted that we have dinner on the inner deck. I switched the recorder off while she talked with the proprietor, who, like her, was a Florentine. She consulted with me and ordered for both of us. She was caring and anxious – and bossy, but I enjoyed being looked after. When the ordering was done, she snatched the recorder from the table.

She said, 'No! No more foolishness. We have only one evening. Do you want to spoil it?' When I was silent, she went: 'Psst! I am still here.' She was in the best of humour, smiling and on the surface far calmer than I was. 'Hey? Coo-ee!'

I said: 'I thought the tape might prove to you that for five weeks now we have been having the same conversation.'

'Ah! Now it makes sense. The same conversation.'

'Pretty well.'

'And you think that I have a ... an *ossessione*?'

'If that means obsession, well, yes.'

'I see!'

'Going on this trip cost me a row at home, and the same row will be there, waiting behind the door when I get back. So do you think we could get through just this one evening without talking about your daughter?'

She laughed. 'Oh, that is very funny, because now you are the one who mentions her.'

'Yes. Okay. Apologies. So let us drop the subject.'

'Good!'

Mineral water appeared. She said, 'Pellegrino, *bravo!*' and made a great show of being vivacious to the waiter. It was not flirtation, but a kind of upside-down ferocity, as if he were the only person who existed in the world; and I knew then that the evening was lost, like all the occasions we had had since the lunch with Thornton at the Coffee Shop.

When the waiter had gone, she said, most reasonably, 'If I think of my daughter, is that an *ossessione*? Silvana has need of work. She does not want to be all day with her father. He is a fussy man, like an old woman. "Do this thing ... no, not like that, do it a different way." She would work in his office, in the same room with him, and when he makes the shipments to foreign countries, he would send her to the docks to be sure he is not being robbed.' Incredulously: 'Robbed of pig-meat!' She sniffed at each of her hands in turn and gave a fastidious little shudder. 'Ugh.'

'We've been through all of this.'

'Yes, well now we finish it.'

'I wonder do we!'

'You have decided it. She will work for Andrew.'

'Fine.'

'No, no, maybe not fine, but she will do it. You refuse to give her a job, so she has no choice.'

She made her gesture of hitting cymbals together. The side of her hand guillotined a breadstick, and half of it became airborne. I thought of the soaring bone turning into a spaceship in Kubrick's *2001: A Space Odyssey*.

I said, 'I've told you until I'm sick and tired –'

'Oh, yes, you are sick and you are tired. Poor you. Go to a doctor, go to sleep.'

'It is not for me to *give* jobs to anyone. When the time comes, Mrs O'Fearna will recommend –'

She mimed a yawn.

'– a person who is qualified.'

'Oh, yes? Qualified to do what?'

'To –'

' … to find out all about a man who is dead. About what he did, about the kind of person he was. Look at me: I who am stupid could do that. You think my Silvana is some kind of idiot?'

'It's highly specialised work.'

'Pah!'

'I told you and I tell you again, the job isn't mine to give.'

'Why do you repeat yourself?'

'Christ.'

'In the restaurant that day, when the April-May Magreedy woman came up and was her charming self, you said to her that you would give the researching to Silvana.'

'I said no such thing. That was Thornton. He said it.'

'He is a good man.'

'It was his idea of a joke.'

She was silent, hurt by my refusal to do a small, sensible thing that was a proof of affection, a demonstration that I was not a man of straw.

'Will you listen to me?'

Through the barge windows, she was looking out at, but not seeing, the trees in Rembrandt Gardens. She turned, ready to hear another shopworn excuse. Her eyes were large with sadness.

I said, 'Look, I could pick up a phone and call the Widow. I could say that I knew a nice, bright girl, just out of school. I could tell her that with a bit of training and patience this girl might make a fist of it.'

The expression was new to her. 'A feest?'

'And the Widow would say –' Stupidly, I remembered a catch-phrase from an ancient play called *Peg o' My Heart*. ' … The Widow would say, "Good, fine, splendid." Except that when the word got out that I had given a job to my mistress's daughter –'

'How could the word get out? Who would know?'

'We live in a town where there are no secrets. You know those new electronic boards that tell you how much space there is in such-and-such a car park? Well, that's how it is. Every time you and I meet, a light goes on on one of those boards.'

'You are insane.'

'And there's a bulletin that says: "TJ Quill and Josie Hand are at a corner table in the Mimosa Garden." Or "Upstairs at the Chez When". Or "Three rows from the back, among the young snoggers, at *Silver Screen 2*."'

'I think you must hate Silvana.'

'You think that, do you?'

'Such a simple favour to do, and you say no.'

'A favour, is that what you call it? You want her to be gossiped about, is that it? You want dirty jokes? – "Quill is knocking off the classic double of all time, a mother and her daughter." You want that?'

Her face became sulky.

I said, 'Then the day would come when I'd get a call from Santa Fe. "Hey, Quill, what the hell is going on over there? What's it with this girl you suckered me into hiring? People are saying that you've been laying her old lady."'

'*Old*?' Josie's look was thunderous.

'It's an expression. Is that what you want? Somebody calling up Kitty O'Fearna and saying I'm putting the archive into bad repute? Is it?'

'You are making this up.'

'Am I?'

'Who would know to do such a thing?'

'Thorn. He knows.'

'Thorn is your friend.'

'Is he? Did you ever hear the story about the frog and the scorpion?'

'*Grazie*, but I think I am not in the mood for stories.'

Our starters were brought. I told the story, hackneyed as it was. The scorpion asked the frog to carry it across a river, and the frog said, 'No, you would sting me and I would die.' The scorpion said, 'If I were so foolish as to do that, then I would die, too, for I would surely drown.' That made sense to the frog, so he agreed to the request, but half-way across the river the scorpion stung him. As he was dying, he asked, 'Why did you do it?' And the scorpion, drowning, said, 'It's my nature.' That was Thornton.

She was not interested. She said: 'Everybody gives a job to a friend. And with Silvana you would save money. I would pay some of her salary.'

This bit was new. '*You* would?'

'It is easy. I give it to you, you give it to Silvana.'

'Dear God.'

'Then you could tell this woman in America what a good businessman you are.'

'Josie ...'

'Yes, *amore*?'

'Don't you have any concept of time?' As she looked at her watch: 'No, not like that. I mean about how little of it there is, and how it is all going down the sink because we are wasting it.'

She said, so honestly that I swam in despair, 'No, my darling, the one who is wasting it is you, because you will not give me – no! you will not give us this simple thing. You make excuses –'

'Yes, I do.'

'Ah, you admit it!'

'I make excuses, and the truth of it is that I'm not going to do it to Greta.'

'To your wife?'

'Yes.'

'You are joking. What has my Silvana got to do with your –'

'I don't know.'

'You don't know.'

'All the other reasons I give you, they aren't lies, they hold true, every one of them. But my gut instinct is that this would be a ... a bad thing to do to Greta.'

'I see.'

'I don't think you do.'

'A bad thing. You fuck me, but that is not a bad thing?'

Her voice was low-pitched, but I was aware that there were other people around. I caught the eye of a woman at another table; she looked away and talked to her companion. I thought of an expression that had just then come into vogue – 'body-language' – and ridiculously I sat up straight and put one hand into another on the tablecloth.

I said, 'I'm trying to be honest –'

'Honest, is that what you call it? You say you care about me, but when it comes to a simple thing, when it is a matter of saving a young girl's self-respect, you ... complain to me about your boring wife –'

'Oh, shut up.'

'What? What did you say?'

'How did I get into this? What the hell am I doing here, away from home and wasting my life listening to this endless *crap*?'

She stared at me, then put her napkin carefully on the table, stood up and walked away and up the companionway. I heard the sound of her heels on the deck above and through the window saw her leave by the gangway. I watched because it was preferable to meeting the looks of the other diners. The proprietor came over. I said, 'The lady isn't feeling well.' I made a show of eating my *antipasto*, asked for the bill, finished my glass of wine – waste not, want not – and went. I walked through Lisson Grove to Regent's Park, where I saw a young couple on a bench and resisted the urge to tell the male to run for his life.

That, I thought as I walked, was the end of Josie. To my shame the gall of regret was made bearable by the smallest tinge of relief. I had had five weeks of eroding, unrelenting, non-stop Silvana, and the prospect of a return to safe boredom was sad, but not one of unqualified dismay. Clearly, I should now find an hotel for the night, and yet in even the grandest gesture bathos lurks, and a dignified exit is none the better for a stone in one's shoe. My toiletries and a change of shirt, socks and underwear were at the Basil Street Hotel, where we had checked in as a couple. So were the pyjamas I had had no intention of wearing. So, too, were the books I had bought that afternoon at Hatchards. I thought of appearing at 'Kate Fortune's Lane' and telling Greta that my overnight bag had been snatched at the airport check-in. Then, knowing Josie, I thought of the same bag and its contents arriving a few minutes later by taxi.

I went to a pub in Baker Street; it was too noisy for a fitting melancholy, so I did an about-turn, walked until I reached Soho, had a sandwich at the Nosh Bar and continued on foot to Basil Street. The turmoil of my brain had begun to subside; the whole Josie thing was becoming as vague as last night's dream. By the time I reached the hotel, the soles of my feet were so tender I could have felt a tenpenny piece underfoot. The bedroom was in darkness, but there was a faint chirping noise that told me Josie was asleep; such was her desire for perfection that at one time, and perhaps frivolously, I wondered if she had somehow had her snore surgically removed. I found my overnight bag in the wardrobe, took it into the bathroom, switched on the mirror light and began to load it with my toilet things. Suddenly, as if with a noise, the full ceiling light came blindingly on.

'*Amore*, what are you doing? Are you mad?'

She was wearing a knee-length white silk nightdress and a black sleep mask which she had hiked up at one end so that her left eye remained piratically covered. I almost expected her to say 'Haargh, Jim lad!'

What she did say, tearfully, was, 'No, no, you mustn't. Be good, be nice. Come to bed.' There was a torrent of what I took to be endearments in Italian.

I said, almost weeping, 'You and your bloody daughter.'

'No more, please. It is finished.'

We went to bed and made love. After I had all but exploded inside her, she sighed. 'I think a little anger has been good for you.' In the morning, by the light that edged around the window curtains, she again reached for me and this time kept the sleep mask on. The pirate image gave place to another. I said, 'It's like fucking Zorro.'

She kept her word and did not mention the Silvana thing again, except to ask me once in a half-hearted way if Thornton might be in need of a secretary. In the end, the girl went to work for her father. I met her at last; she resembled neither Andrew nor Josie. Her hair was blonde but had the sleek, helmeted shine of an old-time movie legend named Louise Brooks. She was quick-witted. 'The job has good perks,' she told me. 'Free scratchings.' She had known from the beginning – had been told, that is – about Josie and me. She lived in perfect harmony with both parents, but for Josie she had a conspiratorial affection, much as a wise mother might indulge a girl who was going through 'phases'.

'There you are,' Thorn said when I told him of this. 'That's how the Eyeties won the war.'

In late October, I went to America for the first time. After months of wrangling, I had been given permission to make videotaped copies of twelve early O'Fearna films at the Eastman Institute in Rochester and of the director's private location footage at the Library of Congress. When Thorn heard of my trip, he told me he had business in New York at the same time and happily changed his dates so that we could fly together. He even used a contact in Aer Lingus to have my ticket upgraded to Club. 'A Gentile is someone who pays retail,' he said, 'and a gob-shite is someone who flies Economy.'

His wife, Prue, drove him to the airport. She was dark and per-fectly oval-faced. She had a Protestant accent that seemed to belong on a raft half-way between Dun Laoghaire and Holyhead. As an actress, she had appropriated his nickname and called her-self Prunella Thorn. She was calm, as she needed to be to manage him; he had chosen well. She excelled in playing well-bred char-acters who were quietly witty. Off the stage, she was the kind of self-possessed woman who could call her husband 'Darling' as naturally as a Catholic wife would say 'Mick' or 'John Joe'. She was too transparently nice to play villainesses. She and Thorn kissed in the departure area. She said, 'Bye-bye, darling. Try not to make us too rich.' I liked cool women. When I had left Greta, at our front door, all she said was 'Mind yourself.'

In the aircraft we sat across the aisle from the hooded-eyed, thin-nosed Minister for Finance and a civil servant, the head of his department. As we crossed the Clare coastline and climbed over the Atlantic, I felt an excitement which over the years would never become jaded. Gift packs were doled out: a kind of wampum for the privileged, including a sleep mask – I thought of Josie and smiled – and what were called 'pampooties'. I looked the word up when I returned home: its source was the Aran Islands, of all places, and it was a name given to slippers made of untanned cow-skin. The Aer Lingus variety were of nylon.

'Are you meeting *Il Mostro* in New York?' Thornton asked. Since our three-sided lunch, it was his nickname for Josie.

I told him that she and Silvana would be stopping over in Washington, DC, on their way to spend ten days on Exhuma. I felt a need to talk about her. He listened while I gave him an account of what I called the Five-Week War, when at our every meeting or, given half a chance, during phone calls, Josie would pummel me with arguments as to why Silvana should come to work at the archive. 'It wasn't nagging,' I said. 'It was as if there was a deep despair at the back of it. She would go on for two, maybe three, hours, and then a week later start up again ... the same thing, only all shiny and brand new. We nearly broke up over it.'

When Thorn said nothing, I asked: 'So what do you think?'

He said, 'I dunno. Menopause?'

'Oh, come on. Josie is only going on forty.'

'Think so?'

'And doesn't look it.'

He said, 'Yes, and she went ten years barefooted.'

'Pardon me?'

He pressed the call button. 'Let's have a jar. Then I'm going to put my head down.'

It had been a long time since I had last heard the jibe about a person going for several years barefooted. I recalled seeing an old Frank Borzage film in which Loretta Young told Spencer Tracy that she was seventeen, and a lone voice earned a great roar of approval from the Sunday night audience by shouting, 'Yis! And you went twenty years barefoot!' It was a derisive way of saying that a particular woman, by paring too many years off her true age, had insulted credulity.

Josie once told me in mock sorrow, 'Soon I will be forty.' Now, high above the Atlantic, I reflected that she and Colleen had been au pairs together when both were nineteen; and Colleen made no bones of it that she herself was now forty-five. To me, Josie's age, whether it was sixteen or sixty, mattered not at all, except for the lie, as white as it was. I thought some more and kicked myself for failing to accept that a woman's age was a movable feast.

As we taxied to the arrivals pier at Kennedy, there was a small comedy. The senior civil servant across the aisle had become so drunk that he attempted, and failed, to pull his shoes on over his pampooties. As he hopped about the aisle, the Minister for Finance said, with the bridge of his thin nose white from rage, 'You malodorous, legless bollix, I'll send you to Fisheries for this.' He locked eyes with Thorn. 'And you mind your own fuckin' business.' As one of the flight attendants came to help, the Minister said to her, 'That's the shaggin' Irish for you. You can bring them nowhere.'

'He'll be Taoiseach one day,' Thorn said, and so he was.

We went our separate ways in Manhattan. I should have caught a flight from La Guardia to Rochester; instead, when Thorn went off to attend to one of the several irons in his fire, I made a brief pilgrimage to the Algonquin Hotel. I had for years devoured the carefully preserved Round Table-talk of Alexander Woollcott, George S Kaufman, Heywood Broun, Franklin P Adams, Dorothy Parker and the other show-offs. None of them would have lasted ten minutes in the ego-fest of a Dublin pub; nonetheless, I wanted to tread the holy ground. It was not easy to be rid of the Irish, however. On the threshold of the hotel Emma Ring, the Ennistymon novelist, almost knocked me down as she fled from an elderly potato-faced elevator-man who shouted after her, 'Yeh think yer two-toilet Irish, but all y'are, ever were and ever will be is shitty-shanty Irish.' An under-manager wagged a finger at him. 'You're gonna get canned, Maguire.'

I was enchanted; it was if a cabaret were being put on to welcome me to America.

That evening, I was in Rochester, where I was received as an honoured guest at the Eastman Institute and spent three days under the guidance of a bright girl with bottle-lensed glasses and pudding-bowl hair the colour of old straw. Her name, to my delight, was Ilse-Lazlo Huneker. Her mother, she told me, had seen *Casablanca* more than sixty times while pregnant.

'If I'd been a boy,' Ilse-Lazlo said, 'guess what she'd have called me.'

'Rick – or Richard – Victor?'

'You got it.'

In the Institute, I was as happy as a small boy in a Christmas toyshop. Ilse-Lazlo showed me how to thread and operate a movieola, and she had not only put my twelve films on video-tape, including the supposedly lost *Silver Hawk* from 1922, but had them translated to the European Phase Alternate Line or PAL system. I took her to dinner, and early next morning she showed me two silents which had yet to be authenticated as the work of O'Fearna. She loved her job, but complained that she was hemmed in by procedures. She was so quick of mind that I called Santa Fe from my hotel and told the Widow that I had perhaps found my researcher.

'What do you mean "perhaps"?'

'Well, she wants a free hand.'

'Then do like the song says. Don't fence her in. And hey, Thady ...'

I swallowed the castor oil. 'Yes?'

'How is Thorn Thornton? What's that fellow been up to?'

'He's opening a restaurant.'

'He'll make out.'

Next day, I gave a green light to Ilse-Lazlo, who shook my hand until she heard the wrist bones click. When I told her that her first job would be to compile a catalogue of Irish-American films, her delight was such that I had to discourage her from smuggling out pirated copies of the two disputed silents, *Dangerous Trails* and *Phantom of the Sagebrush*. As matters stood, I might be in bad odour for poaching an employee of the Institute. Her second job would be to help prepare the ground for my biography, to be called *The Search for Sean O'Fearna*.

When my time in Rochester was up, she drove me to the airport for my flight to Washington National, and gave me another up-and-down handshake. She called me 'sir', as always, and assured me that she would be worthy of my trust. I had no doubt of it until, once airborne, I looked into my overnight bag and discovered a small package. It was a videotape of *Phantom of the Sagebrush*. A card said, 'Happy trails! – I-L H.' I made my mind up firmly to return it to Ilse-Lazlo, knowing I would do no such thing.

As arranged, I met Josie in Washington. She had taken a twin-bedded room for herself and Silvana in a Georgetown hotel with ironwork balconies and had booked a room for me on the same floor. In the daytime, while I worked at the Library of Congress, they saw the sights: the Smithsonian, Arlington Cemetery and the Capitol and the Lincoln and Jefferson memorials. We had two evenings, and on both we strolled as a threesome around Georgetown where, in spite of the month, the summer trees were still heavy and midges swarmed under the street lamps. Later, Josie came to my room when Silvana was asleep.

'Does Silvana know about this?' I asked.

'I don't ask her what she knows,' Josie said, 'and she doesn't tell me. She has learned that people are not like Firenze.'

'Excuse me?'

'I mean like Florence, where you find everything you want under one roof. My daughter knows that in life people must go here for one thing and there for another.'

'That's me,' I said, slightly hurt at being a commodity. 'Your friendly convenience store.'

I was hesitant when it came to telling tell her about Ilse-Lazlo in case it should revive the Silvana dispute, but her only concern was to ask if the girl was sexy. Josie was gratifyingly jealous. 'You as much as look at her,' she said, reverting to B-feature Italian, 'and I break-a your thumbs.'

Towards dawn on our second night, she nudged me awake. 'I must go back to Silvana.'

Coming out of sleep, I managed to say, 'That sounds like a line from *Duck Soup.*'

'But first I want to tell you about Turlough.'

I said, 'Colleen's Turlough?' as if there could be any other.

She said, 'He has been offered a very good job as the art critic for the *Sunday Sentinel.*'

'Great.'

'He was very clever. He gave them what you would call a bribe.'

'And what was that?'

'You.'

'*Me?*'

'He said that instead of writing your film columns for the *Nation on Sunday*, like now, you would leave and go with him and write for the *Sentinel.*'

I switched the bedside light on. She pulled down the sleep-mask, which was across her forehead. Absurdly, I wondered how she could possibly expect to hear with her eyes covered.

'Turlough told them that? Is he gone demented?'

'He said you would do it, because Colleen told him you would.'

'Colleen did?'

'*Si.*'

'And who told Colleen I would?'

'I did. You see, I told her all about you and me. She was a bit shocked, I think, because in a small way she has a fancy for you. Then she got over it, and now she is our friend.' She reached out, blindly. 'Are you listening to me?'

My ears at that moment could have dwarfed Dumbo's.

'And the evening before Silvana and I left to come here, Colleen asked me if I thought you would do this little favour for Turlough.'

'This . . . little favour.'

'And I told her that you would be glad to do it, because it is not only a favour for Turlough, but for Colleen, who you like so much, and for me, who you like more than so much.' She took off the mask and kissed me on the forehead. 'At least, I hope you do.'

I said, 'Josie, I don't want to change jobs.'

She said, 'Of course you do. Don't be silly. My God, look at the time.'

She kissed me again, lightly, and went almost noiselessly out. I was now fully awake and knew that the Five-Week War had not been a war at all but only a campaign. From outside, a police siren reminded me that I was not at home, but in Washington, DC, which was in the American South. I thought of Danny Kaye as the Mississippi gambler, Gaylord Mitty, when answering the call of duty. 'Fort Sumpter has been fired upon. My regiment leaves at dawn.'

Chapter Eleven

At the Ramparts

For several years when travelling to or from the airport, I used the services of a local taxi driver with the faintly comic name of Hilary Hopfoot. A time came when he announced that he was emigrating to open a bar on Lanzarote and said that a new man would carry the torch. 'Has he a name as distinctive as yours?' I asked, trying to raise a smile. 'Not at all,' Mr Hopfoot said gravely. 'He's called Claude Cockshot.'

The new driver, a quiet, stolid chap from Bolton, who served us well until bone cancer claimed him, was waiting when I came in on the New York flight. Because of westerlies, there had been not enough time for real sleep, and I nodded off in the back seat, not waking until the balding tarmacadam of our lane spat against Mr Cockshot's simonized paintwork. Strangely, I thought, Greta, wearing her house coat, rapped on the car window. It was not her usual practice to come from the house to greet her master's return home. I was still dragging my bags from the car boot when she said, 'Shay is out in the back.'

I was so starved for sleep that I actually had an image of Shay as a misshapen latter-day Quasimodo. When I simply stared at her, she said, 'Are you deaf? He's been out in the back garden this half-hour, waiting for you. He landed himself on the doorstep.'

For Shay, an unannounced visit, never mind one at nine in the morning, was unheard of. I might bump into him accidentally in Baggot Street or we would exchange nods on first nights when, out of respect for his ministry, I kept my distance. Every Christmas Day, he came to us with Brigid and the girls, and a week later we saw the New Year in with them at 'Massabielle'; otherwise, he and I met religiously – or atheistically in his case – on Monday evenings at Tish's.

As I dumped the bags in the hall and hurried through to the back garden, Greta said, 'I offered him a cup of tea in his hand, but he said no, it was too much trouble.'

'What's up with him?'

'I don't know. He looks woeful.' This in Greta's lexicon meant simply that Shay seemed less than brimming with good health. As I went through the small conservatory, she fired off a *coup de grace*. 'Oh, and your mother isn't great.'

The house itself shielded the back garden from the worst of the east wind. A hedge that grew higher every year separated us from the Lockes next door, and the garden ended abruptly up against a thirty-foot granite outcrop. In the middle, there was a small pond that was all of nine inches deep, and Shay was standing on the concrete surround, looking into the weedy depths as if he were thinking of his life and of making an end of it.

He said, 'I'm terrible to come out like this.'

'Not at all.'

'I rang the airport from home, and they said that the New York flight was early, so I got in the car and came over.'

'I'm a bit fagged. Will we go in the house?'

'I'd as soon talk on the QT. Could we go for a walk?'

Curiouser and curiouser; and I knew that if I seemed even a whit reluctant, he would be off like a hare, mumbling apologies for being a nuisance. He would take his troubles, whatever they were, back home with him, and probably, while we would still be friends, it would no longer be quite through thick and thin. If Shay and I had a favourite book in common, it was *Great Expectations*, and we would hark back to it on March evenings when a treacherous spring would break its promise and no amount of clothing could withstand the wind from the sea. 'I'll never be warm again, never, not ever,' I would moan (I am a cold creature), and Shay, always the comforter, would insist that, given another week, we would be basking in high summer. 'And then, dear old Pip, old chap,' he would say, 'what larks!' It was perhaps in the nature of things that where Shay and I were concerned, the larks never quite happened, being always larkier in the future tense.

'Yes, let's walk,' I said, almost asleep on my feet. 'The wind'll blow the cobwebs off. Just let me get a quick cup of tea.'

'No, no,' he said, making to be off. 'You're jaded. Have your breakfast.'

'Christ, can you not wait two minutes?'

'Listen, forget it. I ought to have held off till later. I'll give you a ring when you've had a bit of shut-eye.'

'Look, either sit in the kitchen or go out and wait in the lane. What the hell's wrong with you anyway? Did you win the sweep-stake?'

'I drew the short straw, more like.'

I noticed for the first time that his eyes were red, perhaps like mine, from want of sleep. 'Look, this is scary. What is it? What ails you?'

He told me in three words, and while he was mooching up and down the lane outside, I stood in the kitchen swallowing scalding tea and repeated these to Greta. 'Blanaid is pregnant.'

She received the news without blinking, as if I had told her it was raining out. She said, 'Ask him if Brigid knows. I'm sure she must, but find out for sure, and if so I'll give her a call.' It was typical of Greta that although she could become almost hysterical over a pilot light blowing out, she responded to any real crisis with the calmness of a sister in Intensive Care. When I joined Shay outside, I asked him: 'Does Brigid know about this?'

'God, yeah.'

I nodded a discreet yes to Greta, who at once vanished from the front window. Shay and I walked in silence around the corner of the bay, up Vico Road and down to the disused bathing place at the Ramparts, where we sat on the rocks. 'Tell all,' I said.

He waffled: 'This is very good of you ...'

'Give me patience!' I screamed to the seagulls, who screamed back.

The previous evening, he told me, there had been a knock at the door of 'Massabielle'. He answered it and was confronted by the mother of the Midget Mechanic, Mrs Dempsey, who launched into a diatribe which began without salutation and probably ended a moment after Shay slammed the door in her face. He was too taken aback to absorb all of what was said, but her theme seemed to be that, as far as her son and Blanaid were concerned, there had been 'a pair of them in it'. The girl had no claim on her son. She was no better, Mrs Dempsey said, than she ought to be and, if the truth was to be told, an apple rarely fell far from the tree. ('What does that mean?' Shay asked me.) If the girl was in trouble, that was her lookout, and any young one that did not know how to mind her own self in the time that was in it ought not to be let out without a keeper. As for Duane, the few shillings he brought home were scarcely enough to bless himself with, and there was no use coming to him with expectations, for them that had nothing could give nothing. The Lambes thought they were so high up, like tuppence lording it over three-ha'pence, and showing off every Sunday, what with the girls coming from the altar rails with their white lace gloves on them and their eyelashes sweeping the side-aisle carpet like nuns' eyes, and –

It was at this point, when Mrs Dempsey's philippic was verging on the poetic, that Shay had slammed the door. It was all his nightmares come true: he had been made pass-remarkable and bullyragged on his own doorstep, and with worse maybe to come. Of the four girls, Dympna was out playing tennis on a floodlit court in Little Bray, and Maire was attending a class at the *Alliance Francaise* in Dun Laoghaire. Louise, the youngest, was doing her homework upstairs, and Blanaid and her mother had been in the front room watching television. The set had been switched off as Mrs Dempsey's tirade got into full spate, penetrating to the uttermost ends of St Ultan's Park. Blanaid was paler than usual when Shay came in.

'Blanaid, is this true?'

'Say it isn't, say no, say no, say no,' Brigid said, addressing both Blanaid and unspecified saints.

'Is it?' Shay asked again.

Blanaid nodded, but instead of bursting into abject tears, she said, 'Anyway, thank God youse know at last.'

'Thank God we know?' Shay said. 'Is that what you say?'

'Well, I'm sorry,' Blanaid said. 'Honest I am, and I know how yourself and Mam must feel. But ...'

'But what?'

'Well, I mean it's not like we were back in old God's time, is it? I mean it could be worse. At least, people aren't going to look down their noses. In this day and age –'

She let out a little scream, for, as Shay told me, it was the closest he ever came to hitting one of their children. 'That's all I needed,' he said to me as we sat by the broken pool at the Ramparts, watching the high tide peeing in through the cracks in the stone. 'She wasn't being impudent, never that, but I mean my own daughter giving out to me about old God's time and –' with heavy sarcasm – '"this day and age". Christ, you'd think we took her to her christening in a fuckin' hansom cab.'

'She may have a point.'

He gave me a flinty look. 'Oh, she may, may she?'

I trod warily, touched that he had turned to me in his trouble and yet wishing I was getting over my jet-lag in a warm bed at home with the curtains drawn. I said: 'If you don't mind me saying, I think you're still in shock. It's a gut reaction.'

'Is that what it is?'

I chanced another step across the minefield. 'I suppose I'd be the same myself,' I said, 'what with all those pulpit-bashers and craw-thumpers saying as how it's a sin and a disgrace. Come on, now; you know what you believe in and what you don't believe

146

in. Christ, how many evenings did the pair of us sit and talk about it? You're too enlightened to swallow that old guff.'

He said nothing. He was brooding, and I pressed my advantage.

'It's not the end of civilisation as we know it. Blanaid made a mistake and she got caught.' That was a wrong move; the 'caught' suggested badness found out. Mentally, I said 'J'adoube,' and moved my pawn back. 'You know what these young lads are like. They say "If you loved me, you'd let me." They threaten to do a runner, so the girl gives in.'

I was speaking about the young people of Shay's generation and mine, not of Blanaid's. He and Brigid had brought their children up in a now-vanished world, keeping to the rules of what ought to be, rather than what was. If youngsters nowadays took sex freely and on equal terms, that was fine for them, but not for Dympna, Maire, Louise and Blanaid. He said, 'Hey, can you imagine that old bitch, coming to the door and suggesting – the effing cheek of her! – that Brigid or I would make a claim on that little get of hers?'

'At least, now you're rid of him,' I said, throwing crumbs.

'Yeah.'

'Jesus, Shay, this is not a tragedy. Tell you the honest truth, I wouldn't mind having a young one of my own, even if she was up the –' I amended '– in the same fix as your Blanaid. I'd settle for that. There's nights I could die of loneliness.' His head came around to look at me. 'Honest, I'm surprised at this carry-on of yours. This isn't the Victorian age.'

'I know that, I know that,' he said sharply.

'So stand by what you believe in. I mean, now's your chance.'

He said: 'Chance for what?'

I made no reply. Two nights previously and the night before that, I had been shagging Josie Hand, and now I was Shay's moral counsellor.

Shay said, 'Brigid is very cut up.'

147

'So she would be.'

'We were up all last night, talking. Well, we're going to stand by Blanaid.'

'Grand.'

'She's a good girl.'

'I'm sure.'

'What's important now is not what we want, but what she wants.'

'Great.' I lifted my buttocks off the cold stone. 'We're going to get piles sitting here.'

We walked back to 'Kate Fortune's Lane', where Greta insisted that Shay, much against his will, should sit down and eat a proper breakfast.

He said, 'Brigid will be wondering.'

'She knows where you are,' Greta said. 'I talked to her. She's grand.'

She made us poached eggs on toast. He sat and looked miserably at his two eggs, which looked back at him. He jabbed a knife into one of them and watched as the yellow ran. I said: 'You look like King Canute at high tide.'

Greta said, almost snapping, 'What?'

'Nothing.'

She said, 'You wouldn't jeer if it was us.'

'Well, it's not likely to be.' Before she could come back at me, I said, 'I'm not jeering. I'm just trying to tell Shay that he's an old-fashioned fellow, and more power to him, but the world has moved on. Hey, Shay, you're a playgoer, so what about *Juno and the Paycock*, when Mary gets pregnant and goes to the doctor? And the Captain says to Juno, "It isn't consumption she has, is it?" And Juno tells him, "Jack, it's *worse* than consumption." Do you know, whenever that line is spoken today, the audience *hoots*. It wets itself. I mean, the idea that having a child could be worse than consumption! Would you believe it?'

Shay burst into tears.

'This is your fault,' Greta said.

She reminded him of where the bathroom was. A minute later, we heard the clatter from upstairs as the toilet-roll holder fell off the wall.

'How is Brigid taking it?' I asked.

'She'll get used to it,' Greta said. 'They both will. Give them a week or so.'

'Maybe,' I said. 'But I can't see the day when Blanaid will ever be let push a go-cart past number 16, St Ultan's Park.' A new thought occurred. 'What was it you said about my mother?'

She had had what was called a bad turn. There was pain, and the doctor wanted her to undergo tests. 'She's to go on a waiting list,' Greta said. 'Sod that,' I told her. 'We have a few bob now.' For once, she did not give me a look that said mockingly, 'Well, aren't you great!' As soon as I had slept off the jet-lag, we went to Hy-Brasil Lawns.

My mother was not yet sixty-five and looked the same as she ever did, except that for years now the blacklead-black hair had been as white as a snowstorm. There was no sign of illness in her face, only the look of death behind the eyes. What was most disquieting was that while we were there she did not go into one of her fits of weeping; it was as if the cause, whatever it was, had been swept aside. She agreed to go into hospital for the tests. She made tea for us, not letting Greta lift a finger, and said while she was setting out the cups, 'Thady, if it's what it might be, I don't want to be cut into.'

Greta said with great jollity, 'TJ, do you hear her? What a non-sensical thing to say!'

I said, 'You won't be, Ma, I promise.'

Greta said, 'And you're worse to humour her.'

That night in bed, at the thought of her aloneness and the likelihood that she would die, I had a fit of crying, quietly at first, then erupting into a single great sob from the effort of holding it back.

'Stop it,' Greta whispered.

After a time, I reached out my hand and took hold of hers. She neither repulsed nor encouraged; her hand might have been lopped off at the wrist. A ribald corner of my mind thought of Tom Lehrer's sick lyric: 'I hold your hand in mine, dear.' As I was falling into sleep, like a tired climber letting go, her voice said, 'Take hold of Josie's hand.' Or perhaps she had said, 'Josie Hand'.

I said, 'What did you say?'

There was no answer, and her hand was still under mine. Perhaps I had dreamt it.

The specialist told me that it was cervical cancer and inoperable. He said, 'She asked me not to tell you, but of course as next of kin you need to know.'

'Haven't you got this back to front?' I said. 'I always thought it was the sick person who used not to be told?'

He said in a soft, know-it-all voice: 'That indeed was the policy once upon a time. Now we think it best to inform the patient.'

'She's not a patient,' I said, dusting off a cliché. 'She's a bloody person.'

He was unfazed. I had never seen eyeglasses that shone more brightly than his; I wondered if he put them in a solution overnight, like dentures. He had thin fair hair receding to a bald crown. I thought: *If you can't grow hair, you smug, fee-grubbing bastard, how can you treat cancer?* He gave her six months, and I wondered why it was always in multiples of three.

My mother was sent home to Hy-Brasil Lawns, pretending that what ailed her was curable, with Greta and I letting on to be as thick as the double ditch of hallowed simile. We assumed that the verdict of the specialist had at least done away with uncertainty; for, now at ease within herself, she went happily back to her weeping.

Josie returned from the Bahamas, and we met for lunch. She

came into the Mimosa Garden, slapped her hands like a cracking whip and said, 'Well! Tell me your news.'

First, I told her about Shay, whom she had not met, and Blanaid. Before I was half done, she swept them both into a dustbin and slammed the lid. Shay was a boring fool, and the girl was worse. Josie, a caring and provident mother, had ensured that Silvana was fitted with a contraceptive device at the age of sixteen. There was no excuse for ignorance. These people were from the dark ages. 'I mean this kindly,' she said, 'but why do you waste your time?'

I wondered if I could really be deeply in love with a woman who held others in such dismissive contempt. The answer was yes.

When I told her the news about my mother, she was more compassionate. Her own mother, who was older than mine, lived alone in Florence in an apartment on the Via Tripoli, only a few paces from the Arno. She was in uncertain health and wealthier, so Colleen had told me, than God. Josie mused upon the sadness of growing old, then slapped her hands again, like the fairy godmother in *Cinderella* signalling a transformation scene. She said, 'When are you going to keep your word to Turlough?'

'What word to Turlough?'

'To write about films for the *Sentinel*.'

'I didn't give my word to Turlough. You did.'

'You, me, it's the same thing.'

'No, it isn't. I work for the *Nation*. You don't seem to realise that simply to walk out and write for a rival paper would be an act of disloyalty.'

'I don't see how.'

'You don't have to see how. This isn't any of your business.'

Of course it was her business; she had made it so, and the nonsense that followed began in late October and lasted until Christmas and beyond. There were two phases. First, I cut the Gordian knot by confronting Turlough and telling him that I would not be presented to the *Sentinel* as if I were the kind of free carriage clock that new clients received on taking out life insurance. I should have told him the whole truth and said that this was an attempt by Josie to play *eminence grise*; instead, and to save her face, I pretended that I had for a time gone along with the idea, but had funked it. Turlough was angry and told his new editor that I had broken faith with him. Colleen, on the other hand, was aware of Josie's gift for intrigue and so was more forgiving. Josie herself believed that she had been betrayed. I had stabbed her in the back; and although she might have been cheated of her triumph as a puppeteer, she got the worth of it by conducting a relentless post mortem that went grinding into the New Year, dying only of exhaustion.

'If you think so little of me,' I said, 'why don't you go?'

'Is that what you want?'

'No.'

She said, 'Then don't speak of such things,' and resumed the autopsy.

Usually, at Christmas, my mother came to us for two o'clock dinner, and the Lambes arrived in mid-afternoon. The four girls, all with faultless manners, squeezed on to our sofa and watched television as rapturously as if they could not see the same programmes at home. This year, although the thought was not voiced aloud, it would be my mother's last Christmas, and we invited her to stay in the spare room through the holiday. She was bored – she missed her cronies and the poker games at Hy-Brazil Lawns – but agreed so as not to offend Greta. In a tombola, the same Greta had won a set of Christmas door chimes that played *O Come, All Ye Faithful*, and as the notes rang out and the Lambes filed in I prayed that my mother would not take a look at Blanaid, whose pregnancy was pursuing its course, and pronounce her to be a fine lump of a girl, God bless her. In the event, she said no such thing, but Blanaid was burgeoning so obviously as to beget an appalled glance from my mother which asked Greta and me if we were blind.

In early November, Shay had told me that Blanaid had agreed to go for counselling. 'Father Thunder, his name is, but the mildest man you ever did see.'

'A priest?' I said.

Shay smiled. 'I have as little time for that gang as you do. But this fellow is a Jesuit. And with no airs or graces, none whatever. Do you know, he reminds me of Ollie Goldsmith: "And still they gazed, and still the wonder grew, That one small head could carry all it knew."'

I smiled back at him and felt the muscles pulling mutinously under my skin. 'Sensible, eh?'

'Don't be talking. He said exactly what yourself said to me that day at the Ramparts. Told me not to be a Victorian. Told me to ...' He paused, preparing me for the phrase '... to get my act together. He told me to put the idea of sin out of my head. "Unless," says he, "you want to be the one to ..."' And here Shay fetched me a roguish little smile. '"... To cast the first stone." Do you know, it was like a ton weight off my chest. I think I was the one that needed counselling.'

'What did he say to Blanaid?'

'I don't know, and I wouldn't ask. She's ... ah, putting the baby up for adoption.'

'That a fact?'

'Mm. Oh, she made up her own mind. Nobody said yes, aye or no to her. It's like Father Thunder said: "Make a fresh start." You fall, you get up and start again!'

'She fell, did she? Blanaid, I mean?'

'Well, come on! She made a mistake, no one's denying that.'

'The Midget Mechanic.'

'Yeah. And not wishing him a bit of harm in the coming season of peace and goodwill on earth, but may the little bollix die roaring.' Shay laughed, now in the best of good humour.

We had a good Christmas Day. Shay and I played chess and as usual he beat me, three games out of three. At nine o'clock my

153

mother wanted to go and play poker with her friends instead of staying overnight. 'There's the Christmas night game at Lily Mangan's,' she said, 'for 20p openers. Ah, Greta love, now don't oblige me to stay. I might make me fortune.' So Greta packed her few things, and I drove my mother back to Hy-Brasil Lawns.

It was only a five-minute run, and as the electronic gates opened she said: 'I want you to do something for me. I had a think about it, and as soon as we have a fine Sunday I want you to take me for a drive out to Wicklow.'

I thought of the final moment of a western film, *Guns in the Afternoon*, with the mortally wounded Joel McCrea taking a last look at the mountains he loved before falling out of frame. I said, 'Well, sure we'll have lots of spins.'

She said, 'This time I want to go to Calary Bog. Up by the Long Hill.'

It was a road I had avoided, ever since she had become near-hysterical when I made the right turn years ago at Kilmacanoge. I told her 'Sure,' too surprised to ask why and only glad that she was looking ahead. I walked with her the few yards to her door, where I kissed her and saw her safe inside. There was the laughter of women from nearby; the poker session with 20p openers was under way.

When I got back to 'Kate Fortune's Lane', Shay and his brood were leaving. As Brigid and Greta were saying one of the Irish farewells that go on for ten minutes, Shay took me to one side. 'I want to thank you,' he said, his voice thick, 'for having Blanaid this evening.'

I said, surprised, meaning it, 'Why the hell wouldn't I?'

He put a hand on my shoulder and gave me a smile of friendship that told me not to make too light of this. He said, 'There's many a one wouldn't.'

Chapter Twelve

On Calary Bog

Because the Sugar Loaf is cone-shaped and stands apart from other peaks, it looks higher than it is. The four-mile road known as the Long Hill starts at its base and winds like a grey sash around the flank, levelling out at the upland of Calary Bog. By now, the mountain has been demoted to no more than a queer-shaped bald hill you can climb on foot, scrambling over loose stones and boulders. Otherwise, there is nothing to see except an expanse of bogland and, sometimes, the caravans of travellers, mustered for an assault on the city. A generation ago, the travellers were called itinerants, and before that they were tinkers. Those who euphemised the names had either never read or never heeded their own Thomas Moore: '*You may break, you may shatter the vase if you will, But the scent of the roses will hang round it still*'.

Unexpectedly, the second Sunday in February that year was mild and clear like a day in spring, so I kept the promise to my mother. Her illness had made inroads; she looked frail and ate little; nonetheless, I thought to make an occasion of the outing and booked a table for Sunday lunch at the Roundwood Inn.

When the three of us started through the Rocky Valley and up the Long Hill, my mother was trembling with excitement; she hunched forward with her nose all but touching the windscreen. I drove slowly so that she would miss nothing of whatever it was she was at long last willing to face. At the point where the hill ended and the road levelled out, she clapped both hands over her eyes and cried out, 'Thady, don't stop.' As I promptly braked and pulled over to the verge, Greta in the back seat said, 'God, but you're contrary.'

My mother squinted through her fingers, then took her hands down. There was no one on or near the bog road but the three of us. She said, in both relief and disappointment, 'They're gone.'

'Who are?'

'Gone and long gone. My people. Me own.'

I said, 'Ma, do you mean the travellers?'

She nodded, and I knew there and then where she had come from. More than that, I knew where I had come from. I turned off the ignition and got out of the car. The only sound was a gentle soughing from the breeze in the whins. I saw that my mother had opened her door and went round to help her out. She looked about her, then went off alone towards the Sugar Loaf along a rising path that was made from loose flints. Broken glass, a mangled tyre, rusting cans, fire-blackened stones and bits of rag fluttering from the gorse were among the detritus of an old halting site.

Greta climbed out and said: 'Go after her.'

I said: 'Leave her.'

Films had both enriched my life and made of it a cliché, as perhaps Josie, the dream-mistress, had done. I thought of the gospel according to Warner Bros. and wished that if my mother had to die she might do so now, swiftly, easily, in a moment of epiphany, a small dark figure on a mountainside, with music by Korngold, perhaps, instead of in a drugged sleep a few months from now in a bed at the Hospice.

As I watched her walk further away, I covered the thought by saying to Greta, 'Well, how do you like that? I'm a half-tinker.'

If I had expected her to share the joke, I was wrong. Mind, she laughed, first at the notion, then at the reality. The second bout of laughter, loud and hard, went on for a long time. It echoed off the side of the mountain and caused my mother to turn around, smiling, as far as I could make out, and wave to us. Perhaps the mirth was genuine: a simple piece of connubial *Schadenfreude*, and I smiled directly into Greta's eyes to show that I did not begrudge her her tincture of enjoyment. The subtleties in marriage can stretch into infinity. Or perhaps what amused her was her belief that I had social pretensions which had now received either their comedown or comeuppance; choose one. If so, she was mistaken. I thought once again of Batty Kenirons rabbiting on in our car – it was more than a year ago now – about the new Irish who had cut themselves free from the trammel of roots that would hold them back. The past had no claim on them. Reinvention, he had called it. By the same token, the caravans that had once clustered at the Sugar Loaf were part of my mother's life, not mine. My birth date was the year dot, and all that concerned me was that she was confronting her ghosts.

Greta's laughter stopped. She said, 'She's crying now. Go up quick and get her.'

I hurried up the track and led my mother back to the car, making her sit in the back, next to Greta who held her and stroked her hair, saying: 'Shush, now.'

'The creatures,' my mother said. 'I left them. I left me own.'

'Sure we all do what we have to,' Greta said. 'TJ, I think what Mammy Quill would like, and the pair of us as well, is a nice hot Gaelic coffee.' She said to my mother, 'That's the stuff will put white whiskers on you!' My mother laughed. In a small onlooking corner of my mind, I felt admiration. What a magnificent wife Greta would be, I thought, for another husband.

In the Roundwood Inn, eight miles on, my mother's story came out in dribs and drabs. Hardly eating, she cut her chicken Maryland into pieces and pushed them around her plate to create the pretence of a half-eaten meal.

'Just leave it,' Greta told her.

'I can't not eat the good food,' my mother whispered.

'They don't care once it's paid for.'

''Twouldn't be manners,' my mother said.

Out of temper, I settled the matter by using my fingers and thumb like a crane in an amusement arcade, scooping up the chicken pieces, cream sauce and all, dropping the mess into a paper napkin and bearing it off to the toilet. I was back within seconds, with clean fingers and wagging my tail at a job sensibly taken care of.

'Thorn Thornton would have done that,' Greta said in ambiguous praise.

When I had unpicked the embroidery and made a story of it, this is what my mother told us. Although my father had known and married her as Annie Walsh, her name, to begin with, was Ward and she had run away from the Sugar Loaf at two in the morning. Born and reared to travelling, she had a hazy dream of a life that was different. 'Do you mean better?' I prompted, but no, she would not have that word; it spelled betrayal. In country towns, she and her younger sisters, cawing like nestlings, went from one house to the next asking for 'a bit o' help' or 'a few pince'. She stared enviously at girls who worked as maids or in creameries or shops, or went to dances where her sort were barred. She earned a beating by spending her alms on picture houses. She doted on Judy Garland as an Irish girl in *Little Nellie Kelly*.

When she had turned seventeen a match was made for her with a second cousin named Red Hogan. She knew that the choice was either to take him, or refuse and maybe end her days as a tinker's bitch. Money changed pockets and the banns were read below in Kilmacanoge, although neither bride nor groom had a parish. In a sprit of *kamikaze*, the proprietor of an ailing hotel took a booking for the wedding breakfast, while, at the camp site, porter by the keg was laid in, together with a gallon of Waterford poteen. Pubs for miles around were boarded up.

Late on the wedding eve, she whispered to the sisters who shared her mattress that she had to go outside. ''Tis the excitement,' she lied. She crept away from the nest of caravans and started down the Long Hill on foot, listening for the sound of a pony's hoofs and the jangle of harness as her father came after her. Instead, what she heard was the throb and clatter of a truck packed with soldiers who had been on night manoeuvres – it was the time of Hitler's war, or the Emergency, to use the official name for it. She was hoisted up among them, and to show off to her they sang *O'Donnell Abu* and 'We're off to Dublin in the green, in the green.' There was a sergeant who made the men behave themselves, and Annie was dropped off at a hostel on the quays where, starting to give her name as Ward, she changed it in mid-word to Walsh.

With another inmate, she caught a tram to Howth, where they both found work cleaning fish at the harbour. A friendly trawler-man arranged for her to sleep on board a vessel that was dry-docked for repairs. It was snug and warm, like the inside of a travellers' caravan, but after a week or so a local priest came and told her that if she herself was not in moral danger, she was an occasion of sin. He took her back into the city and to Inchicore, where she was put to work as a slavey in a home for orphans. She stayed there for three years, cooking, cleaning and minding children. Perhaps because unpaid help was hard to come by, questions were never asked. She had not taken the step of imagining what awaited her in a world where people lived in houses that were rooted in the earth and never moved, but this was a kind of limbo. She had turned her back on her own and the life they led, and what she had got in return was the price of her. The weeping began.

She slept in the end bed in one of the dormitories and was given some of the cast-off clothes that were donated. She had a half-day off once a fortnight, but rarely ventured into town. At first, she feared that she might be seen and followed and taken back to marry Red Hogan. A worse fancy was that a group of her family might come streeling out of a pub in front of her, and that instead of seizing her they would turn their backs, disowning her for a renegade. Meanwhile, a friendly nun at the orphanage was giving her lessons in reading, writing and sums. It was a kindness that Sister Immaculata came to regret, for Annie learned enough to understand a sign in a window in College Street that said, 'Waitress wanted.'

There, at the Goodwill Restaurant, my father was among her customers and after a month of stares, timid at first and then bold, he asked her out, and after another month, of refusals at first and then maybes, she agreed to an evening at the pictures, and that was her story told.

Greta and I talked about it at home after our outing. 'I'll tell you one thing,' I said in my Freudian mode. 'She's faced up to the past now. She's opened up to others about who she is and where she came from, so that's the last of the weeping.' As usual, I could not be more of a fool, and she wept, as inconsolably as ever, until in March she made a liar of the doctor by dying too soon.

She was buried in my father's plot in Dean's Grange. At the funeral mass, a flautist played 'She Moved Through the Fair' and there was a recording of Judy Garland singing 'A Pretty Girl Milking Her Cow' from *Little Nellie Kelly*. ('It's either that,' I told Greta when we discussed it, 'or a choice between "Singin' in the Rain" and "It's a Great Day for the Irish".') I was in truculent mood, and when the priest asked God to forgive Annie her sins, I wanted to kick him in his allegedly unused balls. He announced to the small congregation that, with Greta's compliments and mine, refreshments would be served at Tish Merdiff's.

Outside the church, it was what my father would have called a ha'sh old day, with curtains of rain sweeping from the north-west. People who were not accompanying us to the cemetery paused to murmur condolences and were quickly gone. There were old neighbours of my mother's as well as the entire population of Hy-Brasil Lawns. The last people to come up were two shy women in late middle-age. They shook hands with Greta and me, mumbled unintelligibly – the last words were the conventional 'sorry for your trouble' – and darted away. They were wearing head scarves, and one was crying and red-eyed. As they drove off in a battered blue Vanette, Greta said, 'Who are they?'

The knowledge and the words came together. 'I think they were her sisters,' I said. Then, and with a sense of loss, 'My aunts.'

Only a few people came to Dean's Grange, and small blame to them – I could imagine my mother shooing them away from the graveside and back to Tish's, out of the weather. Jack Richie had set aside the far end of the lounge bar, laying on sandwiches and drink. Thorn and his wife were there, and Colleen and Turlough, and of course Shay and Brigid. Greta's eyes kept straying towards the door, even when she was hugging people who told us what a great old warrior my mother was.

I said to Greta: 'She got a good turn-out.'

'Grand.'

'And you can relax. Josie Hand won't be here. Colleen says she's in Italy. Her mother isn't well.' I said it not by way of provocation, but to put her mind at ease.

She gave me a cool look. 'Colleen told you that, did she?'

'Mm. Why not?'

She said, raising her voice: 'And why should I care where Josie Hand is?'

'Well, you don't like her, do you? And you haven't taken your eyes off that door.'

'Is that so? Well, the reason is because I was wondering if those two women would come in. I don't believe they're your mother's sisters. I think you're romancing.' With the dignity born of two gin-and-tonics on an empty stomach, she said, 'I think you have your glue.'

'Maybe.'

'If they were travellers, how would their sort – no, I mean your sort, *your* sort, same difference – know about your mother?'

I said: 'It was in the death notices.'

'Oh, was it?'

161

'In the newspapers.'

'Ah, yes, so it was. And I suppose, what with the style of them and all, they would have the *Irish Times* delivered straight to the caravan. You'd know all about that, now wouldn't you?'

She was spoiling for a row, so without answering I moved over towards Thorn and his wife. Before I could reach them, a balding man of my mother's age moved between us and took hold of my hand. He shook it and held tightly on to it. He said: 'You don't remember me, do you?' It was and still is my least favourite question. I smiled, said 'Sorry,' and tried to retrieve my hand. He held on and said, 'Own up. You don't know me from Adam.'

I said, idiotically, 'You hold me with a glittering eye.'

He almost barked: 'What?'

'It's *The Rime of the Ancient Mariner*.'

'Ah.' His brow cleared. 'You're being lit-er-airy. I mean, in spite of the sad day that's in it. The poor oul' mammy is gone and six feet under, but you need to demonstrate your er-u-dit-ion. Well, sure good man, I wouldn't doubt you. Look, do you not remember me?'

'Give me a clue. Your name, for example.'

'Oh, highly humorous.'

'Excuse me, sir.' Thorn, who was now standing between us, took hold of the man's wrist and mine and twisted and pulled the two hands apart as if he were a plumber uncoupling a pipe. In his imitation of an FBI agent, he spoke through his nose, addressing the Ancient Mariner. 'Mr Quill is in breach of regulations that permit a bereaved person no more than ten seconds in which to accept any single message of condolence. Sir, don't leave town without telling us.'

As the Mariner gaped at him, Thorn led me away and giggled: 'How about that, then?'

'Thanks.'

'I'm thinking of starting up my own gobshite annihilation service. I intend to call it GAS for short. Are you bearing up?'

'I keep thinking . . .'

'Thinking of what?'

'Of her. Lying in that . . . in that wet . . .'

'Shut up.'

'Oh, God.'

'No, we'll have none of that. Now quit it.'

'It's a bad day.'

'Oh, sure.'

'And Greta is getting pissed. She says I'm a tinker.'

'Come again?'

'Or at least half a one. And when I mentioned Josie Hand to her, she damn near ate my face off.'

Thorn said, 'I'm not surprised. Confucius, he say that man in hole does not try to get out by digging. Do you think she knows?'

'Who, Greta?'

'About *Il Mostro.*'

I said, honestly: 'I don't know what she knows.'

'You should do like I do: keep your nose clean.'

He winked, and we joined his wife Prue and the Penders in one of the alcoves. Turlough had shaken my hand outside the church, now he did so again. He said, trying to keep it light, but making a hash of it: 'About that job with the *Sentinel*. I got it, would you believe, in spite of you, so all is forgiven. We're pals again.'

Colleen said, 'What a liar you are.'

He said, 'Me?'

She turned from him to face me. 'He does not forgive you. He is like everybody else in this country. Everybody loves you to your face. I am mad about my husband, but sometimes I don't like him much. And Turlough, don't tap your finger against your head behind me to say that I am crackers.'

He said, 'I didn't.'

'Well, you were going to.' To me she said, 'He will be your

friend again. I will see to it!' She patted the seat beside her for me to sit and be comforted. 'I met your mother one day in your house. She was a very nice person.'

'Oh, dear. I never knew her,' Prue said.

Turlough, who was now red in the face, said to Colleen, 'Do you seriously think I would hold a grudge against a man on the day of his mother's funeral?'

Colleen said, 'My darling, you would hold a grudge against a man on the day of his *own* funeral.'

Her tone was so earnest and devoid of malice that we all laughed, earning a scandalised stare from several of the mourners. We were suitably chastened.

Prue spoke up in her cut-glass yet gentle accent. 'Has anyone noticed that a whole generation is being whittled away? One by one ... *insidiously*, that's the word, as if there were someone hoping we wouldn't notice. And meanwhile, our little lot is moving ever so gently to the head of the queue.' She gave a little laugh. 'We're next for the *Skylark*.'

'Thanks for that thought, darling,' Thorn said. 'We needed it.'

The laugh was quieter this time, no more than a gasp, yet again people looked around. I saw that Greta was now with Shay and Brigid, who were on their feet and about to leave. I excused myself from the group and moved over. Greta said, 'I'm glad you're enjoying yourself.'

'It was something Colleen said.'

'I mean with your mother hardly in her grave ...'

'I know where she is, thanks, and I've had one bastard up my nose here today already. So, please, don't you start.' To Shay and Brigid, I said: 'You're not off?'

'They have to go visiting,' Greta said brightly. 'Blanaid has had a baby boy.'

'Get away!'

'One o'clock this morning,' Brigid said. 'Eight pounds.' Shay sawed a forefinger up and down against his nose.

'The first grandchild,' I said.

'Oh, don't be talking,' Brigid said with a little laugh, just possibly not meaning it as a request.

And on this day of all days,' Greta said. 'Well, it's an old saying and a true one. In the midst of life we are in — No. No, I mean ...' She stopped, her brain addled. 'Can you say it the other way round?'

Brigid said to Shay. 'Show TJ the photos.'

'They took thingies,' Greta said.

'Polaroids,' Shay said.

He took the photographs from his pocket. They were of Blanaid, Brigid and Shay, each in turn holding the baby. Shay's attitude suggested that what he was cradling was a swaddled time-bomb.

'Isn't he a dote?' Greta said.

'What is she calling him?' I asked.

'Terence,' Brigid said. 'Today is the 28th, the feast of St Teresa of Avila.'

The mourners had all gone by mid-afternoon, and in the evening I applied myself to the chore of clearing out my mother's one-bedroom apartment. The snapshots, taken on long-ago outings to Dalkey Island and at the Wicklow regatta were the worst part. I was there, between my father and mother, spindle-legged and eyes closed against the sun.

I filled a large suitcase with bric-a-brac and laid her clothes out for Oxfam and the St Vincent. The rented television could go back next day. Her neighbours could have the rest.

When I got home, Greta had been sick and was sober. 'We'll go and visit Blanaid tomorrow,' she said. 'You get flowers in town and I'll find a woolly for the baby.'

Next morning, Thorn telephoned my office. He was rising in the world and had been invited to a dinner party at the home of his role model, Gus de Paor, who lived not far from us. To save the cost of a taxi out, he asked if he could cadge a lift. In rush hour, I was glad of his company; that apart, our friendship had grown, and there had been genuine affection when he rescued me from the Ancient Mariner. He turned up at the archive, smart in a dinner jacket and with hair freshly tousled. As we eased into Westmorland Street, he told me that his plans for the James Joyce Restaurant had met with a hitch.

'Some bollix of a *nouveau riche* upstart has lodged a complaint with the borough council.'

I said, 'How do you know he's *nouveau riche*?'

'Who isn't!' Thorn enjoyed making enemies, but not when they were unknown to him.

At Booterstown, we inched forward through the lights outside Ye Olde Punch Bowl. 'Look to your right,' Thorn said. I did so and, abreast of us there was an Audi containing two blonde women in their thirties. They looked at us as if interested. Thorn said, 'Give them a wink.'

'Like hell I will.'

'Oh, go on.'

'And get arrested?'

Thorn said, 'You're a howl, you know that? Josie Hand, the most gorgeous bit of stuff that ever lived, is mad about you. You and she are having an affair hotter than the innermost hob of hell, and still you're hopeless with women. Give those birds a shagging wink! Do it for pig-iron.'

So I winked, and the nearest blonde responded with a smile that could have lit up a small town. 'You see?' Thorn said, and we giggled like teenagers.

The traffic moved forward, up Rock Road. 'Tell you a story,' he said. 'The other day in town I was in Waterstone's, and I held the door open for a brunette. Mid-thirties, long legs, great figure, not short of a few bob. She said "Thanks." Twenty minutes later, at the Kilkenny Centre, I hold a door open for another woman, only who is it but her again. The same one. She laughs and says, "Oh, hello, there!" She actually lays a hand on my sleeve. Do you know what I did? I caught hold of her and took her to one side. I said to her, "I happen to be a mild diabetic …"'

As I looked at him, he said, 'You didn't know that about me, did you? Well, I am. I said to her: "I happen to be a mild diabetic, and there are lots of things I mustn't touch. But you, whoever you are, will never be one of them."'

'Jesus, that's a great line,' I said. 'That's tremendous.'

He said: 'I swear to you that there and then I could have led her to a hotel room and bonked her to death. It could have been the start of a … *con-flag-ray-shon*. But the rule is, you can wink and you can touch, but you don't follow through. Not if you're married to anyone as gorgeous as Prue. And of course provided the other woman isn't a knock-out like Josie Hand.'

You silver-tongued bugger, I thought. Aloud I said, 'You know, you're like Bernstein in *Citizen Kane*.'

'Say again?'

'He talks about seeing a girl on a ferry wearing a white dress and with a parasol to match. He says: "She didn't see me at all, but I'll bet a month hasn't gone by since that I haven't thought of that girl."'

Thorn said, 'I don't get it.' Then: 'Hey, no, I don't think of the brunette. Not at all. No, what I think about is that remark I made. I ought to have taken out a copyright on it.'

I dropped him outside a high-walled house facing the sea on Ravello Road. I waited with the car window down as he spoke into an intercom and a camera-light came on. There was a buzzing, the gate opened and he was swallowed.

Later, Greta and I went to visit Blanaid in the Blessed Virgin's Manor, which was a contentious name, I suggested, for a maternity home. Shay and Brigid were visiting also, and Greta held the infant Terence and said again that he was a dote. Blanaid was perky and cheerful, and no mention was made of the adoption. She was due to be allowed home, unencumbered within a few days.

As we drove back to 'Kate Fortune's Lane', Greta asked me what the child's father looked like.

'Who, the Midget Mechanic? He's a little fellow, a bit shorter than Blanaid. Well, you yourself met him that day at the press conference when she went off with what's-his-name ... Tyree. Why do you ask?'

Greta said, 'Oh ... my ... God.'

'Why, what's up?'

She said, very carefully, hand-picking every word, 'That was a shocking ugly baby. Mind, I'm not saying a word against it.' I laughed, and she told me to keep my eyes on the road. 'Every new-born child looks all raw and red in the face and squinchy. Except to the parents, that is, and the granny and grand-da. They always think it's the last word. No, but do you know what that infant looks like? Honest to God ...'

'So tell me, Mr Bones,' I said, 'what does the infant look like?'

'Don't be so smart. No, I mean it. It looks like a papoose. For God's sake, watch where you're going. Are you trying to kill us?'

Chapter Thirteen

On Lough Derg

'I suppose, when you think about it,' Greta said, bringing tea to the kitchen table, 'it was only by the mercy of God that the baby was given up for adoption. In St Ultan's Park, he would have stuck out like a sore thumb.'

'Always assuming you're right,' I said.

'Oh, I am, I am, I know I am!'

'A papoose?'

'Did you not see him for yourself?'

'I'm not inclined to look closely at infants.'

'Red in the face and with a sharp little nose, like a bit of carrot.'

'Ah.'

'What kind did you say it might be? A Hopper?'

'Christ,' I said, 'don't get me going. It's a Hopi.'

On the rest of the journey home from the Blessed Virgin's Manor, I had told myself that Greta was mistaken. Assuming that Tyree was the father, the child could not have been more than a quarter of what the Widow had termed a 'native American'; and yet the weasel word 'throwback' would not be evicted from my head. I remembered the day of the press conference when Duane – the misjudged Duane, as it now seemed – had forlornly gone in search of the missing couple. Admittedly, Blanaid had returned home to her parents with a golden opinion of Tyree, who, she said, was a thorough gentleman. He not only wore a Stetson, but knew how and when to sweep it off respectfully. The Code of the West, was what Shay called it. The hat, my mind nudged maliciously, may not have been all he doffed.

'She's calling the child Terence,' I said.

'What about it?'

'Well, I know it has to be a coincidence, but that name is not exactly an ass's gallop away from Tyree.' Greta looked at me with severity and took a sip of tea, which reappeared, streaming out of her nose.

'You can laugh,' I said, offering her the dishcloth. 'But it's hard lines on whoever the adopting parents are. It may be that they live in a St Ultan's Park of their own, somewhere down the country, where people are narrow-minded.'

'And racy,' Greta said.

'You mean racist,' I said.

When the convulsions stopped, I wondered when was the last time she and I had laughed without having to try, unsuccessfully, to remember when the last time was.

When I had bolted the front door for the night and followed her upstairs, we assured each other with the straightest of faces that, never mind about racism, we were no better than scandal-mongers and that in any case the identity of the father was no more than academic. We agreed – she looking out of the window and I untying a shoelace – not to mention such foolishness again. When I next met Shay, life had resumed its gentle ways. Blanaid was home again after what he called her 'trouble', and the baby's new parents had been chosen.

'We're not supposed to know,' Shay said, 'but I hear tell they're professional people. Name of Reddy.'

'*Reddy*?'

'What's up?' he asked.

'Nothing.'

Brigid was not so forthcoming. When Greta and she next did their weekly shopping, they as usual rewarded their exertions with coffee and a biscuit at 'Massabielle' afterwards. 'So tell us,' Greta said. 'How is Blanaid? Is she home and is she well?'

'All that is in the past,' Brigid said, offering a Jacob's fig roll and smiling as if she were forgiving a tormentor.

A door had been closed so gently as to make no sound. Americans, in their restless way with language, have turned the word 'disappear' into a transitive verb, and, as far as Brigid was concerned, that was what had happened to the entire episode. It had been disappeared.

When I next spoke to Kitty O'Fearna to report on progress with the new Irish-American archive, I asked after Tyree. He had moved to Santa Barbara, she said. He and his girlfriend – a small alarm bell went off – were running an agency and school for what the Widow called stunt-persons.

'I'll give him your regards,' she said.

'Do,' I said.

I shivered at the thought of making even the most off-hand mention of Blanaid and her 'trouble'. I could hear the Widow's voice turning as cold as a Pecos winter as she said, 'Is this a shake-down?' No; better, I thought, to let sleeping Hopis lie.

Thanks to the industry of Ilse-Lazlo Huneker, the new catalogue was almost complete. She was not infallible – she classified Virginia Mayo as an Irish actress – but she compiled a list of nearly two hundred films. *Little Nellie Kelly* was among them and, trite and vulgar as it was, the title caused my heart to miss its step. My mother's death had not hit me as hard as the revelation of a life that had been spent in squalor, wretchedness and grief, one after the other. Her story followed me like a black dog, and there was no one to turn to. With Greta, as always, the deeper an emotion went, the more ungivingly she clasped it to her. I felt gladness when the telephone went and the familiar voice that was half a growl asked, 'Can you talk?'

'Yes. Hello.'

'Andrew told me about your mother. Have you a lunch appointment?'

'Today? No.'

'Then come here.'

When I arrived at the house on Raglan Road, Josie said that I looked good. Looking 'good' was a pet phrase of hers; it meant, I think, that I was fanciable. The balance that existed between us had shifted since the early days. In the beginning, she had been the lover and I the loved; now we were on a more equal footing. There were times when I wondered if the scales had come to rest or were still shifting. Today, we sat in an immense day room and kitchen, combined. She gave me an omelette and a glass of wine and spoke of the new films she had seen in Florence, and of the spa – the *termale*, she called it – where she had taken her mother. She had seen and – she had the nerve for it – even approached and spoken to another guest, the director Fellini. When she had taken my empty plate to the dishwasher, she made cymbals of her hands and sat across from me.

'Now. Your mother ... it was sad for you.'

'More than sad.' I told her the story, much as I had managed to piece it together. At one point, she gasped and held her fisted hand to her lips, her eyes huge. She said, 'I knew ... I knew,' and made a sign that I should continue. When I had done, she smiled.

'This is wonderful. *Meraviglioso.*'

'Now what?'

'Don't say it in that cynical way ... please.'

'Sorry.'

'All those times that your wife and you came to Colleen's house, and you and I sat at the same table, I said to myself, "He is the one for me." And yet, what was the attraction? No offence, my darling, but I had not the smallest idea. Oh, you were *simpatico* and you had much to teach me. But, forgive me again, there are many men in the world. If I had been ... how do you say? – hungry for someone – well, I am not bad looking, eh? And I have some accomplishments. And now all is explained. You see, we are the same kind.'

When I said nothing, she refilled my wine glass.

'No, you think I am making the figure of speech. Is not so! This story that you have told to me, I could tell it to you about me. The same story.'

In Italy, did there exist, I wondered, what we called travellers? I had a mental picture of Josie, wearing gold earrings and with her hair caught up in a bandanna, smoking a clay pipe, perhaps, as she perched on the driving seat of a gipsy caravan. The image was short-lived, for at that moment Andrew came in.

On seeing a stranger, he said, 'Oh, forgive me;' then he came forward with hand extended. 'TJ, my dear fellow! I can't say how sorry I am.' Then, to Josie: 'Darling, I'll be in town for dinner at Guilbaud's, so I need a fresh shirt.'

She was already half-way to the door with a gesture that told him to stay put. When we were alone, he asked most anxiously, 'Have you everything you want?'

I could detect no hint of satire. I said, 'Josie very kindly invited me to drop by. She has been cheering me up.'

'No better woman,' Andrew said.

He asked me about the archive. I asked him about luncheon meats. He said, 'My job is nothing as romantic as yours,' and again I could detect no undertones. He was the perfect host, warm and solicitous, and yet he stood as if impatient for his road. Josie came back with the shirt, laundry-wrapped in tissue paper.

She said, 'Have you your briefcase?'

'In the car, and it's full.'

'Then make room and put this in it.'

I said, 'I have to go, too.'

Andrew said, 'No, no, don't hurry. Stay. Please.' He shook hands again, smiled at Josie and went out. The front door slammed.

I said, 'I feel rotten.'

'You are sick?'

'I feel rotten about him. He's such a nice man.'

'Andrew is a charming man, until you cross him, and then he

is vindictive. And he and I have never quarrelled, not once since we are married. Otherwise, you would not be here now.'

'You and I have never quarrelled.'

She smiled. 'Give us time.'

'All the same, I'm in his house, and that stinks.'

She said, 'You take nothing from him that he has use for. He has his club where he meets his friends and where women do not enter. He has his money, his golf every year in Tobago, and his horse in the *Prix de l'Arc de Triomphe*. And, after all that, he has his home where things go like the insides of a clock. He says, "Darling, I need a fresh shirt," and *presto!* it is done. Andrew should thank you for putting horns on him. Because of you, he has a contented wife.'

As I reached for my wine glass, she said: 'Yes, finish that. Then you must go.'

'Oh?'

'Remember that I have my own story to tell. It will not take as long as yours, but today is not the day. It you stay, it will come out too soon and I will make a *sufato* of it. Is that the word?'

'Dunno, but it sounds great.'

When she saw me to the door and in spite of the friendliness of my encounter with Andrew, she continued to be discretion itself. Raglan Road is hardly a place of twitching window curtains, and yet she said in a loud clear voice, 'Goodbye, and thank you very much!' I was mildly surprised that she did not add that she was sure the vacuum cleaner would work splendidly from now on.

Back at the office, there was a message to call Thorn.

He asked, 'Will you do me a favour?'

'What?'

'Don't say "What?" "What?" is a cautious, crappy little word. "What" is a fiddly-piddly little word. Be reckless. Do like everyone else does and say "Certainly, mate! I'll do you a favour and with a will and a half." Then, when you find out what the favour is, break your word.'

'You're in good form.'

'I ought to be. That arch-bollix I told you about, that enemy of mine, whoever he is, has only done it on me from a height.'

'Oh, no.'

'The James Joyce Restaurant is out the window. Planning permission refused.'

'Thorn, what can I say?'

'Do you know any curses that really work?'

I said, 'In that case, and since you've been hard done by, then yes, I will do you a favour. What is it?'

'I want you and Greta to come with Prue and me on the Shannon, next Friday until Sunday.'

'Ah, now ...'

'Yes, go on, then, make my day. Join the club. Chicken out.'

'Greta won't come. No way.'

'Yes, she will. Prue will call her.'

'Anyway, I'd as soon sail on the *Bounty*.'

'Listen, this is not a social occasion. And it's a favour that can cut two ways. Trust me.'

'Next thing, you'll tell me that your cheque is in the post.'

By dint of charm and buttering up, Prue won a reluctant 'yes' from Greta, whereas what was lavished on me was a cornucopia of prophecies of rain, boredom, quarrels, drunkenness, seasickness, and drowning. On the Friday, we drove to Wilton Place, quarrelling as if hatred was to be put on half rations next day, and picked up the Thorntons for the drive to Portumna. Greta's eyes were fixed on the sky of surly grey, while Prue was vivacious, assuring us that the weekend would be fun. Thorn, still fulminating at his unknown arch-enemy, went through a litany of politicians and power dealers.

He said, 'I'll ask Gus de Paor when we see him. He'll know who it was.'

'When *we* see him?' I said. 'Christ, he's not coming with us?'

Thorn put a say-nothing finger to his lips and began to lilt 'Blow the man down'. At the Portumna marina there was, to my relief, no sign of de Paor, whom I knew only by photographs in the press. Papers were signed, and we went on board a six-berth lake cruiser named the *Princess Medbh*. Thorn donned a scrambled-egg cap and a windbreaker that put his identity in question. 'Haargh, Jim lad,' he said, and I had a mental image of Josie in London, in a white nightdress and with a black sleep-mask over one eye. 'Hey, wake up,' Thorn said. 'I'm asking you and Greta to choose your stateroom.'

I had an idea of what we were in for when, instead of instructing me to cast off, he said, 'Untie that cord, will you?' He switched on the ignition, climbed to the flying bridge and rammed the throttle forward with the heel of his hand, spinning the wheel like Edward G Robinson in *The Sea Wolf*. We side-swiped the unoccupied vessel in the next berth, setting up a domino effect the length of the marina. As we slewed down the narrow cut that led to the Shannon, Thorn so over-corrected with the wheel that the cruiser went into a pendulum motion, scything through the rushes on both sides.

'Easy on that throttle,' I said. I took his place at the wheel and put the stick into full reverse. The cruiser all but reared like a horse.

'How come you know about boats?' Thorn wanted to know.

'He's just naturally gifted, dear,' Prue said.

'No, he isn't, no, he isn't,' Greta said.

'Yes, I am, yes, I am,' I said.

I preferred to be thought of as a natural and a born genius, rather than explain that I had lived by the sea for most of my life. We eased downstream through the swing bridge, and minutes later there seemed to be nothing in the world but lake and sky. A chill south-west wind came skimming across the water from the Clare hills; it met the Tipperary hills to the east, came back on itself and churned up a confused sea. The *Princess Medbh* shuddered gently as we passed the first marker. Lake water slapped the forward window.

Greta, beginning to whimper, said, 'He doesn't know what he's doing.'

In my Captain Queeg voice, I lisped, 'Now let me tell you about the thrawberries.'

'Christ,' Greta said, 'now he's doing fucking Bogart.'

To Thorn, I said, 'The wider the lake gets the worse it'll be. What's your landfall?'

'Sorry?'

'Where are we going?'

'Oh.' He pulled a scrap of paper from his pocket. 'Turn right at the fifth black marker.'

We had already passed two blacks. After twenty minutes, two more came in sight, then the fifth. Looking abeam on the starboard side, we could see a tall Victorian mansion in its own grounds a half-mile away. 'There!' Thorn said. 'That's it ... Aquila House.'

Through the ship's glasses, I could make out a low granite breakwater with an ornamental stone mermaid at each end. Praying we would have enough water, I spun the wheel and eased back on the throttle. I told Thorn to go to the bow and watch out for weeds, and managed to keep a straight face as he poked his head over the side and a wavelet smacked into the dead rat. With our speed reduced to no more than a knot, we inched towards the lee shore, yawing as the wind caught us. We slid behind the breakwater to find a wooden jetty and mooring rings. With Greta in her role of recording angel, I would have opened a vein rather than rubbed the pier.

It was idyllic: a tranquil little Shangri-La away from the storms of the lake. A field-mouse performed somersaults on a blade of meadow-grass. I secured the bow rope with a round turn and two half-hitches, while Thorn, handling the stern line, created a tall beehive hair-do redolent of the swinging Sixties.

'You did that well,' he said with admiration. 'If you were wearing suspenders, you could hook your thumbs and stretch them.'

'Yes, well done,' Prue said. 'Greta, wasn't TJ the last word?'

Greta gave me one of her extra-special 'Mmmp's. Thorn brought out two bottles – Chablis and Scotch – and put them on the table. 'You attend to the honours, and I'll see about dinner. And, girls, don't get dressed up.' He went trotting along the jetty.

'Will we be eating here?' Greta asked.

'Right royally,' Prue said. 'Gus says so.'

'Gus again,' I said. 'I don't know Mr de Paor, but I hear tell that his non-goodness goes before him.'

'Oh, he's not too bad.'

'I'm going to change!' Greta said, darting into our cabin.

'Oh, God, then me too,' Prue said.

I supposed that when de Paor joined us for whatever reason, it would be by car. I was wrong. Thorn returned from the house within five minutes and announced all in one breath that we were on the pig's back, as right as the rain and swinging like Crippen. He shook a packet of potato crisps into a bowl, and he and I had our drinks while Greta and Prue changed. After twenty minutes or so, the wives had hardly reappeared when there was a roar and a whirring that quickly became almost deafening.

'There he is now,' Thorn shouted above the noise. 'Everybody out!'

Gus de Paor was arriving by helicopter. As it descended, ripples ran like water across the grass of the lawn, and the surrounding trees had an early autumn. I was reminded of Leni Riefenstahl's documentary *Triumph of the Will*, in which Hitler, godlike, arrived by air at the 1934 Nuremberg Rally. However, as de Paor stepped on to the grass, he looked less like *der Führer* than *il Duce*. He was bull-like, with a massive jowly face that was designed to scowl. To beat God at His own game, he had shaved his head to conceal his baldness. He wore a Dunhill blazer and Gucci loafers and carried a document case. In denims and deck-shoes, I felt like a South Sea islander prostrate before the arrival of the Great Whirly God.

As the helicopter blades slowed and went still, Thorn performed the introductions. De Paor gave Greta and Prue a beefy arm apiece and swept them with him towards the house. Inside, and although there were hours of daylight left, the curtains were drawn, and polished mahogany threw back the gleam of candlelight. A single table had been laid for dinner. A waiter, attired flunkey-style, offered us champagne.

'Is this a restaurant?' I asked.

'Oh, yes,' de Paor said. 'But they don't usually encourage hire craft.' He smiled to say that present company was excepted. 'I took it over for the evening. I wanted us to chat privately. That's why I came by chopper.'

Liar, I thought. *You wanted to show off. You're flash.*

'I'm afraid dinner is Hobson's choice,' de Paor said jovially, inserting himself at the head of the table. 'We can have either sirloin steak or sirloin steak.' The *maitre d'* came and made a note of preferences: burnt (Thorn and Greta), *à point* (me), medium rare (Prue) and almost raw (de Paor). The ritual was hardly necessary; the meat, when it arrived was stringy and tough. My lower jaw soon began to ache, and only our host was undaunted, chomping away like a grinder in a Corporation dustcart. An elderly lady, as tough as the steak and wearing pince-nez and a crooked chef's toque, materialised and asked if everything was satisfactory. 'Superb!' de Paor said. She gave a cavernous laugh and went out again.

The wine was an Australian Cabernet Sauvignon. 'I brought it in the chopper,' de Paor said. 'No matter how fantastic the food is, like here this evening, you can't always rely on the cellar.'

I tried not to meet Thorn's eyes or anyone else's. We talked mainly about show business. Thorn wanted the latest news about de Paor's rock group, The Prince of Darkness, who had lately demolished a hotel suite in Melbourne. 'Scamps,' de Paor said fondly. He asked me about the archive and how time-consuming the job was. I told him that I would soon be no more than a curator. The conversation turned to holidays. Thorn and Prue had been to Marrakech for a fortnight; and de Paor said that he and his lady – I had no idea as to whether he was married or sported what at that time was beginning to be known as a partner – had taken over a small private island near Mustique. 'And where have *you* been this year, my dear?' he asked Greta. His dear truthfully replied 'At home,' and was applauded for her wit.

Dessert was served – a *crème caramel* – and Thorn raised the grievance he had been nursing since Dublin. 'Could I pick your brains?' he asked.

'Feel free,' de Paor said.

Thorn said. 'You know that James Joyce idea of mine? Well, it was more than an idea. I took a lease on the old tram-yard out your way. I went to a hell of a lot of expense. I suppose I should have got planning permission first, but I thought it would be a snip. And now some rat-fink has gone and done the dirty.'

'Yes, I know,' de Paor said.

'You know?'

'I'm the rat-fink.'

There were two silences with Prue putting a feeble 'Oh, really,' between them, as thin as ham in an airport sandwich. To my alarm, Thorn's face began to change colour, darkening from pale to a muddy red. Our host, ignoring him, signalled with his hand, and a uniformed man came into the light; he was the pilot of the helicopter.

De Paor said: 'Now the gentlemen are going to retire to the library to talk business, which will take one hour and not a second more. Meanwhile, as a treat for the ladies, Cathal here' – he indicated the pilot – ' is going to take them for a bird's eye view of the lake, maybe even as far as Limerick.'

'Oh, lovely,' Prue said.

Greta was almost the same colour as Thorn. 'If you don't

mind, I'll go back to the boat,' she said. 'I'm not all that –'

'I won't hear of it,' de Paor said. 'Nonsense.'

She was led out, a ewe-lamb to the slaughter. Prue, following, waggled her fingers at us and said, 'Well, ta-*ra!*'

Thorn said, 'Now, listen, Gus –'

'In a minute,' de Paor said. He said to the waiter, 'Coffee, and three Courvoisiers, large.' He moved, irresistibly, into the library next door, where ripped leather chairs haemorrhaged their upholstery and the books were either Victorian or paperbacks. As Thorn opened his mouth, de Paor said in a low voice, 'Shut up.' From outside the rotor blades of the helicopter began to spin. Then we waited until the coffee and brandies had been brought.

De Paor rubbed the balloon glass furiously between his fat hands and sniffed his brandy as if it were Vick. He leaned forwards towards Thorn.

'First, that fucking restaurant of yours would have been the ruin of the town in which I happen to live.' He looked at me. 'Which is your town, too, by all accounts. From what I see when I drive – or, rather, am driven – through it, it's the dog-shit capital of Ireland; all the same, I don't intend to see it overrun by cunts and wankers and their mucus-running progeny. As it is, I look out my window of a Sunday, and Jap cars are parked the length of Ravello Road. Which is something, give me time, that I intend to put a stop to.' He sat back and looked at Thorn. 'So there's your question answered. Now you know who the rat fink is that put the boot in.

'And second ...' He opened the document case and took out two bound typescripts. He pushed one at Thorn and the other at me. I saw the title *Return to Innisfree.* 'And second, I have a job for you, and I don't want you wasting your time on a Mickey Mouse kip of a restaurant. You can be rich. Maybe not Gus de Paor rich, but rich enough.' As I smiled, his head came around. Sharply, 'Yes?'

I said, 'I was wondering if "rich" and "enough" ever go together.'

He gave me a porcine smile. 'Some people have to make do.' He had long antennae that could measure animosity to within a micron. Probably, he could measure fear as well. He said, 'Tell me now, how much do you know about a fillum –' his use of two syllables delighted me – 'called *The Man from Innisfree*?'

'I know everything about it,' I said. 'I know it backwards.'

'Thought so,' he said with a contented noise that was between a snore and a purr.

'It's one of Sean O'Fearna's masterpieces,' I said. 'It won him his fourth Oscar for best director.'

'Mm. And do you happen to know that there was a sequel?'

'A *what*?'

No, I most emphatically did not know. He reached over and tapped the typescript in front of me.

'*The Man from Innisfree* was what nowadays we would call a mega-hit. It cleaned up at the box office, so the studio, MAP Pictures – which, as you are no doubt aware, is an acronym for –'

'Mom's Apple Pie,' I said.

He paused, not caring much to be interrupted. '... So MAP Pictures paid the original author to write a follow-up. It was never made, of course. Television happened, and MAP was squeezed out of business. The rights of *Return to Innisfree* reverted to the estate of the author, one Donal Dugort, who by then was past tense. I bought it. That's it in front of you – *Return to Innisfree*.'

I said, 'You want to make a sequel to a masterpiece?'

He said, 'I don't just want to. I'm *going* to, and I have ten million dollars of American money that says so.'

'Jesus.'

'Call me Mr de Paor.' *Funnee*, I thought.

'So what's it about?'

'It's a next-generation story, thirty years on. In fact, I'm thinking of Maureen O'Hara in a cameo role. Same character as before, but this time she's the mother. And instead of a big fistfight at the end, there's a foot-race across half of Connemara. Great scenery, and this time out, the one who wins gets the girl. That's part of the story, but we ought to have something else at stake, something more important.'

'Why not have an IRA time-bomb?' I said.

'Hey, hey, hey,' de Paor said, impressed.

'It's due to blow up the Inishmore ferryboat, that has a VIP on board – maybe the Pope – unless the runners can get to it first.'

'That's good,' de Paor said.

'Not to mention there's a werewolf on the rampage.'

De Paor was quiet for a while. Then he threw back his cannon-ball head and emitted a hearty, unforced and well-practised laugh. He said, 'I'm in a very good humour today.' Thorn, who was beginning to shake, took a deep slurp of his brandy, all but drowning the rat.

'I want you to write this fillum,' de Paor said. He turned to Thorn: 'And I want you to produce it.'

I looked at Thorn in time to catch sight of the last of the James Joyce Restaurant vanishing in the north-westerly direction of Connemara.

'And what would *you* do?' I asked.

'Oh, I'm the whole shebang,' Gus de Paor said. 'Clew Bay Fillums, that's who I am.'

'I've never written a film,' I said.

'So what? You're steeped in them. They come out of your every orifice.'

'And I already have a job.'

'Oh, sure. And what was it you said you were? A curator. A minder.'

It was a jibe. I lobbed an invisible hand grenade at him and watched it squeeze past the paunch and go down his trouser-front. I said, trying not to let my excitement show, 'You don't want me.'

'No?'

'Because if I took this job – I say *if* – then there'd be a condition. I'd be answerable to Thorn and nobody else.'

'You mean including me?'

'Especially you.'

'Fine! No sweat. And now *I* have a condition. I'll hire both of you, or neither one. Fair enough?'

I had been needling him, wanting him to tell me to go to hell because I lacked the courage to go there of my own accord. Now he was saying that if I turned him down, Thorn would be out in the cold, and all my fault. Gus de Paor played a good game.

He smiled and extended his right hand.

I said, 'No, I'll still think about it.'

His smile stayed put, but now it was saying that I could be had, and I suspected it was right. The waiter poured more Courvoisier, and de Paor said, 'Leave the bottle.' With the skirmish over, he ignored me and began marking time, consulting a dazed Thorn about locations and casting. After a time, the noise of the returning chopper was heard.

'Ah,' de Paor said, rising. 'Shall we join the encumbrances?' He was a caution.

At ten o'clock, he climbed on board the chopper, waved to us as we returned to the *Princess Medbh*, and ascended, like E.T., into the night sky. We finished our Chablis, had a nightcap, and Thorn told Greta and Prue about *Return to Innisfree*.

'So my fate and fortune, my entire life, my children's lives, the entire caboosh, is in this shagger's hands.' Indicating me, he made a comic shtick out of it. He told Prue, 'Darling, do something. Talk to him. Give him your body.'

She said, 'I certainly will not. Not unless he writes me a nice fat little part. The lady of the Big House, perhaps.'

'Done,' I said.

'So get them off you,' Thorn said to her.

Our cabin was next to the Thorntons', and Greta and I had two single beds with a chest of drawers between. 'I thought I'd die in

184

that effing helicopter,' Greta said as she squirmed under her duvet. 'And my hair's in flitters.'

'So what do you think?' I whispered.

'About what?' Then: 'Oh, *that*? You do whatever you like.'

I put out the light and turned on my side. The cruiser moved gently at its moorings, and there was a pleasant slap of water against the hull. Her voice came to me in the dark, and, getting it back to front, she said, 'If you get up with dogs, you lie down with fleas.'

There was a tapping on the partition between the cabins. 'Are you there?' Thorn's voice said.

'No, I'm not here. I've gone home. What is it?'

'Do us a favour. Lie down with a Rottweiler.'

'Shag off.'

'Because if you turn this job down –'

'Go to sleep.'

'Then you'll never drink lunch in this town again.'

Next morning, the lake was calm, and, with the weekend before us, we put in for lunch at the harbour of Dromineer. Afterwards, Greta said: 'I wouldn't mind a walk.'

'With me, do you mean?'

'Mmmp.'

We left Thorn and Prue in the hotel bar and strolled along the lakeside road towards Ryan's Point on the corner of Youghal Bay. 'Who's paying for this?' Greta wanted to know.

'For what?'

'The hire of the boat. Are Thorn and you going shares?'

'At first, I thought we were his guests. Now I suspect that Gus de Paor is footing the bill.'

'I don't like him.'

'Snap.'

'Are you going to do the fillum?'

'Jesus, don't you start.'

'I only asked.'

'No, I mean don't you start saying "fill-UM". It drives me round the twist.'

'Excuse me for living.'

'De Paor is one hell of a politician. Already he's put the kybosh on Thorn's idea for a restaurant. So if I refuse to do the film, then –'

'Then Thorn is bollixed.'

'Elegantly put. Yes, and on all fronts.'

'He's twisting your arm, isn't he? I mean de Paor is.'

'You're not just a pretty face. So what am I to do?'

'What do you want to do?'

'What do you want me to do?'

'Me? I couldn't care less.'

I said, angrily, 'You make it very easy for me to decide, you know that?'

She said, 'Oh, yes. Blame me.'

I attempted to take her arm and she pulled away. She said, 'Save that for –' and chopped off the rest of it.

I turned.

'Where are you going?'

'Back.'

She trailed after me. When the sails of Dromineer came in sight, she quickened her pace, and passed me without a look. By the time I reached the hotel, she was sitting with Prue at a table that looked out on the harbour and the lake.

'Ah, slowcoach!' she said with a show of perfect friendliness.

'Thorn is inside getting you a pint,' Prue said.

I made no attempt to join him. Either here and now or tomorrow on the drive home, he would remark on how long it had been since the pair of us had had one of our lunches. It was his twist, he would say, and he would suggest Les Trois Cloches or some place equally expensive. Over a liqueur, he would come at me with all guns blazing as he argued or pleaded or perhaps reminded me that he had given me my start with the O'Fearna archive. Thanks to him, I was on a journey which had begun with that one step. I thought of him wheedling and of me yielding, and remembered Greta pulling away from me on a country road. As he came out of the bar balancing the drinks, I said, 'Thorn, to save time and because I hate watching a grown man grovel, I've decided to take that job of de Paor's. Assuming the money isn't insulting.'

Thorn put the glasses down. He said, 'I see.'

'I asked Greta's advice while we were on our walk, and she doesn't care one way or the other. Right, Greta?'

She looked at me directly. 'Right. Absolutely.'

'Well, that makes two of us,' Thorn said. 'Because I honest-to-God don't give a shit either.'

I said: 'You're a liar.'

Prue laughed. 'Boys, boys.' Then: 'TJ, while you and Greta were gone, he said he didn't know what he'd do if you said no.'

'That's my loyal little wife,' Thorn said. He put out a hand to stop a passing barman. 'Get us a bottle of good champagne, will you? Your best, and like ten minutes ago.'

'Let's get this out in the open,' I said. 'It was you who gave me the job I have now. I owe you a big one, but that's not why I'm doing this picture. And neither is it to keep you out of the poor-house. And I'm not doing it, unbelievable though it may seem, to spite Greta.'

'To spite Greta? Why on earth would you want to?' Prue said.

Greta kept a small, bitter smile on her face

I said, 'And it's certainly not because I like the smell of de Paor's after-shave. I hate both him and it. I know he's what they call a role model of yours, Thorn, and that's your business. You're his court jester, and he'd cut your throat as soon as look at you. I'm doing it because all my life I've wanted to write a picture, and this could be the only chance I'll get.'

The barman returned with the champagne and glasses. People looked around at the popping noise. 'I'll pour,' Thorn said, and did so. He raised his glass into the spring sunshine. 'Here's to us, and *Return to Innisfree.*'

Three of us drank. Greta rose and picked up her glass. She smiled at Prue and her teeth chattered. She said, 'The three of you must have Eskimo blood in you. I'm freezing. I'm going to take this inside and drink it there.'

She actually said 'Brrr'. Otherwise it was most convincingly done.

Chapter Fourteen

At the Mimosa Garden

As sure as sunrise, Thorn called me on the Monday. Had he failed to do so after our Shannon weekend, I would have checked the death notices. He said: 'Lunch, yes?'

'Sorry, I have a date.'

'Ah, with *Il Mostro*!'

'Maybe. We should meet, though. Why not for coffee?'

'At your place?'

'Ah ... no, it's a bit cluttered.'

I preferred that our new venture should not come elbowing its way into my office, if only because it was the Widow O'Fearna who paid the rent. I told myself that she would hardly object to my working on a film script in my spare time, especially as the film I had in mind was what the French would call an *hommage* to Sean O'Fearna and *The Man from Innisfree*. And yet I funked the idea of telling her. In a sense, I was on the brink of leading two separate lives; it put me uneasily in mind of Josie the wife and Josie the mistress walking along different streets, both of them in dread of colliding.

Thorn and I met at a coffee shop in Dawson Street. He said: 'Your favourite man in all the world operates out of a suite in Fitzwilliam Square. He's converting half of it into a production office for Clew Bay Fillums and *Return to Innisfree*.' He cackled. 'Mine, all mine.'

'You and he will be co-habiting, then? Cosy.'

'That, as good old Dook Wayne used to say, will be the day. He's promised me: a free hand and no interference, and *I* promised *him*, any messing and he's history. Now that's for real, and don't raise an eyebrow at me, you hoor. Nobody has me in his pocket or ever will have. I may let them think so when it suits me, but I'm a bird-alone.'

'You were, up to now, yes.'

'And will be *in saecula*.'

I told him that Gus de Paor had already been spinning his web. Without troubling to ask me, his people had ferreted out the name of my agent, and by ten-thirty this morning Leon Esterman had called from London. 'This is a film with a pedigree,' he said, 'which already puts it in a major league.' He was being pressed, he said, for my declaration of intent. I told him I needed twenty-four hours.

'What's there to decide?' Thorn said. His voice shook.

'I want things to be right between you and me.'

'They *are* right!'

'So you say.'

Thorn said, 'And while we're sitting here, just the pair of us, please to remember that little speech you made in Dromineer. You said you were doing me no favours, and all you wanted was to write a fillum, full stop. But still and all, without you I would have been up that notorious creek without a –'

'Forget about that.'

'No, I won't forget it. No chance.'

He reached for my arm and got a handful of sleeve. If eyes could catch fire, his blazed and were at too close a range for my liking, and it was neither play-acting nor self-deception. It was as if I had been a close friend of a terrapin who had for the first time gone down-side-up, revealing a soft white underbelly. Out of embarrassment, I said, 'You know, Thorn, you're like an advertisement for a used car. You're guaranteed for life or sixty thousand miles, whichever expires first.'

He said, almost angrily, 'Don't make light of this, you fucker, you. You saved my life.'

'Is that what I've done?'

'Or at least you will do when you say yes to Gus.'

'Then protect me.'

'What?'

'From you. That's why we're sitting here. You're the producer, which makes you the boss. If you don't like what I write, then kick it out. And, if you do, then bugger you.'

'Thanks all the same.'

'But if you do like it, and if you're leant on, then I'm relying on you to protect what we've got.'

'Who would want to lean on me?'

'Who do you think? Gus de Paor for one. And his money-men.'

'Look, mate, you have my solemn word –'

'Spare me the solemn words. Think about it. It might mean putting your head on the block. So be very careful about this, or else include me out.'

He said, 'Trust me.'

'Do you know the last person I ever trusted? Greta, in the Church of the Holy Name, the day she said, "With my body I thee worship."'

He was silent for a moment, then he nodded. It was his turn to do the half-in-jest bit. 'Well, they say that second marriages are the good ones. Fair enough. I take thee for better or for worse and until death. Will that do?'

It would have to; so I said yes, and we talked about the film. I told him that Sean O'Fearna was dead and gone, and master-pieces were thin on the ground, but at least I wanted people to talk about this as 'the kind of picture they don't make any more'.

He said, 'No IRA bombs?'

'The only gun will be a starting pistol.'

'Gotcha.'

We talked so intensely and spun such dreams that it was a small shock to come to and realise that not a word of script had yet been written nor was there one scrap of film in the can. 'What are they putting in this coffee?' Thorn said.

Thanks to our colloguing, I was ten minutes late for my lunch with Josie. When I arrived at the Mimosa Garden, she was telling the Chinese waiter how to cure his backache. She said, 'Oh, I am so honoured you have come. I see that you can't wait to hear my story.'

'You mean today's the day?'

'I need your advice. I need it bad.'

'Bad-ly.'

She locked the adverb inside her head. Being corrected was to her liking. She still went through every day in a tearing hurry, and it pleased her when she could both chat and learn, as one takes two stairs at a time. And I was intrigued, because usually she was the one who gave advice; hardly ever did she ask for it. As the waiter went off, she said, 'I have ordered for you so as to save time. You always eat the same thing anyway. And I have asked him to bring a bottle of Sancerre.'

For a long time, she made no effort to speak. Then she said, 'I am not good at telling a story. For it to be interesting, maybe I could do what you do and put the ... the turn of it ... the ...' She made a gesture.

'Do you mean the twist?'

'*Si*, yes. Maybe I could put the twist at the end, or I could tell it another way, but which? No! I am not doing this to make an entertainment. I will tell it as it is.'

Her story was snarled up and would not come. It was connected, I at first thought, with the holiday she and Silvana had had on Exhuma. She rambled as my mother had done the day in the Roundwood Inn; then she got clear of the tanglewood and spoke of their homeward flight from Nassau to London. While her daughter slept, she had fallen into conversation with a shabbily-dressed man across the aisle. He told her that his wife had recently died. He and she had lived for many years in a slum area of Miami; now he was on his way to his native England to live with a married daughter in Wolverhampton.

He told Josie he was a rabbi. He said, 'Perhaps you are Jewish?'

Josie said, 'So I told him I was.'

I thought: *This woman is beyond belief.* I said, 'Why on earth did you tell a stupid lie like that?'

She picked up a chopstick and stabbed the thin end passionately against her chest. 'Because it is the truth. I am. I am.' She laid the chopstick down very carefully on its silver cradle. 'Or half of me is. What a strange man that rabbi was. He looked at me, and he knew. I tell you, he knew! So I told him all about myself: a story I have never spoken of to anyone, not to Andrew or Silvana or even Colleen, my best friend. I told him, this man, and now I tell you. Where is the bloody wine?'

She was becoming upset. I said, 'Take it easy. We have time.'

She looked at her gold Rolex. 'I have things to do, you know.'

I said, 'I swear that on the Day of Judgement, you will ask God to hurry it up because you need to see your chiropodist.'

She said, 'Now that is funny!'

The Sancerre came and was opened. She poured some into her glass and added mineral water to make a spritzer. She told her story, and if it were not that I had known her incapable of lying – at least to me – I would have taken it for the kind of fantasy a girl might weave in the lazy comfort of a warm bed on a winter morning.

Her father, she said, was Simon – born Shimon – Febreo. He was a left-wing journalist, a native of Rome. When he married a Gentile girl named Bionda Nardoni, his family, who were well-to-do Orthodox Jews, held a funeral service and mourned him as if he were dead. Josie had been told this by her adoptive parents.

I asked her, 'So what's your real name?'

Impatiently: 'I told you, Febreo.'

'I mean, your Christian name.'

'Christian! Now that's funny, too. My name is Miriam.'

In Rome, when the deportations began, Simon and Bionda

193

Febreo fled to Florence, where her uncle was a *monsignore* in charge of the Baptistery. He offered them sanctuary in a grace-and-favour apartment block held under the stewardship of the Archbishop. Here, they could live comfortably as long as they stayed off the streets. There were other Jews – too many – in other apartments, but at first the native *fascisti*, unwilling to make *escremento* on their own doorstep, left them alone. The Germans, too, stayed clear, but with a thinning reluctance. It was at that time that Bionda gave birth, or so the story went.

On June 4th, when news came of the Allied liberation of Rome, the Germans, like robots that could not be switched off, intensified their search for the Jews who had so far escaped the net. One morning, a detachment of the Waffen SS and – the most frightening sight of all – two empty trucks came into the complex. Simon Febreo took his infant daughter and carried her to one of the upstairs apartments. He knocked, uttered the two words 'Per favore,' and thrust the child into the arms of the middle-aged woman who answered.

As I listened to Josie's story, there came the faint sound of traffic on the Bray road outside the Mimosa Garden. The traffic lights changed. A bilingual street sign at the corner had originally said: 'Stillorgan – *Teach Lorcain.*' A jokester, using red poster paint, had crossed out the Irish name and instead translated Stillorgan as *Mici Marbh*, which was pidgin-Gaelic for 'Dead Penis'. The story that Josie was telling me did not belong in Dublin 14, within view of a bowling alley with twenty lanes, where Saturday evening's rubbish still clogged the gutters and no one cared enough to erase a six-month-old graffito. Jews and Nazis and camps were things you had long ago seen in Martian newsreels; there were even those who thought the war was Conrad Veidt being steely-eyed and learning that Claude Rains had rounded up twice the usual number of suspects.

'If you were no more than a baby then,' I said, 'how do you know all this?'

Josie answered without hesitation. 'Because my father knew that one day this might happen, so when I was born, he made a *documento*. I mean that he wrote down all that was necessary about the two families, his own and my mother's, with my name, too, and all that had to do with my birth.'

And with a date, I thought, *that was probably closer to 1939 than 1944*. Still, one white lie hardly made a liar.

She said: 'The Germans took him and my mother away to the camps. My new parents – well, how could they say "No?" How could they say "These young people, these Jews, they have left this *thing*, this *object*, with us?" Once upon a time, these two had said to God, "Thank you, but we do not want any children." And now God said to them: "Do not tell me what you want and what you do not want. Here is a child. Take care of her."

'So, my father, my papa, that is, who is dead for nine years now, he was a man of the nobility, a *principe*, and he went to talk to people who were high in the Vatican. And they went to other people, and these people tore up the certificate of my baptism – phttt!' – she ripped her paper table napkin into shreds – 'and gave me a new one with a new name: Giuseppina Belvedere. In case the Germans came back, you understand.' She smiled 'It is not a bad name!'

'And that became your maiden name?'

'Yes. It was the name of Papa's family. So I became "Josie-not-bad-to-look-at."'

'It fits.'

'I make sure it does.'

'And your real parents?'

'They died in the camp. My father is a hero, you know. There is a road in Israel which is made of gold paving stones, and his name is on one of these because he wrote things against the Nazis. Now, here is our lunch, and the story is already told.' She sounded almost pleased with herself.

'Is it?'

'What do you mean?'

'You wanted my advice.'

'Ah, yes. Now you must tell me what to do, but first, we must eat.' Even so, she could not wait. 'The man on the plane, the rabbi, he asked me if I had ever tried to find my true family. Perhaps, he said, some of them might still be alive.' She took out a handkerchief to wipe her eyes and, in spite of herself, laughed. 'I think he is trying to put me back among the Jews.'

'And *are* there any of them still alive?'

She looked at me in surprise.

I said, 'This was months ago, wasn't it? And you were never one to let the grass grow under your feet. So bring me up to date.'

She glared; I had put her nose out of joint. She snapped at me: 'You are so much like a knife you will cut yourself. How was your weekend in the lake, by the way?'

I said, '*On* the lake, not in it. It was eventful.'

'Oh? I suppose it was a very narrow bed, and you had to share it with your wife. Most uncomfortable!'

'It was two single beds.'

'Too bad, how sad!'

'Never mind my torrid sex life. Tell me what you found out.'

She made a face. 'I have a friend who has a friend who works for a newspaper in Firenze. He says that one person of this family survived the camps. He was a young man then; now he would be maybe seventy. I suppose he could be called my uncle Max. Max Febreo. They say that he has made much money.'

'So?'

'So should I get in touch with him?'

'Well, why not?' For once, she was genuinely at a loss. 'I don't want to go behind my mother's back. She is my family now, and it would not be loyal.'

'She doesn't have to be told. You say she's old.'

'She will soon be eighty.'

'Well, then. All you want to do is mend a few fences. It isn't betrayal.'

'Hmm.'

'Don't you owe it to your real parents?'

She nodded, slowly. And I knew that, whatever I might say, she had already set her course, for in Josie's case nature abhorred a stillness. She had not wanted advice from me, but approval. With finality, she said, 'Thank you! So you see, I am like you. We are both only half of what we thought we were.'

'So it seems.'

'Two halfs.'

'Halves.'

'Halves.' She laughed. 'Then together we are one.'

'Right on.'

'Well, what do you think of my story?'

I said, 'I can't believe any of it.'

She looked at me with her mouth open. A storm began to darken that magnificent brow. 'I see. I am a liar.'

'Not at all.'

'No? No? When you say you don't –'

'What I mean is, it's outside my experience. I can't take hold of it, that's all. I need time.'

She was not appeased. 'I think you are mad. This great ... this terrible' – she made a four-course meal of the word – '*cat-as-tro-fe* happened to millions of people, and yet you say you cannot –'

'I know it happened. All I mean is that because you were a part of it, then now so am I a part of it. I find it hard to grasp, that's all.'

'And yet you believe what I say?'

'Oh, yes.'

It was not quite true. A barb in her story had caught at me; then pulled free, like a hook that had not gone in deep enough. I tried to retrieve it, and, just as it was within reach, she broke the thread. 'I give up. You are a crazy man.'

A chafing dish was set down for our main course. She said, 'Now, you must tell me, this weekend on the lake, in which way was it so eventful? Did your wife make love to you?'

I told her about *Return to Innisfree*, which, when compared with her own story, now seemed piffling. Nonetheless, she was ecstatic. Like the impossible person she was, she said, 'And you wait until now to tell me!' Whatever doubts I had about Gus de Paor were brushed aside. To hear her talk, the film would be '*Citizen Kane* rolled into one'. She begged to be allowed to listen in and share the moment when I told Leon Esterman that I had decided to write the film. She looked at her wrist again. 'But do it now, *amore*, because today I really am very busy.'

She rooted in her bag to augment my change for the restaurant's pay-phone and stood with me when I called my agent. As I should have expected at lunchtime, Leon was out of his office. By the time I gave his secretary a message, Josie had waved a cheery goodbye and was already half-way to the BMW she drove like a Jehu.

Later that week, I flew to London and met my agent in a bistro near Sloane Square. It was a place for high-powered meetings and deals; and on the menu, as he pointed out, the grilled calves' liver was described as 'broiled' in deference to Americans. Leon was hawk-faced, and good company; his thinning black hair was combed from the side in a token attempt to cover his bare scalp. 'All my shortcomings,' he said, 'are out where you can see them.'

As promised, he told me the facts of life. He took a single sugar cube from a bowl. 'This is what they'll pay you for the first draft, right?' He placed the bowl containing the rest of the sugar – perhaps twenty cubes – a few inches away. 'And all this is what you get for the second draft. Lots of sugar.'

He took a table knife and laid it flat between the single sugar lump and the bowl. 'Now this is what is known as the Cut-off. After you deliver draft Number One, the producer will be free to say one of two things. He can say, "Yes, please write the second draft and take the sugar bowl home with you." Or he can cut you off. He can say, "Thank you very much. It was a nice try, but I think maybe we should say goodbye." He took the sugar bowl and tipped the contents into his jacket pocket.

The *patron*, standing nearby, said, 'He does this every week.'

'It's my party piece,' Leon said. 'And shit, I'm a diabetic and my pocket is full of sugar. My wife will cut my throat.'

He retrieved the lumps, one or two at a time. 'Naturally, you want to be employed to write Draft Number Two. So what you do is, you make Number One as good as you know how. The catch is – are you listening? – if you make it *too* good, then they don't need you any more. They take it away from you and give it to some hack for a quick rewrite and a polish. And they pay him two or three sugar lumps.

'So the trick is: walk a razor's edge. Make it good, but not great. Now, do you still want to write films?'

I told him about Thorn, who was to be my producer. He said, 'He sounds like the thorn without a rose. Oh, and by the way, did you ever hear about the Polish actress who wanted to do herself some good in a movie?'

'I'll bite.'

'She slept with the writer.'

I caught an afternoon flight home, and as I boarded the aircraft at Heathrow it came to me what there was about Josie's story that had stuck in my craw. To get to my seat, it was necessary to walk through Club Class to Economy or what Americans call Coach. I recalled that Josie had once quoted her husband Andrew's favourite aphorism: 'There are two classes: First Class and no class.' (And, in parentheses, I thought of Thorn's 'A gobshite is someone who flies economy.')

An image came into my mind of Josie and her daughter in First, sitting across the aisle from a down-at-heel rabbi who had lived and worked in the back-streets of Miami. Perhaps, I thought, his loving daughter in Wolverhampton had paid a

thousand pounds for his ticket and this was the legendary pie –
kosher, of course – in the sky. A likely story. Probably there was an
explanation that was as obvious as it was simple, but one I was
too dim to see. As I wedged my folded raincoat into the overhead
bin, I stowed my doubts away as well, locking them in the drawer
that held jealousies, distrusts and meannesses. Another question
came and tapped the first one on the shoulder. What was this
rabbi doing, not just in First Class, but on a flight out of Nassau?

When Claude Cockshot drove me home, Greta said I must be
tired, making me wonder if she had wrecked the car. She wanted
to know if the film contract was what she called all signed and
sealed. I told her: not yet; a deal would take weeks to be hammered out, but it was on its way.

She said, 'And will we have money?'

'Some, yes. Why do you ask?'

'It came into my head that I'd like to move.'

For an instant, such is guilt, I thought she was intending to
leave me. I felt a chill of dismay: an interesting reaction, I afterwards thought. She seemed taken aback by the look on my face.
She said: 'If you think we can afford it.'

I said, 'Where do you want us to move to?'

She said, 'There's a place here.' She spread out the property
pages of the *Irish Times*. 'You're going to laugh.' I felt her eyes
anxiously on my face as I looked down the page. Her finger
pointed at a photograph of a Martello tower.

I said, 'Jesus.'

It was on the sea, overlooking a beach two miles away. A previous owner had already made 'improvements', so that on the sea-
ward side, high curving windows took up a third of the
circumference. There was a roof garden, and a tacked-on cottage,
ominously described as 'bijou', had been converted into a kitchen,
second bathroom, and spare bedroom – or office for out-of-work
film archivist.

I caught sight of Greta's face a second before she looked

quickly away. Of course I was not to be let know how much she wanted it. She said, and there was a shiver in her voice, 'So what do you think?'

'I hope you know that's two-hundred-year-old granite a foot and a half thick. It would freeze your knickers off.'

'I'll wear thermals.'

'Well then, can we call it "Kate Fortune's Lane"?'

She hooted: 'Oh, you pup, you!'

I told her that next day, I would call the estate agent, but she should not get her hopes up, for Martello towers were attracting queues of eager purchasers. She turned her back to me and hugged herself. I said, 'You want this house, don't you?'

'Mmmp.'

'So what other news is there?'

'Hm? Shay rang, looking for you. Blanaid is having her twenty-first birthday party next month. He says she wants us to come.'

'*Us*?'

'He says it was because we were so good to her in her ...'

'Yes, I know, don't tell me. In her "trouble".'

'So I said we'd go. And let me see, what else? Oh yes! Who do you think I bumped into in town today, only your girlfriend.'

'And who might that be?'

'You know, Josie Hand.'

My heart lurched. Greta's smile was unforced. I had no idea if she was in a good humour because I had been amenable to the idea of our moving, or because it seemed preposterous to her that Josie and I could be having an affair.

'Did you and she talk?'

'Oh, yes. She asked how I was, and I asked how she was. Then she asked how you were. She said she was off to Italy to look up a long-lost uncle. I told her, "It's well for some."'

She laughed like a mischievous child and skipped off upstairs with the property pages of the *Times*. On the landing, she called down 'Will we go out tomorrow and look at the tower?'

'Sure, why not?'

'It's only ten o'clock. Could we go now?'

So we drove along the coast road and looked at the stubby Martello tower with its 'For Sale' sign. It was unoccupied and in a small cul-de-sac. We walked around it, away from the light of the single street lamp and down on to the sand of the beach. It was low tide; there was a smell of rotting weed.

Greta walked up the low groyne and laid her hands against the granite base of the tower. Probably she was more excited than even an 'Mmmp' could say. It was too dark to tell.

Chapter Fifteen

At Celebrations

The roof-garden of the Martello tower cried out for iced pitchers of Buck's Fizz on a Sunday morning in June, with the dog-walking *polloi* staring up in envy from the beach below. There was a suite of garden furniture and a cushioned swing-seat on which one could loll under a peppermint-striped awning. Flowers were bedded in tubs and shallow boxes studded with seashells. The fat estate agent, a comedian, said, 'If you treat yourself to a good telescope, you could be the first to see Napoleon arriving.'

'Yes,' I said, being devil's advocate, 'if the salt in the sea-spray doesn't fog up our windows.'

'If it what?' Greta said.

'If it makes them unsee-throughable.'

She made a face. She wanted the place too acutely to dance the necessary minuet and turn the smallest pimple into a disfigure-ment. I said, 'And of course there's no garage.'

'There's a good parking space at the side there,' Mr Trump-Lenihan said, looking over the edge.

'So there is,' I said, sounding as dour as I could. 'Touch the accelerator in mistake for the brake and you'll find yourself on the beach.'

'Ah, but isn't it great?' he said. 'I mean the proximity. Where else inside of twenty miles from here could you get up in the morning and walk from your front door into the sea?'

'I would die first,' I told him.

He knew that in Greta's case he had found an easy mark, a dove to the dovecote born. 'Come down, ma'am dear, and look at the fitted kitchen,' he said. 'Everything is *Tomorrow's World*. You'll go mad.'

She did, almost certifiably, and it was of no use my telling her that each and every gasp of delight she emitted put another thousand pounds on the asking price. As she poked into cupboards and drawers, I wandered into what would be my workroom and pictured it lined with bookshelves. Mr Trump-Lenihan's waistline butted me from behind. 'This would make a nice den,' he said.

'If we had a lion.'

He gave a Sydney Greenstreet laugh that was like a haemorrhaging volcano, and actually said, 'By Jove, sir, you're a character.' He had seen *The Maltese Falcon* once too often.

The room had a view of the Sugar Loaf seven miles to the south. I thought of my mother. I imagined her looking at the Martello tower with its panorama-windows that could see from Dalkey Island to Bray Head and heard her uttering what in the mouths of begrudgers was a jibe – although in her own life she had envied nothing and no one – 'Ah, *gradh machree*, it was far from it you were reared!'

I told Mr Trump-Lenihan that if we agreed to buy the place, it would be with the condition of a tilly from the vendor. 'A tilly, what's that when it's at home?' he asked, and I told him it was the extra half-cupful a milkman would pour out for his customers in addition to the daily pint. The tilly I wanted was the building of a low wall, a couple of feet high, between the parking place and the beach. 'You'll find the word in Chapter One of *Ulysses*,' I said.

'Well, sir, you won't find it here,' Mr Trump-Lenihan said, looking naked without Peter Lorre. 'The vendor tried to build a wall for himself, but planning permission was denied. They said it would spoil the view from the beach.'

'You and your tilly,' Greta said on the way home. 'I didn't know where to look.'

'Try the inside of my wallet,' I said, 'and say goodbye to whatever you find in it.'

I was spoofing, and she knew it. Thanks to the publisher's advance for the O'Fearna biography, we were already beginning to spread our wings; and, with luck and cunning, I would manage to stay ahead of the posse.

Ilse-Lazlo Huneker was happily beavering away; she had finished her labours in Maine and was now searching through baptism registers in the Connemara parish from which O'Fearna's parents had emigrated in 1882. She had paid me a visit at the archive, where I already had shoeboxes filled with the reminiscences I had cadged from the director's old cronies and co-workers. My part-time secretary – she whom Shay called Voilet – had again become pregnant; and I was fending for myself and making a horse's collar of it. Ilse-Lazlo was obliged to go hopping across a floor covered with sheets of paper. She sighed and hopped back to the door.

'Come on,' she said, 'we're going shopping.'

Within an hour, the Widow O'Fearna, all unbeknownst, had paid for what my researcher called a PC, to be delivered that afternoon, and within two days Ilse-Lazlo had put everything on what she called a hard disc, with – there was no end to the jargon – a back-up on floppy.

'Sir, when you hire a new secretary,' she said, 'make sure she can handle this baby. And *you* could do with a few lessons as well. Now I'm going to a place called Spiddal. That's in the West, right?' It would be another six months, I calculated, before I could actually be expected to sit down and start putting the biography on paper; meanwhile, the screenplay of *Return to Innisfree* would be comfortably done.

When I had driven Greta home from viewing the tower, I let her out at the bottom of our lane. I said: 'I have business in town. And we need to decide here and now about the house.'

'You mean the tower.'

'The bloody tower,' I said, christening it. 'So do you want it, yes or no?' I saw her lips coming together. 'And don't give me one of your *mmmps*, or I'll hit you with something. Are we buying the Bloody Tower or aren't we?'

She said, 'Can we afford it?'

I told her, 'Yes,' and waited.

She had the kind of shrug that could only be removed by major surgery. She said, 'Then I suppose so.' Even that much, she felt, was degrading, and she got out and slammed the car door.

Thirty minutes later, I called Mr Trump-Lenihan from the archive and offered his asking price, less a thousand pounds. He would call back, he said, with the vendor's answer. He gave me another cavernous laugh as a tilly of his own. Meanwhile, both Thorn and Josie had left messages. When I spoke to Thorn, he was walking on air; the Irish Film Awards dinner was next week, and Prue had been shortlisted as best supporting actress. Would we help to make up a table? I told him yes, gladly.

When I returned Josie's call, she said that she was travelling to Florence next day.

'I heard. I gather you're looking up a long-lost relative.'

'That was my message to you. You see how clever I am, to let your wife carry my messages.'

I said, 'I hope you're not poking fun at her.'

'Why? Would that hurt your feelings?'

'Oddly enough, yes.'

'She seemed in high spirits. You must be making her very happy.'

'As a matter of fact, I am. I've just bought her a new house.'

'Never!'

'At least I think I have. I've made an offer.'

'I suppose it is in some lonely place that is miles and miles away, and I will never see you again.'

'You have a nerve. You're in Florence most of the time.'

'My mother is old, and she is sick.'

'What on earth will you do when she finishes her spaghetti?'

'Pardon me?'

I said, 'If this is your way of getting me used to life without you, you're doing a good job.'

I mouthed her standard reply, soundlessly, an instant before she spoke it. '*What*? Are you mad?'

'How long will you be away?'

'As long as I am needed. Perhaps a month.'

When I got home, Greta had declared all-out war on 'Kate Fortune's Lane', and was making high drama of trying to close a cupboard door that had not shut properly in years. 'God, I hate this place,' she said, giving it a vicious slam. 'Nothing works and nothing fits.' As I sat and slowly unfolded the evening paper, she glared at me. 'Well?' She wanted news.

Innocently: 'Yes?'

Her face said that she was not in a humour to be provoked, so I affected to remember a piece of trivia that had slipped my mind. 'Ah, but of course. I had a call from Sydney Greenstreet.'

'From who?'

'The estate agent. Trump-Whatsit.'

'Go on?' Her voice was trembling.

'Offer accepted. We own the Bloody Tower. Oh, and I made him throw in the garden furniture.'

Rather than watch Greta struggling not to be overjoyed I raised the paper again. She went into the scullery, and I heard a snuffle and the rattle of a paper towel on its spool.

Blanaid's birthday party and the Irish Film Awards dinner happened in the same week, two days apart. For the first event, Shay and Brigid had hired a functions room in Paddy Pride's, a roadhouse overlooking the city. Most of the guests were of Blanaid's age; and the few older people, friends of Shay and Brigid, occupied an alcove around a corner from the disco music. One of these was Shay's tall, hare-lipped brother-in-law, Billy Dungan, who, to use the common euphemism for a ruffian, styled himself an entrepreneur. Five years previously, Shay had agreed to be guarantor in the matter of a bank loan and was left to pay when Billy defaulted.

'I hear he's rolling in it these days,' I told Shay. 'Why don't you ask him for the money?'

'I would never do that,' Shay said, firmly. It would have been against the Code. It was in character that among those he chose to invite to Blanaid's party were Billy and his wife – a glamorous creature who, among her marital trophies, counted a solitaire diamond and two nervous breakdowns.

The music seemed to get louder as the evening wore on, and the conversation between the older guests was reduced to either bellowing or a mime play of grins. At one point, Billy led Shay away towards the comparative quiet of the public bar. He came back alone, perhaps twenty minutes later.

'Shay is not feeling all that great,' he said.

I found Shay in the car park, licking a forefinger and pointing it towards the night sky.

'What are you doing?'

He mumbled: 'I'm trying to find out which way the friggin' wind is blowing so's I don't get sick into it.'

'Come with me.'

I led him out and across the road to a ditch with a field beyond. Cattle moved in the dark. On my advice, he took his teeth out and put them in his pocket, and after a few minutes the night air did its work, and he threw up while I kept my eyes trained on the lights of the city. We sat on the raised edge of the ditch. He was still very drunk: a remarkable achievement in only twenty minutes.

'It's Billy Dungan's fault,' he said.

'I know.'

'He toppled me off the wagon.'

'You're entitled. I mean, the one night that's in it.'

The music was faint, but still audible, and through the lighted windows of Paddy Pride's we could see the kids windmilling around.

'Poor old Blanaid,' he said. 'She isn't the worst of them.'

'She's a great girl.'

'You think so, do you?'

I said, 'Yes, I do.'

He had turned his head to look at me, and in the half-dark, I could sense that there was something in his face besides friendship.

He said, 'You think I let myself down, don't you?'

If he had only been sober, we could have talked and put an end to it. I could have welcomed him to the club, where the entrance fee was an acceptance of one's own fallibility. Things had already shifted between us. He came less often to Tish Merdiff's, pleading that he had a play to review or a chore to do. It was no good my suggesting another evening in the week; for him, it had to be a Monday or nothing. Our colloguings had turned into mono-logues; if I brought up a topic – a new play, perhaps, or a piece of political chicanery – he would launch into a kind of verbal analy-sis that went on for minutes and included arguments pro and con, a summing up and a verdict, and ended with Shay dressing the subject in its hat, coat and gloves, escorting it out into the street and closing and bolting the door after it. It was friendship by numbers. I wanted to bring the whole business of Blanaid out into the open, but the open was where it did not belong. I wanted to tell Shay the truth, that he was a more admirable person than I could hope to be, but I suspected that deep within himself, under his very genuine humility, he knew his worth already and treas-ured it like a pearl.

He said, and now there was hostility in his voice, 'You do, don't you, you bugger, you? You think bad of me?'

I got up and said, 'Not at all. Now you take it easy. I want to tell Greta it's near going-home time. And I'll send Brigid out to you.'

As I left him sitting there on the lip of the ditch, he shouted

'Who are you to think bad of me?' I thought of the blow he had aimed at me at the wedding and hoped that this evening would be forgotten in the same way. So it proved; even so, I knew I was for the chop. The court was ready to pronounce sentence, but first it needed the formality of an offence.

On the Friday, Greta and I got dressed up and drove to the Royal Ranelagh Hotel for the film awards dinner. In what Batty Kenirons called her acceptance frock the shortlisted Prue glided rather than walked. 'God, Prunella,' the Oozer said, 'you look piss-elegant. Have you your speech ready?'

Thorn stayed close to his wife. Whenever she was congratulated, he said: 'It's all very straightforward. If they don't give this woman the award, then they're mutton, as dead as. I kill them, it's that simple.'

The room was crowded. The famous and the footling rubbed shoulders. Mutton was dressed as lamb, and lamb as mutton, and cries of 'Darling!' were cooed, cried, shrieked and spat. Household names went by, as real as real and yet unmolested. The frail grand old lady of Irish theatre, known as Bambi-with-Fangs, had never seemed more benign. I caught sight of Colleen and Turlough, who were to share our table. Colleen said: 'Everybody is here.'

'I know,' Kenirons said, adding, according to a logic of his own, 'the food is going to be seriously poxy.' He added: 'And look. The bollix quotient is high.' I followed his nod and saw, bearing down on us, a sky-blue dinner jacket topped by a granite head. Gus de Paor shook hands all round.

'You here?' I said when my turn came.

He said, 'You seem surprised.'

'I didn't see the helicopter.'

He gave a roar of laughter that made it halfway up his face. He said to Thorn, 'A word in your ear', put an arm around his shoulders and led him away without apology.

Prue said, mock-plaintively, 'He didn't congratulate me!'

'Maybe with him you have to win first,' Greta said.

'Well, now,' I said, impressed.

Kenirons gave Greta a bear-hug. 'She's not much for quantity, this one, but by the lord Jasus, you'd never see the bating of her for quality.'

Thorn returned just as the assembly was summoned to table. 'What did Pooh-Bah want?' I asked. 'Nothing,' Thorn said. 'Just playing the big fellow. And you know, you ought to go easy on him. Underneath all the showing off, he's a decent skin.'

Since Prue was a finalist, our table was close to the stage. Sixteen trophies, ready to be presented, were arrayed on a stand. 'The pair of us will be up for one of those next year,' Thorn said as we sat.

There was a still-unoccupied chair. 'It's for my bit of stuff,' Kenirons said. 'She's attending a do and might be running late.'

'Batty, you have a lady friend!' Colleen said. 'When did this happen?'

'Erra, it didn't,' the Oozer said. 'I'm running her in for a friend.' He took a small leather-covered flask from his pocket and poured some of the contents into his still-empty wine glass. 'John Jameson,' he said. 'Antidote against ptomania.'

'What do you mean, you're running her in?' Thorn asked. 'Who is she?'

'She is my solicitor,' Kenirons said. 'No, true as God. She's handling my divorce from Miss America. The Bostonian bitch is suing on the grounds of extreme cruelty – alleging that I bring the coffee pot to the kettle instead of the kettle to the pot.' He was in vintage form. He leaned forward. 'Now all of ye listen to me,' he said. 'What I am about to tell ye is on no account to go beyond this table.'

Colleen, who was so close that she could have eaten his ear, said, 'Batty, don't gossip.'

'This woman' – indicating the still empty chair.

'Your solicitor,' Thorn said, winking at me.

'She is carrying on,' the Oozer said, 'with a certain gentleman, who is in this room tonight under heavy escort.'

'He's married, you mean,' Prue said, 'and his wife is with him?'

'You said it; I didn't,' the Oozer said. 'And no, I don't know who he is, I honest to God don't, and if I did, ye wouldn't get it out of me, not with pincers.'

'Not much we wouldn't,' Turlough said.

'I love you, too.' Kenirons blew him a kiss. 'He is riding the arse off her –'

'Batty!' Prue said, her Church of Ireland soul recoiling.

'And she is so smitten, that she cannot even forego the chance of a glimpse of him across this crowded room. Whoever he is. Anyway, she asked me to do the needful. I am what they call a beard.'

'A beard is a woman covering up for a homo,' Turlough said.

'Erra, poetic licence,' the Oozer cackled.

'Some women are born stupid,' Prue said.

'And most men,' Greta said.

'I myself am a terror with the ladies,' Thorn said.

'Oh,' Prue said, fondly, 'don't we know!' She pointed a finger at her husband. 'That man is the most outrageous flirt imaginable. I mean, I know he's harmless, but God in His mercy help the poor woman who takes him seriously.'

Thorn was all but preening himself.

'Do you know what he did not all that long ago?' I said.

'Now, now,' Thorn said.

'It was in a shop in Nassau Street,' I said, 'and it was the greatest pick-up line I ever heard in my life.'

'Now you're not to tell that cod of a yarn,' Thorn said, his face begging me to do so.

I told the story. It was the one that ended with him saying to an attractive stranger: 'I happen to be a mild diabetic, and there are lots of things I mustn't touch, but you, whoever you are, will never be one of them.'

Everyone laughed, and Prue shrieked: 'Oh, you villain, you! What am I married to?'

Kenirons said, 'Christ, I'll write that down.'

'You're not diabetic,' Turlough said.

'I'll infect meself.'

'Dreadful, dreadful!' Prue said, adoring Thorn. 'Oh, wait till I get you home.' He went red with pleasure.

Food was served, and, as the Oozer had predicted, it was awards dinner cuisine: dried-up roast beef, twice-cooked vegetables and bars of Lifebuoy in the guise of potatoes; and, to disarm any complaints, it was served by grandmotherly waitresses.

When Kenirons abruptly stood up, Colleen said, 'Batty you're not leaving?', but he had done so to welcome his guest, who had arrived at last. She was a petite, thirtyish woman, dark and attractive, in a form-clinging dress. 'I'm sorry to say you're in time for dinner,' the Oozer said. He introduced her around the table as Anna-Livia McGurk.

'I don't use the Livia bit,' she said.

'Go 'way out of that, it suits you,' Kenirons insisted.

'You're a solicitor?' Thorn said.

'The legal kind,' she said, brightly. 'And I'm sorry for being so disgracefully late. One of our partners is retiring, and of course there were drinks. A few too many, I'm afraid.'

As a waitress put a plate of food in front of her, she said, 'Oh, lovely,' and Kenirons said, 'That proves it. She's footless.'

She said, 'I can see you're all friends, and I hope no one minds my being here. Batty is a friend of mine as well as a client, and he insisted.'

She was charming, and there was a chorus of reassurance.

Kenirons said, 'This woman is a fierce liar. She implored me to bring her, so as she could be near her beloved.' To Anna-Livia he said, 'I've been telling them all about you.'

She said 'Oh, Batty, you haven't.'

Thorn said, 'He has.' Then, to Kenirons, 'That's your divorce gone up the spout.'

I thought of Josie and had an image of the only too aptly-named Oozer broadcasting our affairs – affair, that is – across every dinner table in town. Perhaps he had already done so. I said, coldly, 'Batty, you have a mouth the size of Kerry.'

Greta, on my side as usual, said, 'Leave him alone.'

If one looked closely, it was noticeable that Anna-Livia had been drinking; her speech was too emphatic, and one arm, when she gestured, was a stranger to the other. She said, 'Batty is very naughty, but I'm afraid it's true. I wanted to be near the man of my dreams.'

'And do you see him here?' Kenirons asked, enjoying himself.

We all looked around, instinctively. Anna-Livia gave a mock sigh: 'Yes, I see him. So near and yet so far!' She became suddenly demure. 'I'm so sorry. I'm embarrassing all of you.'

There was a murmur of 'No, no' and 'Not a bit of it', and Colleen, honest to the last, said, 'Well, yes, I am embarrassed, but I am enjoying myself.'

We settled down and talked small-talk. Dessert, a fruit salad fresh from the tin, was served. Kenirons topped up his guest's wine glass and said, 'Is it true what they say about you, Anna-Livia, that you have a hollow leg?' She had a warm laugh.

There is a native proverb that says *The nearer the heart, the nearer the lips*, and it was so with Anna-Livia. Once the subject of her lover had been broached, she was reluctant to let it lie. Also, her hollow leg seemed to be filling up. About her affair, she told us she wasn't that kind of girl. We said we knew, we knew. She told us he was a man in a thousand. We said that he must be, he must. She told us that he and she were being discreet and harming no one. We said ah, well, that was the main thing.

Then she gave a little laugh and said, 'Will I tell you how I met him? I mean, this is priceless, and what woman could resist?'

In a sudden crazed premonition, the undigested roast beef all but returned into my throat. Anna-Livia launched into her story and, as in a nightmare, I heard her saying: '... and I bumped into him in two shops, one after the other, and he said as how he was only a mild diabetic, but all the same there were loads of things that he wasn't let touch. And, says he, the cheek of him: "But you, whoever you are, will never be one of them."'

All around us there was the table-talk of perhaps four hundred people and the clatter of cutlery, plates and glasses, and yet my impression was of the silence of outer space. Thorn took hold of the table edge with both hands. He said, 'Actually, that story TJ told was one I passed off to him as my own. It was –'

Anna-Livia saw his face, and we all saw hers. Prue screamed three times. The first scream was quite small, a warm-up; then came a louder one; and finally there was a Fay-Wray-meets-Maria-Callas of a scream that ripped through the ballroom.

There was silence, this time a real one. People stood to see, and one of them was Gus de Paor. Prue ran from the table, and Thorn sat still for too long, then went after her. Colleen said, 'Batty, you had better, please, get this lady out of here.' As the Oozer took her arm, Anna-Livia said 'Oh, my God' several times on a rising scale. She might have been giving a master class in hysterics.

People sat down and talk started up again. I had a mental image of Gus de Paor coming over to ask what was up with Prue. *If he does*, I thought insanely, *I'll tell him she found out that she wasn't one of tonight's winners*. I began to laugh. 'What's up with you?' Greta said angrily. Then Colleen, too, laughed at some madness of her own.

De Paor stayed away from us, and after a time Thorn came back. 'She's gone home,' he said. He looked at Anna-Livia's empty chair. 'Where's the other one?'

'She's gone, too,' I told him.

'Maybe they can share a cab,' Turlough said

Colleen stuck a handkerchief in her mouth and ran towards the ladies', shedding small hiccuping sobs.

'Maybe I ought to go home,' Thorn said.

'You can't,' I told him. 'If Prue wins, you'll have to go up to accept it.'

'Oh, Christ. And say what?'

'Did you ever hear tell,' Greta said, 'or did anybody ever hear tell, of a person in this town saying fuck-all?'

As it happened, Prue did not win, and Thorn was spared a further humiliation. As soon as the award for best picture had been made – it went to a determinedly glum version of *Romeo and Juliet* set on the Bogside – we drove him home to Wilton Place. By then, he was drunk.

'There are two dogs on the doorstep,' he said.

'Those are suitcases,' Greta said.

He rattled his keys, got out of the car, went up the steps and attempted and failed to open the front door. He rang the bell then thumped the door with his fists. The house was dark; no one came. He began to shout: 'Prue, open up.' Across the canal, a light came on. Thorn said, 'You Protestant bitch, you cow, let me in.' He kicked the door. Another light came on.

'Get his suitcases,' Greta said. 'He can stay with us.'

To my surprise, Thorn was docile once I took his arm. 'You're with friends,' I said.

'Friends, yes,' he said. 'What else have I? Take me to Gus's place.'

I was hurt; I was even jealous. 'If you mean Gus de Paor,' I said coldly, 'he's still at the awards.'

'He has servants. He has lackeys. They will give me shelter. You just ... deliver me.'

I nursed a vain hope that he would fall asleep and be quiet during the eight-mile drive to Ravello Road. Instead, he fulminated against Prue, who had dared lock him out of his own house. Who did she think she was? He had no doubt that she was already poisoning the minds of his children. He cursed Anna-Livia McGurk for daring to turn up half-cut, and at our very table. She ought, he said, to be fucking-well struck off. He called Kenirons several kinds of benighted gobshite for oiling the hinges of Anna-Livia's big mouth. I waited for my own turn to come for a whipping, but he took another tack.

'It's people, do you see? You have to turn against them, you have to cast them off before you lose control and they destroy you. Then you're free. That's the badge of integrity. That's where power is.'

I had once told him what was inscribed on Nikos Kazantzakis's grave over looking Heraklion, and he quoted it back at us now with a boozy grandiloquence that sent the Cretan spinning in his box. 'I fear nothing. I expect nothing. I am free.'

'Thorn, nobody wants to be on their own,' Greta said.

'Well, it seems as if I am,' he said. 'And I'm a happy camper.' From the back seat, he said into my ear: 'What am I, then?'

'A happy camper,' I said.

'Attaboy.'

Chapter Sixteen

In Fiesole

When Shay and I met at Tish's on the Monday following Blanaid's party, there was no hint that it was to be our last time.

'I fell from grace at Blanaid's do last Wednesday,' he said.

'What harm?' I said.

'Was I obstreperous?'

'Not in the least.'

He ground his dentures with determination. 'From this out, I'm going to watch myself.'

All was as usual. He drank his three or four pints of alcohol-free and delivered a couple of monologues; we parted amicably, and I took his word for it when, on subsequent Mondays, he pleaded that he was either reviewing a play or being somebody's good neighbour. Perhaps he was.

As for Josie, the earth – or Italy – seemed to have swallowed her. One day, I telephoned the house on Raglan Road, and Silvana answered. She said, 'Mum is still abroad. Granny's not well.' Because of Josie's passion for privacy, I had never asked for her number or address in Florence, nor had she offered either.

The silver lining in both cases was that for six days a week I was able to work on the film script without distraction or let-up. The only interruption was on Saturdays, when gawkers came streeling through 'Kate Fortune's Lane', which now had a 'For Sale' sign in the tiny front garden. The screenplay got into its stride once I had acquired the knack of writing with my eyes rather than my ears, and I touched base with Thorn every other day. For more than three weeks, he was Gus de Paor's house-guest and preferred not to speak or be spoken to on the subject of Prue. Over lunch, we discussed the evolving script with the excitement of two expectant parents.

One of my rare evenings off was when Gore Vidal came to town as part of a lecture tour; his subject was 'The Hollywood Subversives – King Vidor and Others'. The venue was the Irish Film Centre, with a touch-the-hem wine-and-cheese party beforehand, and I had been asked to chair the proceedings. My chum, Liz Meara, was still the director of the Centre and our friendship, so she said, had earned us the nickname in the Centre of Bonnie and Clyde – 'Don't laugh,' she said. 'You're Bonnie.' She and I happily performed an effortless double-act as party hosts – Greta had chosen to stay at home, saying that she had never heard of King Vidor and was not too certain about Gore Vidal.

The evening held two surprises. The first was when I saw Thorn and Prue coming in together. In a kind of vivacious Scott and Zelda performance, they seemed to be joined affectionately at the hip. Thorn said, with a retch-inducing smile, 'I'm back in the old homestead. She forgave me.'

'Don't be too sure,' Prue said playfully. 'He's very much on probation.'

He ferried his coat and hers to the cloakroom. While he was doing so, I said, 'I really am glad the pair of you made it up.'

Prue kissed my cheek and said, 'I know that.' For a moment I thought she was about to cry.

I said, 'Hey, are you putting on an act?'

She said: 'Well, why not? An actress is what I am.'

'What's up?'

'I want to go on *being* an actress, that's what's up. Let's just say that I was advised to give Thorn another chance. Let's just say that I was advised most persuasively. Let's just say I was reminded that I am still a young woman and with a career ahead of me. And –' As Thorn came back, she said loudly, for his benefit, 'but I'm sure I won't regret it.'

'Who advised you?'

She gave me a look, and I held my tongue. I suppose I knew.

The second surprise came a few minutes later. Mr Vidal had arrived and was surrounded by the kind of no-nonsense Irishwomen who knew that homosexuality could be cured by cold baths laced with Lourdes water. Liz and I were greeting the incoming audience, among whom were Silvana, and a boyfriend, Jonathan. She seemed taken aback to see me. I introduced them to Liz and asked, 'How is your mother?'

Silvana said, 'She's fine. As a matter of fact, she's here.'

'She's what?'

'Or she will be when she's found parking. There she is now.'

Josie came towards us. She caught sight of me, and I knew her so well that I could even register the nanosecond her brain took to recover. 'Well, well,' she said, trying on a *pret-à-porter* smile. 'What a nice surprise!'

'Ditto,' I said. 'I thought you were in Florence. When did you get back?'

'Yo-yo,' Silvana said, moving away from her mother.

'What's "yo-yo"?' I asked.

She spelled out the acronym. 'You're on your own.'

I slid an affectionate arm around Liz's waist and made the introduction: 'Liz Meara ... Josie Hand.' Liz, if she was surprised, was nonetheless a quick study; she responded in kind by wriggling her hip affectionately against mine. She unwound my arm and said, 'Excuse me. I think Mr Vidal is being lionessed.' Josie watched her go.

She said, 'She is very attractive.'

'Isn't she! So, how long have you been back from Florence?'

'Four weeks.'

'I see.'

She looked towards the guest of honour. I said, 'You'll excuse me if I don't introduce you to Mr Vidal. Our groupie quota is full.'

The public smile went away; she turned, walked across the foyer, spoke quickly to Silvana and went out into the street. My heart was actually thudding. I was more angry with myself than with her; it was as if I were a one-time cigarette smoker who had thought of himself as almost home free, and then, catching one whiff of the weed, found himself back at Day One.

The guest of honour was at my side. 'Mr Quill, I am told that since this is Ireland I am likely to be the least witty person in the room. I hope you're not going to be too hard on an inarticulate visitor.' Mr Vidal had no need to worry that, as chairperson, I might steal his thunder; thanks to my encounter with Josie, I was ditchwater.

Naturally, she called next morning. 'I don't like to be insulted.'

'I call it to be insulting not to get as much as a hello for four weeks.'

'Yes, I should have been in touch. I am sorry.'

'You're sorry? Is that *all*?'

'Who was that woman?'

'Pardon me?'

'That woman you put your hand on in front of me.'

'That was for your benefit.'

'I thought it was for yours. I suppose, like all the people you suppose are your friends, she makes use of you.'

This was a new one. I said, 'Say that again?'

'You are an important person now, and yet you still have the belief that people like you for yourself.' She said, sadly, wisely, probably shaking her head: 'It is no matter. You will find out.'

I wanted to escape from this. I said, 'The lady's name is Liz Meara. She and her husband are separated. She has a teenage son with motor neurone disease, and she is too busy looking after him to go fucking around with men, married or single.'

'You are in a very bad humour today.'

'I think we should meet.'

'Ah. Now let me see ...'

'And please don't tell me you're busy. As regards what you get up to in Florence, I haven't the remotest idea, and I'm beginning not to care' – which was a brazen lie – 'but here you have no friends except Colleen, who has a family to look after, and all your non-stop running around ever adds up to is sweet fuck-all.'

'That is twice you have used that word to me.'

'Things happen in threes.'

She said: 'I can meet you for coffee.'

I suggested the Nora Barnacle. Coming up to midday, the coffee shops were crowded, but the pubs were still empty; and the walk across town to Baggot Street should have – but didn't – put me in better temper. I was angry at the suggestion, a put-down, that all my friends were hangers-on.

She came in wearing what I thought of as her Arrivals face; whenever we met, she smiled as if that moment was the summit of her day. She said, 'This place is very romantic.'

'Is it?'

'For me, it is. It is where we had our first rendezvous.'

I signalled to the barman for coffee and neither of us spoke again until it was brought. The question I had to ask had only three words in it, but it almost choked me. 'Is it over?'

'What? Excuse me. Is what over?'

'Us. You and me. Is it done with?'

We both spoke together: '*Are you mad*?'

She ignored the sarcasm. 'Yes, it is over, if you want it to be. But no, no, for me it will never be over. What is in your head that you should ask such a thing?'

Meeting in an empty pub had not been such a good idea. The barman had nothing else to look at except two people talking into each other's face in angry half-whispers.

I said: 'Look, don't waste me.'

'Excuse me?'

'Four fucking weeks.'

'Ah, thank you, there is the third one!'

222

'And how many weeks would it have been if you had not come to the Film Centre last evening? Or if I had not been in the company of a woman as attractive as Liz Meara? How many, then? Do you know, I've forgotten what you look like in profile?'

'Profile?'

'Sideways on.'

'What crazy talk is that?'

'We meet at the Mimosa Garden or like now, in a booth. We see each other face to face. I don't even have the small pleasure of sitting next to you. Or of doing this.'

I snatched a quick, cautious glance at the barman, who seemed to be poring over the *Sun*. I reached out and took hold of her breast. She gave a small moan, as of awakened lust, and said, 'Don't.'

I said, 'Am I supposed to think you were turned on by that? That's whore talk. Am I some bogman up from the country, who has to be prick-teased out of the few quid he makes out of selling his cattle? And if you get angry, it's because you're not even listening to me. You say "Eet weel nevair be over," but you couldn't even pick up a phone, not once in four weeks. And when you do call, like today, what I get is a put-down. No, don't interrupt. Let me say this. You're a selfish bitch and a spoiled one, too, but even so you should know that people are not to be wasted, and that includes me. In your case, me especially.'

She looked at me resentfully, like a punished child. 'Are you finished?'

'Not yet. I want something from you. A gift.' Now, I thought, she was listening to me instead of to herself, while she wondered what would send me away appeased. 'I want you to give me back my life. Just tell me to go. It's as easy as that.'

She was silent. When she spoke, she said quietly: 'I can't say "Go," *amore*, because "Go" would be a lie.' She opened her bag and reached for a handkerchief. 'Damn you, damn you. I am not well. I am sick. Now go on, say "seeck" and make more jokes at me.'

223

'Sick? What's wrong with you?'

'I don't know. I am to have tests ... not here, but with my doctor in Firenze. Nobody knows, not Andrew, not Silvana, not my mother, nobody. Only now you know, because you make me afraid I might lose you. You are not to tell.' She fell into stage-Italian. 'Otherwise, I break-a da thumbs.'

'I won't tell.'

'So I said to myself that I would not call you until I was better. Or until I was worse.' She gave a small laugh. 'The doctor, he said it was important not to worry. And now I have that old Jew as well.'

'*What* old Jew?'

'I told you. This man, Max Febreo, who is my uncle.'

'You got in touch with him?'

'I wrote to him, two times. I said, "I want nothing from you except to say that I am the daughter of your brother, Simon. I am telling you that I am alive, that I am in the world."'

'Well?'

Her story took no more than five minutes to tell. Her first letter had gone unanswered. The second was replied to by a woman who said that she was acting for Signor Febreo. Her name was Clara Armetta. She might have been a lawyer, a mistress or a friend of the family; she gave no indication. She proposed a meeting between herself and Josie. They had lunch. She was youngish and friendly in a guarded way. It took only that first meeting for Clara to accept that Josie was not an impostor and had no motives other than to make contact with her only blood relative. 'But Signor Febreo is a very difficult man,' this woman said.

'Clara and I are good friends now,' Josie said. 'But Uncle Max! The old bastard refuses to see me.'

'But why?'

'Why? Because my father married my mother who was a Gentile! Can you believe it? Even dead, he is not to be forgiven!

224

But maybe this uncle did see me. Maybe when I had lunch with Clara, he was at another table, looking at me. Who is to say? Anyway, after all my trouble, after I have exposed myself, this is the end of it. *Finito.*'

The cymbals clashed. She went for her handkerchief again and dried her eyes. She attempted to smile. 'I meet you for coffee, and I have done nothing but cry. First, it is your fault; now it is his.'

'Look,' I said. 'You got in touch. If he chose not to respond, then so much the worse for him.'

She shrugged.

'May I say that word for a fourth time? Fuck him.' Then, being a born phrasemaker, I said, 'You can't win 'em all.'

She reached out as if to touch my hand, looked at the barman and thought again. 'Thank you, *amore.*'

And yet, as if in proof that nothing would ever change, she looked at her watch. I made no comment; this one, I decided, was on the house. Instead, I asked 'When are you going back to Florence?'

'Next week. I must have these tests.'

'But this time, you are to keep in touch.'

'I swear it.'

Even as she spoke, I remembered Silvana's face when she saw me at the Vidal lecture. She had almost said 'Uh-oh,' as if I had been someone not gladly encountered. This time, I was not at all surprised when Josie failed to keep her promise. Six weeks went by, and there was silence. In the meantime, 'Kate Fortune's Lane' had fetched less than we hoped and the Bloody Tower had cost more. Neither Greta nor I was good with money, but Sydney Greenstreet explained all by saying that we had been in a buyers' market when we sold and a sellers' market when we bought.

Josie called my office as I was collating the first draft of *Return to Innisfree.*

'Amore?'

'You? Where are you?'

'In Firenze, of course. Where would I be? Listen to me, the old bastard has been kidnapped, and it serves him right.'

'He's been *what*?'

'In Italy it is an industry. They kidnap businessmen. They send a message: "One million *lire* or we will cut his thing off."'

I was Alice falling down the rabbit hole. 'Thing? What thing?'

'Don't be stupid. The thing he makes pipi with.' She giggled. 'And the best part is, he cannot pay the *riscatto* … the ransom, unless they let him go, and they will not let him go until he pays the *riscatto*. Is this what you call the Catch-22?'

I was still in free-fall. Because of her illness, I had expected Bette Davis in *Dark Victory* and she was giving me Cagney in *Each Dawn I Die*. 'You promised to get in touch and you didn't. How did the tests work out?'

'Bad, bad. I must go. I am with Clara.'

'No, wait. What do you mean "bad, bad"?'

'Is not this the most fantastic and hilarious news?' She pronounced it 'hil-arry-us.' Her gloating laugh was a kind of *heh-heh-heh*. 'Ciao, amore.'

'Hold on …'

Canute had more success reversing the tide. She was gone again, and I hung up and put her into what, as far as I was concerned was the back pocket of my life.

I sent the completed film script to Thorn by messenger that afternoon. At one in the morning, the telephone rang at home. Greta's voice in the dark whispered, 'My God, who's that?' We were still wait-listed for an extension phone, so I went down to the hall. I wondered, against logic, if I would hear Josie's voice giving all of Florence a sleepless night by crowing that the kidnappers had cut her uncle's thing off. Instead, the caller was Thorn.

'I know, don't say it, it's all hours. I wanted you to know that the script is fantastic. I showed it to Prue and she, crafty hoor that

226

she is' – a dutiful whoop of protest came from the background – 'has put her finger on the nub of it. She says that it has Irish charm instead of Oirish whimsy. We're on to a winner, and we'll defend this one to the death. Your agent will have a cheque by the weekend. Now go back to sleep.'

Greta was out of bed and at the head of the stairs. 'Who was it?'

'Thorn. He says the script is wonderful.'

'Is *that* all?'

Sean O'Fearna's *The Man from Innisfree* had been raucous and stage-Irish. It succeeded because he was a genius. He created a world and peopled it with familiar, well-loved screen faces. Now those great faces were gone, and so was O'Fearna himself, which was why, in my script, I had turned the legend back on itself.

My story was of Sean *Og* (for 'younger') O'Driscoll, who returns home from America, as his father had once done. He expects to find an Ireland of colleens and donnybrooks; instead, he discovers that his native village is dying from unemployment and despair. When he attempts to drag the place into a new age, he meets resistance from the die-hards. The climax was still a foot-race, but now it was a marathon in which each runner represented a separate village, and the winner's prize was the franchise for a new mineral water plant. The race would, of course, be the occasion for much attempted nobbling and skulduggery.

A few days after his late-night call, Thorn and I met for lunch. He said, 'I think all your screenplay needs is a weekend of polishing, and Gus agrees with me. At this point, we ought to go looking for a director. What do you say to Creighton Carr?'

Carr was an old-timer who had made two semi-classical Ealing comedies; otherwise his work had the tame, washed-out look of J Arthur Rank cinema. When fashions changed, he dropped from sight. Then, two years ago, he had come back with *A Mongoose Named Mary*, a witty abrasive comedy that was

Oscar-nominated. It was his biggest success. An attempt at a sequel flopped – it was rumoured that the star's temperament had crippled it.

'What we don't want,' I told Thorn, 'is a director who thinks the Irish are as quaint as hell. You know what I mean: Rent-a-Leprechaun.'

'Don't worry,' Thorn said. 'Gus and I are going to London to meet Carr on Monday. We know exactly what we want.'

I said: 'I thought de Paor promised to leave us alone.'

'He promised you, not me. Anyway, Gus is footing the bill, so he has a right to see what he's getting. Oh, and by the way, in case your ears were burning, the cause was his opinion of the script. He creamed.'

'So now what do *I* do?'

'Nothing, until I give you the green light. Then you cross out 'First Draft' on the Page One and write 'Final Draft' instead, and that's virtually that.'

'Sure it is, and the moon is made of green cheese!'

'Hey, trust me. You know my motto: If it ain't broken, don't fix it.'

I said, silently, 'Or else try hitting it with a hammer.'

Thorn looked into space. There was a *Palme d'Or* in one of his eyes and an Oscar in the other.

'*Amore*, hello. Can you talk?'

'Two calls in one week! Lucky me.'

'Listen, I need you.'

'Pardon me?'

'I need you here, with me in Firenze. It is life or death.'

'You mean life *and* death.'

'Do I? Can you come?'

'Are you ill?'

'I cannot explain on the phone. You know I would not ask unless it was most important. I have great need of you.'

'Florence? I wouldn't even know how to get there.'

'You go to London and then to Pisa, it is simple. I would meet you at the airport. Hello?'

'I'm thinking.'

Adultery in London was almost incidental, like wearing the wrong necktie; further afield, such as in Italy, it was as brazen as a loud suit. And the cost of the journey was not something I could take in my stride, even with the payment for the screenplay. Our day for moving house to the Tower was only a month off. And yet Josie had spoken the *sesame* – 'I need you' – so it behoved me to put up or for ever shut up. I told her: 'I could go on Monday, but only for one night.'

'Wonderful.'

'Thorn and Gus de Paor are off to London. I could get Thorn to pretend that I'm going with them.'

'Sure, sure.' Again, she was not listening. 'There is an Alitalia flight from Heathrow every day at twelve-fifteen. I rely on you, yes?'

'But what if there's no room on the –'

'Now I have much to do. Thank you, thank you. *Ciao, amore.*'

I called Alitalia with the small, ignoble hope that the flight would be full; in which case I could ask Silvana to pass on a message. As it happened, there was no need; seats were available. Aware of a twinge of disappointment, I told Thorn that I was using him as a cover. He agreed; he adored intrigue. I imagine that if the dead rat had been waxed at the ends, he would have twirled it.

He said, 'Don't worry. You can trust me not to make a liar out of a liar.'

I winced.

'And where will you be if you're not in London?'

'Florence.'

'By God, you're going it.'

'It isn't like that.'

229

'Well, don't go getting caught with your fly open. Remember me and Anna-Livia.'

Throughout the weekend, I kept myself in a mental limbo, refusing to think of what I was about. The worst moment was at bedtime on the Sunday, when I discovered that Greta had laid out a spare shirt that was new from Christmas, with a scrawled note on top that said 'Mind the pins.'

On the Monday, I arrived at Pisa in mid-afternoon, and the terracotta roofs, light, the balmy air and the smell of jasmine put the puritan to flight. Josie was waiting with a car and driver. As well as her handbag, she carried a bulky cloth satchel.

She said, 'I have booked you into a *pensione* above Fiesole. It is called Bencista. It overlooks the city and it is magnificent.'

'*I* am staying there?' I said. 'Does that mean that you aren't?'

'*Amore*, I live in Firenze with my mother. She is a Catholic lady. What excuse could I give her to spend the night in some other place?' She said with gentle reproach, 'You are usually so sensible.'

I said, 'Did you ever hear the word "oxymoron"?'

'What is that, please?'

'It describes two opposites that cancel each other out. Such as "celibate adultery". Do you know that since we last shared a bed, weeks have become months?'

She said, 'That is at your wish, *amore.*'

'Mine?'

She slapped my wrist lightly. 'This is a beautiful country. It is *my* country. Look at it.' I did for ten seconds, then said, 'May I know what is so urgent?'

'*Scusi?*'

'Why am I here?'

She patted her satchel. 'You will see.'

The *pensione* was just south of Fiesole, with a view of Florence. This, I suspected, was as near to the city as I was likely to get. My room had whitewashed walls and a small terrace. While Josie, as restless as ever, made phone calls, I explored the reading room and found a paperback copy of Belloc's *The Path to Rome*. I decided to steal it.

When Josie had finished her calls, she summoned her driver and showed me the little town, two kilometres down the hill. We walked around the Piazza Mino and looked at the Palazzo Pretorio and the Duomo. As the sunlight went, she led me to a restaurant where the pavement tables had candles in glass chimneys. Just opposite, there was a terrace, with a low wall and the lights of the city below. 'Nice, eh?' Josie said.

As I gave her a sulky look, she laughed and opened her satchel. She said, 'Look!' It was stuffed with money in notes. '*Il riscatto*,' she crowed. 'The ransom. I am paying it!'

Strangely, all I could think of at that moment was the Martello tower, which from the beginning I had looked upon as more Greta's than mine. I wondered if I would ever see it or her again.

Josie, who had been coy until now, was at once unstoppable. 'At first, I said, "Who cares about the old *bastardo*? It serves him right. Let them do what they say they will do to him, and then throw him into the Arno. I hope he sinks." And then I said to myself: "No! That is not the way. He will not acknowledge me. He has disowned me. So I will save him and put him to shame. That will be the best revenge. And then he will come to me, crawling and weeping and running at the nose."' Then, hopefully, picking up a table-knife: 'Maybe he will kill himself.'

It would be wrong to say that she was not herself; she was never more herself; she was Josie-times-ten. I had not seen a performance to equal it since Tosca stabbed Scarpia the year Greta and I went to Verona. Josie again showed me the contents of the satchel. 'Look! A million *lire*.'

My right knee began to jerk up and down violently, as if I were operating a treadle. I said: 'Are you trying to tell me' – I groped for the words – 'that you are going to hand that money over to kidnappers, *while I am with you*?'

'They said I was to come alone.'

'Oh, Jesus?'

'That was the condition.'

'Oh, Christ in crinolines.'

She laughed. 'But I am not so stupid.'

I could have given her an argument on that point. 'When is this to happen? Today? This evening?'

'What time is it now?'

'Just on six-thirty. No, wait ...' I had forgotten to advance my watch. 'It's nearly seven thirty.'

She said, 'Oh, my God,' as if she had missed the six o'clock news. 'Then do you mind? Go over there, sit on the terrace and keep your eyes on me. I don't want to come to harm, you understand me? Okay? Then when it is done and the money is paid, we will have a nice dinner. The *saltimbocca* is *squisito*. Like the name says, it leaps in the mouth! Hurry, if they see you, they will not come.' She splashed wine into my glass. 'Take it. Drink. You are on holiday!'

I took the glass and crossed to the terrace, where there were wooden picnic tables and benches. The lights of Florence shone below; a mandolin was playing; it was an Ernst Lubitsch film set, except that when I drank, the glass rattled on my teeth. It has always been a weakness of mine to see both sides of every story, and I found myself wondering if Josie was a free spirit who lived life to the utmost, and I was a craven milquetoast, or if, maybe, the reverse was true. Maybe I was the civilised norm, and she was unhinged? No, that was unkind. I was trying to find a half-way point between eccentric and barking mad when I saw a man rise from a table in the restaurant and approach Josie. He had perhaps been there all along, and, if so, he had seen me.

He reached her table and sat across from her. They talked. It was too dark to see him clearly at the distance. He pointed to me. He might have been Raymond Burr staring at James Stewart in

Rear Window. He leaned towards her, aggressively. He snatched the satchel from her and stood, but instead of walking away he came towards me. As he emerged into the light, he was real for the first time. He was of medium height, dark and in his thirties. There was a scar, or it may have been a birthmark, caught up in his left eyebrow; it was not vivid enough to be a disfigurement, but it was there. He stood over me, looked and kept looking. I knew enough Italian to say – boldly, I hoped – '*Buona sera.*' He was holding a lighted cigarette and after a moment he deliberately dropped it into my wine.

He turned, swinging the satchel, and walked downhill around the corner and out of sight. I crossed the street to Josie.

She said: 'Well, it is done. What happened? Did he speak to you?'

I said, 'No. But I'll know him the next time?'

Josie laughed at this. 'The next time? It is not very likely. Sit down and let us have a beautiful dinner.'

He had given her his name, or *a* name: Michelangelo. I told her that she had probably been the victim of a hoax and that the woman who called herself Clara Armetta was a confidence trickster. Josie pooh-poohed the idea; by midnight, she said, the old *bastardo* would be free. She spoke of her mother, who was now an invalid; she said that she must spend more time with her. Perhaps she would return to Dublin and train a full-time valet to look after Andrew. When I asked about her illness, she said she was having treatment, and as soon as the time was ripe, there would be an operation. She wept for a few moments and said that she had had a good life. I said, not very sympathetically, 'Yes, you have.'

The evening dragged; after Michelangelo, there was a sense of anticlimax. I was glad to go back to the *pensione*, knowing that tomorrow I would be home again. With a sense of shock, it came to me that I was tired of her company. Perhaps I had been emptied, but, for the first time, she bored me.

Seeing that I was lost in thought, she waggled her fingers at me and said: 'Coo-ee!'

I smiled back and told myself it was over.

Chapter Seventeen

With Thorn and Shay

Well, I tell a lie; of course it wasn't over. Like many another convalescent, I thought I was cured when I was no more than in remission.

Thorn came back from London to say that Creighton Carr was undoubtedly the ideal director for *Return to Innisfree*. 'Cry loves the script,' he said. 'He says you're a natural.' I had hardly begun to blush with pleasure when he said that 'Cry' would come over later in the week. He had a few suggestions that I might care to incorporate in the final draft. I was anxious to learn from an old hand; after all, a film script was not writ in stone.

The day came, and Mr Carr greeted Thorn and me in a VIP suite of Judge's Hotel in Ballsbridge. He was a slight, dapper man in his early seventies with a mane of silvery hair. He wore Gucci loafers and tailored slacks and had a blue silk scarf tucked into his open-necked shirt. His handshake was firm and his voice as silken as the scarf. He wore a hearing aid and a gold bracelet.

'Now, my dear fellow, what am I to call you?' he asked. He spoke in what from previous encounters I identified as a Pinewood accent.

Thorn said, with a grin, 'He's called Thady.'

I said, 'I would prefer TJ.'

Mr Carr said, 'Then TJ it is. And I am called Cry. That isn't just a diminutive of Creighton, but because I'm a sentimental old cuss.

Once or twice, by the way, I very nearly shed a tear over your script.'

Thorn and I sat on a sofa in front of a glass-topped table. Cry sat opposite, with my screenplay, a notepad and a bottle of sparkling Ballygowan before him. He had been through this ritual a hundred times. He smiled; 'Shall we get the tiresome bit over with? And do forgive me. I'm a most uncouth kind of chap. I have absolutely no small talk. Aren't I dreadful?'

On the contrary, he could not have been more charming. We smiled back at him, and, whatever about Thorn, it was to be my last smile for several hours. The top sheet of Cry's pad was covered with small methodical notes in blue-black. I wondered how many pages there were.

He said, 'Now, may I kick off with a whopping great, impertinent generality? What a dear script you have written, TJ. It's a crime even to look askance at it, but forgive me, haven't you rather got hold of the wrong end of the stick? I mean, here you have an absolutely idyllic little Irish village, and yet you want us to look upon this ... this ghastly bottled water industry as a Good Thing.'

He poured himself some of the Ballygowan. I thought he was setting up a sight gag; perhaps he would do a double-take and toss the bottle aside, like Claude Rains with the Vichy water in *Casablanca*. Instead he sipped, looked at me, said, 'Mm?' and adjusted his hearing aid.

I said, 'Well, the way I see it is that this bottling plant *is* a good thing.'

Cry murmured 'Good God' in ingenuous wonder.

'An industry of some kind is necessary if the village isn't to die. There's a well of spring water, you see, and it flows through limestone –'

Cry laughed, mildly. 'My dear chap, I did read the script.'

'The village is at its last gasp,' I said. 'The plant will bring it into the modern world.'

236

'Yes, well, what I say, and with the very greatest respect and in utter humility, is that Irish villages don't *belong* in the modern world. They are synonyms for charm, and where's the charm in a lot of beastly machinery? I happen to know a little bit about comedy, you know.'

'Yes, I do know ...'

'I've worked at Ealing with dear impossible Bob Hamer and Sandy Mackendrick. We were the Trinity, so-called, and what every one of our films cried to the rooftops, loud and clear – in our very British, poker-up-the-arse way, of course – was that so-called Progress was the deadly enemy of Charm.' His little homily had moved into capitals. 'Now shall I tell you my idea?'

I looked at Thorn and had the impression that someone had painted a smile on a piece of cardboard and stapled it to his moustache. He said nothing, electing me to make the epigrams. I said, 'Do.'

Cry said, with what I took to be humility, 'I'm not a writer, of course.' Later on, I realised that this, an opening gambit at every story conference, was the verbal equivalent of a lobbed hand-grenade.

He went on. 'Let us by all means have the foot race, as is. And our hero, Sean Og' – he pronounced it 'Ogg' – 'is determined to win. Then he notices the sheer breathtaking beauty of the country he is running through. It is enchanting – mountains, sea, islands, barefoot girls – colleens, yes? – digging up peat in the bogs, and so on. And Sean Ogg says, "Oh, shit! All this loveliness will be for ever gone if I win this marathon." So he loses it. He throws the race.' Cry was so overcome that he reached into his pocket, produced a tissue and dabbed at his eyes. 'Ha-ha, here I go, blubbing. Most un-English! Now bear with me. In the story, as I see it, losing the race is not altogether that simple, because, you see, Sean Ogg happens to be in love with a local girl. I rather thought of Jamie Lee Curtis. And she has promised to marry him if he wins!'

I said, 'Oh, balls.'

His eyebrows went up. He said, 'Oh, yes?'

I said, 'Please forgive me, I was thinking out loud. I mean, what kind of a silly cow would base a marriage, a family and an entire life on whether a man could run fast or slow?'

'My dear chap,' Cry said. 'Can it be that you don't realise? What we are about is not realism; it is romance.'

Thorn stood up. 'Look, I'm going to leave the pair of you to it.' I stared at him. 'This is all technical stuff.'

As the door closed behind him, I knew the day was lost. Creighton Carr loathed and abominated the script, and I was to be the lone defender of the garrison. With Thorn gone, he said, 'Well, shall we get down to what our departed friend calls the technical stuff?'

He started at page one and went through the scene of Sean Og's arrival at the railway station of his native village. I had intended this as a satirical echo of his late father's first appearance in O'Fearna's *The Man from Innisfree.* In my script there was a taxi which broke down because the driver could not afford to buy petrol. Cry would have none of it; he wanted a jarvey who resembled an exhumed Barry Fitzgerald.

'But that was in the previous film.'

'Exactly!'

He virtually undotted my every *i* and uncrossed my every *t.* Now and again, he would hesitate with his pencil – it was red, of course – poised like a Stuka on a bombing run before saying, 'No point in our messing about with this, seeing as we'll be throwing it out, anyway.' At lunchtime, he sent down for smoked salmon sandwiches and coffee. I asked for a Scotch.

He said, 'You drink on the job, do you?'

'I do, today.'

'Of course, I forgot. You're Irish, what, what?'

He may not have uttered the 'what, what', but I resolved that in my memoirs he would say it. A few minutes later, made reckless by the whisky, I said, 'May I hazard an observation?'

'My dear fellow, this is your peat. Or should I say your turf? Do feel free.'

'It's this. I think you want both me and my script off this film.'

I had overturned the chess board. Probably he would think I was a lout for not playing by the rules of the game. In the film world a knife inserted anywhere but in the back was looked upon as unsightly. I expected incredulity, protestations, but instead Cry smiled angelically.

He said, 'What a clever chap you are. I do believe you're getting the point.'

There was nothing to do except stand up and leave. It took a conscious effort to put one foot in front of the other. As I reached the door, he said, 'You're off then, are you? Well, cheery-bye.'

I fought off tears of fury in the taxi that took me from Judge's to the archive. Awaiting me, there was one telephone message. It was not from Thornton, as I had hoped, but from Josie, in Florence.

She said, 'Hello, are you ever in your office? I want to tell you, I was right and you were wrong. It was not a hoax, so I thumb my nose at you! They have released my uncle Max, and he has paid me back the money I gave. So there! And would you believe, the ungrateful old *bastardo* still says he will have nothing to do with me. Well, I don't care. He can go home to hell. *Ciao, amore.* Oh, and have you been writing nasty letters to Andrew? He says –'

The message came to the end of its recording time, and I had no way of returning her call, even if I wanted to. I asked myself why I should want to write even a friendly letter to Andrew Hand, never mind an offensive one; but my immediate concern was with contacting Thorn. He stayed clear of his office until after four, and, when I reached him, I said, 'You ran out on me.'

'I had to. It was either that or kill the old shite. Honest to God, he wasn't like that in London.'

'He wants me off the film.'

'He what?'

'He said so, plump and plain. The alternative is to do his rewrites.'

'Which amount to what?'

'Not much. Just the story and all of the dialogue.'

'Jesus.'

I said, 'Look, we've got to talk to Gus de Paor. I mean, today.'

Thorn said, 'I've already laid that on. He's heading for a gig in Cape Town, but he'll pick us up on his way to the airport.'

'Twenty minutes, big deal.'

'Look, it's our script, yours and mine. I said I'd defend it to the death and so I will. Our bottom line is that Cry either has to do it as written, or else get off the pot. Okie-dokie?'

'Thanks, mate.'

'For what? It's my script, too, you know.'

We had a drink around the corner from de Paor's office. When we came out, a fine, piercing April rain had begun to fall. Neither of us was dressed for it, and we ran to a where a silver Bentley was waiting. De Paor, with a secretary holding an umbrella, came down the steps. When he and Thorn were in, I took the jump seat; facing them.

De Paor said: 'TJ, I thought you made a condition that you need have nothing to do with me. And yet here you are. Why am I honoured?'

I said, still loathing him, 'I was wrong and I apologise.'

He weighed this, then nodded. Don Corleone was appeased. 'So?'

I said, 'Creighton Carr is a dinosaur. He belongs in the fifties. He had a big hit with *A Mongoose Named Mary*, but the sequel was a disaster, and now he's running scared. So he wants this to be the kind of film that worked for him back in the old days.'

Thorn chimed in: 'People don't want leprechauns any more.'

De Paor said, 'Creighton wants a *leprechaun*?'

'You know what I mean.'

I said, 'What he's proposing is a tired rehash of *The Man from*

240

Innisfree. Audiences won't accept it, and I won't write it.'

De Paor said, 'Thorn?'

Thorn said, 'I agree with TJ. It's not the fillum we set out to make. And I like what we've already got.'

'Uh-huh. And pray tell me, what are you doing on this fillum?' Even in my distress, I thought of Thorn and de Paor as half of a barber-shop quartet. At any moment, they would launch into *Lida Rose*.

Thorn was taken off-balance by de Paor's question. He said, 'Well, I'm the producer.'

De Paor said: 'Then why don't you produce? In London, you were all for hiring this Creighton Carr.'

'I think he was putting on an act.'

'Then get rid of him. Start earning your bread. Carry the sodding can.'

He told the driver to stop. We had reached the junction of Tara Street and Burgh Quay. He said to Thorn, 'I hired you to take responsibility for this fillum, so start doing so. This meeting was highly unnecessary, and now I'll happily excuse both of you.'

He pushed the door open. As I got out, the jump seat snapped like a Rottweiler's jaws, and Thorn followed me and slammed the door. The Bentley moved across Butt Bridge and was gone. The rain, scything up the river, had become heavier and colder, so we ran to a pub at the corner of D'Olier Street.

'I don't feel like a fillum producer,' Thorn said, panting. 'I don't think I look like one, either.'

I looked at his moustache. He was a drowned rat wearing a drowned rat. We ordered drinks. Thorn said, 'Well, he put us in our box and no mistake.'

I said, 'He's a bollix.'

'So, did I keep my word? Did I or did I not stand up for you?'

'You did.'

'Did I or did I not?' As Josie would have said, he was dipping his bread in it.

241

'You absolutely did, and I'm very grateful.'

'You can't say I let you down.'

'No way.'

My Scotch and his G&T were served. Thorn said, 'G'luck,' took a swallow and said, 'Okay, now that we're on our ownsome ...'

'Yes?'

'Do the fucking rewrites.'

Today, years later, I remember how it was at that moment: the dirt of the pub, the steam rising from wet clothes, the traffic outside and the hiss of tyres, the damp soaking through the shoulders of my jacket, the smile on my face turning stupid as I realised he was in earnest.

Even so, I said, 'Thorn ... now come on.'

He said, 'Come on where? Why should we stick our necks out? I was thinking all afternoon: we're first-timers, if we make a balls of this, we'll never get another chance. We'll be bollixed. Creighton Carr is an old-timer; he's been through the mill. He'll do a professional job, whatever else. Let him take the risks, it's what he's paid for. Do the rewrites.'

'No.'

His smile was knowing, easy. 'Yes, you will. Go home and sleep on it.'

'No.'

Gently: 'And I say, you will.'

'How short is your memory? This is something we believed in.'

'Ah, the days of innocence!'

'Don't make a joke of it. We said we'd protect it. I told you at the outset, if I didn't have your word of honour then I'd as soon throw my hat at it.'

He said, 'So now I'm a ... a what? A man of straw, is that it?'

'I'm not calling any names. All I'm saying is –'

'Don't go getting up my nose on this.'

'... is that I'm not going to do those rewrites.'

'Then –' He stopped short, his upper teeth on his lower lip to form the *f*.

'Go on. Say it.'

He said, 'TJ, would you ever grow up? It's only a fuckin' fillum.'

If there was a sin against the Holy Ghost, that was it. I said, 'Goodbye, see you, then.' I walked for half of the way back to the archive, and squelched the other half. A red-headed girl was sitting at Voilet Mooney's desk reading, of all things, *Riders of the Purple Sage*. She had come at five o'clock for an interview as my secretary, and it was now a quarter to six. 'The cleaning woman let me in,' she said. She told me her name was Mattie Mundow.

I asked her if she could handle a computer. 'That yoke?' she said, pointing. 'Tha's a pudden.'

Out of embarrassment at having forgotten the appointment, I gave her the job. She reacted by saying, 'Well, I don't want you dyin' on me,' with which she sat me down, knelt, took my shoes and socks off, put the shoes upside down on the radiator and hung the socks next to them.

'Where's the coffee?' the treasure said. The phone on my desk went, and she got to it first. She made a face at me, not knowing how to address the caller. 'The Fillum Archive,' she announced. Then: 'It's a Mr T'ornton.'

'Yes, Thorn?'

He had not wasted his time. He said: 'TJ, I'm at Judge's Hotel with Creighton Carr. And I'm speaking as producer of *Return to Innisfree*. I have to ask formally, are you prepared to do the rewrites as required by Mr Carr?'

'No, I am not,' I said. 'Because –'

'Well, that's your lot, then,' he said and hung up.

Mattie was looking at me uncertainly. 'It's all right,' I said. 'I'm fired, but you're not.'

It was as I had once said to Josie. Thorn and I were scorpion and frog, and he had stung, not from ill-will, but because it was his nature. I thought, too, of the evening when Prue had found him out with another woman and we drove him home. A man could not prove his integrity, he had said when in his cups, except by standing alone. He would punish her, too, one day for taking him back.

When my socks had stopped steaming, I drove Mattie home to where she lived with her parents in Irishtown and continued out of town to 'Kate Fortune's Lane'. Greta called from the living room: 'We have visitors.' It was a warning not to come in wearing what she called my *Old Dark House* face. Our callers were Colleen and Turlough.

'We were visiting a friend in hospital in Loughlinstown,' Colleen said. 'So we went to look at your Martello tower, and then we thought we would come here and tell Greta how wonderful it is.'

'It's great,' Turlough said, using his rubber stamp.

Greta made fresh tea while I went upstairs and changed my shoes and socks. When I came back, Turlough said, 'How goes the film?'

'I'm afraid "goes" is the wrong word. It's gone. I've been dumped.'

The visitors gasped and said, 'No!'

Greta said, 'Well, thanks for telling me.'

'It only happened today.' It could have passed as a scene in a bad sitcom. 'I refused to write an entire new script, and Thorn told me to feck off.'

'*Thorn* did?' This from Turlough, blowing his BAFTA.

Greta's contribution was 'I told you. Didn't I tell you?' Then, almost accusingly: 'Well, I hope Prue is still talking to us. I'm fond of Prue.'

Trying to raise the level of the script, I assured her that the quarrel was between myself and Thorn, who would as soon share a lover than an enemy.

Colleen said, loyally, providing the comedy relief, 'You are right. He is what they call a controlling freak. I think you are well off out of it.'

There was more tea and sympathy and slander, and, as the visitors were setting off, Turlough said to Colleen, 'Tell them the news about Josie.'

I looked mildly interested: 'What news would that be?'

Turlough knew about Josie and me, and he had not altogether forgiven me for declining to leave my niche on the *Nation* and move with him to the *Sunday Sentinel*. In front of Greta, any talk of Josie was mischief-making, and Colleen would pay him back for it on the way home.

'There is no news at all,' she said with a look at him, 'except that Josie is going around with a crowd of artistic people who are exploiting her. She does not care as long as they tell her what she badly wants to believe, that she is not getting old and is still – what is the expression? – the bee's knees.'

'I hear,' I said, 'that she hasn't been well.'

'Oh? Who told you that?' Greta said.

Colleen said, 'The doctor says that she has a touch of asthma. And he has made her give up the drug – Premorin, is it? – she takes to look young.' I had a not displeasing vision of Josie as the girl in *Lost Horizon* who goes into the outside world and turns into a raddled old hag. 'I think that you do not know Josie. If her life is boring, she invents herself over again.'

'She's a born liar,' Turlough said.

'She is not. It is simply that she wants to eat every food that is on the table. She is a sad person.'

Turlough asked: 'Were you ever in Florence, TJ?'

He knew, of course, about my trip the previous Monday. Josie had told Colleen, and Colleen had told Turlough.

I said, looking him straight in the eye, 'No, never.' I took an umbrella from the hall stand and saw them both down the lane to where their car was parked. When we got to it, Colleen punched him hard in the small of the back and said: 'You have a big mouth. Get in.'

To me, she said: 'Josie says that Andrew has had a letter without a name on it, and she thinks you sent it.'

'Me?'

'It tells him that like a fool he pays the money for your air fare so that you can go to Florence and do you-know-what – I do not like to say the word – with his wife.'

I said, 'I pay my own air fares. And why would I write an anonymous letter against myself?'

She said, 'I know. Maybe this is one more of the stories she makes up. Turlough is right. She is a liar. My God, she is a liar!' She kissed me. 'Be careful.'

Back in the house, Greta said: 'What's going to happen to us?'

'How?'

'If you're not doing the fillum, will we lose the new house?'

'No. I still have the book to write. Matter of fact, now I needn't put it on the long finger. I can start it whenever I like.'

She said, 'If you hadn't given up the good job with *Sunrise,* this wouldn't have happened.'

I told her, 'If I hadn't given up the good job, we couldn't have afforded the new house.'

She said, bitterly, 'You always have a good answer.'

That Englishman we are for ever quoting said that sorrows do not come single spies but in battalions. Perhaps one day we will find out if there is a natural law at work; if so, it was in full swing that week. The American humorist Mort Sahl was appearing at the Royal Hospital in Kilmainham, and we had been invited. Greta wanted to go, but had promised to visit a girl friend home from Canada, so I took my willing standby, Liz Meara. As we stood in line for tickets, I saw a white head in front of me. It was Willie Cooney, looking naked without the *bodhran*-playing light-o'-love.

'All alone?' I said.

'We couldn't get a sitter,' he said. 'Anyway, Siobhan is expecting again, and she thought it best not to venture out.'

'Congratulations,' I said.

I remembered how Greta had flown into a babbling rage on hearing of Willie's previous incursion into fatherhood. Probably the news that he had done it again would have twice the effect. And there was no way I would keep it from her; she got so little pleasure.

'Your mate, Shay Lambe, is here just ahead of us,' Willie said.

'Oh? I haven't seen him in months.'

'Don't tell me there's a row on.'

I said, 'Shay and I don't have rows. No, he's just been busy.'

As I said it, I felt that the excuse was woefully thin. I took my ticket and walked with Liz towards the bar. Willie tagged after us. Shay, holding a glass of Fanta, was there with Brigid, and I sensed that he was less than pleased to see me. As we approached, Willie said, fatuously, 'You do know Mr Lambe, I presume?'

I said, 'Yes, we meet at first nights.'

Shay was silent for a moment, then said, 'I don't have to take that. Come on, Brigid.'

He and she walked into the auditorium.

'I thought you and Shay didn't have rows,' Willie said with a smirk.

'What was that about?' Liz asked as I led her to the bar.

'Search me,' I said.

I could not tell her that five testily-spoken words – 'We meet at first nights' – had been used as an excuse to end twenty years of friendship. I wondered if Shay himself knew it for no more than the feeble excuse it was. He had let himself down over Blanaid's 'trouble' and had made of me an unwilling witness, who must therefore be disposed of. Another person would have picked himself up, limped for an hour and then done what men are best at: the forgiveness of themselves. Shay's standards were too high for weaselling out, or so I mistakenly thought. Years later, when one of their other girls married and gave birth, Shay and Brigid called the infant 'our first grandchild'. It was then I realised that I had done him too much honour. The Blanaid thing had simply never happened. Nor, for that matter had I. At any rate, he never spoke to me again.

I did Mort Sahl poor justice that evening, and Greta was home from her visitation ahead of me. She said, 'How was the show?'

By then I had forgotten about Willie Cooney and the pregnant light-o'-love. I told her about Shay. She said, 'I suppose that means I'll be next for the high jump. With Brigid, that is.' She was silent for a while; then she said, 'You'll miss him.'

'Yes, I will.' I was surprised and grateful that she had let slip the chance of scoring off me with a joke. I said: 'You know what I thought you might say? That I had managed to lose two friends in the same week.'

'How do you mean?'

'I mean first Thorn and now Shay.'

'Thorn?' she said. '*Him?*' She laughed and used an expression I had not heard since, years ago, my mother used it about a neighbour she distrusted. 'He's a go-be-the-wall.'

Chapter Eighteen

At Dublin Castle

Moving day came and went. The son of the man who, thirty-five years previously, had put up the shelves in my mother's kitchen on Chapel Road came and fitted my bookshelves in the annexe of the Bloody Tower. By way of a surprise for Greta, I had our window curtains operated by a bedside switch. Now, as in full Cinerama, they glided open through 120 degrees to show a great expanse of sea, unbroken to the horizon, with Dalkey Island and Bray Head peering in at opposite ends. At night-time, there was the double flash from the Kish lighthouse, seven miles out.

On our first morning, when the curtains opened, Greta sat up in bed and said: '*Oh ... my ... God.*'

'Do you like it?'

'Mmmp.'

'That good, eh?'

When we had been in the tower for a couple of months, we gave ourselves the treat of seeing a new play at the Abbey. I could still remember a time when people dressed up to go to the theatre; now first nights were collar-and-tie-optional. Afterwards, I asked Greta if she wanted to go to the bar for the obligatory post-mortem – the 'pilgrimage to Knock', as it was called by those who knocked the hardest. She said: 'No, it's like a pub. We'll go home.'

As we made our way up the aisle, we found ourselves shuffling cheek-by-jowl; with Shay and Brigid. I looked from a range of eighteen inches at Shay, who kept his eyes fixed on the door ahead. Brigid was like a walking waxwork, giving neither of us a sign of recognition. As we let them draw ahead, I said to Greta: 'You seem to be in the doghouse, too.'

She said, 'Brigid and I had a row.'

'You and she?' It was unheard of for Greta to quarrel with a living soul, myself excepted. 'You never mentioned it.'

'You don't have to know everything.'

'What happened?'

She shrugged.

We had retrieved our car and were at Merrion Gates before I managed to winkle out what had happened. Two Wednesdays previously, Greta had driven Brigid home from their weekly shopping, and over coffee she had quite suddenly said, 'It's a pity about TJ and Shay. I hope they make up.'

'Shamy never makes up,' Brigid said proudly, as if declaring that Shay never went into a Protestant church or skipped a Hail Mary while saying the rosary. 'TJ gave out to Shamy in the Royal Hospital. I was there. I heard him.'

'He says he told Shay that they met at first nights.'

'Yes, but sarcastic, like. And he said it in that voice of his.'

'I don't know who else's voice he could say it in.'

'You weren't there,' Brigid said.

'Well, all I can say is that, if you ask me, Shay is very easily gev out to.'

'I hope you're not going to take TJ's part.'

'Catch me!' Greta said.

'I mean, husband and all, I'm surprised you stick up for him.'

At which Greta said, 'Oh, now; oh, now. Brigid, *I'm* not going to be gev out to, either. I'm sorry, but next Wednesday you can go to Tru-Valu with someone else.'

'No trouble at all!' Brigid said.

As if by intention, the split between Shay and me had widened, so that now he and Brigid had brushed off any shreds of liking that might weave together and mend the tear. I was grateful to

Greta, but saddened that she had lost a friendship. For whatever the reason – perhaps moving to the Bloody Tower had something to do with it – a *détente* seemed to have set in between her and me. We had our house-warming party on a July evening, and the weather was so balmy that, when the sun set beyond Sorrento Point, as unreal as a crimson backcloth, the guests overflowed on to the roof.

Liz Meara was there, and also my new treasure, Mattie Mundow, and Ilse-Lazlo Huneker, who had finished her researches in Connemara. Mattie had by then taught me to operate a PC, and in turn I was trying to convert her away from the heresy, peculiar to Ireland, that *film* was a two-syllable word. At one point in the evening, she said to me out of the corner of her mouth, as if she were Effie Perine tipping off her boss, Sam Spade, 'After you went home today, there was a phone call.'

'Oh?'

'A woman with a voice out of a spy fillum. She said to tell you to call her at home.'

'Did she leave a name?'

'I don't t'ink she had one,' Mattie said.

Next morning, I took a chance and called Raglan Road, ready to hang up if the wrong voice answered. It had been so long that I had to look up the number. Josie answered at once. 'Ah, thank you for calling.'

'You're back in town, then.'

'I don't know for how long. My poor mother has been very low, and I could be called to go to her at any time. And to make it worse, I have been in hospital.'

'Oh, yes?'

'It was for an operation. I told you I was not well. Obviously you have forgotten.'

We were fifteen seconds into the conversation, and already I was in the wrong. 'I remember perfectly. Was the operation a success?'

'They say they think they caught it in time. I do not know. Oh, God, I hope so. Well –'

'I know. You've had a good life.'

'You are not very nice today. Is something the matter?'

'Should there be?'

'You have changed. At one time you were affectionate.'

I said, 'Oh, that was a long time ago. I haven't seen you since Fiesole.'

'Because I have been in Firenze, so how could you?'

'True.'

'So listen to me.'

'I'm all ears.'

'You sound so strange. I don't think I like you this way. Well, no matter. Yesterday, I came home, because Saturday is Andrew's birthday, and there must be a cake and a party, you understand. Well, last evening we were having dinner, just he and I, and he put a piece of paper in front of me. It is another note that is not signed.'

'About me?

'It is the same as the one before. I will read it. It says, "Your wife is using your money to pay for Thady Quill to fly to Italy to go to bed with her." Only it does not say "go to bed".'

'You mean it says "fuck".'

A hesitation. 'Yes.'

'So this would be the second note.'

'It is the second one that he shows me. *Amore*, how many people know that you were in Firenze?'

'In Fiesole, I think you mean. I never got to the Uffizi. Well, there was you and me. We knew.'

'Don't be stupid.'

'And there was Thorn. I told him because I needed an alibi. God knows who *he* blabbed it to. Gus de Paor, maybe, although anonymous notes aren't in his line. And I know that you told Colleen, who of course told Turlough.'

'Well, forget about Colleen. And you did not write this note?'

I said: 'No. Did you?'

'I wish you would not make jokes. I told you a long time ago that Andrew is a bad person to offend. He is a gentleman all the time, yes, but the people around him and the people he comes from are wild.'

I said, 'You're not so tame yourself, love.'

She said, 'I have no time for this. I must go. Think of me, and be very careful. *Ciao, amore.*'

That year's Dublin Theatre Festival was scheduled for early October, and it featured an Italian company presenting the Pirandello trilogy, *Six Characters in Search of an Author, Each in His Own Way* and *Tonight We Improvise.* Ordinarily, I would have mentally doffed my hat out of respect and steered clear, but by way of a cherry on the top there was to be the Irish premiere of the Taviani Brothers' film *Kaos*, based on four Pirandello short stories.

Liz Meara rang and said, 'May I call in a favour? After the film, the Italian embassy is holding a posh buffet supper at Dublin Castle. Could Greta spare you?'

It threatened to be a late evening, so that morning I left the car tucked into its space next to the tower, took the DART into town and planned to return home late, by taxi or the last train. The film was visually ravishing but, at more than three hours, it was a long haul for non-Sicilians, and afterwards the audience straggled across Dame Street and through the gates of the Castle. The supper took place in St Patrick's Hall, which was already crowded, and among the first people I saw were Gus de Paor and Thorn. In accordance with pecking order, the former was smoking a Monte Cristo No.3, the latter a cheroot. Thorn caught sight of me, and, unlike Shay and Brigid, he did not look elsewhere, but stared and scowled as if a hated enemy had come into view. I deliberately thumbed my nose and waggled my fingers. As I turned away, I saw Josie.

She was talking to a dark, youngish man who was holding a glass of red wine, and I knew at once that they were lovers. I knew because she had often looked at me in the same way and touched me, as she was doing to him, when I spoke to her. It was hardly touching at all – she was not one for public intimacies – rather her fingers might have been a daddy-long-legs that for a fraction of an instant fluttered against his arm, his wrist, his shoulder. She could not keep her hands from him. I felt the acid taste of jealousy.

My instinct was to walk out, but an absurd notion came and I needed to see the man close up. When Josie caught sight of me, the insect folded its wings. She said, 'Well, *hello*!' with her best and widest smile, but it was hard work.

I nodded at her companion. 'Who is this?'

She said, 'This gentleman is Signor Carlo Vanuti of the *Compagnia dei Giovani*. He is here with the Pirandello plays.'

'Carlo?' I said. 'Not Michelangelo?' I was looking at what I had come closer to see: a scar – or perhaps it was a birthmark – across his left eyebrow. I said, 'I think I met this gentleman in Fiesole.'

He smiled, puzzled. For the moment, he had forgotten me. Josie said, as I knew she would, 'Are you mad?' I had never known her to be so pale.

Her companion said something, probably asking her who this madman was. I said, '*Momento*,' and walked the few steps to where Thorn and de Paor were colloguing. I said, 'Do you mind?' and took the cheroot from between Thorn's fingers. He was too surprised to protest. I returned to Josie and her friend.

I said, '*Scusi*,' and dropped the cheroot into Carlo's glass of wine. I told Josie: 'Now maybe he'll remember me.'

As I walked out under the ceiling portrait of St Patrick preaching to the heathen Irish and past George III supported by Liberty and Justice, I knew that it had been a good and cherishable moment, but it could not erase the knowledge that I had been a puppet in another's fantasy. The ground was shifting beneath my feet. Had there ever been a kidnapping? My thoughts ran backwards towards the year dot. Was there a curmudgeonly uncle named Max Febreo? Or, further back, a heroic Jewish father and a Gentile mother? Were there ever such people as Nazis? Or camps? Or a young lawyer in Miami who had killed himself for love? Was it all an elaborate hoax from the beginning, or did Josie Hand so badly need to live other lives that she ate them whole?

I waited at the hatch of the cloakroom while the girl found my coat. I felt my face burn as an image came of a fool sitting on a terrace overlooking Florence, half afraid for his life and half savouring his own gallantry. I thought of how Josie and the man – Michelangelo there, Carlo here – would have laughed later that night. It was probably laughter in bed.

I put my coat on, and, as I reached the front step, the forgotten Liz came after me holding a plate of pasta. She said: 'Hey, what's up, mate? Are you dumping me?'

As I turned to make an excuse, Andrew Hand appeared out of the dark and moved between her and me. As always – in Hong Kong suit, Jermyn Street shirt and Lobb shoes – he could have stepped out of a bandbox.

He said to Liz, 'Excuse me.' Then, turning to me, 'TJ.'

I put my hand out. 'Andrew.'

Without responding, he said, 'I'm glad I caught you. Greta said you'd be here.'

'Greta did?'

'On the phone. I've just been having a long chat with her. And it's a good job you're not going home. You'd have been in for a hot reception.'

I said, 'What do you mean, I'm not going home?'

He tapped my shoulder twice and went past me into the building. Only afterwards did I realise that he was pointing me out. Two men took his place. They were wearing donkey-jackets. I had time to think that they did not belong at the buffet supper when one of them hit me a hard blow in the eye and the other kicked the feet from under me. Next thing, I was kicked again, this time in the face, and the noise of a bone breaking sounded louder inside my head than out. I had landed on the cobblestones, face up, and remember thinking that the night sky was overcast. Liz was screaming: 'Stop that!' I heard the noise of her plate breaking. One of the men kicked me in the ribs several times and a voice, either his or his comrade's, said, 'There now, you hoor's melt.' Their footsteps were soft as they went away, and I thought: *Thank God, they were wearing rubber-soled boots.*

Liz looked at me and said, 'Oh, my God' two or three times. She helped me sit up and that was when the pain began. Two of the Castle security men came up. One said, 'Do you know who did it?'

I said, 'Meat-packers,' and almost fainted.

The other security man said, 'Give us a dekko at you' and shone his torch in my face. He said, 'They were amateurs. You're lucky.'

His mate said, 'Still, I'll call an ambulance.'

I said, 'No,' and dribbled what I thought was saliva, but wasn't. 'I want to go home.'

'What's he say?'

'He says he wants to go home.'

'They always want to go home.'

It was like Old Mother Riley and her beautiful daughter Kitty, only funnier. I said, 'Get me a taxi. I have to talk to Greta.'

'Hospital first,' Liz said.

'No, I want Greta.'

She said, 'Then I'll drive you. Home first and then hospital.' She added, unnecessarily, 'Wait there.'

The security men helped me to my feet and kept watch over me. My side hurt and my left eye was already closing. A woman, arriving late for the supper, stopped to look at me and said, into

my face, 'Is he drunk?' as if I were deaf as well as in bits. Liz came
back after a time, and the two men helped me into her car. As she
made an illegal right turn at Trinity, she said, 'Can you talk?'

'A bit.'

'So what was it about?'

'The fellow in the good suit. I'd had a thing with his wife.'

'Uh-oh.'

'It was a while ago.'

After a time, Liz said, 'Was she the one you introduced me to at
the Gore Vidal evening? You wanted to make her jealous.'

'That was her.'

'She was too old for you.'

'Not that old.'

Liz said, 'She's at least two thousand.'

And no, it was not cattiness. Even through the pain, I thought
of Walter Pater, the *Gioconda* and the age of rocks. My mind was
addled; I began to savour the pain, urging it past a finishing post,
like a rider wielding a whip. Then I fell asleep until I was nudged
and heard Liz say, 'Something's up.'

We were nearly home, across the DART railway line and
approaching the tower. There was a flashing light from a police
car, and in our parking space I could make out a high yellow
tractor-like vehicle with a crane attached. There were men
clustered around and a few late-night gawkers. Liz, her voice
shaking, said, 'Oh, TJ mate, be afraid. Start being afraid.'

We had arrived in time for the main event. There was a spring
tide, and the tractor was at first towing, then lifting a car out of
the sea and back over the groynes. Water poured from its insides.
Some of the men guided it clear with their hands when it swung,
airborne, and a small cheer went up, as it was lowered on to safe
earth. The front wheels were splayed out like a can-can dancer's
legs. There was no sign of Greta. I thought: *Let her not be dead.
Let her not be in the sea.*

As I got out of Liz's car, I shouted Greta's name aloud with both kinds of pain. A uniformed Garda said, 'Christ, what happened to *you*?'

'I live here. Where's my wife?'

'Ah. You would be the householder?'

'Yes!'

'And this would be your vehicle?'

'Jesus God, will you tell me what's happened to her?'

Another Garda, with sergeant's stripes, said, 'The lady has had a bit of a knock and a bit of a wetting and apart from that and a few cuts, she'll be grand. But by Jasus, you've been in the wars.'

'Where is she?'

'Down the road at St Columcille's.'

I gathered that Greta had driven forward at speed, over the groynes and into the sea itself, knocking herself out against the windscreen. The tide had been on the flood, and by the time the car had been spotted by a late-night dog-walker she had been waist-deep in the sea.

At the back of the Sergeant's mind, the idea began to form, based on my appearance, that maybe I was the one who had driven the car and that I had fled the scene. Liz set him to rights while I went into the tower and looked up the number of St Columcille's with my good eye. I was put through to a ward sister who said that Greta had been concussed and was asleep.

'Are you the husband?'

'Yes.'

'Your wife was very distressed and said she doesn't want you to visit her. But she'd like you to bring her her spare glasses. The good ones got broke.'

That was Greta, as ever was, eating her cake and having it. I found the spectacles, and Liz drove me to the hospital, a mile away. She said, 'They won't let you see her, you know. It's after twelve.'

I said, 'Why did she do it? '

The police had called ahead, and at the hospital I was all but dragged from the car and into Casualty. When a nurse made to take my jacket off as well as my blood-stained overcoat, I said, 'No, not until I see my wife.' There was no argument; instead, she consulted with a sister, who told me, 'If you waken her I'll skin you.' I was taken upstairs and along a wheezing, coughing, snoring, hawking corridor lined on one side with what would have been cubicles except that the only partitions were thin curtains. One half-expected to meet Florence Nightingale and Sairey Gamp, arm in arm. I was shown Greta. She was in a corner bed, fast asleep. The impact had driven the spectacles into the soft skin of her upper nose. She wore a wad of cotton wool and had two black eyes, which made three between the pair of us. I left the spare glasses on her bedside table and went back to Casualty, where I thanked Liz and kissed her – it even hurt me to pucker up. I allowed myself to be felt, poked at and given pain-killers, and at my own insistence was bedded down on a cot for the night.

Next morning at eight, I went upstairs to Greta. She was sitting up, eating two boiled eggs for breakfast. Her eyes were blacker than before. She said, 'What happened to you?'

'Andrew Hand got two of his bully-boys to give me a going over.'

She said, 'Serves you right.'

'Thanks.'

She asked, 'Are you a patient here?'

'I'm to be X-rayed when I go back downstairs.'

'Don't let me keep you.'

'I was kicked in the chest and in the face.'

She said nothing but dipped a finger of toast into one of the boiled eggs. Her sympathy was spread as thin as the Flora margarine. A gubby old woman in the next bed had her ears out on stalks. I dropped my voice.

'What made you do such a stupid thing?'

'What?'

'Trying to ...' I whispered '... to do away with yourself.'

'Are you mad?' For a moment she sounded like Josie.

'Oh, now come on,' I said. 'I saw the car.'

She said, 'What about it? I was going home.'

'Home?'

'Home to Mammy. After I found out about you and that rip. Would you expect me to *stay*?'

'You drove into the sea.'

She said, viciously, 'Well, I was in a tizz. I got mixed up. My God, could you not tell that I was going home? Were you blind? Wasn't my suitcase in the boot?'

'I didn't look in the boot. Matter of fact, I don't think we *ought* to look in it.'

She said: 'You're not going to tell me the damp got in?'

'Damp? *Damp*? The car's awash!'

'Oh, Christ, me good clothes.'

In her rage, she crushed the empty eggshell in her fist. The woman in the next bed sniggered.

I said to the old faggot, 'Are you enjoying yourself?'

She showed me her gums and said, 'It's as good as a fillum.'

I ignored her and took hold of Greta's wrist. She looked at my hand as if it were unclaimed lost property. I said, 'Greta, I don't want you to go.'

She said, 'Are you still carrying on with that one?'

'No, not in a long time.'

'How long?'

'I honestly don't know. A good bit.'

'But you were carrying on with her?'

'Yes. You knew that. You must have.'

'I wasn't sure. And Andrew Hand says you went to Italy to meet her.'

'That's a lie. I never did. Not ever.'

'Honest?'

'Honest to God.'

She believed the lie and looked at me with wounded eyes. I

thought how very convenient it had always been for me to take her muteness for licence.

There was a silence between us, then a familiar voice said, 'Oh, my God, look at the two of you!' It was Colleen. 'I don't believe it. It is like a horror film.'

I said, 'What are you doing here?'

Greta wiped her eyes with the bedsheet.

Colleen said, 'Don't you know? You are in the newspaper.'

She showed us the *Irish Times*. On page three there was a small library picture of a Martello tower that was not ours, and the heading was 'Car Drives into Sea'. The text said, 'Greta Quill, wife of the film archivist and writer TJ Quill, was injured when her car drove into the sea at her home near Cobawn. Mrs Quill was not believed to be badly hurt.'

'Christ, now I'm in the papers,' Greta said, wailing.

I said, 'I'll leave you two alone. Colleen, would you mind running me home after I get X-rayed? And later on I'll come back and collect Greta?' To Greta: 'All right?'

Greta said, 'I suppose so. And bring clothes. I have nothing.' To Colleen she said, 'I know him. He'll bring an evening dress.'

'That's it, give him lackery,' the old woman cackled.

After the X-rays, I was told that I had two cracked ribs and a broken cheekbone which could result in a disfigurement unless I had surgery. When I had been taped up, Colleen drove me back to the tower. I told her Josie's story about her uncle Max, the kidnapping and the ransom, and she laughed so hard that she was obliged to stop the car.

'You are a fool,' she said.

'I know.'

'You don't know. You don't begin to know. Oh sure, there was a kidnapping, but it was an Italian politician she was carrying on with. He is married, with children, and Josie paid the what-do-you-call-it ... the money.'

'The ransom.'

261

'I suppose the idea of a kidnapping was too good to waste, so she turned it into an old uncle. A Jew, ha-ha. I cannot keep up with her.'

My mind could not contain any more. We had reached Ballybrack, and she pointed out of the window. 'Is that a public house? If so, will you buy me an Irish coffee?' We went inside, and she said, 'This is the first time I ever had a drink with a man when Turlough was not with me. I think maybe I have led a wasted life.'

I said, 'I'm honoured'.

She said, 'These people are too clever for you. They are too rich or too ambitious, or their blood is too old.' I thought of Liz in the car last evening. 'These are people who do not know what to do with their money or their blood or the poor ones who love them. I thank God I am just a little bit wise instead of a good bit clever, and that I am not beautiful and will never be rich.'

I said, 'I might be some day.'

'Do you mean as rich as Andrew Hand?'

'Why not?'

'Then go back and get born again. Get new parents.'

'So what do I do about Greta?'

'How the hell do I know?' Colleen said. 'What a stupid question. Deserve her, maybe.'

When she had driven me home and went off along the coast road, waving an arm out of the car window, I took Greta's sodden suitcase from the boot of our wrecked car. I was lugging it into the tower when the telephone rang.

For the last time, the voice said: 'Can you talk?'

'Just about,' I said. 'Thanks to your husband's thugs.'

'I don't know what you mean. And how dare you?'

'Excuse me?'

'How dare you be rude to Mr Carlo Venuti who is a most respected actor as well as a friend – a most platonic friend – of mine? You insult him, you call him by some wrong name and then you drop a cigar into his –'

262

I hung up, pleasantly surprised at how easy it was. A few seconds passed, and the telephone rang again. I sat and looked at it, and after a time it stopped.

Chapter Nineteen

Dinner and Afters

According to the *Readers' Digestive* school of psychology, if you ask yourself whether or not you are happy, then by axiom you aren't. For the same reason, I shied away from the folly of asking Greta if I was forgiven. As two quite separate beings, we lived in the Bloody Tower, whereas as a married couple we had regressed the two miles to the battleground of 'Kate Fortune's Lane'. The mark of the stitches across the top of Greta's nose was hidden by the bridge of her glasses. For myself, I had not bothered to have my face mended. Looking in a shaving mirror, I said, 'Hello, Claudette!' I was thinking of the star, Claudette Colbert, who famously had to be photographed from the left because her right profile did not quite match. Also, my mind held the idea that, thanks to Andrew Hand, I had paid my dues, and a dented face was my receipt.

We went into the long tunnel of winter, and I was by now more than half-way through the first draft of *The Search for Sean O'Fearna*. It was my plan to take the story as far as the autumnal years and finish the book with a 15,000-word interview – still to happen – with the Widow O'Fearna. Meanwhile, news of *Return to Innisfree* came, uninvited. Creighton Carr would not, after all, direct it; he died of hepatitis in January. I had a momentary fantasy of Thorn, proving himself a sheep in wolf's clothing by declaring that my screenplay had been reinstated and imploring me to forgive and forget. I cannot, as I told Josie Hand years before, let go easily. But Thorn, as I should have known, thrived on his hatreds. To replace the late Cry, he hired a television director: a *wunderkind* from Wexford who had had a surprise hit with *Sister Lizzie*, a sitcom set in a nunnery on the fictional Atlantic island of Fartin Mor.

In February, Greta and I had a visit from a genial American academic named Holmes, whose parents had waggishly christened him Westering. Wes, as he begged me to call him, was a friend of the Widow O'Fearna and a fan of both her late husband and the old-time cowboy actor, Harry Carey, whom he even mimicked by cradling his left forearm in his right hand. He and I hit it off; we sat up long past midnight, he drinking what he called Southern Discomfort, I on Scotch, and watched videos of *Desperate Trails* and *Satan Town*. A long-standing dream of his had been to set up a Chair of Western Film at Santa Fe University, where he taught motion picture theory and technique. This, with the aid of a grant from the Widow, was about to come true.

He said, 'Hey, why don't you come out to New Mexico for the first year as professor-in-residence? What about next September?'

I told him that my education had stopped short half-way through the Christian Brothers. He said, 'Hell, we'll give you a degree. What do you say to Doctor of Humane Letters? And we'll make a heroine of Greta and call her Dallas, like Claire Trevor in *Stagecoach*.' That, I said, mimicking the Dook, would be the day.

It was 2 a.m.: the time for pipe-dreams, easy promises and apple pie in the sky. And yet Wes had not been home for a month when his offer came. In the fall, as he quaintly put it, would I go to Santa Fe for a year as guest lecturer on western films?

'Do,' Greta said. 'Go, if you want to.'

'Not without you,' I said.

'Me? I'm not going. You're out of your tree.'

I said, 'Fair enough. Let's forget it.'

'Oh, now,' she said. 'None of that lark.'

'What lark?'

'Blaming me. Now I'd be standing in your way.'

'I'm not saying that.'

'Not out loud.'

I said, 'Whatever's to be done from this out, I think we should do it together.'

It was as far as I dared go, given that Greta used silence as others used words. If things had been half-way right between us, she would have laughed and thrown the idea out of the window. Instead, she sat at the breakfast room table for a long time. Then she said, 'Skyscrapers.'

'There aren't any in Santa Fe. It's low-rise.'

'And the Alamo.'

'That's in Texas.'

'A whole bloody year!'

'Not really. It's two semesters of sixteen weeks each. You could come home in between. You could stay home if you didn't like it.'

'Leave me alone.'

'And it's six thousand feet up, so it's not sweltering. In fact, they have winters.'

'Will you just shut it?'

'And a house is provided. A very nice house.'

'Jesus, so it ought to be.'

She was not convinced, not willing; but, like thistledown, the idea was settling. I asked Wes Holmes to allow us a couple of weeks to decide. I left coloured brochures on Greta's side of the bed; and, cunningly, Wes sent us Polaroids of the house.

'It has a pool,' I said.

'Handy to do the Monday wash in,' she said.

After two weeks, I heard her talking to a girlfriend on the phone. She was saying, 'There's this possibility of us going to would-you-believe New Mexico.' It was my cue to say: 'It's time I gave Wes a firm yes or no. Will I tell him we'll go?'

'You're forcing me into this.'

'No, I'm not. So will I?'

To my delight, she gave me a look of pure hate and said, 'Mmmp.'

In April we were invited to two May weddings. The first was of Ilse-Lazlo Huneker, who had kept it a secret that while in the west of Ireland she had fallen in love with a man who made figurines from Galway crystal. They were to be married in Clifden – the next parish to America, Ilse-Lazlo said. We accepted and were glad. At the wedding breakfast, there was a choice of rabbit stew or Dublin coddle; the music went on until four in the morning and the drinking until eight, and Greta, half-cut, went round telling people we were traipsing off to America, and weren't the both of us three-ha'pence short of a shilling?

The second wedding was of the Widow's stepson, Tyree, to his partner, whose name was Dee-Anne. The ceremony was to take place in Paris in, of all places, Notre Dame. Greta flatly refused to go; her excuse was that it was too far. The set of her face told me not to argue; she would have stayed away if the wedding had only been up the road in Killiney. Her suspicion that Tyree was the seducer of Blanaid and begetter of what she called the papoose had hardened from a half-joke into certainty, and now he was escaping with a clean pair of heels. 'If that poor girl he's marrying only knew!' she said.

I said nothing – there was no way in which I cared to refresh her views on sexual misconduct – and sent our regrets off to the Widow. Strangely, this crossed in the post with a hand-written card:

Mrs Kitty (Catherine) O'Fearna
regrets that her previous invitation to the wedding of her stepson,
Tyree O'Fearna to Dee-Anne O'Shaughnessy
must now be withdrawn.

'Maybe the wedding is off,' Greta said. 'Maybe she found him out.'

'It doesn't read like it,' I said. 'It reads like we've been dis-invited.'

'Not at all,' Greta said.

At first, it was no great matter; then three weeks passed, and late at night there was a call from New Mexico – the Bloody Tower, unlike 'Kate Fortune's Lane', was blessed with a bedside telephone. The caller was Wes Holmes, asking, 'Are you and Kitty O'Fearna on good terms?'

The cancelled wedding invitation flickered in and out of my mind. I said, 'As far as I know, yes. Why?'

'Hold on to your hat. She says she's going to oppose your appointment.'

'Oh?'

'And she can do it, too. The foundation is her baby and she has total power of veto. Can you hear me?'

'I wish I couldn't.'

'Who is it?' Greta hissed.

'Today or tomorrow,' Wes said, 'she's heading out for Europe for a wedding, and when she gets back there's to be a board meeting at the university. That's when she says she's going to pull the plug. I asked her why, but she's singing dumb. Look, the job is no big bananas, but hell, you'd have had a good time, and so would we. Could you sort this out?'

'Me?'

'Well, call her. Find out what gives. She sounded good and mad, I can tell you that.'

I said, 'She can't do this.'

'Yes, she can. G'bye, now.'

'Who can't do what?' Greta wanted to know.

I told her to hush a minute and looked up the Widow's home number. The voice that answered was difficult to understand; then I remembered Thorn telling me that there was a Japanese manservant. *Rashomon* and *Seven Samurai* apart, he was my first Jap. He told me that Mrs O'Fearna was frying. I assumed that she was in the kitchen until it came to me that she was airborne. Tomorrow, the servant told me, she would be at the Annariffy and the next day at the Litz. I made him repeat this. It sounded even worse the second time, but with a compass and a set-square

I worked out that the Widow was breaking her journey in Dublin and staying at her old haunt, the Anna Livia, before continuing on to the Paris and the Ritz.

'The wedding's there,' Greta said, 'so what's she coming *here* for? What's going on?'

I told her what Wes had said, that our year in Santa Fe was under threat. Mentally, I tossed a coin as to whether she would be pleased or disappointed; instead, she was angry. She said, 'I've gone and twisted my mind one way to suit you, and now you're twisting it back again. What happened? Now what have you only gone and made a balls of?'

'Nothing. I don't know.'

I rang the Anna Livia, and was told yes, Mrs O'Fearna was expected on the morrow. Greta's face was beginning to crumple. 'You make me want what I didn't want to want, and now you take it off o' me.'

I said, 'I'll find out what's up. Whatever it is, I'll fix it. Go to sleep.' She turned on her side, not facing towards me, and said in a voice of misery, 'If I had a duck, it'd drown.'

Next morning she wanted me to call the hotel. I said that Widow would surely have gone to bed after her flight.

Greta said, 'I thought you said she never gets jet-lag.'

I said, 'That's right. She says she takes erbs.'

'She takes *what*?'

I left for work and promised to call home as soon as I had news. There was no message in my office, and the phone stayed mute. At eleven-thirty I could no longer wait to telephone the hotel. The operator put me through to her suite.

'Mrs O?'

'Quill, I don't think you and I have anything to talk about.'

I said, 'Whatever is wrong, I want it face to face.'

A pause. 'Then get over here.'

She was already sitting in the foyer, a little older and now becoming leathery. She wore a smart trouser-suit in authentic

Donegal tweed that proclaimed her, loud and clear, as an American. She was in a temper; she looked like Bette Davis when crossed.

She said, 'What happened to your face?'

'A jealous husband had me beaten up.'

She made as if to stand. 'Well, if you're going to make with the jokes ...'

'It's true. You asked and I told you.'

She sat again. 'Oh.'

'So what's the problem?'

'No problem. I don't want you at Tyree's wedding. I don't want you at the University of Santa Fe. I don't want you in the O'Fearna Archive. In fact, Mr Quill, that's why I stopped off here, to tell my lawyer to find a way to break that contract I signed. Oh, and you can forget about the long interview for the biography. I'm not going to do it.'

'You promised to give full co-operation.'

'So sue me.'

'The publishers will.'

'I can afford it.'

I said, 'What's this all about? Am I to be told?'

She said, 'Okay. It says in the trades –'

'In the what?'

'The trade papers ... that you've written a load of shit called *Return to Innisfree* which is a rip-off of my late husband's masterpiece.'

For more than a year, this had been crouching, ready to happen, and I should have guessed. I said, 'The trades are wrong.'

'They're never wrong.'

'This time they are. What I wrote wasn't shit and it wasn't a rip-off. It was intended as an *hommage*.'

'That's a French word, isn't it?'

'Yes.'

'It means "theft".'

270

'For another thing, I was sacked from that film more than six months ago.'

'Sacked?'

'Fired.'

'But you wrote a screenplay.'

'A first draft.'

'Without my knowledge.'

A pause, now. 'If you like, yes.'

'I like.'

'If *I* hadn't written it, they'd have got somebody else.'

She looked at me. Her eyes were very dark. Even to myself I had sounded like Adolf Eichmann. I tried again.

'I wanted to come to you with a finished script, one that Sean O'Fearna would have wanted to make. It was a gentle story. He'd have liked it.'

She still said nothing. The third time, I told the truth.

'I just wanted to write a film. I was given the chance by a man named Gus de Paor. He said take it or lose it, and I grabbed. I told myself that it had nothing to do with you. Well, maybe it had, but only morally.' At this, she almost smiled. I said, too late, 'No, I mean sentimentally. So I went behind your back.'

She said, 'I can stop this picture.'

'Do, for all I care. Only I don't think you will.'

'I can delay it. I can injunct. I can plead that it impugns the integrity of the original.'

'Big words.'

'I can tie them up for five years in lawsuits. And I can start with you.'

'Why should you?'

'Why? You worked for me.'

I said, 'Right! It was a job, that's all it was. It was business, and now all of a sudden you're making it personal. And blocking Greta and me from going to Santa Fe, that's just vindictive. All you want is to lash out.'

She stopped a passing waiter. 'Could I have coffee? Regular, and just for one. The gentleman isn't staying.'

She turned her attention back to me. 'I got a call the other day from an old friend in Hollywood. She used to be in musicals. A big star. She said, "Hey, Kitty, what's with this sequel to *The Man from Innisfree*?" I told her, "Annie, I know nothing about it." She said, "Are you kidding? The screenplay is by a guy named Quill, who runs the O'Fearna Film Archive in Dublin, Ireland. He's working for you, and he's written this movie, and you say you know nothing about it?"' I thought the Widow was going to do what was an unnatural act, and weep. 'Quill, do you know how that made me feel?'

I said, 'I'm very sorry.'

She said, 'Have you any idea?'

I said, 'Yes, I do. I ask your pardon.'

She waved her arm wearily. 'So go away. Get lost.'

I stood up. I said, 'Mrs O, you don't have to see a lawyer today. I'll be out of the archive by this afternoon. You can go straight on to Paris and have your wedding.'

It was not a ploy on my part, but I would have been a fool to think that she might match my quixotry with her own. The Widow was what Thorn had once called her: a tough biddy. She said, like a small pair seeing a broken straight, 'Well, Mister, I'm going to take you up on that.'

She looked at me steadily. I nodded goodbye and started for the stairs to street level, then changed my mind and went to the bank of telephones. I called Greta. I told her, 'It turns out that all this is because I wrote *Return to Innisfree*. The widow-woman thinks she was stabbed in the back, and maybe she was.'

Greta said, 'We're not going to America, then?'

'You may as well know the lot. I quit the job.'

'You what?'

'At the archive. There's no way I could stay on. So I'm afraid it's back to whatever the square is before square one. Sorry.'

She said nothing for so long that I wondered if she was in shock. After a time, she asked, 'What time will you be home?'

'The usual. Sixish.'

'Okay.'

She made the word sound almost chirpy as she hung up. I went to the bar, ordered a large Scotch and drank it. As I crossed the foyer, the Widow was having her coffee. A page-boy, brandishing a card on a stick and calling her name, almost bumped into me. I directed him, 'Over there,' and wondered who, apart from myself, knew she was in town.

I had a bar lunch in Davy Byrne's and balked at the thought of going back to the archive to tell Mattie Mundow that she was now jobless. It was a fine spring day, and to use up the afternoon I drove out of town, into Wicklow and to the Vale of Clara. There I sat by the Avonmore and tried to summon up a sentimental flashback. Instead I nodded off and, of all people, dreamt about Shay. He was wearing a row of pens in his breast pocket. He said: 'You made me keep them out of sight, and now I'm getting my own back.' I woke with a sour mouth and for the first time in years wanted a cigarette.

I got home early, before five. As I was about to let myself in, Greta looked over the parapet of the tower and said, 'I'm up here.' I climbed to the roof by the outside stairs, ready for a catechism, but when I said, 'The Widow is some woman,' Greta simply said, 'Mm' and affected to look out to sea. She had made herself iced tea and had the cordless phone and a paperback – *The Silence of the Lambs* – on the ironwork table. I asked if there had been any calls; she said no. She seemed on edge. She said nothing about the lost job, and I was about to call the inquest to order, when the phone went. She jumped and all but screamed.

I said, 'What's the matter with you?'

'Nothing.'

I picked up the phone. As a likely caller and in a field of ten runners, the Widow O'Fearna would have come in last. And yet she romped home, saying with an air of jollity, 'Is that the bold Thady Quill?'

'Hello?'

'Hey, what the hell am I paying you for? I keep calling your office, and that girl of yours – say, is that a Dublin accent, because it's cute? – she doesn't know where you are. Listen, I'm at the airport, Paris bound. Wasn't there an old play with that title, *Paris Bound*?'

'Yes, there was. They made a film of it. 1929. Fredric March and Ann Harding.' I was treading water.

'Quill ...'

'I'm here.'

'I think we should let bygones be bygones. Faults on both sides. Let's give it another chance. Okay with you?'

I had no feeling in my limbs. The sea was a daub of blue-grey paint. Greta was refusing to look at me. I said, 'Fine.' I could hear the background echo of a flight announcement.

'That's good. You just stay cool, and I'll see you in Santa Fe in September. Both of you. That's some wife you've got there, Quill. Sharp as a tack. See-ya!'

The line went dead. I looked at sharp-as-a-tack Greta. She was shivering. I said, 'Don't you want to know who that was? Or what was said?'

Her shoulders rose and fell. 'Mmmp.'

A memory came from earlier in the day of a page-boy calling the name of Mrs Kitty O'Fearna. I recalled wondering who, besides myself, knew she was in town. Now, looking at Greta, it was my turn to shiver.

I said, 'Greta, did you call her? After I rang you from the hotel. Did you?'

She said, as if it was hardly worth mentioning, 'I gave her a buzz.'

'A what?'

She began to whinge.

274

I said, 'Don't do that. Whatever you do, don't cry. Not yet. Jesus, Greta, don't tell me you begged her. Not for me or for us. If you did, I swear I'll kill you.' I looked at the parapet. 'You go over the edge, you hear?'

She was genuinely indignant. 'Beg? Who me? How dare you? Me, go on my knees to that one? To *anyone*?'

'Then what did you say to her?' I took her by the arms and shook her. 'Tell me.'

'You're hurting.'

'What? What?'

Her voice fell to a whisper. 'I . . . mentioned the young lad.'

'Who? What young lad? Do you mean Tyree?'

She might have been a child at her first confession. 'And Blanaid.'

I let go of her and then took hold of her. Through the horror of it, the only poor consolation was that blackmail was not as bad, could never be as bad, as pity.

We went to Santa Fe, and Greta stayed for the full two semesters with a trip home in between. The work was not onerous, and meanwhile I finished the book. The American publishers liked it, and there was talk of my doing a lecture tour: 'The Invented West'. When our time in New Mexico was over, we returned to Ireland and the Bloody Tower. Not much had changed. Seeing me, a man in our local pub took up the traces of an argument he had left unfinished a year before. The Oozer Kenirons had won a Whitbread Award for poetry. *Return to Innisfree* had been made on a reduced budget; it failed to get a cinema release and was going direct to video. Thorn Thornton was putting on a show called *Three Sopranos and a Contralto*. Prue had once again bolted the door against him, and this time had changed the locks. Shay was still reviewing. And Colleen invited us to dinner and served her speciality: paella.

'This will be a change for ye,' Kenirons said. 'In America they have peculiar tastes in grub. For instance, they think Indian food is buffalo.'

There were new faces around the table, but it was soon like old times, and Colleen and Turlough were impressed by how well Greta looked. America, it was agreed, suited her. There was rarely a lull at a Penders' dinner, but as empty plates were being passed up the long table, the Oozer said, 'Any word about the Hands? I saw the bold Josie in Nassau Street the other day, and *anno domini* is beginning to catch up.'

Turlough looked at me. 'Her mother died, did you know?'

'I didn't,' I said.

'If you ask me,' he said, 'I bet the old lady's been stretched and in her box these five years, and Josie's been singing dumb about it so's she could go off to Italy to fly her kite. Several kites.'

'That is not true,' Colleen said.

'So is she home now?' Greta asked.

Colleen answered her, but the words were aimed at me. 'She is not very happy. She finds it hard now to get away. Andrew watches her.'

Greta cackled happily.

'How old is this lady?' someone asked.

Turlough said, 'Too old.'

'And then some,' the Oozer added.

I had business to do in town next day and took the DART in rather than drive. I walked up Westland Row, through Lincoln Place and made for Grafton Street, hugging the railings of Trinity. After a few yards, I crossed over to the Nassau Street side where the people and the shops were. I asked myself why I had done so. It occurred to me that although Josie and I were in the past, one day, inevitably, we would meet. I wondered what would happen.

After all, and as I keep saying, it's a small country.